PRAISE FOR *THE WINDING WAY HOME*

As a one-time English professor, having absorbed countless works of fiction, I have never read a novel more devastating nor more beautiful.

> — Patricia Browne, Former Professor of English, St. Catherine's University, St. Paul, Minnesota

This is a novel I can heartily recommend. It is contains profound insights about the sometimes extremely weird workings of the mind, shocking struggles with monstrous evil, the challenges of family relationships, the maturation processes of children with different characters and backgrounds, and, most of all, the healing power of human love. Wildman's characters are sharply drawn and engagingly different. Their complicated interactions with one another constitute the unifying theme of the novel. The novel is evocatively religious in its sensibilities without references to anything supernatural. It poses haunting questions and tentative answers to these questions, each of which merits serious reflection.

> — Donald A. Crosby, Professor of Philosophy Emeritus, Colorado State University

In this hauntingly beautiful novel, Wildman demonstrates that even the most heinous tragedy can be transformed through the alchemy of agape love. *The Winding Way Home* wilds mysticism and metaphysics to explore the intricacies of the mind, overcoming unspeakable trauma, relatable familial struggles, the bondage and freedom of death, and the resilience of the human spirit. It is an enthralling journey.

> — Bishop LaTrelle Miller Easterling

Wildman creates an engrossing multigenerational narrative of present-day America that resonates with *East of Eden* and *One Hundred Years of Solitude*. He also brings to us the mind and heart of Jesse, a quintessential religious naturalist, who creates a fascinating version of reality.

— Ursula Goodenough, President, Religious
Naturalist Association and Professor of Biology
Emerita, Washington University in St. Louis

The Winding Way Home is traumatic, transcendent, and exhilarating. Through a cornucopia of characters, arresting themes, and captivating plotlines, Wildman explores the duality of joy and sorrow and the meaning of life. In less capable hands, the darkness might obscure the graceful beauty that emerges from the lives of ordinary people. There is nothing cheap about this grace. Rather, there is an affirmative spirituality in the face of the awful things that fate brings our way.

— William David Hart, Margaret W. Harmon
Professor of Religious Studies, Macalester College

In *The Winding Way Home*, Wesley Wildman integrates his theological background with the life concerns that confront human beings daily. The story raises questions about what does and not have priority in individuals' and families' lives, whether there is anything that impacts those lives from beyond day-to-day contexts, and how to connect with a loved one now absent or deceased. The family dynamics include both traditional and non-traditional settings, with happy and struggling relationships, personal growth and change, experiences of connecting beyond the visible to the invisible. I found myself pondering what is (or is not) real and how the Holy might (or might not) impact my experiences and those of others. I strongly encourage others to immerse themselves in the story as well as in the spoken and unspoken questions raised in it.

— Bishop Susan Hassinger

The Winding Way Home is a multilayered, page-turner of a novel about a family living, loving, and learning to be human in the wake of an unspeakable tragedy. The story focuses on the father's spiritual attempt to join devotion to his daughter's memory with loyalty to the moral complexity of a world saturated with value but shorn of the supernatural. The novel shows us how one man strives to live meaningfully in the world as it is, rather than as he would like it to be, and in so doing, how he learns to revere its staggering beauty and goodness along with its pain, loss, and violence.

— Michael S. Hogue, Author of
American Immanence: Democracy for an Uncertain World

Disturbing, inspiring, daring, heartwarming, this is a novel of family, of terrible events, of deep and patient love (the erotic is not neglected), and of ultimate experiences and mysteries. The prose is engaging, the storytelling deft and resourceful, the vision of life opening into a larger vision of Being itself.

— Brian Jorgensen, Professor Emeritus,
Department of English, Boston University

The Winding Way Home is a captivating novel in which Wildman draws on various religious, philosophical, and scientific perspectives at strategic points in a well-crafted, human-interest story dealing with heartbreak and hope. Realistic, complex characters create a warm patchwork quilt – many personalities, talents, and challenges pieced together with strong relational threads throughout the story. The narrative moves at a comfortable pace with authentic dialogue appropriate to the situation, which richly contributes to the plot, to character development, or to psychological insights. Wildman conveys tragedy and its emotional aftermath with sensitivity, often reflecting the turmoil and spiritual struggles within his characters' psyches. The novel's multifaceted layers of misfortune, frustration, and resilience make it an ideal book club selection.

— Joyce Ann Konigsburg, Department of
Religious Studies, DePaul University

The Winding Way Home offers a different kind of answer to, or perhaps an exploration of, the age-old question of how people make sense of their suffering. In addition to a compelling story about how an extended family deals with the aftermath of heinous crimes, the novel explores questions of theology, spiritual technology, and the sometimes fuzzy lines between madness and genius. Wesley Wildman brings his formidable and edgy thinking about religion and spirituality into the form of a novel for everyone to encounter.

— Daniel J. Ott, Dean of the School of Theology, Humanities and Performing Arts at Eastern Mennonite University

The Winding Way Home is a story about constructing meaning after unspeakable evil renders reality absurd, about the power of love to transfigure traumas that are beyond the reach of healing, and, ultimately, about the immense beauty, unspeakable wonder, and infinite spiritual vitality of everyday life. Providing a searing vision of the depth dimension of human existence shorn of all supernatural obfuscations, it's a must read, especially for the spiritual but not religious crowd.

— David Rohr, Center for Mind and Culture, Boston

TS Eliot wrote that 'humankind cannot bear very much reality'. This sophisticated and searching novel is about just that - bearing reality, in the face of almost unimaginable trauma. Skillfully chronicled, it also breaks innovative ground in understanding the human imagination. Warmly recommended.

— Christopher Southgate, Professor of Theodicy, Exeter University

The Winding Way Home is an astounding and achingly beautiful story about what love can do—the enduring love of an ordinary family searching for healing in the face of unspeakable tragedy, the fierce love of an extraordinary mother protecting her children from monstrous evil, and the mystical love of a less-than-ordinary sannyasi learning to see, accept, and even worship the world as it is most truly, intensely, profoundly. The novel is a slice of life that opens out onto reality as a whole, reality in all its wonder and possibility, complexity and depth, wildness and ambiguity, grace and horror. As readers, we are invited to taste the bliss of surrender and given a glimpse into a strange but adventurous spirituality, a spirituality of suchness, a spirituality that reveres—yes, loves—what is, without the illusory comforts of supernatural fictions. Wildman's courageous novel belongs on the shelf of anyone who has become disillusioned with traditional religious "answers" to the problem of suffering or has tried to find meaning, hope, and authentic spiritual sustenance in the midst of trauma and unredeemable loss. In the closing words of the luminous protagonist, "Love conquers nothing but it changes everything."

— Demian Wheeler, Associate Professor of
Philosophical Theology and Religious Studies,
United Theological Seminary of the Twin Cities

— THE —

Winding Way Home

a novel by

WESLEY J. WILDMAN

For Sam and Ben
fellow diner denizens

CONTENTS

PROLOGUE

I was with my adoptive father when he died. Jesse was eighty-seven but in such good health my brothers and I expected him to live another decade. I was working on a canvas on one side of my studio, and Jesse was in his wrinkled leather recliner and staring out the open window, at one with the trees and every other living thing, which was his way in later years.

"Sweetheart," he said. "I think I'm leaving now. Will you be okay?"

I ran over and knelt beside him and held his hands. He smiled so brightly it seemed like he was about to laugh or tell me a joke. But those were his last words. He closed his eyes and left, just like that. So gentle and content, like falling into a blissful sleep.

My kids and I had come to live with Jesse and his beloved Alexandra twenty-three years earlier. We'd escaped horrific circumstances and needed a safe place to land, a place to heal. Jesse and Alexandra took us in and put us back together. They taught us how to live again.

Jesse was well known in philosophical and scientific circles but I never knew much about that side of his life. He rarely spoke of it, preferring to devote himself fully to family when he was home. And by the time I came to live with him, he was already sixty-four. Most of his books and lectures were behind him, and he spent as much time as he could with his children and grandchildren. I doubt I would have understood his books even if I'd tried to read them. But in my years with Jesse I did pick up a thing or two, and

I also learned something about his private spiritual life, which he never talked about in public.

In Hinduism there's a person called a sannyasi. The sannyasi gives up everything for enlightenment. He moves to the forest, begs for food, and meditates as much as he can.

Jesse wasn't a traditional sannyasi. He loved his house and his family, his food and his friends. He never felt the urge to leave any of that behind. But in our quiet Boston neighborhood, he was on a quest that I think any sannyasi wandering the woods would have understood.

In his will, Jesse appointed his son Matt to decide what to do with his writings—which to everyone's surprise, included a memoir. We'd known that Jesse kept hand-written journals, but it wasn't until after his death that any of us knew he'd been quietly writing his life story.

In a file cabinet, in a folder marked "Ephemera," Matt found not one but two manuscripts, along with a note explaining that he'd tried to write a traditional memoir but didn't like how it turned out—so he rewrote the whole thing as a novel. Leave it to Jesse to learn a whole new art form in his eighties.

As a way of honoring his life and also as a way to say goodbye, the five of us—Matt and his wife Jenny, Josh and his wife Oli, and me—gathered on a Saturday afternoon to read Jesse's preferred version together. I was too self-conscious about my reading to participate, but the rest of them took turns, reading aloud and handing off the manuscript when they got hoarse.

At the end of the day, we decided to publish Jesse's book. It was not an easy decision. Jesse wrote it as a novel but its contents are true, and it includes personal details about each of us. I in particular have an ugly history that many people would rather not know, and at times would like to forget about myself.

But one of the lessons I learned from Jesse helped me find the courage to let my story go out into the world. Jesse never bought into perfection. Neither did I. But he believed in healing, even if it left scars. I think he took up his weird suburban sannyasi spiritual quest to deal with a deep gash in his soul—one that Matt and Josh share and that he describes in his book. I'm trying to find my own healing and will probably be doing that work the rest of my life. Jesse gave me courage to try to heal, and I want other people to have that, too.

Matt asked me to write this prologue, which I feel honored to do. Now that you know the circumstances of what you're about to read, I think Jesse's story will speak for itself. But there's one final thing I want to say, something that Jesse couldn't write: I miss my father. Terribly. Joyfully. Endlessly.

Maddy
In Boston on New Year's Eve, 2048

Part I
The Way Things Were

A THOUSAND FLYING DIAPERS

Jesse steered the car home with a relief that verged on elation. He was done with another tense yet tedious faculty meeting, which more often than not seemed to devolve into a bunch of Ph.D.s fighting over scraps. He never knew whether to remain silent so as not to prolong the agony, or try and intervene. Probably best to stay out of the fray—he was aware of the blank stares and barely suppressed sighs when he contributed. Well, fine. Let them have their petty conflicts—he'd save his energy for Alexandra and the boys.

He was still shaking his head over pointless university politics when he strode into the kitchen and saw Alexandra at the table, her long fingers wrapped around a steaming cup of tea, her beautiful face pale.

Jesse frowned and sat down opposite her, wrapping his cold hands around hers. Instantly, his mind conjured the competition inside Alexandra's hands between the warmth of the cup and the cool of his hands, deploying heat-conduction formulae, estimating conduction coefficients through skin and bone and tendon, and seeing it all unfold dynamically in his mind, with billowing blooms of cold blue and hot red swirling around one another and gradually merging and fading, with little spiraling tendrils of chaos shimmying along the interface where the warring forces of physics met. The mental movie was so instinctive he wasn't even a little distracted from what was happening in the moment.

"What's wrong, sweetheart?" he asked.

Alexandra groaned.

"Are you sick?"

Still nothing.

"You look pale," he tried again. "What's wrong?"

"Oh *Jesse*," she finally said, and he could hear the gathering tears in her voice. "Take a wild guess."

Jesse stared at his wife, his beloved of almost twenty years, and all at once he got it. His frown dissolved into a smile that blossomed into a beaming grin.

"You're pregnant?"

Alexandra groaned again.

"You're pregnant!" A new mental movie instantly appeared. This one depicted the developing fetus, cells dividing and differentiating, structures bending and migrating, DNA regulating factors switching on and off, activating some proteins and closing others down right on schedule, creating the miracle of life one more time.

"I take it you're not too happy about it," he said, almost laughing.

"And you're grinning like an idiot," she said, finally smiling.

She pulled her hands from his and covered her face. Jesse was visualizing forces in the triangular arrangement of table, forearms, and face, when Alexandra suddenly slapped the table with both hands and said, "Good lord, Jesse. What're we going to do?"

He knew what she meant—he was forty-one, she forty-three, and they thought they were long done with child-rearing. A new visualization pressed into his mind, co-existing with the previous two, still vividly present. He saw Alexandra's life settled and happy, Alexandra flourishing in a meaningful career, and all that now invaded by a thousand flying diapers that looked like tiny, stained storks. To his amazement, the countless flying diapers started dancing in a choreographed display, like high-kicking Rockettes.

He placed his hands on the sides of her head, and her eyes filled with tears. "Hey," he said. "Alexandra, look at me. Hey, I get it, okay? I get it."

He drew her around the table, and Alexandra collapsed into his lap and started sobbing, her face against his shoulder.

Jesse held his wife tightly and absorbed her distress. At the same time, his mind filled with images of a daughter. Her arrival would upend one family system and give birth to another, and the process took shape in his imagination like one of the boys' mechanical transformer toys, starting as an innocent-looking suitcase and unfolding with clanks and hisses into a sleek, futuristic vehicle. He drove with Alexandra beside him, the two boys flanking the baby girl safely ensconced in a car seat in back, all of them happy. The little blonde being was absorbing everything, growing and learning, playing with Josh's hands while Matt chatted on in his interminable way about entries he'd been reading in the family encyclopedia.

Back in the real world, he caressed Alexandra's slender back as she synced her breathing with his—a gift they'd given one another a thousand times when one of them was upset.

"Hey, listen to me," he said. "We will be okay. I'm telling you, I can *see* it. We will be okay. All five of us."

"What we'll be," she said, "is past sixty when this kid goes off to college. Oh my—we could even be grandparents by then!"

Jesse laughed. "This kid!" he said. "How about Rebecca? Let's call her Rebecca."

Alexandra sat up and stared at him. "So it's a girl, is it?" She finally smiled a little.

"Why the hell not?!" he said.

He pulled her into a full-bodied hug as a classic image of a fat, blonde cherub floating on clouds filled his consciousness. He laughed in delight.

"We'll figure it out, Alexandra," he whispered in her ear. "We'll make this work."

THE 403RD BOYS' BREAKFAST

"I'd like a baby brother or sister," said nine-year-old Josh.

Matt was shocked enough to pause his usual speed-eating at Boys' Breakfast, where he was making a terrible mess of a stack of pancakes. He was eleven but they were still working on his fine motor skills, not to mention his manners. Jesse, too, put down his fork, not so much in shock as amazement. His youngest son's intuition had always been downright spooky.

"A baby!" said Matt, and wiped syrup from his mouth with his sleeve. "Where'd that come from?"

"Dunno," said Josh. "It just seems like we should have a bigger family, and I'd like to take care of a little baby."

Who *was* this child? Every time Jesse thought he had his boys figured out, they surprised him.

"What do you think that would be like?" Jesse asked.

"I'd hold her and feed her," said Josh. "I'd play with her and teach her how to do stuff, like ride a bike." Josh went on for a while, his imagination firing as he thought through every big-brother skill that might be involved.

Matt grimaced. "Babies poop a lot and they smell bad and they cry all the time," he said. "Also, you can't play with them because they can't do anything."

Jesse laughed.

"Well, you're partly right," he said. "Babies do poop a lot but you change them. When they cry you comfort them. They smell amazingly good most of the time. And they can't do anything at the start, but their brains are wired to learn amazingly fast, and you can watch them learn to do everything you can do."

"That's so cool," said Josh.

"Blech," said Matt, and fell in on his pancakes.

"Josh, you're talking about a baby sister, not a baby brother," Jesse said. "What's that about?"

"Either would be great but I guess I just imagine a sister," said Josh.

"Doesn't matter, anyway," said Matt. "Mom's too old to have a baby."

Not for the first time, Jesse smirked at Matt's over-confident pronouncement. But he also sensed trouble. Josh would adapt effortlessly, but Matt was going to *flip* when he realized his mother was actually pregnant. Even a change as small as a pear rather than an apple with his peanut butter sandwich could trigger an outburst, and God help them all if school was canceled or there was some other major disruption to his routine. He'd been diagnosed with an autism spectrum disorder when he was two, and much of the reason he fared as well as he did was Alexandra's training in child development and children with special needs—and her tireless patience and love. Jesse could only imagine how Matt would react when he realized there would be a pooping, crying baby who would demand much of his too-old parents' time, who would disrupt Matt's cherished routines. This unexpected new family member was going to change everything.

THE 407TH BOYS' BREAKFAST

They broke the news to the boys when Alexandra was three months along.

"What do you think Matt's thinking?" asked Alexandra.

They were in bed, Alexandra folded around Jesse's large body and unconsciously playing with the curly hair on his chest while he stroked her back. So far everything was fine, without even a trace of the morning sickness she'd had with Matt and Josh.

"No idea," said Jesse. "He didn't freak out, though."

"That's exactly what worries me," said Alexandra.

While Josh had been beside himself with excitement, Matt had said nothing.

"You're right," said Jesse. "I was so relieved there was no blow-up I wasn't thinking about how suspicious that is."

"You should investigate at Boys' Breakfast tomorrow."

"Will do," said Jesse. "But maybe he'll surprise us. I think he's doing okay with it."

Alexandra was quiet for a moment. "For now, maybe," she said. "We'll have to keep an eye on him, though."

"You remember what he was like when Josh was born?" asked Jesse. "It's like the new baby wasn't even there. Not a point of happiness, not even annoyance. Just not there at all."

Alexandra sat up on one elbow and looked at him. "I actually don't remember that," she said.

Jesse laughed a little. "Well that's not surprising, is it, given you were dealing with an autistic two-year-old and a newborn? Not to mention awash in hormones."

She flopped back down beside him. "All true," she said. "Still, stuff like this worries me. I don't want to become like my mom. Or *her* mom. I mean can you imagine? Not to remember anyone by the end, and think you're surrounded by strangers?" She shuddered.

"I know, sweetheart," he said, "but I wish you wouldn't worry so much about your memory. Events stick in people's minds differently. I probably recall Matt's weird behavior because I was so vigilant about protecting the baby."

"And I can recite all of my workshops and lectures by memory and never forget a name," she said.

"See?" he said, reassuring her with a hug. "There's absolutely nothing wrong."

At Boys' Breakfast the next day, it was Josh who brought up the pregnancy.

"Dad, did you guys make a baby because I told you I wanted one?"

Jesse laughed so hard he drew stares from the neighboring table. "Actually," he said, "your Mom was already pregnant by then."

Josh was visibly relieved. "Is it a girl?"

"Well, we don't know yet," answered Jesse. "We could find out if we wanted but I think we might wait until the baby is born and see for ourselves."

"How do you find out when the baby is still inside?" asked Josh.

Matt jumped in and at great length, in astonishing detail, explained about ultrasounds.

"Matt, how on earth did you find out about all that?" asked Jesse.

He shrugged. "Encyclopedia."

Matt had no idea how strange it was that he knew so many facts about the world.

"Hey, I just thought of something," said Josh. "If it's a girl, is Boys' Breakfast over?"

Matt suddenly stopped eating and looked at Jesse with real fear. "Dad?" he said. "*Dad.*"

Jesse reached across the breakfast mess and held his son's hands. If he couldn't head this off at the pass there would be a full meltdown, and that was no fun with a boy as large as Matt was—especially in public. "Matt, Matty, look at me."

Matt's eyes roved around wildly.

"Matty, eyes on mine," Jesse said. "Now, deep breaths, like we practiced, okay? Breathe with me."

Josh put down his fork and joined in. This was second nature to them all.

In a few moments Matt's shoulders relaxed. He nodded. He still wasn't fully himself but they'd passed the danger zone.

"Brilliant, Matt, excellent job," Jesse said.

He was about to answer Matt's question when Josh spoke.

"Boys' Breakfast will never end," he said.

Jesse stared at his son.

"Well it's got to end *some* day," Matt said. "Because all of us will be dead."

"Well I didn't mean *literally*," said Josh.

Literal was the only way Matt thought.

"I think what your brother is saying," said Jesse, "is that he can't see it ending for the foreseeable future. As long as we're all around, Boys' Breakfast will continue."

"So if the baby is a boy, he has to come too," said Matt.

"He's not," said Josh. "I mean, the baby is a girl."

"How would you know?" said Matt. "But that would be good, actually—if she's a girl, she stays at home with Mom."

"Okay, time out," said Jesse. "We'll just have to wait and see about the baby's gender. And then let's have a discussion, man to man, about how to carry on with Boys' Breakfast. Agreed?"

"Agreed," said Josh, and Matt nodded.

"Hey, what number is this anyway?" Josh asked.

"Four hundred and seven," Matt said. He was the keeper of facts—Alexandra referred to him as the family's external hard drive—and his tally of weekly Boys' Breakfast outings was always flawless, which Jesse knew because he logged them in his journals.

"Tell us about number one," Josh said.

"C'mon, you've heard that story tons of times," Jesse said.

"I'll tell it," said Matt.

"You'll screw it up," complained Josh.

"Let him try," Jesse said. "You can fix anything that goes wrong."

"Fine," said Josh.

As usual, Matt seemed oblivious to his little brother's disappointment, no matter how patently Josh displayed it.

"It was when Josh was six months old and I was two and a half," began Matt.

"Is that right?" asked Josh.

He knew it was. This was more an attempt to derail Matt's story than a serious question. Again, Matt was oblivious.

"Yep," said Jesse. "Carry on, Matt."

"Josh was in your bedroom and he woke up. Mom fed him and he went back to sleep. Then I woke up and climbed into bed with you. We all went to sleep but then I woke up again so you took me downstairs so I wouldn't wake Josh or Mom. While I was playing with blocks you heard Josh crying again so you ran upstairs and brought him down so Mom could sleep. Then you took both of us out to breakfast to make sure Mom could stay asleep. And that was number one."

"That was a bad story," said Josh.

Matt didn't look offended in the least. All that mattered to him was that he got the details right.

"Hey, Josh, take it easy," Jesse said. "Matt nailed the main points."

Matt resumed vacuuming bits of pancake off his plate. Josh was still grumpy. He didn't know how to say it but Jesse knew he liked more drama in his stories.

As he gazed at his sons, the two of them so different, his mind hit Play on the mental movie projector. Images of their second Sunday morning in Boston, right after moving into their new house, filled his mind with astonishing force. This was a multi-sensory memory, sounds and smells and tastes and sensations shot through a tapestry of his video-like recall. These high-definition memories—which he could play back on super speed without losing detail, or on slo-mo to savor every little moment—had been with him all his life. He was Matt's age when he began to realize his memory capabilities were out of the ordinary. On this occasion, with the boys still debating the story and restaurant chatter tumbling around him, the memory played back in hyper-speed.

Happy, Buddha-like Josh was just starting solids, while big noisy Matt was a whirlwind with food. He and Alexandra were both perpetually exhausted from having two very young, very high-needs children, but Alexandra, as the one with boobs, rarely got to sleep in. Sneaking the boys out for breakfast was nothing more than a natural reaction that Sunday morning when she was particularly exhausted. Matt did have all the details right, but what he couldn't recall was the little striped pullover he'd worn that day that came home smeared in strawberry jam, the way Josh, in a highchair, craned his neck to stare and smile at every passing patron, the server named Sarah who greeted them by saying "Well what can I get you three gentlemen this morning!", the way sunlight had started to bother Matt's eyes and Sarah adjusted the blinds automatically, the sweet rich taste of the fresh-squeezed orange juice. There were a thousand more details, all present to Jesse as if they were happening this very second, all occurring while he was still fully attentive to Matt and Josh bickering over how best to tell a story.

The first Boys' Breakfast had been a success all around: no diaper blowouts, no launching of pancakes across the dining room, no tantrums. Best of all, Alexandra got to sleep in.

They'd now been doing this every Sunday for nine years. Apart from the weekends he had to travel to give lectures or attend conferences, they'd only missed two Boys' Breakfasts: once when the whole family had stomach flu, and once when a Nor'easter shut down the state—a statistic that Matt could have furnished without even thinking about it.

The truth was, Boys' Breakfast had become a precious tradition for all three of them, and Jesse had no idea what would happen to it once the baby was born.

And he was as nervous about that as Josh and Matt were.

AN ENGINEERING PROBLEM

"You're kidding me!" said Jesse.

Alexandra paused sorting through the mail and stared at him, daring him to go on.

He decided to take his chances. "*Another* workshop?" he said. "You could have this baby any minute now!"

"I'm perfectly aware of my due date," she said. "But my clients—"

"You told me your clients are actually *worried* about you, sweetheart. And just think—if you'd take some time off, no one else could ask you if you're having twins."

She laughed and patted her enormous belly. The pregnancy had gone smoothly despite Alexandra's "advanced maternal age," but her belly seemed like nature's idea of a cruel joke—gigantic and cumbersome, far bigger than she'd been with Matt and Josh. Jesse privately wished she'd go into labor early, just to get some relief.

"But I'm just now breaking through to a new group of potential clients," she said. "It's taken me years to get here. The timing is just really, really bad."

Jesse shook his head and spoke in his best schoolmarmish voice. "It'll all end in tears, I tell you."

He walked over and gave her an awkward hug. "You'll build it all back," he said. Alexandra had been running her own educational consulting business for years, and she was right—she was just on the cusp of expanding when this surprise pregnancy threw a wrench into everything. "Listen, sweetheart," he continued. "Your clients love you. They're in your corner. It'll be fine."

"Let's hope you're right," she said.

"These are pretty good, though, aren't they?" He gently squeezed her swollen breasts and she let him, as usual. He would be forever grateful for a partner who not only tolerated but liked his boyish antics.

"Why are you squeezing Mom's boobs?" asked Josh, unexpectedly walking through the kitchen.

Alexandra brushed Jesse's hands away and stood there grinning at him, waiting for his answer.

"Uh, just dealing with an engineering problem, Josh," he said. "You know, bigger breasts stress the bra and all that."

"Gross," said Josh, and left.

Alexandra snorted. "I'm an engineering problem?"

"Yeah, your poor bra, it's really struggling," said Jesse, weighing a breast with his hand.

"Still doing engineering inspections, Dad?" asked Josh, as he passed through the kitchen in the opposite direction.

"For Pete's sake!" exclaimed Jesse. "Why don't you people announce yourselves?"

"Off to my room now, Dad."

"Why don't I hear them coming?"

"Something else on your mind, I guess," Alexandra said, giggling. "And by the way, your pitiful attempt to distract me didn't work."

"Oh, I don't know, I reckon it might have worked a little," he said, leaning in for a kiss. It went on a bit longer than usual, conveying an intensity they both welcomed.

"Another engineering problem?" asked Josh.

"Sweet Jesus, Josh, are you doing this on purpose?"

Josh just laughed and kept moving.

"Wear some noisy shoes, boy!" shouted Jesse.

Alexandra smirked, her body open, leaning back on the counter. They'd both been delighted to discover that this pregnancy, despite the physical awkwardness, had done nothing to diminish their appetite for each other. Jesse glanced at his watch and grimaced.

"Rain check?" he asked.

"You know where to find me," she said.

Alexandra's final professional event, a workshop for educators at a Catholic preschool on working with autistic children, was mere days before her due date.

"It's often called a sensory integration disorder," she told the teachers. "For instance, as a three-year-old, my son Matt wasn't able to locate his favorite toy in a messy playroom, and he couldn't handle playground chaos or busy crowds. If he got overwhelmed, he was liable to lash out. There were times when he hit me or his dad or brother, or worse, a kid on the playground."

The class murmured in sympathy.

"When you intervene in a moment like that, it's wise to ask if you can touch first, to avoid a reflex punch—these kids often don't hit out of anger, but in an attempt to cut down on the sensory confusion they're feeling. Make sure everyone's safe, and once the child has calmed down, you anchor in a familiar routine." Alexandra shook her head. "I'll be honest—there were times it felt like Matt would never gain control over himself in chaotic situations. But he did get there eventually. He learned by practicing and by being self-aware."

An attendee raised her hand. "Why does sensory integration disorder happen?"

"Good question," said Alexandra. "To begin with, it helps to realize that we don't have to see it only as a disorder. You can also see it as a different way of connecting with the world that can be very creative. Matt didn't have the brain machinery to shut out the irrelevant details and focus on what he cares about. But that also means he was incredibly observant, capable of noticing details that most people miss because they filter sensory information so much better than he does. Matt has an absolutely uncanny ability to—" Suddenly Alexandra gasped. "Uh... Oh, Jesus, Mary, and Joseph..."

She leaned on the table in front of her.

The class started to talk all at once. There were voices asking her if she was okay, if they should call an ambulance, if they should get the director, if she should lie down. A student helped her ease into a chair and someone else offered her water. Then the frizzy red hair and friendly face of the center director, a buxom woman named Connie, was beside her.

"How about we get you to hospital, dear?" she suggested.

"Um... yeah, *owww.*"

"Tell me where we're going and then you can call your...husband?"

Alexandra nodded through gritted teeth.

"Just follow me," Connie said.

As thirty teachers waved goodbye and wished her well, Alexandra waddled off with Connie to her office, phone to her ear.

"Sweetheart, it's time," she said. "She's coming fast. Or he."

There was total silence on the other end.

"Jesse?"

"I'm sorry—what? No, I mean where. Where are you?"

Alexandra groaned. "Can you get the boys sorted?"

"Of course, of course. But where are you? I'll be there as soon as I can."

"Honey there's no time. The preschool director will drive me. Meet me at the hospital, okay?"

"Wow. Okay, listen, sweetheart, don't worry about a thing. I'll take care of everything at home, and I'll be there within an hour."

"Okay. Hurry. I love you."

Alexandra's water broke when they were ten minutes from the hospital, and by the time she was wheeled inside, she was whimpering from pain and already six centimeters dilated.

The labor progressed quickly—horribly quickly. A mere three hours after the first contraction, Alexandra and Jesse were gazing down at a brand-new baby girl. Jesse had arrived just in time for the pushing.

"Precipitous labor!" Alexandra said. "That's a fancy word for what just happened. That was more like…I don't know, a cataclysm."

"I can't even imagine," said Jesse, caressing her hair. "You were brilliant."

"It was unspeakable," she said. "But look at this beautiful, perfect little being. I'd do it all over again for her."

Jesse marveled anew over the female of the species. A force of nature, they were.

"She's so tiny compared to our two ten-pounders," he said.

"Wow," said a nurse, overhearing the discussion. "Your first two were really ten pounds?"

"Ten three and ten seven," said Alexandra, "and you should see them now. They're going to be as big as their dad, maybe bigger."

"Well, congratulations," said the nurse. "You make a beautiful family. I'll leave you three to get to know each other."

"So… any more thoughts about names?" asked Jesse.

"Jesse, honestly, I'm still not sure. I just want to catch my breath—and stare at this perfect, angelic face. I really don't know that I've ever seen a more beautiful newborn." She glanced up at him. "And don't you *dare* tell me this is adrenaline and oxytocin speaking."

Jesse laughed. "You know me through and through, sweetheart!" He kissed the top of her head. "And actually, I fully agree with you. She's extraordinary."

While he was immersed in the moment, in awe of his wife and beautiful daughter, not even an hour old, his mind was off on its usual mental gymnastics. He was visualizing the facial recognition system, already genetically and structurally primed, going to work as each second of staring at faces trained the tiny girl's brain, creating a staggeringly efficient algorithm for recognizing patterns, identifying people, and reading their emotions and thoughts. The visualization was spectacular, a biological version of a furiously busy shipyard with the hulk of a giant ship of neural pathways emerging within a dry dock, glittering in ever-gathering complexity.

"You know, I think Rebecca will do nicely," Alexandra said.

The visualization vanished. Jesse leaned over and kissed their new daughter. "Rebecca," he said. "Welcome to the world."

VIPARINAMA DUKKHA

It might have been a mistake to schedule a baby shower after Becca's arrival. Alexandra's reasoning made sense at the time—she didn't want anything to distract her from work—but hosting two dozen women, mostly friends from church, was a lot. Becca was only three weeks old and Alexandra was even more exhausted than normal because Becca had a bad case of colic.

The event was organized chaos. Becca was awake for about half of it and spent most of that time crying. It helped that so many of the women wanted to try their hand at settling her.

Jesse stood back at one point and took it all in while one part of his mind visualized the incomplete development of Becca's digestive system, which he had researched in detail to make sense of why their lives with this newly arrived little being had been so difficult.

Most of the ladies were arrayed around Alexandra in the living room. The air was filled with "Ali this" and "Rebecca that" but Alexandra didn't look like she was enjoying being one of the two centers of attention. She caught Jesse's gaze as he stared at her from the dining room. She smiled weakly, trying to make the most of an event that ordinarily she would relish.

Alexandra's best friend Meg was sitting in the dining room with twelve-year-old Matt. Matt was cowering from the chaos, which seemed incongruous because he was a huge boy. A loving and practical woman, Meg was an experienced teacher—like Alexandra, expert in children with special needs—and had taken care of the boys on many occasions. She and Alexandra would do anything for one another. Jesse realized that he didn't have any same-age friends quite that close but he let the thought slide as he tuned into Meg's conversation with Matt, who was staring blankly into space.

"Matty," Meg said, "remember what we talked about? Look people in the eyes when you talk to them."

"Why Meg?" he asked.

"It's a social convention. It tells people you care about them and are interested in what they have to say."

"I'm not interested in what they have to say Meg."

Jesse stifled a guffaw, which Meg heard. After a quick sidelong smile at Jesse, she responded to Matt.

"It is polite to pretend that you're interested."

"Why Meg?"

"It's another social convention. When people think you're interested in them, they behave more calmly."

Matt seemed happy with that and the questions stopped.

Jesse gazed at Meg in wonder. Maybe it really did take a village to raise a child, he thought, and his mind billowed with a visualization of a highly differentiated social network capable of instantly adapting to the addition of a new little human and reforming as needed around a human with special needs. It was a miracle of cooperation, so many minds building adaptable, caring cultures.

Josh walked into the chaos of people with a tray of hors d'oeuvres. He floated smoothly around the room, chatting easily, the perfect host. Jesse experienced a strange mix of pride and jealousy toward his almost ten-year-old son, who always seemed to know what to say in complicated social settings.

Jesse was hit by a memory of the first time he had been seriously impressed by his second son. It had been Josh's second day of preschool. Jesse watched Josh settle in with a group of four other kids sitting in a circle inside an open wooden house. They were playing with toys and Jesse could see from the way Josh was staring that he wanted the truck another boy was holding. Josh asked the boy whether he could play with the truck and the boy said no.

Josh waited a minute and then asked another kid whether he could play with her toy, while keeping an eye on the truck. He asked in a way that made the boy with the truck want the girl's toy. The boy put down the truck and snatched the girl's toy. Josh unobtrusively picked up the truck he wanted all along. Very sneaky. Jesse had laughed on and off all the way home.

Which of the boys was he more like? Today he figured he was most like Matt. After all, he was doing exactly what Matt was doing, staying out of the fray. He told himself he didn't want to distract from Alexandra's event but knew better. He was incapable of small talk. He forced himself to get another tray of food from the kitchen and did the rounds with it, self-consciously mimicking Josh's graceful manner.

He went to sit beside Matt, Meg having left to circulate. He put his hand on the giant boy's knee and gave a gentle squeeze. "How are you doing with the chaos, Matt?"

"I'd rather be upstairs but Mom says I have to stay down here," he said.

"It's not just your Mom, your Dad says that too," Jesse said. Matt just stared ahead. "At least our guests are not misbehaving and don't need anyone to keep them in line," teased Jesse, calling to mind Matt's tendency when he was young of policing unruly children, sometimes in quite violent ways. He had been ejected from one preschool because of it. Alexandra had been outraged over the preschool's inability to manage Matt, which she saw as a failure of basic competence and a betrayal of professional standards.

Matt smiled grimly, too tense to play along. "Do I really have to be here Dad?"

"Hey, we've handled worse than this, right?"

"Yeah, I s'pose."

"Viparinama dukkha, Matty. Viparinama dukkha."

Jesse put his arm around the man-child's broad shoulders and gave him a squeeze as Matt closed his eyes and took a deep breath. Jesse's mind was flooded with a precious memory, which played out in multi-sensory technicolor.

They were on holiday in the California summer. Jesse whisked the kids away for Boys' Breakfast, and Matt suggested they tell each other "Highs and Lows" from the previous week, something they did in his kindergarten class. Jesse tried to explain how, on this occasion, his high and low were the same: yesterday's long plane ride. He was thrilled to be leaving for vacation, but not at all happy about his seat being kicked.

Matt couldn't stop kicking the seat in front of him, in a car, on a plane, or anywhere else. So they'd buy four plane seats with three in a row for Alexandra and the two boys and one for Jesse in the seat right in front of Matt. Better Jesse than someone else.

After breakfast, they went for a walk on a quiet mountain road. Jesse held Josh's hand in that special parental way: his entire hand around Josh's fist and wrist while Josh gripped his Dad's index finger with his whole hand. Josh was always running away from them, with no concern for his own safety. The little imp was going nowhere without him, at least when they were close to roads and cliffs and animals.

Jesse remembered the luminous California summer air as a taste: clear, cool water. Matt ran in and out of the trees, picking up stones, and bringing them back to Jesse to hold in his free hand. Few of the stones seemed visually interesting, but Matt found something alluring in each one.

They carried Matt's stones to the motel, where Matt made a display of them in a corner. Over the next few days he added to the collection with ferocious dedication. Alexandra looked at Jesse, worried. Matt was blissfully unaware of the looming problem.

A few days later, all four of them were out walking. Matt's stone collection had grown to unmanageable proportions and he was still collecting. It was time to say something.

"Matt, how many stones do you have now?" said Jesse.

"127," Matt said, "not counting the new ones."

"Do you remember how we got here, to California?"

"We flew on a plane," he said, still focused on the stones scattered on the ground.

"That's right, and you kicked me the whole way, didn't you?" There was no response to that comment. Jesse knelt and gathered Matt into his arms, where he relaxed happily, leaning backwards against his Dad's chest, both of them looking at the newly selected stones, lying in a little pile on the ground.

"Sweetheart, we have to fly back to Boston soon and we can't take all of your stones with us."

No response.

"You can choose some stones to take home but we'll have to leave the rest here."

Still nothing.

"Matty, do you understand what I'm saying?"

There was a pause and then Matt finally spoke. "Dad, I want to take the stones home." And then he broke down.

Matt hung onto Jesse's neck, crying with deep sobs and ragged breathing. Jesse lifted him up and gently moved him, soothing him. He could see Alexandra watching; she knew what was happening and trusted him to manage it, so she concentrated on keeping Josh out of the picture. Jesse was thinking they should swap places; she was so much better with Matt than he was.

Between shuddering breaths, Matt tried to say that he wanted to take the stones home. Jesse told him to take a deep breath and showed him how. He copied his Dad and after a while his breathing became steadier. Jesse sat cross-legged on the ground, with Matt in his lap, his head against Jesse's chest where they could see each other's face. Jesse wiped Matt's face with a free hand and brushed his hair as the boy calmed down.

Jesse remembered feeling Matt's trust, the burden especially but also the honor of it, as he instinctively counted on him to help ease his pain. Jesse also remembered feeling out of his depth. He had a powerful urge to call Alexandra for help. But he didn't want to be a failure in Alexandra's eyes and he certainly didn't want to let Matt down. He took a deep breath and tried to reach his son.

"Matty, I want you to repeat something after me. Will you do that?"

He nodded, still breathing raggedly.

"Dukkha," Jesse said. Matt repeated it easily.

"The next bit is tricky. Vi-pa-ri-na-ma." After a couple of tries Matt could say it.

"Now put it together: Viparinama dukkha." He practiced a few times. Then Jesse took the plunge.

"Matt, viparinama dukkha is the reason you're feeling so upset about the stones." Matt was listening intently. "Everything changes, Matt. When you hold onto things because you don't want them to change, you suffer terribly. That's viparinama dukkha. The way to be happy is to let things change. You collect the stones. You enjoy the stones. You let the stones go. You're happy."

Staring at his tear-streaked face, Jesse could tell that Matt understood at some level that was relevant to him. He gave Matt a stone to hold. Matt looked at it, grasping it with both hands.

"It's beautiful, isn't it?" Jesse offered.

"Yes Dad."

"Can you enjoy it and then say goodbye to it?"

"Yes Dad." Jesse's heart broke as he beheld this little being determined to manage his life the best he could.

All four of them said goodbye to the stone collection in a special way. They helped Matt put the little objects in the woods the way he wanted, nestled under a bush. In the end he took no stones back to Boston with him. That was his decision.

Saying those words to ease Matt through some difficult moment of attachment while trying to control his spinning world had become a ritual. Jesse kept this one just between himself and Matt, though. Josh didn't know about it and it wasn't Alexandra's style to whisper ancient Sanskrit phrases to her children. The bizarre dimensions of their family life were Jesse's territory.

Jesse patted Matt on the shoulder and rose to distribute another round of snacks to the visitors. He passed Josh on the way into the kitchen as he headed out with another tray. With their free hands, they exchanged a wordless high five.

Just as Jesse finished getting the next tray ready, Matt appeared at his side, looking like he was in a better place and wanted something to do other than sit by himself and stare into space.

"Would you like to pass these around?" Jesse asked. Matt took the tray and headed out. "Thanks, Matty."

Jesse leaned against the kitchen table and all at once the whole history of Matt's twelve years of life filled his mind as a multi-tracked symphony of visual and auditory strands. He was alone in the kitchen so he closed his eyes to feel the full force of it. He felt the whole of it as a masterclass in determination, in persistence and resilience, overcoming limitations, learning basic social skills that other kids take for granted, managing panic and swirling emotions, choosing a life and fighting for it.

Then Josh's life joined the visualization, another symphonic creation, sparkling with ease and wit, effortless, undisciplined, emotional, risky. The symphonies interacted, interfering with tension and resolution, refining one another.

With the symphonic visions twirling like ice dancers, Jesse remembered the day Alexandra had worked with the two boys to transform the living room into a gigantic tent. There were chairs and tables for support, sheets and blankets everywhere, different rooms for different activities: drawing, jigsaws, blocks, eating. Alexandra had been roaming around in there with Matt and Josh while Jesse sat on the floor just outside the entrance, reading a book, taking it all in. His mind filled with shame thinking back on it. Matt and Josh would say hello to their Dad but they never asked him to join in. They had figured him out and knew that he was no use for that sort of thing. But Alexandra...just beautiful.

The intertwining visual-auditory symphonies still playing, Jesse was filled with the overwhelming urge to make worshipful love to his beautiful life partner, to thank her for who she was, living where he could behold her and treasure her, to bless her for being such a brilliant mother for these two boys, and now Becca.

In the middle of this glorious vision of family bliss, a single, bell-like soprano rang out. It was Becca, a life forming in the midst. Jesse felt the thrill of the voice as a tingle pouring—not creeping, but flooding—up and down his spine.

And then, just as he was afraid he'd collapse or cry out from the improbable bliss of it all—how and why had such happiness come to him, while others suffered unspeakably?—in a corner of his consciousness, he felt something else rising, something unfamiliar, brooding, unwelcome. He was just turning his attention to investigate when a flash of nausea doubled him over.

"Jesse!"

He opened his eyes to see his beloved standing beside him.

He hugged her ferociously. He could tell she was shocked, but after a moment she melted into the embrace.

"You were off somewhere when I came in," she said. "I watched you for a while—you had no idea I was here. It looked like you were on cloud nine, at least until one minute ago. What's going on?"

"Do you have a sec?" he asked. She nodded. Like young lovers escaping a party, Jesse led her by the hand into a quiet room where they wouldn't be interrupted. He sat down and pulled her into his lap and kissed her deeply, his hands on her face as her hands moved from his chest to his neck and hair. They broke apart reluctantly, both breathing heavily.

"My goodness," she said, and took a deep breath. "So you were leaning on the kitchen table, thinking of my child-ravaged body and getting horny?"

"Partly," he said.

"Hey, Jesse," she said, grasping his face with the hands he so loved. "For real. Lemme in."

"I adore you," he confessed, his eyes filling with tears.

She kissed him again. "You're so damn good at deflecting," she said. "Just give me a little. Please, Jesse. I want to see what you see when you disappear like that."

"It's—well it's difficult to explain," he said.

"Try me."

Jesse smiled. "I see us," he said. "The five of us. It sounds like merging symphonies, it looks like miraculous sparkling colors, and it feels so beautiful and intense I can hardly stand it."

She regarded him for a moment. "That sounds wonderful, Jesse. So why are you so shy about these amazing states of mind? Why do you keep me out? I can't understand it."

"I'm not sure I understand it myself."

"Damn it, Jesse." She stared at him for a second and tried once more. "Tell me what *I'm* doing in these visions of yours. Make it good or I'm going to punch you as hard as I can."

"You hold everything together, part glue, part goddess. Sweetheart, it's just my strange mind."

Sure enough, two fists landed on two pecs.

"Ow!" he cried. But what was the point of telling her anything about his bizarre mental way of life? It was impossible to put into words, and he didn't want to frighten her.

"I don't know whether to give you a black eye or screw you silly," she whispered.

"I know which I prefer."

"Be serious," she said. "You know I want to know about this stuff, right?"

"I know."

"And you know you drive me nuts when you won't tell me, right?"

"I'm getting that impression, yes," he answered, mock-rubbing his chest.

"So what are you going to do about it?"

He leaned down and kissed her, one hand on a milk-swollen breast and the other gripping her ass in a nearly desperate way. "Alexandra," he said, "I want you. As in right now. I need you."

"Hey," she said, separating slightly. "It's ok, Jesse. You've got me, ok? Doesn't matter what you say or don't say. I'm yours, all yours, ok?"

His eyes brimmed with tears.

"Jesse!" she cried. "It's ok. I'm right here!"

"I know, sweetheart, I know."

"Listen," she said, "can we talk about this more tonight? I have to get back out there. And you, my love, need to stay here for just a bit until you calm down. You can't be wandering around the church ladies with a raging erection." She reached down to flick his penis affectionately through his dress pants. Jesse laughed. She hugged him and then she was gone.

Jesse sat down heavily in the chair, leaned back, and closed his eyes. He was instantly flooded with the same vision as before, the entwined symphonies of the boys, the goddess glue of Alexandra, the bell-like soprano of Becca, the music rising and swelling, the colors glowing and sparkling. And then, once again, at the edge of his consciousness, he sensed it—something dark and dreadful, steadily encroaching. He couldn't see it, couldn't interpret it, couldn't draw it out. It hovered there, just beyond reach, threatening, predatory. The nausea rose again, and he didn't know if he'd ever been so scared in his life.

He opened his eyes and shook his head, hard, to clear the image. There was no way he would ever tell Alexandra one word about the terrifying presence in his visualization of their family.

Part II
A Growing Family

THE 535TH BOYS' BREAKFAST

It was a chilly March in Boston. Two-year-old Becca was at home with Alexandra while the boys were out for their weekly breakfast. It was time for "Highs and Lows."

Josh had just turned 12 and Matt was a huge boy at 14, already six feet tall and over 200 pounds. and looking like he'd eventually be even bigger than his father. Josh was sprouting, too, and probably headed in the same direction. The boys crowded into one side of a booth opposite Jesse.

Jesse reported on something annoying about work and something enjoyable about the family. The boys paused, respectfully, as their tradition required. "Always listen, never interrupt, never rush" were the rules.

"My turn?" Josh asked.

"Sure, go ahead," Matt said.

"Well, last weekend at youth group, something weird happened." He looked over at Matt, who wore a half smile but stayed silent. "After the Junior High meeting I was out in the parking lot, waiting for Mom. It was dark and cold and nobody was around. Then Paul shows up and decides this is a good time to beat me up. Probably because I told him to shut up when he'd been picking on a kid at the meeting. He came at me hard, knocked me to the ground, and was about to start punching me when, out of nowhere, Matt shows up, drags Paul off me, puts him in a choke hold, backs him up against big metal garbage container, and then throws him into a snow pile. It was awesome!"

Josh had said it all so breathlessly. Jesse was speechless.

"Anyway," Josh continued, "that was my low. And my high."

There was quite a long pause, oddly full of energy. Then Matt crossed his arms and said, "Well, he shouldn't have attacked my little brother."

What was Jesse supposed to say? Trot out the ridiculous parental non-violence line? Ask Josh if he was okay? Demand to know where the adult supervision was? He was being invited to see the world from the middle-school viewpoint of his sons, a rare privilege, and simultaneously sensed that his values were on trial. Sons it was.

"You guys rock," Jesse said. "That's a great story, one for the ages."

Now the boys were beaming, the tension around possible paternal disapproval completely dispersed. After a moment, Jesse continued. "We'll have to break it to your mother carefully…"

The boys descended into happy chattering while Jesse's mind roamed. Josh always seemed to be getting into trouble. Jesse remembered him as a two- or three-year-old running after large and potentially dangerous animals, from geese to dogs, and running heedless in front of traffic, resulting in one rescue drama after another. Why couldn't the kid detect when he was in real danger? How would he manage the teenage perils that lay just around the corner?

Jesse revisited the now-familiar symphonic visualization of his family. Over the past couple of years, it had become even more vivid—taken on depth and texture and nuance, like a photograph coming into focus. But the foreboding presence still haunted the scene off to one side, not quite accessible. Jesse had embarked upon an amateurish form of zazen meditation, "sitting with" the visualization and trying to "make space" for the foreboding presence to fully manifest itself. The only thing to emerge from that experiment was feeling like an idiot. So he was trying to be content with the visualization as it was—enjoy the blissful family part while not denying that worrisome note of foreboding or get too worked up about it. The most likely explanation was that this was his brain's way of registering the anxiety he had over Josh. Would the boy finally do something so monumentally stupid that everything would change for their family? Nightmare scenarios—Josh in a fatal car crash, Josh in an accident that left him paralyzed—weren't out of the question when it came to this kid. The thoughts were so appalling that, had he been a superstitious person, Jesse would've crossed himself on the spot.

He was dragged back to the conversation by a question.

"Dad, Matt says it's unhygienic for Becca to play with my fingers and face because she puts her fingers in her mouth," said Josh. "Is that true?"

"I know what you do with those fingers," said Matt.

"But don't we all share the same germs anyway?" asked Josh.

"Doing that *guarantees* passing any bad germs along," Matt pointed out.

"But it also strengthens her immune system, so you could say I'm actually doing her a favor!"

"Let me tell you what I read about immunity…" Matt began, and then they were off on their own again.

Jesse's mind wandered, this time remembering Josh play-wrestling with his little sister. Caring for Becca was the sole arena where Josh was completely responsible and trustworthy. Jesse didn't doubt for a minute that if the house were burning down or some other calamity beset them, Josh would risk life and limb to get his sister to safety. It was as if all the heedlessness he exerted toward his own body found its exact opposite in Becca. He was so gentle with her, so full of care, and she never had a reason not to trust him completely. Matt, meanwhile, had adapted better than expected to his little sister's arrival, but he wasn't smitten with Becca like the rest of the family were. He was interested in her in more of a cerebral way, and only intermittently. He lacked the physical coordination needed to safely get physical with a tiny human, but he also didn't mind Becca clambering up or scrambling all over him. Watching her treat his big body like a play structure—Becca squealing in delight while Matt stoically endured—left Jesse, Alexandra, and Josh doubled over in laughter.

Jesse was about to tell the boys they should be heading back soon when the glorious visualization of family bliss bloomed in his mind with surprising force and speed. This time all five of them were walking on the shore of a white-sand beach, a gorgeous sunset lending an orangey glow to the whole scene. He laughed a little at the postcard image. He and Alexandra were walking hand in hand, as usual, Matt and Josh were off to one side, and Becca was in the middle, stomping happily in the lapping waves. She fit in so beautifully, like a jewel in the center of a complex necklace. They were so happy it hardly seemed possible.

Surely it couldn't last. Nothing that good lasts forever.

Then it hit him—of course it couldn't last. Nothing, good or bad, lasts. Wasn't he the very one always coaching Matt not to get attached to things? How blind he'd been, to presume this didn't apply to him, too.

Instantly, the hovering threat took center stage and came into focus. In some terrible parody of those dreaded faculty meetings, he saw a celestial committee of cosmic deities, cartoonish in appearance but formidable, assembled to wreak havoc on unsuspecting humans. These malevolent gods got off on arranging events to maximize cruel ironies and deliver existential shocks. "Let's allow that arrogant twit's life to be as close to perfection as possible—and then rip it apart!" "Oh, fabulous idea! Are you thinking what I'm thinking?!" "Of course I am. Let's do it!"

Jesse was deeply shaken, seeing his little family as the target of some cosmic conspiracy. He must be going crazy—he didn't believe in deities, conspiracy theories, premonitions, or portents. Yet all of this felt so very, very real. He could hear the cosmic committee cackling with evil glee even now.

"Dad! Dad!" said Josh. "Are you okay?"

"What?"

"Dad, we've been saying your name for like ten minutes!" Josh said.

"More like 40 seconds," said Matt.

"What*ever*," said Josh. "The point is, you looked all weird and spacey and then you got kinda pale and you wouldn't answer us. I thought you were like, having a stroke or something!"

His fearless son was on the edge of tears.

"I'm sorry, boys," he said. "I just…remembered something I have to do for work, and I got carried away thinking about it."

He was so stunned and afraid he wasn't even lying coherently. And he couldn't stop wondering what was going to happen to his beautiful boy.

WHAT A STRANGE
PROBLEM TO HAVE

It was early Saturday morning in the Boston spring, a few months after Becca turned three. The horrific experience at Boys' Breakfast had faded, lost in the tumult of academic responsibilities, home life, and three kids' busy schedules. And, so far so good: Josh had sustained a sprained ankle in a soccer game, but by Josh standards that was a minor inconvenience, and in fact he'd delighted Becca by giving her crazy, loping piggyback rides while on crutches. Cosmic deities be damned.

Jesse awoke to see Alexandra sitting up in bed, staring out the bedroom window at the old oak trees, illuminated by the faint predawn light. He rolled over and nestled his head in her lap, with an arm around her hip. She instinctively began caressing his neck and hair.

Just as sleep was ready to reclaim him, Alexandra spoke.

"Have you noticed anything weird about the way people stare at Becca?"

"Hmm? What do you mean?" He was drifting, sleep so close, his beloved beside him. It was all so blissful.

"I dunno," she said, "I feel like she gets a lot of stares. Too many."

Well then. No more sleep. "Well, she does strike me as exceptionally cute," he said. "But I figured that was just my parental bias."

"You're right about the bias, but I swear she gets double-takes. I've also had lots of strangers come up and tell me how beautiful she is."

"I'm sure they're just being nice, sweetheart. And don't people tend to stare at young kids anyway? Put disproportionately large eyes and a button mouth on a robot, and evolutionary programming kicks in and people will try to protect and feed the thing. There've been studies where—"

"Oh I'm sure there have been plenty of studies," Alexandra said, with a laugh. "But I'm more concerned about *this* child. Our child. Don't you think people stare at Becca more than other kids?"

"Not that I've noticed. We can devise our own study, sample size one, to check it out, though."

"What do you mean?"

"We've got that lunch today," Jesse said. "Let's observe how people look at her."

"But they won't do it if they think we can see them," she said.

"We can work around that."

Alexandra looked down at her husband. "Aren't you the clever amateur scientist?"

"Well, I haven't noticed anything creepy and you have, so looks like I'm not much of a scientist."

"You know, that's actually a reassuring point," she mused. "Normally you *would* notice everything. Maybe I'm just imagining it."

"Maybe; we'll see," he said, and pulled Alexandra back down into the warmth of the bed. "Sleep," he whispered.

"I'll try," she said.

She was asleep again in moments. But Jesse was wide awake, aching with shame. Why wasn't he sharing his premonition of peril with her?

Later that day, just after they ordered lunch at an outdoor café, Jesse initiated the plan.

"Boys, Mom and I are going for a short walk while we wait for the food. We'll be just over there, on that bench. Do you see it?"

"We see it," Matt said.

"Brilliant. Take care of Becca, ok?"

Josh rolled his eyes as if to say, "Well *duh.*"

Jesse and Alexandra settled in on the bench. It only took moments before Jesse saw it.

"Holy Moses."

Alexandra was right. Almost everyone was staring at Becca, virtually ignoring the other children. They were all beaming, seemingly helplessly, as they watched this little blonde kid in her spring dress playing with a spoon and talking with her brothers. Men, women, young, and old: they were all gawking at Becca.

"I guess you're seeing what I mean," Alexandra said.

"Am I ever," he said. "Why didn't I notice this before?"

"I spend more time with her," said Alexandra, "and my head isn't off in wherever it is yours goes." Then she giggled. "And I may be less intoxicated by her."

Jesse smiled, even as he struggled with a rising discomfort. "Guilty," he said.

Alexandra squeezed his hand tightly, brow furrowed. "We're going to have to contend with this forever, you know. And it's only going to get worse as she grows up."

"Holy Moses," Jesse said again. "I don't even want to think about that."

"Nor do I," said Alexandra. "But it's best we be prepared."

"What a strange problem to have," he said. "I never thought about it before—never had any reason to, with my rather mediocre looks—but I guess beauty can be a liability."

Alexandra smiled and kissed him on the cheek. "I like your looks just fine."

He looked into his wife's eyes. "And I sincerely think you're the most beautiful woman I've ever seen."

"You're such a dope," she said, beaming.

"True. But okay, what are we gonna do about this unaccountably beautiful child?"

"We'll do the best we can, like always," said Alexandra. "And it doesn't hurt that she has two huge brothers, one of them on his way to earning a black belt."

"And one who would move heaven and earth to protect her," added Jesse.

Alexandra exhaled. "Okay," she said. "I can't tell you how much better I feel. We'll be just fine. All of us. Let's get back to the kids."

"Let's do," he said, and they walked back hand in hand.

HER PERPETUAL
HOST OF WATCHERS

Becca was four and her parents were taking her to the zoo while both boys were at school.

As they approached people near the zoo gates, the staring began. Jesse could always feel it coming, and it always came.

"Hey," Alexandra said. "Ease up. Nothing new here."

"Sorry," he said. "I should be used to it by now, but it makes me so angry."

"What makes you angry, Daddy?" asked Becca, perched in his arm. Jesse was momentarily speechless.

"Daddy wishes he could come to the zoo more often, sweetheart," offered Alexandra, leaning over to kiss him as they walked.

While Alexandra stood beside the empty stroller, staring at the map and planning the route, Becca pointed out shiny balloons on sticks and Jesse walked over with her, hand in hand. Everyone was watching her, as usual, with furtive glances or, in some cases, brazen stares.

"I want a balloon," she declared. "That one." She pointed to a pink balloon emblazoned with a photograph of a baby gorilla in a mother gorilla's arms.

"We can get one on the way out," Jesse told her. "After we see all the animals."

"I want it now, Daddy," she said, staring into his eyes like a hypnotist.

"But then we have to carry it around all day," Jesse said. "First the animals, then lunch, then the balloon, okay? Let's go see Mom."

Becca beckoned him to bend down. He squatted next to her and she held his face in her hands, then looked around at the several dozen people nearby. Jesse watched the usual wave-like effect of people averting their gaze when they were caught staring. "Daddy," Becca said. "I want that balloon now." Then she started to cry.

My God, he thought, this was entirely calculated. The little monster knew it would be harder for him to say no with everyone watching.

Alexandra said he tended to process certain feelings too quickly, and not always the right feelings. On this occasion, he sensed a glorious jumble of emotions. He felt honored to be played by such a young master. Part of him wanted to give her a high five but she was still crying and he needed to take care of her. He was also angry, but most of all he was in awe. If she was this smart—or should he say shrewd—at four, what would she be like at fourteen? They had a real firecracker on their hands.

"All right, kiddo," he said. "Time to join Mom." He pointedly ignored the disapproving looks as he walked a sobbing Becca back to Alexandra and got her strapped into the stroller.

"What was that about?" asked Alexandra.

"She wants a balloon. I told her later when we go home." His observation about his daughter employing her perpetual host of watchers to manipulate him could wait until later. "She'll settle," he added, and started walking.

"There wasn't a better way to handle it?" Alexandra asked.

"Not that I could find," he said. "Not without buying the balloon anyway."

Alexandra had him stop the stroller. She knelt beside it and ran her hands through Becca's wispy blonde hair. She wiped tears away from the girl's gleaming blue eyes, and Becca's sobbing subsided.

As they headed to the recreated African savannah to cast their eyes on the absurdity of displaced giraffes and elephants and rhinos, Jesse realized just how out of his depth he was with this child.

But he was also enormously proud of her, and so sublimely happy that he really didn't care.

FIGURE IT OUT!

Becca sat in Alexandra's lap, flanked by Josh and Jesse, everyone perched on fold-out chairs waiting for Matt's black-belt kung-fu test to begin. Becca was playing with one of Josh's hands, but eventually got bored so she climbed into his lap. She pulled at the hairs sprouting from his chin and upper lip, his first attempt at fashionable facial hair. She tugged on his lips and ears but Josh didn't mind. Josh never minded. She stood up and started jumping up and down on his lap, periodically hugging his head, and singing an unintelligible song to him, to herself, and to everyone watching the cute little girl playing. She had no idea how hard Josh was working to protect her from hurting herself as she jumped all over the unstable platform that was his lap.

Just that morning they had found Becca, once again, sleeping at the foot of Josh's bed. Any time she had a nightmare, she crawled into bed with Josh. Jesse sometimes felt a disconcerting sense of jealousy, but mostly he was glad and grateful: Becca seemed to be the one thing keeping fifteen-year-old Josh, who'd been caught smoking and drinking more times than Jesse cared to recall, from going off the deep end.

Jesse leaned over to Alexandra. "This is an amazing moment," he whispered.

Alexandra beamed. "Just think how far he's come," she said, leaning her head on Jesse's shoulder.

"And you!" Jesse said. "He never would have stuck it out if you hadn't gone through the training with him."

"He's a lot better than I am," said Alexandra.

"But you're only one belt away. You'll get your black belt before he graduates next year."

She gave him a peck of thanks on the cheek. "If I ever get that black belt," she said, "it'll have nothing to do with me being able to defend myself in a dark alley. It'll be because sensei sees my determination and hard work, and takes pity on me."

"Look, there's Matty!" shouted Becca, pointing at her big brother as he walked out in the line of black-belt candidates. She jumped up and down and waved but Matt was being very formal and didn't even look in her direction. "He's not waving at me," said Becca, pouting.

"Shhh, time to sit down, Becca," said Josh. She nestled in his lap and leaned back against his huge body.

Throughout the testing of forms and fighting Josh was masterful in handling Becca, distracting her when she became impatient, keeping her quiet, and doing it all gently. In the end Matt and his cohort received their belts, and everyone applauded.

The second the ceremony ended, Becca ran to her newly honored brother. She held out her arms for Matt to pick her up, though he rarely did. On this occasion, he held her hand and walked with her over to where the family was smiling proudly. Everyone congratulated him, and Josh—now almost as large as his big brother—wrapped him in a giant hug, which Matt returned. Jesse felt nearly faint with happiness—but immediately the thought of the committee of cosmic deities assailed him. *Just you wait*, he could hear them say. He frowned and shook his head, hard.

"Jesse?" Alexandra said.

Becca's shouts preempted further conversation. "Matty! Up!" she said.

Becca grabbed hold of the black belt around his waist and attempted to climb up his body.

"Help me!" she cried.

"Figure it out," Matt responded.

"No, help me! Matty, help!"

"You can't always get what you want, you know, Becca," he teased, and she started pounding on his giant thighs with her tiny fists. He suddenly grabbed her, swung her around, held her upside down, and tickled her into gales of laughter. They had all seen it a hundred times.

Matt was the only one of them who seemed immune to Becca's charms. Josh didn't mind being manipulated and relished being the teenage idol of Becca's life, and Jesse found himself giving in to her at least half the time, despite his best efforts to maintain consistency in his parenting. Even Alexandra, the trained parenting expert, found herself melting before Becca's cuteness from time to time.

Becca's appearance was truly striking, like something out of a fairy tale. Long golden hair, eerily bright blue eyes, perfect rosebud lips, flawless skin. Where had this creature come from? Her coloring matched her genetic endowment, but the beauty seemed out of place in their otherwise normal-looking family. Jesse often found himself looking at Becca in amazement, no different than the strangers who were always doing double-takes. The cuteness response wasn't driving the public gawking anymore; now it was definitely her stunning appearance. Could a child so young be beautiful? It was hardly fathomable, but Becca was. Alexandra and Jesse often wondered what she'd look like at eighteen, and how her appearance might impact her future. How odd to have such a problem to contend with—if a problem is indeed what it was. Jesse, who'd navigated the world through his intellect since he was Becca's age, was at a loss when it came to his daughter.

Her personality was still developing but she was above all sweet at that age. Despite all the manipulative moves, Jesse sensed not even a hint of malice in her. She was polite, obedient, loving, and affectionate. Unlike Matt, she wasn't particularly curious about the world. Unlike Josh, she was not particularly insightful. Rather, she was an intuitive presence, moving through her world with a sense of entitlement—an assumption grounded in her short but powerful personal history.

WHATEVER

Something was pulling at Jesse's sleeping mind. It was annoyingly insistent. The phone. He fumbled for it and said hello—and was stunned awake the moment the caller identified herself. It only took a few moments to get a report on the situation. Holy Moses.

Alexandra turned on her bedside lamp. "Who was it? What's going on?"

"The local police," said Jesse. "No one is hurt, but they have Josh."

Alexandra gasped. "It's 2am, Jesse! What happened?"

"Apparently Josh was pulled over driving Matt's car."

"He *what*? He's only just fifteen!"

"Precisely what I said," said Jesse, pulling on some clothes.

"Wait for me. I'm coming too," she said.

"What about Becca?"

"Aarrgghh. Okay, you go, but we all talk when you get home," she said.

There was a knock on the bedroom door and Jesse answered it.

"What's going on?" Matt asked.

"Your brother got caught driving your car tonight," Jesse said. "I have to go pick him up from the police station. And since you're up, either you or your Mom should come with me so we can collect your car from wherever it is."

Before Matt could volunteer, Alexandra jumped in. "Matt, would you please stay and deal with Becca in case she wakes? I'd like to go with Dad."

"Sure, Mom. No problem." Matt looked at Jesse. "Is this the first time he has taken my car in the middle of the night?"

"I don't know for sure, Matt," answered Jesse. "But you and I can both do the math."

"Did Josh have permission to drive that car?" asked the officer.

It was a strange question and Jesse sensed a trap. If he said yes, the permissive parent would be in trouble; if he said no, Josh could be charged with auto theft. But it was a small suburban town; there had to be a better way.

"Look, I'd rather not answer that," Jesse said. "Is there any way we can take him home and deal with him ourselves?"

"Harshly," Alexandra added. She had been quiet on the ride over, but Jesse had never seen her so angry.

The officer took in the parents, one obviously anxious and one obviously furious, calculated the amount of hot water the teenager was in, and relented.

"Thank you, officer," said Jesse.

The officer retrieved Josh and Alexandra marched him out by the arm. Not a word was spoken on the way to Matt's car until they were about to get out.

"You," said Alexandra. "You're coming with me. Get in the car. *Now.*"

Josh got out and slunk into the passenger seat of Matt's car. Jesse did not envy him that ride home.

Becca hadn't roused so the four of them sat around the kitchen table for a heart-to-heart in the middle of the night. Josh was hard to read, avoiding eye contact and seeming put out by the whole thing. Alexandra started to speak but Matt cut her off.

"Have you taken my car before tonight?" he asked.

"Jeez, so I'm getting it from all three of you?" Josh said.

"That doesn't answer my question," Matt said. "Have you taken—"

"What do you think?" said Josh. "Look, Mom already ground- ed me until I'm like twenty. Doesn't that settle it? Can't we all just go to bed?"

"Just go to bed?!" Jesse said. "Josh, if you hadn't noticed, you were picked up by the police tonight! You should be thanking your lucky stars—and your mom and me—that you aren't in jail."

"Whatever," said Josh. "Mom has already given me the whole spiel—I scared everyone half to death, I'm so irresponsible, I should feel lucky I didn't blah blah blah."

Jesse was astonished. What had happened to his sweet, empath- ic son who was, or had been, so compassionate, so mature for his age?

"So the answer is yes," Matt said. "You have taken my car with- out permission, multiple times. Are you going to do it again?"

"Nope!" said Josh, his sarcasm lost on Matt.

"*Josh*," said Alexandra.

"His word is good enough for me," said Matt. "I'm going to bed."

And just like that the matter was settled for his first son. Jes- se envied him: his uncomplicated trust, his faith in his younger brother.

Jesse stared at his second son as Alexandra launched into what he could only assume was a more forceful reprisal of the "spiel" she'd given Josh in the car. Part of the freak squad, Josh had just finished his second year of high school and clearly didn't think much of it. Extremely intelligent and perceptive, he possessed a massively over-developed crap-detector. He saw piles of crap in the hidden corners of every institution he encountered: school, church, government, industry, advertising, the military. He was letting his hair grow long, exploring pot and sex and alcohol, getting hooked on nicotine, and aching for something that was truly capable of captivating his tired soul. Even Alexandra had been stymied by his sudden rebelliousness, and nothing they did— grounding him, trying to reason with him, threatening him with ever-increasing consequences, trying to scare him back into model behavior—seemed to work. But he obviously also wanted to stay connected with the family, especially to Becca, who idolized him, so Jesse had always felt Josh would eventually come back around.

But now he wondered. His visualization of the family beckoned him as they sat at the table. The gods who got off on playing around with human lives for their own amusement were having a blast right now—he could see them all snickering at him, his ignorance, his arrogance. *You actually thought you were going to get off scot-free, didn't you?* one of them said. Another doubled over in laughter. *No one hides from the gods, you simpleton!*

Jesse shook his head and covered his face with one hand. Who was supposed to be in the hot seat right now, him or Josh? The brain was such a funny thing, capable of such complex, convincing tricks. But he couldn't shake the feeling—no, the certainty— that something was about to break. The gods were done playing around. They were coming to claim his son.

Part III
The Gods Speak

WEDNESDAY EVENING, JULY 15, 2009

It was eight o'clock on a hot and humid Boston summer evening, bedtime for Becca. She was six-and-a-half, enjoying the summer after her kindergarten year, and looking forward to first grade in the fall. She'd flourished in school, was already reading independently, and had made a number of new friends. Jesse was hopeless at keeping up with their names and all the birthday parties and playdates, but thankfully, not only was Alexandra great in that arena, she delighted in it.

Josh, too, had been an enormous help. He was still a mess, failing two classes only for neglecting to turn in work, still drinking and smoking, but his devotion to Becca was unfailing. It was Alexandra's idea to give him more responsibility regarding Becca's care, and the arrangement worked beautifully. It was Josh who picked up Becca from school each afternoon, Josh who helped her with projects, and it was Josh she still turned to when she had an occasional nightmare. She brought out the best in this wayward, struggling boy, and not a day went by that Jesse didn't take a moment to be grateful for Becca's existence, Josh's safety, and Matt's dogged perseverance to make his way in the world. They were all still more or less okay. He was embarrassed at having got so worked up, yet again, over the taunting of nonexistent cosmic deities, at letting his worries get the better of him.

That night Alexandra was tired from a day of conferencing, so Jesse carried Becca upstairs and got her ready for bed while Alexandra found the books for the night. Reading to the children had been Alexandra's favorite activity, right from the beginning. She read thousands of books to the boys, gradually working through the local town library's holdings. With Becca, she got to revisit old favorites as well as explore everything newly written since the boys had been little.

Jesse kissed Becca good night, then sat in the rocking chair in the corner while Alexandra perched on the edge of the bed for the nightly reading of P.D. Eastman's "Are You My Mother?" Becca was way beyond this board book by now, but it was her favorite, and part of their ritual. Alexandra used different voices for the various animals, none of whom was the right mother for the lonely little bird—except one, of course. Then, after reading a chapter from whatever "big girl book" they were onto now, Alexandra hugged and kissed Becca goodnight, and Jesse kissed Becca's forehead and ran his fingers through her hair, which she loved.

"Goodnight Becca. I love you."

"Goodnight Daddy. I love you."

"Goodnight Becca, I love you," said Alexandra.

"Goodnight Mommy. I love you."

It was their simple parting ritual. Alexandra and Jesse walked away, pausing at the door to look back toward their daughter, the most unexpected surprise that had turned out to be the most precious gift. They embraced, side-by-side, watching her drift off to sleep.

THURSDAY MORNING, JULY 16, 2009

As usual Jesse was up at six, and he crept out quietly to keep Alexandra asleep. The boys slept like teenagers so he didn't expect to see them until midday. Becca, however, normally woke between six and seven, and sometimes joined him in his office.

On the way to the kitchen, Jesse peeked into Becca's room. He grinned to see she'd beaten him to the punch today, already getting breakfast by herself—the sign of a growing girl. Soon enough they'd both be in his office, he tapping away at the computer, she in one of the leather recliners, with a pile of books.

The kitchen, however, was not occupied. And neither was the playroom. Jesse sighed—poor Becca must have had nightmares again. He went back up the stairs to peek in on Josh and Becca, but Josh was alone, dead to the world. Becca never crept into bed with Matt, but Jesse looked there too. No Becca. Maybe she'd got past him somehow. He started over. The master bedroom had Alexandra in it but no Becca. Knowing it was absurd but unable to help himself, he looked in the boys' rooms again. No Becca. Becca's room was empty, as were the bathroom and the attic office. Jesse ran downstairs to Alexandra's office: no Becca.

"What's going on?" he said aloud.

Basement: no Becca. External doors: dead-locked. He was starting to panic, but she could be hiding. He checked the usual spots. Nothing.

"Becca!" he called. "Come out immediately—game over!"

There was nothing but an eerie, intolerable silence.

Jesse bolted upstairs and woke Alexandra.

"Honey, I can't find Becca. Have you seen her?"

"What? No, I was asleep—wait, what do you mean?"

"Oh sweetheart," he said.

Alexandra sprang out of bed and they rushed to Becca's room to start looking all over again. They both called out her name. Nothing. Alexandra looked under the bed and in the closet. Jesse thought to feel the bed and announced that it was cold.

"Check the window," Alexandra said.

Jesse yanked up the blind. The window was closed, but when he pushed it, it opened easily. His heart sank. "Unlocked," he said.

The look on Alexandra's face was too terrible to behold.

"Well," he said, "we don't check the upstairs windows every day...."

"Jesse."

"No," he said. "Don't say it."

It suddenly occurred to him that the screen should have been in place. He stuck his head through the window and saw the screen lying, bent, on the front lawn.

"Oh no." He said it quietly, his pulse pounding, his heart attempting to escape his chest.

"Alexandra, don't touch anything else," he said. "We have to call the police. Now."

Alexandra sprinted downstairs for the phone. Jesse ran outside. The screen was slightly crumpled, which meant it had been forced open. He could detect indentations in the grass beneath the window, where a ladder might have been placed. But that didn't explain how the window had been unlocked. Or why the shade was down.

Jesse went back inside to check on Alexandra. The 911 operator had told her to stay on the line until officers arrived, so she was still standing there, phone to her ear, tears streaming down her face. Jesse gave her a hug and she started moaning. He found her a chair and started to tell her not to worry, that everything would be okay, but he could already hear the committee of malevolent gods snickering.

"I'll get the boys up," he said.

Josh first. Jesse shook his shoulder, harder than he'd intended.

"Josh, listen. Wake up and listen. Becca is gone. We can't find her. The police are on their way. Please get dressed and come downstairs. Don't touch anything." Josh stared at him without moving, horror overtaking his face. "Quickly, please. Your mom needs you."

Josh was out of the bed in a flash. He grabbed at the pile of clothes on the floor and tossed on the first thing he found.

Matt next. He was immediately into a weird kind of pseudo-alertness, as usual, even before Jesse told him the news. It took him a couple of tries to comprehend.

"Wait, what?"

"We can't find Becca."

"What?" Jesse couldn't tell how much was sleep and how much was disbelief. But he told him again, slowly and plainly.

"Come downstairs, Matty. And don't touch anything, okay?"

"Okay."

By the time Jesse got back to Alexandra, she was sobbing freely, this time into Josh's shoulder. Matt was soon pounding down the stairs. Jesse grabbed the phone from Alexandra and told the 911 operator that two police cars were pulling up out front. He hung up.

Jesse met the officers outside, told them what he knew, and pointed out the window screen and the indentations in the soft ground. Inside he showed one of them Becca's bedroom while the other began interviewing Alexandra and the boys.

"So we'll find your prints on the window?" the officer asked.

"I'm afraid so," said Jesse. "Alexandra's too, from who knows when, but I hope you'll be able to find something else. *Someone else's.*"

He could not believe he was saying these things, that any of this was happening. *Please, please,* some part of him reflexively said, *let her be okay. Bring her back to us.* He was the last person in the world to think there was any supernatural being who heard humans' pleas, much less did anything about them, but his instinctive superstition was being brutally unmasked.

"We'll do everything we can, sir," the officer said.

Two more police cars arrived. The officers asked lots of questions, repeating themselves ad nauseam. Jesse and Alexandra answered everything clearly, helpfully—and fast, because a lot was at stake in the timing. Alexandra gave them a recent photo of Becca. The police issued an Amber Alert with impressive speed.

Soon there were forensic experts dusting for fingerprints, scouring for stray hairs, and looking for scratch marks that might explain the unlocked window. An officer helped Alexandra figure out whether anything else was missing from Becca's room or from the rest of the house. Nothing was missing. Just Becca.

After a couple of hours, the four of them sat in the living room, blankly staring at nothing in particular. Josh was fastened to Jesse's side in a most un-teen-like way, wrung out from sobbing. Alexandra was beside Jesse as well, utterly desperate, but quiet. Not even Matt was speaking, which somehow frightened Jesse more than anything. He just sat on the edge of an armchair, eyes unnaturally wide and watching the three of them.

The police had called for a social worker, and she was in and out of the living room, fussing about with kind but ineffective gestures. Mrs. Buxton was a robust woman in her mid-40s, drably dressed, very sympathetic, and completely useless. Poor woman. What was she supposed to do? She had asked them whether they wanted her to arrange for a local clergy person to visit and Alexandra and Josh said "no!" simultaneously and with a degree of vehemence that took Mrs. Buxton and Jesse by surprise. She described resources, explained procedures, offered to call friends or relatives, yada, yada. Jesse took it in, more or less. Matt probably did too. None of them was really attentive.

A policeman came in to report no movement on the Amber Alert. The forensics people wrapped up and left, leaving instructions to stay out of Becca's bedroom. The police left, promising to share any news as soon as it came to hand. Mrs. Buxton left, somberly offering to be available whenever the family might need her.

And then there were four.

Josh was lying on the floor, staring at the ceiling in a profoundly disturbing way.

"Josh?" Matt ventured. No response.

"Josh, are you okay?" Alexandra said.

"Leave him be," Jesse said, quietly.

"No!" Matt boomed. "We need to know everyone is okay!"

"I'm okay," said Josh, almost inaudibly.

Jesse leaned into Alexandra and whispered. "We have to do *something* or we're going to go absolutely crazy."

"But what can we do?"

"I'm going to make breakfast," he said.

"Nobody's going to eat it."

"Doesn't matter. It's what we do. It's what I need to do."

Jesse stood. Alexandra held out her hands so he could pull her up off the couch. He was pounded by the memory of Becca reaching out to him, arms fully extended, so he could pick her up. He collapsed to his knees, put his head in Alexandra's lap, and gave in to the sobs he'd been holding back.

At midday Jesse started moving around the kitchen to make breakfast food that nobody would eat. He started some bacon frying, whipped up pancake batter, scrambled eggs, cooked toast, warmed a few plates.

Six hours had passed since the discovery that Becca was missing, almost that long since the Amber Alert had gone out. Jesse was losing his mind, entering a bizarre state of calmness. The ritual of cooking breakfast kept him in touch with reality, or maybe it was keeping him out of touch with a reality he didn't want to face.

He moved smoothly, with practiced flips and scrapes and whips, making the timing work so that everything was finished together.

Alexandra set the table and they put out the food. Jesse went back to the boys, still sitting in the living room.

"You don't need to eat," he said. "But we do need to sit together. C'mon."

They slowly migrated to the dining room table, moving gingerly as if nursing broken bones.

Once everyone was seated, Jesse said, "I don't feel like eating but I'm going to make myself. You can eat or not eat. There's no normal way through this."

As he stared as his plate, the familiar visualization of his family screamed at him. The formerly hidden darkness had appeared and spread, dulling the colors, and the symphonic music was an unintelligible cacophony, dominated by a screeching chorus of cackling divine laughter. Right then, he knew with irrational certainty that he would never see his daughter again. He fled to the bathroom where he repeatedly dry-heaved into the toilet bowl. Alexandra ran after him and held onto him as the boys stared at their parents from the doorway.

The gods' sadistic laughing crescendoed to a head-splitting volume and Jesse instinctively clawed at his ears. They cackled and gibbered and jeered, and to his deep horror, they began to morph into demonic forms. These were cartoonish demons and ghouls he must have seen in some childhood storybook or television show, but somehow all the more awful for their fatuous absurdity. "No," he said. "No!" He was aware that Alexandra was speaking to him but he couldn't understand her. The demon gods laughed even harder. Jesse clutched at his head and squeezed his eyes shut. "Go away!" he shouted. "Leave us alone!"

Alexandra's sharp slap to his face snapped him back. "Jesse! Jesse!" It was clear from her tone she'd been screaming at him for some time.

Jesse opened his eyes.

"Sweetheart, I'm so sorry!" Alexandra said. "You kept going on about how you couldn't make it stop, and I didn't know what else to do! Jesse, what's happening? Should I call 9-1-1?"

Jesse looked at his family ("your *remaining* family," the gods whispered), and saw the terror in their faces.

"No," he said. "No, I'm—I'm back now. I—I just need to catch my breath."

"Boys," Alexandra said. "Would you give us a moment?"

"Sure Mom," said Matt, who grabbed Josh's arm and led him away. Alexandra, who he now registered was on the floor with him, kicked the bathroom door shut.

"Jesse, what *was* that?" she said.

"I'm honestly not sure," he said. "But I think the worst of it has passed."

"It was one of those vision things, wasn't it?" she said. "You lost control of it this time, didn't you?"

Holy Moses. Was he *that* transparent?

"Mmm, something like that," he managed.

Jesse sat up and leaned against the side of the bath. "Come here," he said, and pulled Alexandra close. "Where are the boys?"

"Probably listening just outside the door."

"What did they see?"

"All of it."

"Sweet Jesus." He looked at her. "I'm so sorry."

"Jesse, I know this is a terrible moment—the worst moment of all our lives," she said. "Which is all the more reason you shouldn't try and go it alone. Now tell me what just happened."

Jesse gazed at his wife—his beautiful, smart, strong beloved, who had no idea she'd just vanquished a contingent of slavering demons. "Oh sweetheart," he said. "I feel terrible that I frightened you. Nothing like that has ever happened to me before. My whole life, since I was a young boy, I've always been able to stop a visualization that troubled me. This time, when I'm under such terrible stress, I guess I—."

"Wait, *what?* You've been having these experiences since you were a boy and you never thought to tell me?"

"I didn't want you to worry, sweetheart."

"Don't you dare 'sweetheart' me! I can't believe this!"

"I'm sorry, Alexandra."

"I hope so," she said. "This is too big a deal to keep to yourself."

"Fair enough," he said.

"Okay then," she said. "Tell me more. And Jesse, I mean in detail. None of your usual evasiveness."

"Right now?"

"Right now is what matters most," she said.

Jesse was suddenly aware of how angry Alexandra was. He was hurting her. He would tell her about the visualization—absent the demonic "visitation," which he was already writing off as an aberration, a reaction to extreme stress.

He took a deep breath. "Okay, this may sound crazy, but what I'm seeing is that we've been the victims of a cosmic prank. A bunch of sadistic deities are partying, laughing their asses off at how perfect the whole thing turned out. And by that I mean tragic, horrendous. They've been waiting for years for tragedy to befall our family—all because we're too happy."

"Oh Jesse," she said.

"No but wait, it's not all bad," he said, aware of how completely cracked he sounded. "In the background is the visualization of family bliss I described to you years ago, at your baby shower."

"You call that describing?" she said.

"The visualization is normally so captivating—and such a source of comfort and joy," he said. "Nothing at all like today. The boys each have a symphony with sparkling colors and they merge so beautifully, sometimes in tension, sometimes in harmony. Becca is a crystal-clear soprano voice, which fits perfectly while also going its own way, and I see her as a bright rainbow thread spooling out across everything else. You're the goddess who holds everything and everyone together. You're white light shooting through all the other colors. Sometimes parts of your body become visible but you're so all-encompassing that everything else is tiny by comparison and so the action seems to take place inside of you. I get to watch from the edges, no music or visuals. Alexandra,

I have savored this visualization and developed it for years, ever since the baby shower when it first came to me."

Jesse gazed at her, as earnestly as the day he vowed to be hers in their wedding ceremony. "But here's the part I haven't told you, and I'm sorry for that. Right from the beginning, there was something not quite right about the visualization. I could sense a patch of darkness off to the side, just out of sight. It's not unusual for half-formed feelings to show up—it can take me a while to figure out what's going on—but this one felt vaguely threatening, like a premonition. I thought maybe it was about some disaster befalling Josh, but it was never clear. Anyway I tried a thousand times to figure it out, but I couldn't make it show itself. In the end I decided it was an expression of my incredulity at how wonderful my life had become—a kind of certainty that things couldn't stay this good forever.

"So I savored the visualization, the happy family part, and ignored the unpleasant bit. It went on like that for years, until one day I finally got an inkling of what the threatening presence was. I got the visual of that committee of gods who torture mere mortals like us, especially happy ones, as if to underline the futility of human efforts to be happy."

"Oh Jesse," Alexandra said again.

"I know," he said, with a weak smile. "Your husband is a bit cracked."

"Maybe a little," she said. "What about now? What are you seeing now?"

He shook his head.

"Oh come on, Jesse. Don't get shy on me now." She leaned over and kissed the top of his head.

"It's—it's not good, Alexandra. It's all so dark and ominous."

"You underestimate me, Jesse."

His eyes filled with tears. What would he do without this woman? What would any of them do without her?

"Right now the darkness has flowed into the visualization, like blood poisoning a clear stream. The music is distorted and cacophonous. Becca's soprano is just a scream that goes on and on and on…. And you—you feel like a Picasso painting, with parts of your body connected up all wrong, and blood all over you. And behind everything is this horrible, super loud, cackling laughter. It's like something out of a horror movie."

He gripped her so tightly she gasped. But she put her arms around him and didn't let go.

"I thought the premonition had been about Josh," he cried. "But I was wrong—it was about Becca all along!"

He started to weep, and Alexandra held on. After a few moments the door slowly inched open, and Josh poked his head in.

"Dad!" he said.

Matt was right behind him, and they crowded into the bathroom, where all four of them gathered on the floor. Soon they were all crying.

Exactly how much agony was sufficient for the amusement of sadistic deities?

THE FOLLOWING TWO DAYS

The next forty-eight hours were unspeakable.

YOU CAN TRUST THE
POLICE CHIEF

On Saturday morning, the family received a visit from the Chief of Police. In his deep, gravelly voice, he admitted he had no good news to report: nothing on the Amber Alert, nothing from forensics, and nothing from people calling in with possible sightings. No active leads. Over fifty hours had passed.

Jesse had done his homework. He knew it was pretty much over.

Even the closed but unlocked bedroom window had led nowhere. They hadn't been able to think of anyone who might have had an opportunity to unlock it from the inside, and forensics had been unable to detect anything that might have led to it being unlocked from the outside. Was it possible that Becca had opened it, standing on a chair, maybe in response to someone outside? She knew how to do that. But her chair had been where it always was, beside the rocking chair they loved to sit in, with Becca. Maybe the person who took her had moved the chair back—probably would had to have done that, in fact, to get in and out. Maybe that person closed the blind and the window as well, before leaving. But Becca had been well trained in stranger-danger matters. Maybe it had been someone she knew. Maybe it had been someone dressed as a fireman telling her that the house was on fire and promising to help her. Jesse chided himself for touching the window that terrible morning, possibly hiding Becca's prints or damaging critical evidence. But whoever took her was probably wearing gloves anyway.

As his mind spun around in useless circles, Jesse felt himself subtly switching from hoping to recover Becca to hoping she was safe. Maybe she'd been stolen for money, sold to a grateful family who'd love her and take care of her. The alternatives were imponderable, unbearable, unforgivable. He didn't dare share this bizarrely detached line of reasoning with Alexandra.

The police chief's update delivered, Jesse led him outside and asked him point-blank what the chances were that Becca would be cared for by a reasonably loving family.

He looked darkly at Jesse, sizing him up. "Five percent." He sighed. "Honestly, less. I'm sorry."

"Thank you for being straight with me," said Jesse.

"Do you want me to get the press more involved? It'll probably turn your house into a media zoo for a few days but it might increase the odds of finding Rebecca."

"Yes, I think so," Jesse said. "Is there someone you trust that you can recommend? Someone with good national reach and who won't sensationalize this situation?"

"Anna Feld," the chief said. "I'll have her get in touch, okay?"

"Okay. Thanks again."

They shook hands and he left. Jesse thought he saw him shaking his head as he moved away. He knew it was pretty much over, too.

They'd already been contacted over the phone by the media, following the Amber Alert. That started on Thursday afternoon, right after the disastrous brunch. A couple of trucks had come by and taken photos of the house. But nobody had been camped out on the lawn or stalking them. Missing children were tragically common. Jesse was sure they wouldn't have bothered at all if it hadn't been for the extraordinary photograph of Becca that went out with the Amber Alert. People probably stared at that photograph the way they stared at Becca in person.

The police chief's contact, WDRZ's lead anchor Anna Feld, arrived at the house at 6pm on Saturday with a camera crew. Somehow every other news outlet found out and were arriving outside the house as well, cameras and microphones and reporters everywhere.

Alexandra and Jesse met Anna on the front porch. She was tall and fit with coifed blonde hair, as though she was ready to be on camera at any minute.

"We're talking with you on the basis of the police chief's recommendation that you're professional and well-connected," Jesse said with uncharacteristic bluntness. "Was he exaggerating?"

Anna took the question in stride. "You can trust the police chief," she said. "Most importantly, I have strong personal connections with anchors in three of the major national television news networks, and in a dozen high-profile national newspapers. I won't bore you with the details but the connections are real."

"It's important to us that you keep our two boys out of the media coverage. Just my wife and me, okay?"

"No problem. I'd do the same in your situation," she replied. "How about we get started with an off-the-record conversation? No crew."

Alexandra nodded weakly. "Please come inside, Anna."

The camera crew remained on the porch, two of them sitting on the swing that had so often held Alexandra and Jesse, with Becca in their laps.

After an hour of conversation with the whole family, the boys went upstairs and Anna spelled out her plan.

"I think the best way to get Rebecca back is for me to tell a compelling story that spreads Becca's picture as far and as fast as possible. Sound right?"

Jesse and Alexandra nodded, sensing a glimmer of hope.

"I know what to do," she said. "It will involve a couple of interviews, which are best done with both of you together. One of them will be with me and my team. I think at least one of the national current affairs programs will pick this up and that will lead to at least one other interview. There could be others, which is up to you. My plan will also involve a potentially complicated news conference, again with the two of you present. What I'll have that nobody else will is the inside story of Rebecca's life and character—and that's what people get invested in. All of a sudden it's not 'some anonymous kid' who's missing, but a very particular, very special little girl from a very particular family. A family who loves her very much and desperately wants her back."

"We understand," said Alexandra.

"You need to know this is going to be crazy for a while," said Anna. "You'll see Rebecca's picture everywhere. You'll probably read some things that are false and maybe even some things that are sick or malicious—about Rebecca, about your family, about you as parents. You'll meet people who'll try to exploit you and your situation without a moment's hesitation, and you'll see a culture of news hounding that will abandon your story and your daughter as soon as it picks up a stronger scent. Are you ready for this?"

Jesse glanced at Alexandra. She looked determined.

"Yes," she replied. "We'll do anything that could help bring her back."

SLEEP NEEDED AND NASTY

"That's right, good! Now try going backwards," shouted Jesse. He turned to Alexandra on the snowy shore and yelled, "Look at your clever daughter, skating like a pro!" Mother and daughter waved at each other. Suddenly an ominous sequence of cracking sounds filled the air, and Jesse turned to see Becca frozen in fear. "Daddy?" she said, voice quavering. He was moving before he realized it. As he drew close he dove and fanned out his limbs and slid along the ice on his belly toward his terrified little girl. But he was too late. The ice gave way and she fell into the freezing water. He heard Alexandra scream. Jesse slid up to the hole and plunged his arm in after Becca but he couldn't feel her. He slid back and there she was, staring up at him through clear ice, her hands clawing and her mouth shouting "Daddy!" He flipped over and threw all his weight into his skate, aiming at a point beside her, and then scrambled up and jumped repeatedly, bringing down all his weight on the ice. "Becca! Swim!" he screamed, frantically motioning toward the hole where she'd fallen in. She was staring up at him, terrified, struggling one last time before she began to sink.

As if from a great distance, Jesse heard his own voice screaming as he woke, his heart pounding harder than he ever remembered it. "Becca!" he shouted.

"Jesse!" cried Alexandra. "Jesse? Sweetheart, you're dreaming."

"A dream? My God, again," he said. The sheets were soaked in sweat.

"Just a dream," Alexandra repeated, rubbing his forehead as though she could somehow extract the nightmare from his mind.

It was early on the Saturday night after Becca's abduction. Every time they tried to sleep since that day, if sleep came at all, it came briefly for both of them, and laced with poisonous nightmares for Jesse, which often woke Alexandra, too.

She rolled her body up onto his. "Breathe," she said, and they took deep breaths together. They kept at it until his heart rate slowed.

"Same dream?" she said.

"Same one," he said. He wrapped an arm around her. "Maybe we should be in different rooms for a while. At least then one of us could get some sleep."

"We need each other just as much at nighttime as we do during the day," she said. "We'll find some other solution."

They lay there in the lamp-lit room, completely still. Jesse was comforted by her body weight on top of him.

"Maybe I could distract you and help you relax," she said, starting to move her hips above his.

"I don't have it in me," said Jesse. There was no way he could allow himself the pleasures of making love under these circumstances. The very thought felt like betrayal.

"Not even for medical purposes?" she asked.

"Doesn't feel right."

She was silent for a moment. "It's all right," she finally said. "Let's try sleeping again." She rolled off him and switched off the light.

THE 748ᵀᴴ BOYS' BREAKFAST

During the day, Jesse would think of Becca's beautiful face or see one of her toys, and it was everything he could do not to scream. At night, the terrifying dreams continued, and half the time, he did scream, waking the whole house.

He tried to work but for the first time in his life couldn't focus. Instead, he found himself obsessively surfing the web for information on missing children. Every statistic was grim, and nothing boded well for Becca. A little more than half of kids abducted by strangers returned home—usually within 48 hours and often much faster, and all of them came back traumatized. Another 40 percent were found murdered, usually within 72 hours—the mark they'd just passed. The other five percent of cases were never solved. Most of the victims were girls, most were targeted for sex, and most were stalked carefully before being taken. Very few were as young as Becca.

Jesse knew the odds of Becca coming home weren't good and were getting worse by the hour. In the unlikely event she was still alive, it was because someone wanted her alive, and they'd strive to keep her alive. And well hidden.

All the more reason to pour every resource into the search. They'd all been scouring their memories trying to recall even the tiniest detail that would help, but none of them could remember anyone following them or watching Becca any more strangely than usual for her. Mrs. Buxton said pictures were key, so they supplied more. Anna would have the TV newscasts working for them. Meg was leading a group of Alexandra's friends from church in contacting online missing children sites and plastering public bulletin boards with posters of Becca. They weren't taking no for an answer from anyone. Becca's adorable face was making their sales pitch easier.

Jesse was starting to realize that this situation might be with them a long, long time. They were all changing, permanently. The committee of cruel deities was smirking with satisfaction.

Shortly after eight Sunday morning, Jesse remembered it was time for Boys' Breakfast. He sighed heavily, not knowing what he'd face when he woke the boys.

Matt first this time. Matt, the lover of patterns, was up quickly. He dressed at the same rapid speed as usual.

Josh. Jesse knocked on his bedroom door and sat down on the bed.

"Hey, buddy. It's that time. Breakfast, okay?" Josh didn't stir. "Josh, wake up. Let's go." He rolled over and sent visual daggers Jesse's way.

"We're *not* going to breakfast."

Jesse paused and then reached out and touched Josh's shoulder. "I need to go to breakfast, Josh." Jesse said it softly. Eventually his troubled son started to move. "Thank you," Jesse added.

It occurred to Jesse, belatedly, that he shouldn't go out without making sure someone was at home when Alexandra woke. This would be the first time in days he'd gone further than polite-voice distance from her. So he called Meg, knowing she was always up at an ungodly hour, and asked if she'd come to the house and wait for Alexandra to wake while he took the boys out. Meg was grateful for an opportunity to help and arrived within minutes, before the boys were even ready to leave. When Jesse met her on the porch she just stared at him, shook her frizzy-haired head, and gave him a hug.

"Go take care of your boys," she said. "I've got Ali."

A few minutes later they were sitting in the car, still inside the garage.

"This is a weird situation," Jesse said. "None of us feels like breakfast but we're going to do it anyway. So where shall we go?"

"Somewhere different," Josh grumbled.

"Does that suit you, Matt?"

"Yeah. Somewhere new. But not just a different fast-food place."

"I think I know a place," said Jesse. "It'll take some time getting there."

"Good. We'll miss church," said Josh.

"Okay, then. Let's go."

It was a quiet trip.

Jesse drove over an hour from Boston to a diner on Cape Cod.

"We don't have to eat but we do have to order, okay?"

Service was slow. They waited in silence, ordered, and then waited in silence again.

The food came and they started picking at it. Josh broke the silence.

"Dad, what're the chances that Becca's still alive? Like for real. I Googled some stuff but it was all so awful I gave up."

The question had to come up sooner or later.

"Matt, have you been looking into that too?" Jesse asked.

"Yes," he said. "Nothing I read made me feel any better."

Jesse flipped over a paper placemat to the blank side, grabbed a nearby crayon, and drew a graph upside down so the boys could read it on their side of the table. On the vertical axis he wrote "% alive" and on the horizontal axis he wrote "time." Then he drew one of the most depressing curves in modern western civilization and explained the details.

"It's been over three days now," said Josh, "so the chance that Becca is still alive is pretty low, right?"

"Right," Jesse said.

"But the graph goes flat in a couple more days, right?"

"Yep."

"So that means if she's alive now she'll probably stay alive."

"Yep."

"That means we should keep looking for her," Matt said, with a trace of hopefulness.

"That's right, Matt," said Jesse.

"But we have no idea where to look, do we?" said Matt.

Jesse fought back a sob. "I'm afraid that's right, Matty."

"That sucks," said Matt.

"But we're not giving up," said Josh.

After breakfast, Jesse drove to the canal that divides Cape Cod from the rest of Massachusetts. They parked on the east side and set out to amble north along the bike path at the edge of the canal. It was pleasantly warm and the gentle breeze sent ripples through the clinging gloom that enveloped them.

Matt picked up the pace and pounded ahead. They were used to him dealing with things his own way. Jesse put his arm around Josh's broad shoulders for a moment, feeling nervous because their relationship had been so strained lately. Jesse felt he needed to take the initiative to ease Josh out of his particularly tortured form of their shared darkness.

"Is there anything else you want to ask me?" Jesse said. "I know you feel protective of Becca and there are a lot of natural questions we haven't discussed yet." He lifted his arm off his son's shoulders. They paced ahead slowly, uneasily. Then Josh took the plunge.

"I'm worried about...you know, abuse."

Jesse steered him over to one of the benches dotting the edge of the canal. They watched Matt power onwards, seemingly purposefully. Jesse took a deep breath.

"Josh, there's no easy way to say this, so I'm going to speak straightforwardly, okay?"

"Good," he responded.

"Most children taken in these circumstances are girls, most are taken for sex, some are tortured, and many are murdered." Jesse felt dirty, saying out loud what he'd been learning. And he felt he was betraying Becca. His mind bloomed darkly with horrifying images of what could be happening to his little girl right at that moment.

Josh's face was deeply serious, but unreadable. "I think I knew that," he finally said. "I just didn't want to believe it."

Jesse put his arm around Josh again, just for a second. The boy leaned his head on his shoulder, but it didn't feel right. They both straightened up. Their need for comfort was impossibly large and all they had was each other. It wasn't enough, by a wide margin. So they sat quietly, in exquisite agony, watching the boats float by, and waiting for Matt to return.

When they arrived home late that morning, Meg had left. Jesse looked for Alexandra everywhere. He thought he heard a noise as he passed Becca's room, a door they now kept closed. He hated walking past that bedroom and couldn't bear entering. He put his ear to the door. It was Alexandra. Sobbing mournfully. His hand rested on the doorknob for a moment. And then he turned away.

IT'S A BAD SIGN THAT SHE'S INTO THAT TYPE OF THING

Two weeks after Becca disappeared Jesse was at his wits' end. He'd lost ten pounds along with his ability to sleep. He was gaunt, with pits for eyes, and shooting pain in his legs. He was hypersensitive to noise and light, irritable, and plagued by appalling images of what might have happened to Becca.

"Jesse," Alexandra whispered. It was just after 1 a.m. and he was perched on a window seat in their darkened bedroom staring out at the trees. "Jesse?" She climbed out of bed and sat on the other end of the seat, facing him in the half-darkness, the skin of their entangled legs illuminated in the light of the just-past full moon.

"Another nightmare?" she asked.

He nodded.

"Same thing?"

He nodded again. He looked at her in despair, and the tears began to trickle down his face.

"Oh sweetheart," she said, moving around to hold him.

They stayed there, clinging to each other, for the better part of an hour. The quiet was infinitely empty, as though even their thoughts were being sucked into the enveloping darkness, their minds stunned into stillness.

Alexandra finally spoke. "Jesse. Stay with us. I need you in one piece."

All he could do was stare at the moon.

"We have to get help," she added.

He nodded slowly.

"Come back to bed. Let's try to sleep again."

A couple of days later they were driving to an emergency meeting with a therapist who specialized in trauma and anxiety disorders; she'd come highly recommended by Meg. Lily was the second therapist they were trying out. The first candidate, from whom they'd just fled, was all gooey sweetness, devoid of insight and intelligence. They left early, as politely as they could. Once out of earshot, they repeated some of his lines, as if to convince themselves that it had really happened. It was the first moment of humor in over two weeks.

Jesse expected therapist number two to be no better. Apparently she had a side interest in shamanism and soul retrieval. He wouldn't have minded if she'd been into daughter retrieval but shamanic soul retrieval sounded like one more fantastical framework for triggering useful psychological effects. Or worse, a moneymaking scheme that preyed on desperate people. Then again, he was a desperate person.

Alexandra was determined to remain openminded. "Just please give her a try," she said. "We aren't going to her for soul retrieval."

"Well it's a bad sign that she's into that type of thing," he said. "She'll probably want to tune our chakras."

"Look, you ninny, that's not what this is about. I know you, Jesse, and I've never seen you morose and anxious like this, so maybe I shouldn't say this, but get over yourself, okay? You need some help, and this is worth a try. Lily did wonders for Meg."

Jesse took a long breath as he watched her lithe figure maneuver their car through the suburban traffic. As he took in her lovely form, his mind filled with shameful awareness of the added burden he was forcing her to carry.

"I'm sorry," he said. "I'll try."

"Thank you." She smiled. "By the way," she added, "tuning chakras has nothing to do with soul retrieval. I know you know that. Are you trying to baffle me with your fancy academic BS?"

They chuckled. Doing something practical—getting help they could reasonably expect to receive—was making a difference whereas their Becca-search activities seemed to be getting them nowhere.

"What can I do for you?" Lily asked, after preliminaries. Her face was an asymmetrical assemblage of mismatched pieces, like a Picasso painting, but somehow the overall effect was friendly. Her office was homey with knick-knacks and framed photographs. Jesse looked at Alexandra and she started.

"Our six-year-old daughter was taken two-and-a-half weeks ago and we're—well we're unraveling. Neither of us is sleeping much. Jesse's having recurring nightmares and suffering from high anxiety—I've never seen him like this. He can't work and he can't sleep and he's just not himself. Our daughter needs us to be sharp, our two sons need us to be there for them, and we need each other for support. So—we need help. A lot of it."

This was the test, thought Jesse. Was Lily going to blow it by gushing excessive sympathy, or would she figure out quickly who was in her office?

"I know about Rebecca from the news," she said. "That's one heavy burden for a family to shoulder. What kind of help are you hoping to get from me?"

Good response. Jesse's mind visualized a soccer stadium scoreboard and a vast throng of people cheering as Lily's score turned from zero to one.

"We need someone to help us understand our options, from medication to therapy, or things we haven't thought about," said Alexandra. "We don't want to waste our time on interventions that won't work. Staying stable and high-functioning is urgent for us."

"Does Alexandra speak for you on this, Jesse?"

"That's about the size of it, yes," he replied. He paused and, miraculously, the conversation didn't continue. Lily somehow knew to wait for him. So she was intuitive as well. Score another one for Lily.

"There's something else," Jesse said. "Honestly, I'm ashamed of not coping better with this situation. I think of the horrors that families have endured over the millennia and my anxiety-ridden response to Becca's disappearance seems spineless." He paused again before continuing a step further. "I feel like I should be able to wake up from terrifying nightmares, recognize them for what they are, shake my head clear of them, and move on. I should be able to keep working even if I'm exhausted. I should be able to support Alexandra, who's bearing exactly what I am—and who appears to be weathering this whole catastrophe far better."

"You have incredibly high standards for yourself," Lily said.

"That'd be an understatement," said Alexandra, rolling her eyes.

"Your standards seem unreasonable to me," said Lily.

Wow, score three for Lily.

"Maybe they are," Jesse conceded, "but maybe you're conditioned to expect weakness sitting across from you."

He caught himself. This is exactly what Alexandra was afraid of: him destroying a promising relationship with someone who could help them. He could feel her silently glaring at him. But Lily smiled. Score four.

"What I'm inelegantly getting around to," Jesse said, "is this: the practical meaning of my prideful attachment to unreasonable standards for coping is that I'd strongly prefer to avoid medication. Short of being seriously mentally ill, medication to me would be a kind of failure of character. I like my standards. I'm looking for advice and information that's consistent with them."

He didn't have to look at Alexandra to know her eyes were on the ceiling.

"Fair enough," said Lily. "For now. Let's talk."

And that was the match for Lily.

"You're a bad man," Alexandra said, as they got into the car. "I thought you'd blown it, insulting Lily and all her clients in just a few arrogant words!"

"It was a test, sweetheart, just a test. And Lily passed with flying colors."

"A test, right," she said. "More like you hate being weak and needy so much that you'll insult everyone around you to maintain the illusion of emotional invulnerability."

"Sounds about right," Jesse mumbled.

"What? What was that?" she asked, on the edge of laughing.

"Oh, nothing."

Then she did start laughing. He loved watching that woman laugh, even when she was laughing at him.

At home, as they were changing into more casual clothes, Jesse noticed something under the pillow on Alexandra's side of the bed. He waited for her to go the bathroom before investigating. He lifted the pillow to find P.D. Eastman's "Are You My Mother?" lying there. Becca's favorite. He couldn't even bring himself to touch it. He just replaced the pillow and left the room.

Jesse climbed the stairs to his attic office, sat in his black leather recliner, and tried to block out the wall of pain he was feeling, made worse by seeing little hints of how Alexandra was trying to manage her own agony. He shook his head to dispel the memory of her weeping behind Becca's closed bedroom door. Maybe it'd help to focus on the page of instructions Lily had given him.

He'd studied meditation extensively both scientifically and philosophically, so he was already aware of several different meditation techniques and the various challenges a practitioner might expect when pursuing each one. But he'd only ever tried meditation in an idiosyncratic way, to figure out what was haunting the blissful symphonic vision of his family, and that was a complete failure. He'd certainly never personally explored meditation as a spiritual or health practice. It was time to change that.

Jesse closed his eyes and took slow breaths, inhaling deeply and exhaling completely. He pictured breathing in energy and breathing out anxiety. He allowed his thoughts to come and go without fighting them. He focused on each muscle group from his toes to his head, relaxing them as he went. Then he resumed focusing on his breathing, slow and relaxed, in and out. His mind quietened and he sank deeper. He lost himself for some time, thinking of nothing at all. After fifteen minutes, he breathed his way back into normal consciousness.

When he had fully regained his senses, he experienced a profound shock. He had been completely absorbed and deliciously relaxed. How was that possible? For a blessed few minutes, he wasn't thinking about Becca's empty bedroom, his gutted sons, or the child's book that kept Alexandra company in the darkness.

That night he enjoyed his first half-decent sleep in two-and-a-half long weeks. Like always, he woke up terrified, heart pounding, mind racing with horrendous images of Becca, trapped and begging for help that never came. But apparently he hadn't screamed this time because Alexandra didn't awaken. He sat up in bed and tried the deep-breathing method Lily recommended.

It had seemed easy enough earlier in the day, but now he had trouble breathing from his diaphragm and keeping his breath steady. His mind was still racing. But he kept at it, and slowly his heart rate dropped and his breathing became steadier, deeper. He started thinking about the silliness of being afraid of fear and let that thought go. He grew calm and began getting some distance on the nightmare. After fifteen minutes, feeling almost normal again, he deliberately visualized the scene from the nightmare, but his heart started racing again. Too much, too soon. He backed off and returned to just breathing. After thirty minutes, he felt almost calm, and no longer afraid of going back to sleep.

He woke up at a decent hour the next morning. He stayed in bed waiting like an excited child for Alexandra to wake up so he could tell her what had happened. Eventually he gave up and selfishly woke her by cuddling up against her. She was thrilled with his progress and eager to help him celebrate properly. But as soon as she opened her body to him, Jesse shrunk away.

"What's wrong, Jesse?" she asked. "You haven't touched me in weeks. And you're not letting me touch you. It's so unlike you."

"I'm sorry, sweetheart, it still just doesn't feel right," he said.

He swept out of the bed, abandoning Alexandra to her confusion.

In the bathroom with the door locked behind him, Jesse stared at himself in the mirror. He felt a powerful urge to run back and beg Alexandra for her forgiveness, but an inarticulate resistance was even stronger.

"What the hell are you doing?" he said quietly to his gaunt mirror image. "Just get a grip, will you?"

He sighed heavily. Now he could add talking to himself as a symptom.

Well, there was no forcing his grip to return. In the meantime, he'd keep up with the new meditation practice, which was off to a promising start, and research, which had long been a refuge. This time, however, he'd explore psychological maladies and the entire array of treatments—even if it included a little chakra-tuning. What did he have to lose?

POWER ANIMALS

They saw Lily three times the first week. In their third session, Jesse told her about the success of the relaxation meditation she had recommended. She was guardedly pleased.

They met with her twice the following week and kept up that pace for a while. Three weeks in and almost six weeks since Becca disappeared, Lily said it was time for a talk.

"Let's take stock," she began. "Becca is still missing, and there are no leads. Matt and Josh are both seething with anger and Josh is depressed but neither he nor Matt seems to be in any immediate danger of self-harm, violence to others, or psychological collapse. Ali: you're angry, feeling helpless and violated, taking out your frustrations at the gym where you can fight through to a kind of relaxation, and your sleep is slowly returning to normal. Jesse: the tension you're feeling is manifesting as anxiety, with recurring nightmares as well as intrusive thoughts and images throughout your waking hours. The relaxation meditation is working to calm yourself when needed, but nothing seems to be ending those nightmares."

"That all sounds about right," Alexandra said.

"I want to talk to you both about a treatment option for Jesse that goes beyond calming anxiety," Lily said. "For some people, this treatment decreases the frequency and severity of their nightmares and day terrors."

"You're talking about a PTSD treatment?" Jesse asked.

"That's right, Jesse. I do think you're grappling with post-traumatic stress disorder, as well as nightmare disorder. You have many of the classic symptoms: recurring nightmares with high distress, intrusive unwanted thoughts, hypervigilance, uncharacteristic irritability, feeling detached from your surroundings and your loved ones, and intense guilt that's irrational and persistent."

"Isn't it too early to diagnose PTSD?" asked Jesse. "I thought you had to wait a few months to see if the symptoms abated without special treatment."

"I see you've been doing your homework," Lily said. "No surprise there, I guess." Alexandra rolled her eyes and Lily continued. "After six weeks with no easing of any of the symptoms except the irritability, I think post-traumatic stress is the most likely explanation. But the treatment options for your cluster of symptoms are the same whether or not you call it PTSD with nightmare disorder."

She waited for him to process that. Lily never rushed him.

"Okay," Jesse said, "what's this treatment?"

Lily gave her customary wonky grin. "Given that you've been reading up on this and you still don't want meds, what treatment options do *you* think might help?"

Damn. She was good. She wasn't going to box herself into a corner by recommending a treatment that he might have studied extensively—and he'd studied all of them, reading dozens of research articles. Meanwhile he could feel Alexandra mentally warning him about bad behavior again. Both women were demanding to see the cards in his hand. Fine. He'd show them, but he'd keep one hidden up his sleeve.

"Okay, so from what I understand, cognitive processing therapy can probably help with the irrational guilt, but that will most likely ease by itself. Stress inoculation training doesn't seem indicated because I'm already handling most day-to-day stress in the ways that particular treatment targets. That leaves prolonged exposure therapy and eye movement desensitization and programming therapy, both of which seem relevant to the anxiety problem and the nightmares."

Jesse paused but Lily wasn't taking over.

"I imagine you'd recommend the exposure therapy because it's most likely to be effective in mitigating the potency and frequency of nightmares and intrusive thoughts."

He paused again but she stayed silent, obviously expecting him to express his own opinion, not just predict her recommendation. Jesse didn't know why he was being such an adolescent about this. Fine. He'd give her what she wanted.

"I reckon prolonged exposure therapy has the best chance of working in my case."

Lily smiled. He had been comprehensively handled by these two women, who silently steered him away from juvenile behavior and kept him in the zone of adult communication.

"That's a good assessment, Jesse," offered Lily, "and you're right: I would recommend prolonged exposure therapy. It would involve sitting with me or another therapist trained in this technique, repeatedly talking about every facet of the traumatic event and your nightmare images, steadily reducing the potency of those thoughts in a safe and caring environment. If the treatment works, eventually you should be able to go into Becca's room again, the nightmares should decrease in severity and frequency, and the intrusive daytime thoughts should abate. Combine this technique with the relaxation meditation, which already seems to be working unusually well, and you may have a well-rounded solution to your anxiety problem."

"I read that people can run prolonged exposure therapy on themselves," said Jesse.

"True. They need some training, but it's important for most people to learn to do it themselves eventually so they increase their sense of personal control over their own emotional reactions." Lily smiled. "And let me guess: you've already started some DIY exposure therapy."

Jesse grinned. "Guilty."

"Jesse!" Alexandra said. "Did it not occur to you this is massively irresponsible, given your mental state? And by the way when on earth have you been up to this?"

"I'm afraid the insomnia has given me a lot more hours in the day," he said.

"And let me also guess," Lily said, "that you don't plan to involve any professionals in this part of your treatment, aside from informing me how it's going. Is that about the size of it?"

Jesse, feeling a bit like a plucked chicken, again marveled over Lily's percipience. Apparently he was paying a feather-stealing mind-reader for a therapist. And he had been worried she'd be peddling shamanic treatments and power animals! Maybe he actually did have a power animal after all—a pathetic, scrawny chicken with one proud, unpluckable feather.

"That's right," Jesse said.

"How did it go when you tried it?" Lily asked, genuinely curious.

"Yes," Alexandra said. "We're all ears!"

There would be hell to pay when they got home. All the more reason to keep the more controversial details of his DIY therapy to himself. "The first time it was overwhelming, so I backed off and stayed focused on relaxation," he said. "But it's worked better with practice."

"Are you saying you combine exposure self-therapy with relaxation meditation?" Lily asked.

"Well, I tried to, anyway, and I plan to keep trying. Is that a problem?"

"Well, it's unusual, Jesse—in fact, I don't think I've heard or read anything about it. I would be concerned that you might lose the benefits of the relaxation meditation if you also employ it as an environment for prolonged exposure to traumatic thoughts and memories." Again she paused to size him up. "But I expect you've already thought of that...and you're planning to use your capacity to maintain relaxation as a measure of how far to take the exposure, right?"

He hadn't wanted to admit that, but she had his number. "Right," he said.

"Well then!" Lily said. "Let me know how it goes. And Jesse—"

"Wait a minute," Alexandra said. "You're actually condoning this?"

"Do you think we have a choice?" Lily said.

Suddenly he felt terribly sorry for Alexandra. On top of everything else, now she had to worry about yet another permutation of her husband's weird mental machinations. "I promise I'll be careful, sweetheart," he said.

"You *must* be careful, Jesse," Lily said. "Please don't push yourself too hard and too fast on the exposure thing, okay? We'll keep up with our meetings, and the minute you feel you need a hand, I'm just a phone call away. Agreed?"

He nodded. Alexandra rolled her eyes at Lily.

A few minutes later, Jesse had the distinct sense that his chicken power animal with its single feather led his beloved Alexandra and him, in as dignified a way as a mostly plucked chicken can, out of Lily's office and back into the terrifying and beautiful world.

Jesse was instantly and unaccountably fond of his ridiculous power animal. The single feather on that scrawny bird represented his absolute refusal to risk Alexandra finding out that he was using his visualization skills to engage in a horrifying form of exposure therapy: deliberately entertaining gruesome images of their daughter in pain. But he saw no other way through this nightmare, and hadn't Lily herself recommended this very form of therapy? He might have talked about it with her if Alexandra weren't there. But under no circumstances would he divulge the details of his visualizations to Alexandra.

He didn't think he was being irrational in fearing how she would react. The visions in his nightmares and day terrors were often truly macabre, the very worst of his fears of what could be happening to Becca. He pictured her dead in the woods and eaten by animals, alive and trapped in an attic, sold to the highest bidder, tortured and abused, buried alive in a crate praying for him to find her. He moved among the images, treating each one as a shard-like perspective on a fear-inducing, darkly humming crystalline monstrosity. He was brutal, too, contrary to Lily's advice, punishing himself by confronting the horrific images, crushing his repulsion, his disgust, his moral objections, his emotional resistance.

So no, there was absolutely no way he could tell Alexandra that he was visualizing these terrifying and repulsive things on purpose. Just the chance that she might be morally offended by it, or see him as a monster, was utterly paralyzing to him.

So the stupid chicken kept its feather. Meanwhile, the stupid chicken owner was aware that he was crossing some invisible line and, for the first time, was keeping something important from his wife.

This was darker than his other failures of late. He had left Alexandra to mourn alone in Becca's room because he was too afraid to enter. He had failed to express solidarity with her in the wake of finding Becca's book under Alexandra's pillow, Becca's colorful hairclip in Alexandra's purse, Becca's church shoes nestled in Alexandra's closet, and Becca's cup on the kitchen windowsill, where Alexandra stared at it every day. Worst of all, he had robbed Alexandra of his touch. Those were forms of neglect born of cowardice and fear. But now he was committing to a large-scale lie. The shame was almost overwhelming, but his power animal was even stronger.

HOW YOU FIX THAT

Seven weeks into the family's sojourn in hell, Jesse and Alexandra were in their offices when they heard an almighty crash followed by a screamed "Fuck!" Three pairs of feet were immediately running to investigate. They found Josh sitting on the floor in the bedroom hallway, a few feet from Becca's closed door. His head was bowed, his hand was bloody, and there was a fist-sized hole in the wall above him.

Nobody said anything at first. Matt slid down the wall and sat on the floor beside his brother, putting his arm around Josh's shoulders. Jesse sat down opposite his sons while Alexandra retrieved some supplies. She then joined them on the floor and reached for Josh's battered hand. She gently cleaned it and kissed it. Josh started sobbing, his tears splashing on the wooden floor. As Alexandra worked on the damaged hand, they all started weeping.

When they were cried out, everyone stood up and looked at the damage.

"Lemme show you how you fix that," said Jesse.

THAT'LL HOLD ME
FOR A DAY OR TWO

In the early fall, a little more than three months after Becca's disappearance, Jesse walked into the kitchen and found Alexandra washing dishes. Before he'd given it any thought he crept up behind her and hugged her. On the windowsill in front of them, he saw the cup with Becca's name inscribed. Alexandra lay her head back on his chest and suddenly he felt a wave of guilt and a creeping sense of dread and pulled away.

"Sorry—I think I need to go lie down," he said.

He made his way to their bed and immediately began his relaxation meditation practice. What was happening? He missed Alexandra and he knew she missed him, but the thought of being intimate…well he just couldn't bear it.

In a few moments Alexandra joined him. She lay down beside him, close, but not touching, as he continued deep, diaphragmatic breathing. After a while she reached over and stroked his arm, then put her head on his shoulder.

"This is nice," she said. "As close as we've come to being intimate in three months. Thank you."

He managed a small nod.

"Jesse," Alexandra said, "I'm going to say a few things. You can tell me if I'm off base." She took a deep breath.

"I miss touching you and being touched," she said. "I miss it terribly. I know you still love me. I also know you feel guilty about Becca, though I've never been able to see any reason why you should. I think you're punishing yourself by denying yourself pleasure. I get that—it feels wrong to enjoy yourself when she's not with us, when she could be going through God only knows what. I've been patient and I'll continue to be, but this is hurting me, Jesse. So here's what I want, what I need. No sex for a while longer is okay if that's what you need. But I need you to touch me in other ways and I need you to let me touch you too. We need to be affectionate…we need to hold hands, maybe even give each other massages."

Jesse finally opened his eyes. But he still couldn't look at Alexandra.

"Hey. Jesse," she said. "You need to tell me if you're okay with what I just said. Any answer is fine but you can't leave me in this by myself."

"You're right, sweetheart," he said, "and I'm sorry. I'm okay with what you said—but I'm not sure if I can do it."

"Would it be easier if I tell you what I need?" Alexandra said.

"Maybe."

"Okay, then. I need something from you right now. No touching required, okay?"

"Yes, okay."

She locked the door even though the boys were at school. "Take your shoes and socks off and stand up on your side of the room facing me," she told him, which he did.

"Do what I do. Say what I say," she said.

He nodded.

"I love you," she said, as she unbuttoned her shirt and pulled it off.

"I love you," he repeated, taking off his own top.

"You are the only person in the world for me," she said, as she unbuckled, unsnapped, unzipped, and peeled off her jeans.

"You are the only person in the world for me," he answered, stripping off his own pants.

"I adore your body," she said, unhooking her bra and letting it float to the floor.

"I adore your body," came the reply, his undershirt coming off.

"Your body makes me feel at home and safe," she said, slowly slipping out of her panties.

"Your body makes me feel at home and safe," he echoed, pulling his boxers off.

They stared at one another in silence. For five intense minutes, they took in every curve, every muscle, every wrinkle, every mole, and every bulge. At forty-eight and fifty, their bodies were so familiar to one another.

"Listen Jesse. I need you in every way. I need your support. I need your presence. I need your body. It's not just about pleasure. It's also about strength and partnership. I've tried very, very hard to let you be and not burden you with what I'm going through, but I'm also suffering here, okay? I think about Becca every moment of every day, and sometimes I don't even know if I can go on."

"Oh *sweetheart*," he said. "I'm so, so sorry."

"I don't need your apologies or even your sympathy, Jesse," she said. "What I need is you. I need you to be here in some form or other, as much as you're able. So I'm counting on you to solve whatever problem you've got with touching me and letting me touch you. This will help me so much. And I think it will help you, too."

"I promise to try, sweetheart," he said.

"That's all I need," she said. "Now, can you stand a hug?"

He smiled and held out his arms. They held each other for many long moments.

"Thank you," Alexandra whispered. "That'll hold me for a day or two."

God bless this woman.

A couple of days later, Jesse found Alexandra just as she was coming in from her workout.

"Hey," she said, obviously tired but happy to have put herself through her paces at the gym, which was her main way of coping with everything stressful, and vital for her mental health under the current circumstances.

"Hi," he said. "It's been two days. I guess you need an intimacy recharge."

"Well sure. What do you have in mind?"

"I was thinking I could give you a massage to work the kinks out of those sore muscles before you take a shower."

"That would be wonderful, Jesse," she said.

"I have everything set up," he said. "Come upstairs when you're ready."

A few minutes later, she entered their bedroom to find a large towel on their bed, some mood music and lighting, and some warm massage oil.

"Strip down to your underwear and hop up." She shed her shoes and socks, her shorts and top, leaving only a sports bra and a thong. She lay on her front.

"This is so sweet, Jesse," she said. "I can't believe you—"

"Shhh," he said. "All you have to do is relax."

He started on her large muscle groups, being very respectful of her covered areas, just as a professional masseur would be. She whimpered when his hands swept along the inside of her thighs, almost but not quite reaching her crotch. He had her flip over and he tackled the front of her thighs and gently worked over her toned abdomen. Then it was onto the hands and fingers, feet and toes.

When he was done she stretched languorously. "That was... perfection," she said.

"Time for a shower," he said.

She lay there staring at him. "I can't shower yet," she said. "Do you have any idea of how much that turned me on?"

"Oh!" he said.

She giggled. "For such a genius you sure can be a dolt sometimes."

"What can I say? I'm a man of extremes."

"Listen, I'm going to have to..."

"Oh!" he said again. "Oh, of course. Sorry, I didn't think of that."

"Do you want to leave?" she asked. "It's fine if you want to stay. But I can't wait so you decide while I get started. It's not going to take me long."

Alexandra slipped her hand under the elastic waistband of her underwear. Jesse sat beside her and rested his hand on her knee, watching her hand and her face.

"I'm imagining your big strong hands taking care of me," she said, eyes closed, her other hand reaching for her breasts. "It helps me feel closer to you, even when you're not with me—"

Suddenly she cried out and closed her legs on her hand as she climaxed.

Afterwards, she kept her eyes closed, as tears gathered in his. He waited for her to open her eyes, not caring at all if he looked like a foolish, crying child.

"Would it be okay if we shower together?" he asked. And that's what they did.

That night, Jesse asked if they could cuddle in bed, another first in a long time, though he had never asked before. They spooned with him behind her and his hand on her belly. Just as he heard her breaths slow and deepen, he moved his hand to her bare breast. She was instantly wide awake. She wrapped her arms around his hand over her breasts, locking it in place.

"Alexandra," Jesse said, "I want to say thank you for what you've been doing with me. Your patience. Your courage. Your leadership. You're reading me so beautifully. I think I've never felt so loved. I know I'm a mess but I'm working on it."

"Oh Jesse, I could only take those risks because I trust you so completely." After a skip, she added, "You've no idea how restrained I've been."

"What would you do if you weren't restraining yourself?"

"I shouldn't say," she said. "I've been corking that stuff up for months."

"I asked," he said. "Go ahead."

"Okay. Well, I'm as wet as a leaky faucet and I can feel you're hard as a rock so I would roll you over, jump on top of you, and ride you like a wild woman."

"Let's give that a try," he said.

"Oh my God, really?"

"Really," said Jesse, as Alexandra turned around and kissed him all over his face, showering him with whispered "thank yous" before doing exactly as she had promised.

NONSENSICAL WISDOM

Within a few months, Jesse noticed that the tone of his exposure-therapy visualization process had changed: there was now an unexpected note of experimentation, of curiosity, of play—familiar feelings from his lifelong visualization habit.

He understood how morally depraved that might seem to others. How could extracting enjoyment of any kind from the rotten fruit of an abducted daughter be morally respectable? He heard that question in Alexandra's baffled voice, as her challenge to him, though she didn't know enough to issue it. Would Alexandra be right to think of it that way? He asked himself the question over and over. Should he abandon the visualization process, or rein it back in to focus on managing anxiety? Jesse kept following the wordless advice of his one-feathered power animal, who he had come to call Chester the Chicken, and said nothing about his visualization methods to anyone. With Alexandra and Lily, he only talked about taming the recurring nightmares and managing his anxiety.

Visualizing Becca in every imaginable situation didn't feel wrong when he was doing it—far from it. But picturing Alexandra's reaction left him worried enough that he wanted to talk about it with someone who wouldn't—couldn't—spill the beans, someone who would focus on moral evaluation rather than therapy. There seemed to be only one option, and he could scarcely believe it as he reached for the phone. Chester flew into a panic, silently squawking his protest. Jesse hesitated. The little bird flung his scrawny body over the handset in an effort to prevent Jesse from crossing some mysterious line of secrecy.

"Damn that looks real," said Jesse. "You know you can't actually stop me from calling, you ridiculous bird," he said.

Jesse suddenly realized that he was talking to a very real-looking
hallucination. He sat back, stunned. What precisely was the difference between that and what people suffering from schizophrenia
did when they were psychotic?

"I'm *not* psychotic," he said aloud. "I don't have disorganized
thoughts and I can navigate my world just fine."

But then again he was seeing chickens and talking to himself.

"Sorry Chester," Jesse said. He made the call.

Three days later he was in a meeting with the priest of their
Catholic church, Father James, or Jimmy as the kids and some of
the adults liked to call him. Jesse had no interest in the supernatural
mumbo-jumbo this parish or any other offered, but he did have respect for tradition, and for Alexandra's desire to be involved with a
faith community, so he went with her most Sundays. Furthermore,
he agreed that Matt and Josh should have some sort of religious
education, and he admired this parish's commitment to social justice issues and their practice of getting children involved as early
as possible. That Father Jimmy—keenly intelligent, warmhearted,
and profoundly nonjudgmental—was the priest sealed the deal.
They had now been members of St. Theresa's since Matt was a
toddler, and everyone, including Father Jimmy, tolerated Jesse's
skepticism. Jimmy knew their family well, and his flock was active
in supporting them—public prayers offered in church (for whatever that was worth), meals delivered to their door, and friends
(including Meg) coordinating leaflet and outreach campaigns.

Jimmy had come out from behind his desk and they sat in
two comfortable chairs, half facing one another and half facing
the large office's windows, which overlooked the playing fields
stretching behind the church buildings and parish school. It was
an almost pastoral view, with middle-school kids running around
on the grass and the woods in the distance.

"How can I help you, my son?" said Jimmy in his most formal priest voice.

"Seriously?" asked Jesse.

"Sorry. Going for a little priestly humor there, you know, lighten the moment and all that. We haven't talked like this in a while!"

Jesse appreciated the lilt of Jimmy's Nigerian accent, even in his sermons, which in his estimation were filled with the nonsensical wisdom of an alien worldview.

"Actually I do need your help," said Jesse. "And I don't mean the bazillion impossible things you believe with such apparent confidence."

"You'd be surprised how many unbelievers there are in this parish, in every parish," said Jimmy. "They are just as much my flock as the annoyingly confident people who toe the orthodox line."

"There are degrees of unbelief, surely," said Jesse.

"You're not the only atheist black sheep, Jesse. Now let's cut to the chase. You are Catholic—at least technically. You can enter into the rite of confession with me. I am constrained, as a mediator between you and the God you don't believe in, to keep what you say confidential. Does that answer your question?"

"Yes. But can we dispense with the usual guff that goes along with confession?"

"Sure," said Jimmy. "There shall be no 'how long since your last confession?' and 'say five hail Mary's for penance' in response to a mildly jealous feeling toward a neighbor."

"We'll certainly be heading in a different direction than that, if you're willing," said Jesse.

"I'm always willing, old friend," said Jimmy. "First, though, look at this," and he handed over a photo taken at Becca's baptism, with the baby wearing beautifully embroidered clothes and resting in the priest's arms while Jesse and Alexandra stood either side of him. Seeing his daughter felt like a punch in the gut but Jesse tried not to show it. Jimmy, of course, was trying to be kind.

"It's a beautiful photo," said Jesse. "Happier times."

"A happy moment for me, also," said Jimmy. "So, onwards. What's on your mind, Jesse?"

Jesse took a deep breath to fend off crippling sadness and shook his head to regain his focus.

"Okay, you'll need a bit of background first. There's a psychological trait called 'image control'...it varies from person to person, from high to low, and has a bunch of dimensions."

"I take it a person with high image control can hold pictures in mind without loss of detail, is that right?" asked Jimmy.

"Yes, exactly, that's one of the dimensions. Other dimensions relate to rotating and panning images, combining different images, movie-style playback, lucid dreaming, and so on."

"Okay, I'm with you. And let me guess—you have high image control, yes?"

"Freakishly high," said Jesse. "It's been a feature of my mental life since I was a kid. Just imagine how useful it was as a hormone-ravaged teen." They both chuckled.

"Jesse," said Jimmy, "I've gotta say, this is a lot more interesting than hearing about how Mrs. Smith failed to return Mrs. Jones's casserole dish because she accidentally-on-purpose left it in a cupboard in the church kitchen."

"I'm glad I can be of use!" They laughed again and then Jesse turned serious. "But okay, here goes," he said. "I have beautiful, high-res, dynamic visualizations of Becca, mainly memories from before she disappeared. It's like a playlist. Or really, more like an old-fashioned jukebox with a stack of video clips instead of records. I pull out one and experience it fully before replacing it and pulling out another from the stack. I've done this all my life, but the ability has grown much, much sharper since Becca disappeared. It's been incredibly comforting to me."

"I can imagine," said Jimmy.

"But there's a downside. I've also been struggling with recurring nightmares of what might have happened to her. I've been seeing a therapist, who's diagnosed me with PTSD. I've been working through all that and am slowly getting back to normal...but there's an aspect of my healing process that I want to talk with you about."

Jesse paused, looked at the priest, and pressed onward.

"In my nightmare images and day terrors, I see just about every imaginable possibility for what Becca's life has been, alive or dead, since she was abducted. It's grim, Jimmy. Very grim. These visualizations have been constant, unwelcome companions since she was taken. I'd go so far as to say I feel terrorized. The therapist is helping. She got me into relaxation meditation to stabilize my anxiety, and then we moved on to exposure therapy, aiming to defang the negative images. But as it happened I had already found out about that and was doing it myself. I would contemplate a terrifying image from a nightmare until I felt overwhelmed, and then retreat back into relaxation meditation—back and forth, back and forth, trying to make the brutal image more tolerable."

"Jesse, this sounds extremely difficult to say the least," Jimmy said.

"But wait, there's more!" Jesse joked, lamely.

"I'm sure. Carry on."

"At the outset, I scrupulously kept the two kinds of Becca visualizations separate. The happy memories were for comfort. The terrifying images were for mastering anxiety. In time, though, I learned how to blend appalling images of a little girl dead or in desperate circumstances with my real memories of Becca. This was Becca's life to me, now—the mixture of wonderful memories and terrifying possibilities I could only guess at.

"There was a key moment in this process that I remember vividly. I conjured one of the pictures from my nightmares, of Becca flung over a fake fireman's shoulder and thrown into the rear of a windowless van in the middle of the night. Becca's terrified, and this fake fireman tells her her old family died in a fire, that she's the only one who made it out and he's taking her to her new family. That's my best guess as to how she was taken from the house and the story she's been told—if she's still alive. I held onto that picture in mind as my fury surged, and then I slowly, angrily inserted it into the happy and comforting image stack. It was part of who Becca was for me now, so that image belonged there.

"And then…well then I just kept at it. I let every scary image come. I documented my worst fears, laying them out where I could see them. Hate them. Love the little girl who suffered in them. Be present to her no matter where she was or what had happened to her, even if she was dead. I felt like it would've been cowardly and self-indulgent of me to escape only into the happy-memory stack of Becca images. Anyway, eventually I was able to float freely among *all* the images, the beautiful, real-life memories and the horrors my mind conjured up."

"And how do you feel about picturing what might have happened to Rebecca?" asked Jimmy. "I don't mean how you feel about what might have happened to her, I mean how you feel about picturing it. A lot of people wouldn't go there."

"You've put your finger on my problem exactly," said Jesse. "For one thing, given my type of mind, I visualize everything—I can't really cork it up and I just have to manage it. For another, I started picturing those awful things deliberately in order to survive, to fight back against the power they held over me. I could tolerate doing what seemed necessary, though I've never told Alexandra how macabre those images are, and I won't be telling you either. But things have progressed from there. As time went on, I had less and less anxiety, and my dominant emotion actually became *wonder*—wonder over the little girl Becca was and the light and joy she'd brought into our lives, and eventually wonder at everything, even at the horror that overtook my daughter and the unrelenting fury and frustration I felt.

"And *that's* why I'm here, Jimmy. There are two sides to this I have to explain and then I want you to tell me what you think about the morality and advisability of what I'm doing. You with me?"

"I'm right here, Jesse. Please carry on."

"Okay, good. On the one hand, there's Alexandra. I'm desperately afraid of how she might react to my visualizations, with their strange neutrality and distancing, the transformation of tragedy into wonder. I'm worried it will look to her like a self-indulgent, spineless escape from pain. Or that she'll think I'm outright mad! So I haven't told her about it, and I don't think I can. I love her so much and I don't want to risk her hating me. In fact, you're the first person I've told. I fear losing Alexandra's trust more than anything. But apparently I don't trust her to understand this part of me. The part of me that doesn't trust Alexandra to grasp what I'm doing is much the same as the part of me that wonders whether I am, in fact, morally depraved and spineless. Perhaps I'm merely deceiving myself, using mental tricks to avoid pain under the guise of deliberately causing myself pain that I can learn to control." Jesse paused. "How crazy does that sound?"

"Let's say fair to moderate," said Jimmy, with a wink. "What's the other side?"

"The other side is Becca," said Jesse. "When I'm not worried about what Alexandra might think of me, I believe I'm seeing Becca more truly than ever, her actual past and her possible futures pressed together into a glorious multidimensional visualization of her life. And it really is glorious to me—the horror and the happiness woven into a seamless tapestry. Emotionally, it's staggeringly complex, with rage and joy, despair and hope, panic and calm, all held in suspension. Whatever the truth about Becca is, I'm facing it squarely rather than abandoning her to go through it alone. In what feels like a very real way to me, my beautiful little girl is with me, receiving my love and my comfort no matter what she's experienced.

"So that's about it, Jimmy. My fear of Alexandra's reaction is keeping my self-doubt high. Maybe I am mad. Maybe I'm *bad*. Yet something is drawing me forward, like a moth to a flame. Coping with anxiety is the part of my motivation I show to Alexandra. The deeper part of my motivation is solidarity with Becca, refusing to abandon her."

"Can you say something more about the wonder part of all this, Jesse? I think I need a little help there."

"As long as you can handle a little amateur theology."

"Whatever it takes," Jimmy said.

"Your sermons describe a divine being who can do things, change circumstances, answer prayers. And this God is good in a humanly recognizable way, most of the time. Right?"

"Close enough," said Jimmy.

"Well as you know, I'm betting there is no such divine being. I think when people talk about God they're really referring to something else: the amazing possibilities inherent in life, the pathways we chart through those labyrinthine possibilities, and the groups we form and the meanings we create in the process. You want to worship what I think of as a useful fiction. I want to worship the way things are, unscaled to human moral concerns, full of grace and threat, pervaded with inevitabilities and serendipities. So when I think of Becca the way I do, the beautiful memories and the horrific possibilities all pressed together, I feel like I'm worshipping what is, surrendering to it, even though I hate some parts of it. My worship feels like wonder. Of course, most people can't picture that infinite network of possibilities. But my peculiar mind lets me do that easily. Wonder equals worship equals accepting things as they are equals solidarity with Becca equals love. That's my equation."

There was a long pause. Jimmy rested his head on his hands, his elbows on the armrests of the chair, staring at Jesse. Jesse mentally visualized the impression of perfect stillness before him even as the earth spun on its axis and rotated around its star, the solar system wheeled around the center of the Milky Way galaxy at blinding speed, and the Local Group of galaxies receded from others even faster. Perspective was everything.

"It's a mild fall day and the leaves are turning," Jimmy finally said. "How about we take a walk?"

They started out in silence. The confessor had his hands clasped behind his back, looking mostly at the ground, deep in thought. The penitent member of his flock thrust his hands into his jacket pockets, taking in the trees with their colorful leaves and children at play on the fields.

Jimmy drew to a halt, and placed his palms on Jesse's broad shoulders.

"You're deliberately visualizing Rebecca, a little girl, tortured, raped, and murdered," said Jimmy. "You see that in high-resolution technicolor, right alongside your happy memories of her. All this together, despite the horror, feels like worship, full of wonder, recognizing the way the world truly is and staying as close to your daughter as you possibly can. Do I have it right?"

"You've got it exactly," said Jesse.

"I can see why you'd worry about Ali's reaction," said Jimmy, pocketing his hands. "You're asking me for a moral evaluation, but our theological differences complicate the question. If you're right and I'm wrong about God, then I think I see no moral problem— and in fact, a moral *obligation* to do exactly what you're doing. But if I'm right and you're wrong about God, then I think I see profound moral danger. Unfortunately, we never covered your worldview in seminary and I wouldn't like to second guess a man far smarter than me about such things. But obviously my conclusion is that theological perspective matters here."

"So I'm gambling my sanity *and* my soul," said Jesse.

"Trust a priest to cook up such a dilemma for you," said Jimmy.

"And Alexandra?" said Jesse. "Should I tell her everything?"

"At this point, you seem to be operating from a place of fear in your marriage with Ali. Honestly, I think many marriages would benefit from a touch more fear about what a partner might think; it would certainly inspire improved behavior. You seem solicitous toward your wife, Jesse, but your fear strikes me as rational and justified. I believe you may be gambling with your sanity, your soul, and your marriage."

"That's not much of an answer, Jimmy," said Jesse.

"Ah," Jimmy replied, "you can trust a priest in that regard, too. But tell me this. Why are you so confident that Alexandra would not understand? This is fundamentally about solidarity with Rebecca, right? Wouldn't she support that and understand the price you must pay to do it?"

"She probably would understand," answered Jesse. "But there's a *chance* that she wouldn't and that finding this out about me would destroy us. That might happen in a big explosion, or it might happen like a creeping infection, as she slowly becomes aware of how strange—and possibly sick—I really am."

"Jesse, my friend," said Jimmy, "you sound profoundly ashamed of who you are. Yet are you not being authentic? Does not Ali love you in your strangeness? Every couple must decide how intimate to be with one another, again and again. That choice is before you, once more. Fear is the enemy of intimacy, and shame even more so."

Jesse left the meeting with Father Jimmy calculating probabilities. He weighed the marginal returns associated with the likelihood that Alexandra would understand his spiritual quest against the catastrophic consequences of the low-probability outcome that she might be repulsed by him. He could not bear the slightest risk that he might evoke disgust in his beloved. Yet it also felt risky to limit their intimacy in this way.

Chester the Chicken wasn't hiding how he felt about the situation. Jesse wondered why he didn't have a power animal for the other side of his mind, the one that longed for ever-deeper intimacy with Alexandra.

Meanwhile, Jesse's intimacy with Becca—part remembered, part imagined, all of it richly visualized—was growing more profound every day. And his spiritual quest to surrender to the world—the world as it is most truly, most profoundly—was taking off into full flight.

Part IV
The Shapes of Endless Waiting

THE 1,000ᵀᴴ BOYS' BREAKFAST

On the first anniversary of Becca's disappearance, Matt had insisted they all spend the day together. Despite Josh's grumbling, he went along. They didn't do much; in fact, the day was nothing short of horrible. But being together was better than running away from one another and pretending that everything was alright. The four of them went for a walk in the woods after lunch. Normally the boys would run off and do their own thing but for that hour they were never far from their parents. And that's the way it was the entire day.

The same thing happened spontaneously the next year. And the next. And then it was an inviolable tradition. But it never became remotely like an enjoyable family day. It was about sheer survival, from before dawn when insomnia drove the early risers out of bed until late at night when they fell exhausted back into the sweet relief of sleep.

They approached the fifth anniversary with heavy hearts. It might have been something about one year for each finger in a child's hand.

The Sunday before the fifth anniversary, they hit the thousand mark with Boys' Breakfasts. They had been going almost 21 years at that point, and only Jesse's travel and lately the boys' availability had stopped the number from being quite a bit higher.

Jesse scanned back through his journal entries documenting Boys' Breakfast, calling to mind some of their discussions. "BB 961. J and me. Climate change and fear of having children." Or "BB 627. M, J and me. Sex." They didn't often talk about sex but they would go there sometimes. How else was a young man like Matt supposed to figure this stuff out? Jesse was sure both he and Matt could learn a thing or two from Josh but they never went into that much detail.

The boys were home for the dark anniversary, as always, so the 1K milestone was a three-way affair rather than just Josh and Jesse, as it had often been in recent years. Josh drove them down to the Cape Cod breakfast place they had visited the first Sunday after Becca's disappearance. The mood was weird and no one said much. They could all sense it: they were steeling themselves for the descent into hell that was this accursed week for them every year now.

After breakfast, they parked beside the canal and the three of them walked the east-side pathway, just as they had done five years earlier. This time, Matt walked with them instead of charging ahead.

As the quiet mood continued, Jesse pondered Alexandra's answers to questions Anna Feld had asked in a recent follow-up interview to remember the five-year anniversary. Anna had wanted to interview him but he thought that was pointless. So he sat with them while Alexandra did the talking. He replayed the memory to savor his wife's untangled and practical optimism. He wished he had a touch more of that, even though it looked like tragically fragile optimism to him.

"Can you share some of your memories of Becca?" Anna asked.

"She was an unexpected gift for our family," Alexandra said. "She made us closer and happier. She was endlessly affectionate, loved to play, full of energy, wanted to be with people non-stop. She was kind and happy. I was scared she'd one day become cynical and angry when she found out how cruel the world can be. Maybe she'd be a target and people would try to take advantage of her. So Jesse and I were talking about how to help her be wise without losing her innocence. Raising any child is complicated but... I guess we'll never know."

"Do you still think about the night she disappeared?"

"Not so much anymore. It doesn't seem like the sort of thing we could prevent. We don't have Secret Service protection so if someone really wants to take our six-year-old child, they'll probably find a way to do it. It's horrible misfortune, for us and for Becca, but if it hadn't been that night through a bedroom window, it probably would have been some other way at some other time."

"Alexandra, I know this is difficult—and don't answer if this question makes you feel too uncomfortable—but do you think Rebecca might still be alive after all this time?"

"That's not a difficult question. We don't know, obviously, but I think she might be. I don't sense her anymore, the way I thought I did at the beginning, but I haven't given up hope completely. Unfortunately, we don't know how to look for her, because we've tried everything and nothing worked."

"What do you think your relationship with Rebecca would be like if she hadn't disappeared?"

"At age eleven we'd be very close. I had a happy childhood and Becca was happy partly because I tried to do what my mother did. In a few years from now, it would have been a different story. But parenting is easier when there are two people to share the burden. Jesse and I would have found a good way through. He'd have helped keep Becca and me close no matter what happened, and I'd have done the same for him and Becca."

"How have you and your family been managing the uncertainty of not knowing what happened to your daughter?"

"My husband is a professor, a thinker, so he copes by meditating and writing. I'm all about action, so I've been volunteering at a shelter for homeless families helping single parents figure out how to raise their children well. Doing something practical has been meaningful for me. Our youngest son is still in college but he's talking about becoming a social worker so he can help struggling families; I reckon Becca's disappearance is influencing that decision. Our oldest son is headed to law school; to me, he seems to be managing the best of the four of us—and I don't mean because he wants to be a lawyer! He seems more able to accept that this horrific thing has happened whereas the rest of us seem to be stuck fighting it in vain. We've all handled Becca's disappearance differently but we have a couple of things in common: we don't feel right and never will, and we're holding strong as a family."

"What do you want to say to people about how they can help families who're forced to go through what you've been through these last five years?"

"I'd say that the most important single thing people can do is to care: pay attention to the pictures of missing kids, memorize their faces, and keep your eyes open. A lot of people tried hard to help us find Becca—our friends, especially, were amazing. I still wonder whether reaching one more person with a photograph of her beautiful face might have made the difference."

The interview ended with a photo slideshow of Becca, which included a few heartbreaking pictures of the three of them together. Alexandra had been firm that no photos of Matt and Josh would be included, even though they bore little physical resemblance to the younger, more innocent boys they'd been when Becca was still with them.

Jesse was relieved that Alexandra hadn't mentioned Josh's problems with alcohol and possibly drugs. That information didn't need to go out into the world. Josh had been very quiet about that part of his life, but they knew he was attending Alcoholics Anonymous meetings. The one time it had come up at Boys' Breakfast, Jesse had asked a blunt question.

"Are you abusing drugs and alcohol because of your sister? As I recall, you might have been headed that direction even before she disappeared."

"I don't know, Dad," Josh had replied. "I don't know. But it sure as hell hasn't made things any easier."

THE WOODEN RAIL FENCE

On the Sunday after Anna's report aired, for their 1,001st breakfast, Matt, Josh, and Jesse were eating brunch at a new restaurant. Jesse fielded one approach from strangers about the television interview but nobody else seemed to recognize him. Jesse knew that, just as with the original media blitz, people would soon forget their faces, and stop approaching them on the street. That's probably what happened with Becca's face as well.

"Guys," Jesse said. "I've been thinking. We're living with this perpetual clinging darkness that threatens to destroy our souls and rob our lives of every possibility for happiness and contentment, right?"

That got them laughing, grimly.

"Things could be worse, though." Jesse could tell what they were thinking: *here he goes again.* "For example, we could all be suffering from hemorrhoids..."

They cracked up laughing.

"...instead of just Josh..."

Now the laughter had become so raucous as to draw stares.

"...and we could still be haunted by perpetual hovering darkness that consumes our joy and leaves us empty husks of men, flailing in futility against our fate."

Suddenly, right in the middle of the laughter Jesse felt a horrific surge of fury. He reached across the table for both boys' hands and hung on for dear life, riding the surge. He breathed and trembled. And breathed some more. Soon he was crying quietly, the tears running down his face.

"I still miss her, terribly, and I don't think this pain is ever going to stop," he managed to get out. The boys had an arm around each other on the opposite side of the table and they were all weeping.

Then, somehow, with one more effortful breath, Jesse consciously started letting it all go. He closed his eyes, focused on his breathing, and relaxed a hundred muscles. He opened his eyes and stared at his boys.

"You mean the world to me," he said.

Josh wiped his eyes. "You know we feel the same."

"Yes," Matt said. "Yes we do."

As they were leaving, Jesse saw her: long, straight blonde hair, shining blue eyes, a girl about eleven years of age, perched on top of the wooden rail fence bounding the parking lot. She was staring right at him.

He was about to tell the boys when something stopped him in his tracks. The girl's whole body flickered, like an out-of-tune TV picture. He gasped audibly and experienced a palpitation so forceful it hurt. His body flooded with adrenaline.

"Dad, are you okay?" asked Matt.

"I'm fine," he lied, desperately trying to regain control. He was still staring at the girl, hoping Matt would take it for pensive thought rather than what it appeared to be: the onset of a mental breakdown.

She flickered again. Jesse could feel his anxiety building towards panic as she kept staring at him and he kept staring right back, feeling increasingly out of control of his own mind. Then something happened, something that comprehensively changed the tone of the experience: the girl smiled at him. That smile floated downwards, falling gently like the drifting silk thread of a tiny air-borne spider, looking for a home. It came to rest deep within Jesse's soul. His breathing slowed, his heart rate dropped, and his anxiety eased a notch.

"What's going on, Dad?" asked Josh.

"Nothing. I'm just thinking. Sorry guys," he said.

He unlocked the vehicle and the boys climbed in. The girl was still perched on the fence, smiling at him with what he felt was the simplest, purest love he'd ever seen on a face.

Jesse folded himself into the driver's seat, losing sight of her because of the intervening cars. He measured his state of mind and willed himself to be calm enough to drive safely. As he maneuvered the car through the parking lot, driving by where the apparition had been balancing on the fence, he looked for her through the passenger's window. She was gone.

Somehow he knew what was happening with overwhelming certainty: Becca was coming back to him, just as he'd finally found a way to let her go.

STUPID AND STUBBORN

Jesse feigned normalcy as he drove home. The boys seemed to stop worrying. As soon as he parked, he retreated to his office.

He closed the door and stood in the middle of the room, feeling woolly-headed and confused, his mind flashing with images of the girl on the fence, increasingly mixed with horrific images from his nightmares and visualizations: Becca bound and tortured, Becca buried alive and suffocating, Becca trapped and terrified, Becca praying for help and no help arriving. He sat down in one of the black leather recliners, closed his eyes, and tried to reset his state of mind. He was breathing slowly and his heart rate wasn't far above normal but his mind was not right and relaxation meditation was not working.

The fuzzy feeling deepened and took hold of him. Every thought moved slowly, against great resistance, with no continuity and no discernible purpose. He felt trapped in a vat of treacle, fighting in vain for a single clear idea. He was going to drown as anxiety rose higher, heading towards full-blown panic.

He thought about reaching out for help but he couldn't move.

Minutes passed. The anxiety peaked and maintained a high pitch, images of the girl on the fence and from his dreams flashing threateningly. Jesse just sat there, desperately afraid and helpless, his mind useless, the rest of his body frozen, meditation impossible, time and awareness slipping, waiting for the terror to relent.

He became aware of Alexandra leaning over him, talking, but he couldn't understand her or communicate. After that there was a small group of men in uniforms. Then he was being moved. Then there were bright lights and chaotic noises.

Behind Jesse's closed eyelids a clear light appeared. The anxiety didn't ebb and the treacle didn't drain from the vat. Rather the entire horrific mental state slowly disintegrated, evaporating in the light like a stranded puddle in the summer sun.

After an indeterminate amount of time, he was back. He felt anxious… and drugged… but his head was available for limited use. He heard voices nearby and found he could move his fingers. He opened his eyes and took in a hospital Emergency Room.

Alexandra was speaking with a doctor. The doctor noticed Jesse move and they both came into the room. Alexandra sat on the bed, brushing the hair back from his forehead.

"Jesse?"

"What happened?" he asked.

Alexandra turned to the doctor, a tall woman with frizzy black hair who looked like she was just out of med school.

"Hi Jesse. I'm Dr. Morse. We're still running some tests but we think you suffered a panic attack. We don't see anything else wrong with you at this point."

"That was a panic attack?" He suddenly felt frightened again, this time of his body's ability to betray him. It was very different than the experience of panic on the day of Becca's disappearance when he couldn't shut down the screeching laughter in his mind.

"Yes, Jesse," answered Dr. Morse.

"But I don't get panic attacks," he said. Chester the Chicken picked himself up off the floor, hobbling and covered in a tire track, his single feather blackened and bent, his spirit quavering, trying to regain his shredded dignity.

"Well, it looks like you just had your first one, and a serious one at that," said Dr. Morse.

"Really?" he asked again. "That was a panic attack?"

He turned to Alexandra, who nodded, and he noticed that she had been crying. Jesse gently brushed her cheek as she continued to run her fingers through his hair.

"Are you under the care of a psychiatrist?" asked Dr. Morse.

"No," Jesse answered.

"You should be. I'll give you some recommendations."

There was no way Chester was going to be happy with him seeing a psychiatrist or taking meds.

"When can I leave?" he asked.

"Wait another 30 minutes for the rest of the test results to come back. After that I should be able to clear you to leave so long as you feel able to walk," she replied. She pulled the curtain mostly closed behind her and left.

"Brusque," he noted, turning again to Alexandra. She nodded and weakly smiled but then tears welled up in her eyes.

"Oh sweetheart, I'm sorry. But I'm fine now," he said.

Her beautiful eyes darkened and the tears started to roll down her face. "You're not fine, Jesse. You're just not."

She held his hand in both of hers, shaking her head as though she knew he was going to be pridefully stubborn about this. Chester was walking around the foot of the bed, quailing before Alexandra's determination.

"Look, we'll get out of here, sit down and have a good chat about it, and you'll start feeling less worried," he said, with more confidence than he felt.

Alexandra slapped him on his chest with one of her hands. Chester looked up, outraged.

"Jesse," she said. "You're being stupid and stubborn."

"Am I?" he said. He pretended to take her seriously, but he didn't think he was being stupid or stubborn, and Chester was in total agreement.

"As usual," she added, the hint of a smile at one corner of her mouth.

"Can we just get out of here?"

Alexandra drove home. Dr. Morse's psychiatric referrals were tucked into Jesse's shirt pocket but he knew he wasn't going to follow up with them. He also knew he wasn't going to get any time to himself until Alexandra had thoroughly talked this through with him.

They sat in his twin office recliners and he prepared himself for a delicate conversation.

"You have to take care of yourself," Alexandra said. "Are you even going to see one of those psychiatrists?"

"Alexandra..." he began, and she snapped.

"Don't you Alexandra me! Stop trying to control this situation and stop trying to control my feelings!"

Wow, she meant business. "Hey, take a step back, will you?" he said.

She stayed silent, eyes blazing.

"Okay, obviously, I have an anxiety disorder," he began, making a concession to disarm her. She said nothing but he could tell what she was thinking: "Duh."

"Until now it's shown up in recurring nightmares and intrusive thoughts during the day. Lily thought it could be treated with relaxation meditation and exposure therapy, and she was right. There was no repeat of the problem I had the day Becca disappeared. And I've been fine for several years, right?"

"Right," she acknowledged.

"What we really need to know is why the change. Why did this panic attack occur?"

"Okay then, why the change, Jesse?"

He couldn't tell her the truth about hallucinating Becca, so it was going to have to be an excellent lie.

"Earlier today, at Boys' Breakfast, I had this moment of fury about what happened to Becca, followed by a spectacular kind of cathartic release, letting the whole horrible thing go. The boys and I were crying but it felt good to relax my tight grasp on the situation, to let it be. Right after that, I had this barrage of intrusive thoughts about the worst things that might have happened to Becca, which really threw me. I steadied myself enough to drive home and then came up here to relax. And that's when the panic attack happened, before I could even get started on meditating."

He paused to take in Alexandra's reaction. She seemed to be buying it. And why shouldn't she? It was mostly true, after all. All excellent lies are mostly true.

"That cathartic release was a one-time thing," he continued. "So I think the panic attack has to be a one-time thing also. If I have another panic attack, I'll get psychiatric help. I promise."

Alexandra just looked at him. In fact, she looked right through him. Under her loving gaze, Jesse suddenly felt like a child, short on emotional resources and grasping for anything to make himself feel better.

"Okay," she said at last. "But I have two conditions. First, if it happens again, we get you help, no arguments or bizarre rationalizations or manipulative re-framings. Agreed?"

"Yes," he replied. Wow. She had his number.

"Second, you go talk to Lily about this. All of it. And I want to know how that conversation goes."

He nodded, feeling as though he had both won and lost this power struggle.

"And Jesse," she continued, "you really don't have to try this hard to control everything. It's okay to need help."

No, it's not, he thought. But he nodded at her again.

"I should relax, maybe meditate," he said.

"Okay." She rose from her chair and sat down in his lap, nestling her head on his shoulder. "I'm sorry I hit you," she whispered. "You are not invulnerable, no matter how much you pretend to be." He caressed her slender back with one hand as he held her close with the other. They sat quietly for a long while, savoring each other's oh-so-familiar presence.

Jesse felt like an idiot. She was just so much more mature than he was, more emotionally perceptive, and stronger in every way. All he had going for him was intelligence, and evidently he was willing to use it to deceive the love of his life in a vain attempt to hide from reality. Maybe this withholding of crucial information was getting out of hand. He thought back to Father Jimmy's perceptive comments about marital intimacy, five years earlier.

Just as he was about to make a full confession, Alexandra lifted her gorgeous head, gave him a peck on the cheek, and left.

The moment of truth had passed and Jesse had said nothing, intensifying the lie. Filled with self-loathing, he dropped into meditation and before long recovered a deep sense of relaxation. The experience of the panic attack had scared him silly, totally defeating his carefully constructed resistance to anxiety.

In the relaxation state, Chester appeared, looking haggard and terrified, his single feather dragging on the ground. Jesse's ridiculous plucked-chicken power animal offered just the dash of comic relief he needed.

After pulling out of the relaxation state, Jesse remained in the recliner, trying to make sense of what had just happened—not the half-truths he'd told Alexandra but the real story. He took stock and decided he felt fine, physically. But he was worried about a serious emotional collapse. Then he remembered his promise to speak with Lily.

Jesse picked up the phone and left a message. Five minutes later Lily called back. After the usual greetings, she asked how she could help. He realized he hadn't figured out a good strategy for talking to Lily. The dissembling was getting complicated and exhausting.

"Our conversations are confidential, right?" he asked, playing for time.

"That's how it works, yes," answered Lily.

"So you can't talk to Alexandra about what I tell you?"

"That's right," she said.

"Okay. I'm just out of the Emergency Room having suffered what they tell me was a serious panic attack. Alexandra and I are both worried about my mental stability. She insisted I speak with you and she wants a report. From me or you, I'm not sure. But I care about the confidentiality thing."

There was only a short pause.

"I don't normally meet with clients on Sunday but I have some time and could meet with you in a half hour if it suits your schedule," Lily said.

Jesse left a note for Alexandra and headed out.

I'LL BE THE JUDGE OF WEIRD

Thirty minutes later Jesse was thanking Lily for seeing him at short notice.

"Always happy to make time for my most... enigmatic client." She smiled wonkily but warmly, as Chester marched back and forth behind her head on the top of the chair's backrest, concerned that Jesse was about to say too much. "So, a panic attack. And Ali had to twist your arm to get you to come here, I suppose."

"Something like that," he said. "It hit from out of the blue and I'm... I thought I had the anxiety thing under control."

"How are the nightmares?" she asked.

"Far less common than they used to be, easier to manage."

"What do you think triggered the panic attack?"

Chester was really worried now. He had stopped pacing and was now sitting, one of his scrawny wings covering his face, expecting the worst.

"So here's the deal," Jesse said. "A few minutes before the panic attack, I hallucinated Becca—a girl who looked just like the age-progressed images of her we get from the police. And that was immediately after a cathartic release of anger about what happened to her, to us—this occurred while I was eating breakfast with the boys. It's been five years... I didn't think... I thought..." He took a deep breath. "I haven't told Alexandra about seeing things but it's got me scared silly. I didn't know my brain could do that."

"Seeing *things*? Plural?"

Holy Moses, this woman was annoyingly observant.

"I mean seeing Becca." Chester poked his head above his wing, glad at least that Jesse was showing some discretion. Jesse had gotten so used to seeing Chester that it was only now, with the bizarre juxtaposition of a hallucinatory chicken beside his therapist's head, that it occurred to him how worried that hallucination should have made him. He was like a man with a drinking problem, trying to reassure himself that his drinking was under control while mindlessly downing another scotch.

"Why haven't you told Ali about the hallucination?" Lily asked.

"I don't want her to worry," he said. He could tell that Chester, his coach in all things concerning lying, approved.

"Don't you think she'll figure out you're holding out on her?"

"I think that's partly why she insisted I speak with you. Even if I don't tell her everything, she wants to know that I'm telling someone."

Lily leaned forward and stared intently at him. "So she's already worried and you think she already knows you're not being completely forthcoming. I don't buy the 'don't want her to worry' thing. Why haven't you told her, Jesse?"

Jesse had never seen Lily this confrontational, but he'd also never been alone with her. Another half-truth should do the trick.

"You know me," he said. "I like to be in control so I want to make sure I know how worried I should be about this—the hallucination and the panic attack—before I drag her any deeper into it."

Lily appraised him for a full minute. Jesse was starting to feel uncomfortable when she finally spoke.

"Working with you seems to require that I break all of the conventions in the therapist handbook." Then she seemed to make up her mind. "Okay, catch me up on the highlights for now," she said. "Last I recall, your strategy for managing anxiety was relaxation meditation that quickly expanded to a visualization practice, exposing yourself to nightmare images, and using your capacity to find a relaxed state as a measure of how well you were coping. Are you still doing the visualization thing with Becca?"

"Yes," he said.

"And practicing visualization in a crazy disciplined way, I assume."

"Right again," he said.

"So how has your visualization practice developed?"

"What do you mean?"

Such a stupid thing to say. So transparent to someone like Lily. It was like marking that theme with a big red X and telling her to dig right at that spot.

"I mean how are you visualizing Rebecca these days?" Lily said. "And what else are you doing besides visualizing Rebecca?"

Jesse paused. How much should he evade her? He was flooded with shame once more. Chester quailed in fear.

"These days, I picture Becca in every way I can," he said. "The way I remember her. The way she appeared in my nightmares. And also, in every way I could possibly imagine, from dead to trapped to tortured to..." He shook his head. "You get the picture. I do it to stay present to her the only way I know how. And I feel close to her when I do this."

She stared at him intently, waiting for further details. Jesse experienced a flash of anger at himself for attempting to orchestrate this meeting, for trying to control his obviously uncontrollable conversation partner. Lily raised her eyebrows, inviting him to get serious. Something in him broke and relief started to rise as he opened up and told Lily about the original stack of Becca images and how comforting himself with those images eventually felt like spineless retreat from the reality of Becca's life. "So I started adding the terrifying images from my nightmares into the stack," he said, "slowly making it a realistic representation of my fears about what happened to her."

"How many images in each stack?" Lily asked.

"Over a hundred."

"And they're like color movies, right?"

"Yes."

"And I guess by now you know those images so well that all the feelings merge into a kind of whole."

"Yes."

"And you love that."

"Exactly. And with practice I learned to move through the images quickly. I only feel one at a time in detail, but the accumulating feeling is... amazing. It's mostly wonder now. Awe. These days, it's not primarily about comfort or defanging terrible nightmares. It's about solidarity with my little girl, no matter what she went through, or is still going through. It's joyful and sad and awesome and... I'll admit it, addictive."

"And this is what you're afraid of telling Ali?"

Jesse wasn't sure if Lily was belittling him but he felt annoyed by her question. He answered honestly anyway.

"I think there's a chance that Alexandra would see this as exchanging pain for play, abandoning Becca and her, a kind of betrayal. I think she might be deeply hurt. She might understand, but there's also a real chance she might be repulsed by the idea of me experiencing wonder as I behold our daughter in pain and feeling desperate."

Lily stared at him again. Jesse thought she was assessing how accurate his judgment of Ali was. But her next question changed the direction of the conversation.

"How long did it take to achieve this awe-filled state of mind when meditating with the stack of Rebecca images?" she asked.

"About a year."

"That was almost four years ago. You'll have tried other visualization tricks since then. What are you doing now?"

"Because of the Becca-stack experience, I started to feel drawn to something new: I wanted to feel everything I'd learned about the world in a single, luminous state of blissful awareness. Maybe it was the ultimate distraction from constantly thinking about Becca's fate. Whatever the motivation, like an athlete finally breaking the four-minute mile, but sensing I could go even faster, I was wondering how far I could take my mental gymnastics. Not wondering, really—more like obsessing. I've been utterly intoxicated by the siren call of seeing everything I know all at once, revering the world exactly as it most truly is."

"I'm not following you," said Lily. "What do you mean?"

"It's hard to explain. I'm pretty sure it's weird, too,"

"I'll be the judge of weird," she said.

"Okay. So, I've invested my life in learning everything I possibly could," said Jesse. "Every topic under the sun. I've experienced intense wonder with each new insight. A mathematical proof, the general theory of relativity, cellular metabolism, the fit between human cognition and social life, quantum entanglement, ecological niches that drive evolutionary adaptation in plants and animals, simple kindness between animals, food webs and pervasive predation, glorious art and sculpture—everything is wondrous to me and I have beautiful visualizations of much of it. But the Becca-stack experience made me realize I was frustrated with being able to enjoy these insights one at a time, like reading a book. Since they're true all at once, I figured I should be able to sense their truth simultaneously, and in detail. To visualize these incredible perspectives simultaneously is as close as I could ever come to omniscient bliss in this world. So that's become my spiritual goal."

"You're describing this as a spiritual practice, then, not mere escapism?" asked Lily.

"Yes," he answered.

"Wouldn't Ali grasp that?" she asked.

It was a good question. Jesse acknowledged that Alexandra would grasp that if it didn't involve doing the same thing with the horrors that Becca had faced, and perhaps was still facing.

"Maybe," he said. "But if I tell her about that she'll know that I've been doing something with Becca images and I don't even want to try to explain that to her. I'm terrified I'll break her heart and she'll never look at me the same way again."

"Jesse, you're probably right about how she'd react," Lily said. "But it'd be transitional, wouldn't it? A passing reaction until she understood more deeply what you're doing in that odd brain of yours. But you don't want to take the risk."

He looked up into her eyes, confirming her suspicion.

"That's got to be because you're of two minds about it yourself," she said. "You're still feeling powerful guilt, and at some level you sense that your spiritual quest is a betrayal of Ali and

Rebecca, even though it makes you feel close to your daughter, bonded to her."

There was a long pause then.

"Okay," she said. "Let's try something else. Rebecca is the only image you've seen with eyes open while not meditating, right?"

"Yes," he said, staring over Lily's shoulder at Chester and lying through his teeth. "And I've only seen her once, this morning."

"Have other images ever intruded into your meditation states?"

"Oh, sure," he said. "Everything from normal, run-of-the-mill images from daily life all the way to a flash of my dead grandpa, or talking animals or weird gigantic beings with faces like molten metal. I can find the memory traces for all of them and I don't take any of them seriously. It's just my brain's simulation machinery throwing off images like steam from a boiling kettle."

"And you're saying that these things appear unbidden, that you're not meditating on them or trying to visualize them, right?"

"That's right," he said.

"Is there anything else I should know?"

Chester shook his head and Jesse followed suit. "No. That's it."

"Okay, then. You asked me how worried you should be about your mental health. Here's a preliminary diagnosis. You definitely have an anxiety disorder, and you've had it for at least five years now. Today's event confirms what we already knew—that it's serious. Treatment with meditation but not medication appears to have been fairly effective, until today. Other than associated low-level but persistent depression, which is understandable under the circumstances, you don't appear to have a mood disorder. But now it appears that you have tendencies to psychotic states, and maybe even developing schizophrenia. Apart from the panic attack associated with today's eyes-open hallucination, the eyes-closed hallucinations or intrusive visualizations haven't upset your functioning, right?"

Jesse nodded.

"So I'll put this to you bluntly: I'd say you're on the edge of a serious mental breakdown. I recommend that you cease this visualization practice immediately before something even more serious happens. I urge you to come clean with Ali and protect your primary relationship."

She seemed tired, as though she knew that telling him this was futile.

"Schizophrenia? Psychosis?" he said. "Is it really all that serious?"

"Intrusive images, increasing in severity, culminating in an eyes-open hallucination that temporarily destroyed your ability to function. So tendencies to psychosis and maybe schizophrenia, yes. Worse is on the way, Jesse. I actually believe you're in grave danger. Stop what you're doing with visualization right now. Stop it or risk losing your mental health and damaging your marriage, your family, and your career."

Well, he'd got what he paid for: a blunt appraisal of how worried he should be.

"You're not going to stop, are you?" Lily said.

He didn't answer as he rose from the seat.

"I'm not going to see you again, am I?"

Jesse still said nothing as he smiled at Lily and walked to the door.

"Jesse," Lily said, "please, please, be careful."

Jesse made his way to the car feeling angry and agitated. Lily just didn't understand. But Alexandra probably wouldn't understand either, and certainly not if he told her what he'd just told Lily.

Three things happened in that moment.

One. Jesse resolved then and there to keep this part of his life hidden from everyone. Chester approved from his perch on the dashboard.

Two. There was no way he was stopping this spiritual quest. More than ever, he wanted to see all of reality, from every possible perspective, simultaneously, consistently with the best human wisdom arrived at through careful inquiry, and with the intensity of wonder that those insights deserved. That would be an experience he could trust wholeheartedly because it would be an intensification of the very best knowledge about reality that our species has assembled, knowledge that he'd learned through great effort, independently of his meditation practice. This was his spirituality, his religion, his worship. To hell with Lily's dire warnings.

Three—and this dawned on Jesse with the blinding luminosity of a candle being lit in a pitch-black cave—Becca would be right there, woven into the glorious visualized fabric, her pointless suffering making as much sense as it possibly could. Fictional religious reassurances—God wants Becca's company, God will punish the evildoers, God must let the world go its own path, this is just one life of many, you'll see her soon in heaven—enraged him. There was no way to rationalize what happened to Becca so the best he could do was to tell himself the truth, to situate that horrific event in as wide a field of view as he could possibly muster, a vision rich enough to encompass all suffering right alongside hers. Jesse was instinctively drawn to this integrated vision of reality because he needed to relieve his agony, to protest religious fictions that did not comfort him, and to worship the severe and serene intensity of reality. His worship was a surrender to suchness, shorn of fictive comforts. And making sense of Becca's disappearance was driving him there.

Jesse was awestruck by this revelation. Seeing the why of it supercharged his determination to achieve his meditation goal. Lily was overreacting. This was weird but not dangerous, and he'd find a way to handle the side effects. He would do it for Becca.

THE POWER OF ICE CREAM

In the days following the Becca hallucination, Jesse's meditation practice took a surprising turn. No matter what he tried to focus on, Becca would be there, in his mind. She looked exactly the same as in the diner parking lot.

He'd be focusing on that astonishing moment in the early universe when electrons could finally bind to atomic nuclei without getting smashed off by some passing particle, thereby allowing photons to roam freely, making the universe transparent for the first time, releasing what we now call the cosmic microwave background radiation. He'd be juxtaposing that mental simulation with reflection on the evolved social and cognitive miracle of humor, trying to see both realities together in the same state of mind instead of merely flipping back and forth between them. Becca would intrude right in the middle of this challenging task, her laughing face framed by the Big Bang.

Or he'd be picturing the spontaneous formation of amphipathic phospholipid molecules into bilayers, their electrically neutral carbon-chain tails crowding together away from surrounding water molecules. He'd be holding that simulation in mind while thinking about the forces acting on the Golden Gate Bridge in San Francisco, which he used to stare at every day when he lived in Berkeley, fog gods permitting. Becca would appear, floating around the towers of the bridge within a transparent spherical bilayer bubble, happy to see him.

Jesse tried not to get frustrated. When another meditation session ground to a halt, wrecked by Becca, he'd sit still, eyes open, trying to see the funny side of the mental gymnastics he was performing. Chester would get all huffy and it helped to laugh at him.

She was in his dreams, too. Those dreams afforded the most control he'd ever experienced up until that time. He could determine what happened in the dreams generally, like a movie director. But he couldn't control or influence what Becca did. She was an unruly actor, moving however she wanted, an active participant in the environment his lucid dreaming created for her.

Jesse concluded that he'd passed some threshold in his visual simulation abilities. Something about his mental self-cultivation efforts was throwing off Becca appearances like water from a twirling sprinkler.

Thankfully there had been no recurrence of the paralyzing experience of bodily and mental collapse, though it had only been a few days. With any luck, welcoming Becca into his meditation states and dreams could help him avoid another panic attack.

Jesse was riding the train home after a rare summertime faculty meeting. He was leaning against the window, staring out at the trees flashing by between station stops in the late afternoon sunshine. As they approached the station before his, the train slowed. He took in the golf course with its stately trees.

Then he saw Becca. She was thirty feet away, sitting on the ground, leaning against the trunk of a giant pine, looking relaxed. She watched him the whole time the train unloaded passengers and he stared back at her. As the train pulled away, she turned her head to follow him, just as she'd done in the diner parking lot.

When she was out of sight, Jesse stared at the back of the seat in front of him, his anxiety rising. Would the terrifying physical and mental paralysis return? He tried to rein in his anxiety, knowing it might trigger what he hated and feared all by itself. He told himself that the preceding event had been a simple faculty meeting, not a cathartic release, so he'd be fine.

He disembarked from the train and was about to start walking home when he had an idea: he'd get an ice cream from the train station's little shop. If ice-cream distraction worked for three-year-olds, maybe it would work for him.

He purchased a cone and started to walk. He focused on the cold, the sweetness, the contrasting textures of ice-cream and wafer. He tried to look up and around at the trees, to feel the gentle breeze, to sense the energy all around him. He tried to smile and be grateful for his life. He tried not to think about what happened last time he saw Becca.

As he turned a corner, he thought he saw Becca walking a good way in front of him, her blonde hair in a ponytail this time. The hair bounced as she moved. She didn't turn around to look at him and there was no flickering in his visual field so it occurred to him that she might be a real girl from the neighborhood. He picked up his pace to see. As he drew closer, she disappeared.

It had been Becca, twice in the space of a few minutes.

He finished his ice-cream as he arrived home. Alexandra was out so he went straight to his office and sat in the same chair he'd been sitting in when the anxiety-ridden paralysis state hit him the first time. He was daring it to come back.

Nothing happened after a few minutes. Nothing happened after half an hour.

Jesse closed his eyes and dropped into a relaxation-meditation state to calm down. After a few minutes, Becca appeared in his mind, as usual, this time with Chester. He tried to be happy to see her. But he could feel himself resisting the image, resenting its intrusion into his life. Chester was strutting around pompously, annoyed with Becca.

He opened his eyes, suddenly, dragging himself out of the relaxation state.

"This won't do, dammit!" he said out loud.

"Viparinama dukkha, Daddy."

Holy Moses. She'd spoken. And he'd heard her voice even though he couldn't see her.

"Okay then," he answered, out loud. "I'll just let it be. You can come and go how you want and I'll stay light-hearted about it all. I'll just go with the weird flow."

He was aware he was talking to a non-existent person, a disembodied voice, which would have set off alarm bells for anyone, most notably, his therapist and his wife. In this instance, though, Jesse reasoned that just going with the flow and letting it happen was striking a blow for mental health. Maybe it would even be fun. Eventually.

NO WONDER THEY
WANT YOU BACK

"How did the farewell party go?" Jesse asked Alexandra. She'd just arrived home after an evening celebration at the shelter where she'd been volunteering. She paused brushing her teeth as they got ready for bed.

"It was fun," she said, her words garbled from toothpaste froth. "They know we'll only be gone a year and I think they're working hard to get me back when we return."

Jesse had landed a coveted year-long fellowship at Princeton during his upcoming sabbatical.

"They're celebrating because they value what you do," said Jesse, wrapping his arms around her from behind. He stared at her face in the mirror, and then at her naked body, taking in her shapely breasts and then her belly—stretched by bearing three children and yet toned from the unrelenting rigors of working out for two hours, six days each week. He adored her belly, a sacred icon of their shared love for their children.

"What are you staring at?" she asked, smiling.

Jesse responded by cupping her breasts, his eyes locked on hers. "We should celebrate, too," he said.

A few minutes later, right in the middle of their lovemaking, with her moving easily above him, she picked up the thread of the conversation begun in the bathroom.

"There's this amazing young woman in my group at the shelter," she began. "Geena, African American, eighteen, a two-year-old son called Noble, dropped out of high school when she got pregnant. She was gang-raped and has no idea who the biological father is; she knew only a few of the men who raped her and never pressed charges. Everyone encouraged her to have an abortion but she couldn't bear the idea. Her mother has addiction problems, her father is in prison, and her step-father is violent. So she lives at the shelter."

"You're doing it again," said Jesse, grinning at his two-tracked wife.

She looked down at his beaming face. "Surely it's a lot more interesting for you to listen to a story under these circumstances," she said, with the barest hint of a smile. "Anyway," she continued, "as I was saying before I was so rudely interrupted, when Geena first arrived, she was like most of the other mothers, thinking that parenting is obvious, easy, natural. They welcome the support but don't think highly of any type of parenting education. But within a couple of weeks, Geena had this flash of realization: you can be better and worse at parenting, and hard work can make you a lot better than you ever imagined possible. She's been totally different ever since, a powerhouse of determination. She landed a job and found a way to sort out childcare, all by herself, which is unusual. She plans to leave the shelter soon and I'll probably never see her again. But I'm certain she's going to make it."

"That must make the volunteering feel worth the effort," said Jesse, trying to concentrate on two things at once, which was surprisingly difficult given how thinking of multiple things simultaneously was the hallmark of his mental life.

"It does," Alexandra said, shifting slightly and momentarily closing her eyes to absorb the sensations. "But what's amazing is how rare people like Geena are. The traumatic circumstances of her life, along with the built-in disadvantages she's been forced to confront, are incredibly difficult to overcome. She's rare. I wish there was a formula for helping deeply traumatized women move toward healing but, if there is, I don't know what it is."

"Maybe it's built-in resilience, like Matt," said Jesse. "Something to do with genetics."

"Maybe," she said. "But I want it to rub off on the other young moms. I see the way they deal with their little kids and it's all about discipline, trying to force the child to do what the mom wants. Geena was like that a while ago but not anymore. She's now fighting to see the world from Noble's point of view. It's going to have a hugely positive effect on his development."

"You did that," said Jesse, as they picked up speed.

"Geena did that and I was privileged to witness it," answered Alexandra, eyes closed again, her full attention shifting back to her lover.

"No wonder they want you back," he said softly, but she didn't seem to hear him.

The next day, Jesse found himself thinking more about Geena and Noble. He realized that each story of a child who was recovered after being abducted also represented the near annihilation of a life, leaving a severely traumatized child and almost insurmountable challenges in any journey toward wellbeing. Was Alexandra right about how rare Geena's resilient drive was? If so, the situation for these survivor children was grim indeed. He wondered what it would it be like if Becca were recovered. Would she be in the small minority like Geena, or like the large majority, permanently disabled by what had been done to her?

When even the most hopeful aspects of a situation are poisoned, you know the situation is dark indeed.

A WISE PRINCETONIAN

A few months later, Alexandra and Jesse were walking among the old stone buildings of Princeton University, under the arches and glowering gargoyles. They'd left the boys in Boston, where they were supposedly looking after the house while both were working and Josh was studying.

"Why do people make such a big deal out of the gargoyles?" Alexandra asked, idly.

"Don't know," said Jesse. "Maybe it makes them feel a nostalgic connection to the old European universities."

"I think they look cute, not scary," she said.

They wound their way through the campus, pausing before the eerie metallic tigers at the entrance to the football stadium.

"Scary, not cute," Alexandra said.

They wandered down toward the canal on the south-east side of the town. It was too early in the autumn for a bright blaze of color but a few trees were getting a head start. The water was still and reflecting the brilliant world above as the afternoon transitioned to evening.

"This is amazing," said Alexandra. "I wish I could record these memories forever."

Jesse immediately understood the source of his beloved's anxiety.

"Sweetheart, just because your mother had dementia doesn't mean you will," he said, squeezing her close as they walked.

"But we both know it's strongly heritable," she said.

"But lifestyle matters, too," said Jesse, "and you're doing everything right."

"Mmmm," she said. "Well I'm going to enjoy this beauty right now even if I can't remember it later."

Jesse could see Becca walking ahead of them on the trail, her blonde ponytail bouncing. Now and then she'd look over her shoulder at them, her face friendly.

He hadn't told Alexandra about the apparition. He hadn't told anyone. Even Lily only knew about the first appearance. The possibility of a psychiatric condition such as schizophrenia or delayed PTSD did cross his mind occasionally. But he'd been giving the matter quite a bit of thought, and his theory was that Becca's ghostly presence had to be a manifestation of the strain associated with the hard, hard fact that her fate remained unresolved: she was always absent yet always present. He figured his rigorous mental simulation training had enabled the hallucinations—that it had created a psychic opening for her to appear and the ongoing stress had pushed her through that opening and into his awareness.

So if he were being really honest, he wasn't keeping Becca a secret because he feared a psychiatric diagnosis or that he was indeed going crazy. He kept her a secret because he didn't want anyone to take her away from him. Not only was he untroubled by her bizarre hallucinatory presence, he was enjoying it.

And he meant to enjoy it while he could. He figured she'd leave, eventually, when he was further along in the process of acceptance.

He'd now seen Becca eyes open a dozen times since that first occasion in the diner parking lot a few months earlier, usually in the evenings. The first couple of episodes had been terrifying, but after he'd decided to go with the flow he started to feel comforted by her presence. By now he was fully relaxed when she appeared, and seeing her even made him chuckle at his brain's colorful expression of pain and longing.

On this occasion, walking beside the canal, watching Becca ahead of them, Jesse actually laughed out loud.

"What's funny?" asked Alexandra.

"Nothing, sweetheart. I'm laughing at the weird workings of your husband's mind. I'm not sure you were wise to team up with him."

It was an old joke between them.

"I couldn't be happier," she said.

Practically everyone else Jesse knew would take his teasing as an opportunity to tease back. Maybe they'd say, "Oh, you'll do" or "I don't know, I think we did alright." But in the entire time he'd known her, Alexandra had never once picked up the invitation to tease back. Jesse had been confused by this at first, not least because teasing was an expression of affection in his family. Alexandra had been confused by his teasing as well, finding him difficult to read. But they'd figured it out. His teasing became ever so gentle, she learned to read him, and she was so sincere in response. He'd come to treasure that about her.

But he was not going to tell her what her husband's strange mind was conjuring that very minute.

Jesse felt privileged to know brilliant people in a host of human endeavors. In particular, he had a large number of friends who studied human minds and brains. One of them, Jerry, happened to live in Princeton. An MD PhD, Jerry also happened to be a psychiatrist with a research specialization in schizophrenia and knew a lot about hallucinations and other symptoms of psychosis. He was, in fact, part of the reason Jesse had applied for this fellowship. If he wasn't going to talk to his family about the Becca apparition, and if he wasn't going to see Lily again, then he figured he should at least have a chat with Jerry.

At the very moment he had this thought, Becca appeared again. He was in his office in the home they were renting and he could see her through the doorway, standing beside the television, staring at him. Becca smiled, and he shook his head in humorous disbelief. Yes indeed—it was time for a chat with Jerry.

Jerry, as usual, was happy to hear from him.

"Jess!" he exclaimed. "You guys settled in? How's things?"

"Weird, actually. Do you have a sec to talk?"

"Hang on a minute." Jesse could hear him moving away from some happy ruckus into a quieter location. "That's better. What's up?"

"You know how we did that study together on hallucinations of dead loved ones?" Jesse began.

"Yes, of course. It was a blast," Jerry replied.

"You remember us talking over dinner in Rome about how it's weird that most people experience these hallucinations as comforting rather than terrifying? And that we had no personal experience of what we were studying?"

"Yes," said Jerry.

"Well," said Jesse, "I now have my own comforting apparition. Of Becca. It's persistent, beautiful, non-threatening, and actually really cool, though it didn't feel that way at the start. I'm hoping it's not a tumor symptom—but I don't think it is. Whatever the cause, I'd like to understand it better. Could we get together and talk about it?"

"*Wow*," said Jerry. "Wow. Of course, yes, let's talk. Can you do lunch tomorrow?"

They met outside the quiet restaurant Jerry had chosen. They happily embraced and exchanged pleasantries as they made their way inside and settled into a booth and ordered food.

"Okay," Jerry started, "I gotta say, I could barely sleep last night for thinking about the million and one questions I want to ask you, but let's start with this: you don't sound particularly worried about your hallucination. In fact, you sound more curious than anything. Am I reading you correctly?"

"Yes," Jesse replied. "The first couple of times I saw Becca, and especially the first time, I had a major negative reaction, which I'll have to explain, but I got past that. Sometimes I get annoyed with her intrusiveness, because she shows up in dreams and meditation states as well as in these eyes-open hallucinations. But mostly, I'm just fascinated. I don't currently feel the need of any psychological help or medication to manage whatever condition is making this recurring hallucination possible. But I'm not talking to Alexandra or the boys about this, so I want to make sure there's at least one person who'll both understand what I'm experiencing and tell me the truth about my state of mind."

"And that person is me?"

"Who better?" said Jesse. "I'm living in Princeton this year, we did study this stuff together, you're an expert on hallucinations, and we're friends. I thought the glove fit. Do you want to wear it?"

"Yes, I think so...." Jerry said.

"Let me assure you I feel perfectly in control of my faculties, and I'm not looking for therapy," said Jesse. "What I want is to understand what's happening to me—and I also want to make the most of it. And I'd appreciate a warning from you at the first sign that things strike you as weird." Jesse chuckled. "I mean weird in the sense of unhealthy."

"God help me, this actually sounds like fun," said Jerry. "If the apparition is stable, we might even be able to experiment with it, run it through its paces, so to speak. You'd be training yourself to control your hallucination, a bit like lucid dreaming."

"I'm in," Jesse said. "That sounds like a blast."

"But Jess," Jerry added, "we also have to look into this as a sign of a possible health problem, okay?"

"Of course. I've been thinking a lot about that and can probably save you some time there. Schizophrenia doesn't seem to fit because my thinking isn't even a little bit disorganized, even when I see her eyes open, and the hallucination is visual, whereas schizophrenic hallucinations would normally be auditory. My mood is steady so bipolar manic psychosis or depressive psychosis doesn't fit. Delayed PTSD could be a factor. Physically, I'm trying not to think about tumors or mini-strokes and all the rest...."

"Don't worry too much about all that for now," Jerry said. "We'll look into it. But that doesn't mean we can't explore the experience along the way. So, first things first: catch me up on how and when all this began."

Jesse recounted the first time Becca had appeared, the terrifying aftermath, and the trip to the Emergency Room. He quickly sketched the other occasions, ending with her appearance the previous evening. He also filled Jerry in on the visual simulation aspects of his meditation practice.

Lunch arrived just as Jesse was ending his story, but by now Jerry was in full clinical mode. He ignored his food and launched into a series of questions.

"How does she appear? Does she fade in, does she move into your field of vision, or do you just notice her?"

"I just notice her."

"Does anything else in your visual field change or does she just appear within it while everything else looks as it usually does?"

"The latter; she's the only different thing."

"Have you seen her partially obscured by intervening objects?"

Jesse thought for a minute. "Yes."

"So the hallucination is deeply plugged into your visual field, behaving much like real-world objects," Jerry mused. "When does she usually appear?"

"In the evenings, normally, but the first time was midday, right after the cathartic brunch episode."

"You've seen her moving her head when she watches you. You've seen her smile. And you saw her move her entire body when she was walking with you on several occasions. Have you ever seen her move her hands or mouth as if she were trying to communicate?"

"No."

"Have you ever heard her make any sound, even footsteps?"

"I heard her talk that one time, when I couldn't see her. Otherwise, no."

"You described her as being a fair way off initially, and quite close yesterday. Has there been a trend toward her getting closer over these few months?"

"Nice one, Jerry. Yes, she's been getting closer, consistently, I think. And she's becoming more interactive, though not communicative."

"Wow. Okay. Is she always wearing the same clothes?"

"Her clothes have varied, and sometimes I feel as though I recognize them. One time I thought she was wearing a larger version of a dress Becca used to wear as a six-year-old."

"Makes sense. Have you tried to talk with her?"

"No. I've talked to myself in her presence, mostly about the strangeness of the situation. No, wait, I did address her directly once; that was after I heard her voice without seeing her. But there was no reply."

"Have you ever focused in on particular parts of her body to see if the image stays steady? Like if you focus on her hair, does it stay visually stable or does it wobble or get covered in static?"

"I haven't tried to do that."

"Maybe she's been too far away. Have you tried moving closer to her?"

"When I'm walking and she's walking ahead of me, she keeps a constant distance. If I try moving closer, she disappears."

"How does she disappear?"

"There's no fading or moving of the image. It's more like I stop noticing her."

"Have you ever felt as though you wanted her to stay but you couldn't stop her going?"

"No. After the initial episodes, I've happily let her appear and disappear. I think I've figured out how to take the whole thing lightly and so I haven't tried to make her arrive or stop her from leaving."

"That was going to be my next question. Has she ever appeared when you didn't want her to, like when you were doing something private?"

"Good question. No. She's only showed up in wholly innocent contexts."

"She's always in color, like the first time, right?"

"Yes."

"And the colors are natural, right?"

"Yes."

"Okay." Jerry paused. "Let's talk experiments. Do you think you could make her appear? Do you think you could move closer to her? Do you think you could get close enough to study the quality of the image? Do you think you could communicate with her?"

Jesse laughed at his friend's eagerness. "I've no idea, Jerry," he replied. "I'd be happy to try."

"Excellent. First off we have to schedule a battery of medical tests. And I need to do an in-depth interview about your lifestyle and that crazy meditation practice of yours. And I need to find out about those dreams."

"Understood. But Jerry, there's one big caveat: I don't want to tell my family about the hallucinating, at least not yet. I'll make up something about visual abnormalities as the reason for the tests. Can you live with that?"

"Entirely your call, Jess. I'll let you know if I get concerned."

"Fair enough."

They ate in silence for a few minutes, and then Jesse asked for Jerry's bottom-line interpretation of the Becca apparition.

"Jess," he began, "I know I've said this before, but first let me say again how very sorry I am that this happened to you, to Rebecca, and to Ali and the boys."

"Thanks, Jerry."

"I can't imagine what it's been like to go through," Jerry continued. "But I can say two things. Since I've known you, I've been more vigilant about my own children. And the quality of your apparition says a lot about your attachment to your daughter."

"I'm sorry about the burden of vigilance," Jesse told him. "Our story does seem to have that effect on people. One bad aspect of this is that we now know that parental vigilance can't necessarily stop an abduction of this sort."

"Horrifying thought," Jerry said.

"So tell me what you mean about the quality of the apparition."

"Well, it sounds as though you have a hi-fi simulation going on there, my friend. Nothing but the best for Jess."

Jesse laughed. "I appreciate your open-mindedness," he said.

"Well, it helps that we know each other pretty well," Jerry said. "Anyway, on the hallucinations, high-quality visual and auditory hallucinations can be confusing at first: people can't quite tell whether they're veridical or not. Low-quality visual hallucinations flicker and shift and can't stand up to concentrated attention. But even high-quality hallucinations have resolution limits. A skilled manager of psychosis can learn to detect the telltale signs of a hallucination, before saying or doing something embarrassing in public."

"I didn't see flickering after the first time," said Jesse. "What's going on with that?"

"I think you're improving the fidelity of the simulation with time," said Jerry. "If you're patient, you may be able to communicate with it eventually. Some people believe they get information from their hallucinations but I think the evidence is stacked against that, and I know you agree. The best that communicating hallucinations can do is deliver information you already possess but of which you aren't fully aware. For example, a hallucinated person might help you recall something or surface an only-partly-formed intuition."

"Yes," said Jesse, "my dead grandfather, who sometimes appears during my meditation sessions, once drew my attention to a pattern in my behavior of neglecting Alexandra. I think I was starting to sense the pattern but Dead Grandpa said it in plain language. So to speak."

"Fascinating. I'll have to find out more about Dead Grandpa," Jerry said.

"And shiny beings and talking animals," Jesse added sheepishly, noting that he kept Chester the Chicken private.

"Okay, them too," said Jerry, brow furrowed.

"Is there any danger in cultivating this hallucination?" Jesse asked. "A psychologist I saw gave me dire warnings about a looming mental-health catastrophe."

"You're as mentally healthy as a mentally healthy ox, my friend, at least from what I can see before formal testing."

Jesse laughed. "I'm not sure if that's supposed to make me feel better!"

"Seriously," Jerry went on, "I rarely see someone take vivid hallucinations in stride the way you are. The paralysis event and panic attack after the first appearance seems to have been a one-off, though I wouldn't be surprised if it happened again in the presence of special stressors. I don't yet see any other signs of psychosis and you seem solid as a rock, psychologically, apart from the persistent mild depression and low-level anxiety, both of which seem entirely understandable given your family situation. If you want to cultivate the simulation, I'd say go ahead. Just stay in touch with me. Check in regularly to share data and to make sure you're doing okay. And we have to do testing, soon."

"Thanks for taking on the check-in job," Jesse said.

"I'm honored. And hey, think we'll get a paper out of this?" Jerry asked, not completely joking.

"A paper? Maybe. It'd have to be anonymous though."

"I'll start taking notes," Jerry said.

"Anonymous notes as well, right?"

"Yes, anonymous everything."

They both paused.

"You're right," Jerry said. "This is absolutely fascinating. I wouldn't mind experiencing such an apparition for myself, though I'd not want to go through that anxiety-filled-physical-paralysis-mental-treacle state. Thanks for sharing this with me, Jess. I know it's tender but it's also really, really cool. I hope nothing too disastrous explains your new-found mental abilities."

IS IT OKAY IF I STUDY YOU?

Jesse was walking back to his office after lunch with Jerry when he saw Becca ahead of him. He was so excited about having a plan to cultivate his relationship with the hallucination—and frankly, so relieved Jerry hadn't recommended immediate admittance to a mental institution—he had to remind himself to calm down and be patient. His first task was to study the quality of the apparition.

Becca looked over her shoulder and smiled. She was almost five feet tall, slender, dressed in jeans, boots, and a light jacket, with hands in her jacket pockets—all appropriate for an eleven-year-old kid.

Jesse sought in vain to recall an episode where he'd been able to see her hands.

He quickened his pace until she was about fifteen feet in front of him. He studied her hair, as Jerry had suggested. When he focused on a patch of it, the texture and color held up pretty well. He'd only seen it long, straight, and even, or in a ponytail like it was right then. The wind didn't seem to move the hair, though it bounced about with the movement of her head.

She wasn't walking any quicker than she had been yet Jesse was walking faster without getting any closer. He reasoned that there must be a kind of slipping of her feet on the ground so he looked for something odd. Sure enough, as he watched her feet he stopped noticing her altogether.

So she was good in large-scale visual characteristics but weak on physics. She couldn't do wind in hair and had trouble interacting with the physical world. And the simulation system avoided complexities such as hands and mouth movements beyond smiling. He made a mental note to watch for shadows next time.

Jesse was working in his office later that same day, concentrating on writing up a complex argument. He swung around on his chair to pluck a book off the shelf when he saw Becca in the chair across the room.

"Hi there." He'd said it out loud, spontaneously, before giving it any thought. It just seemed so natural. Before it really dawned on him what had happened, Becca smiled and said, "Hi Daddy."

Holy Moses.

He stared at Becca. "Is it okay if I study you?" he asked. Apparently his professional research habits had become so ingrained that he felt the need to secure informed consent—from himself, no less.

"You can study me, Daddy." Jesse wondered what the human subjects review board at his university would say to that.

"When you speak your mouth doesn't move quite right," he told her.

"You haven't finished building me yet," Becca replied, her mouth already matching her words better.

"You have a shadow. I hadn't expected that."

"Static things are easiest," she said. "But my shadow shape mightn't be right." Jesse looked but couldn't tell because of the way the shadow fell over the couch, floor, and nearby wall.

"Makes sense," he said, appreciating the way he was telling himself things he already knew but hadn't been thinking about right at the moment when Becca said them. "But I can't tell how good the shadow is."

"You're a clever simulator, Daddy. You put me in a place where I wouldn't move and in a posture so that you couldn't detect flaws in my construction."

"You don't talk like an eleven-year old."

"I'm almost twelve," she said, giving a wry smile.

"I've simulated a girl who can make fun of me," he said. "Jerry is going to love this." He'd spoken out loud, unsure if he was talking to himself or to Becca, and immediately wondered if there was a difference. He chuckled once more at the ridiculous situation.

"Becca," Jesse said, "why can't I see your hands?"

"Hands are hard."

"Pull them out of your jacket pockets and rest them on your legs." She'd done as Jesse suggested before he finished speaking the words. "Now move them." Again she obeyed the command before he finished telling her to do it, as if the thought was all that was needed. When her hands moved they were an indistinct blur.

"You're really high resolution most of the time," he said. "Will you get better in the hands and around the mouth?"

"I don't know. I guess it depends on what you want and how you concentrate."

"I'm going to call Jerry. Can we learn to say goodbye so you just don't vanish?" he asked.

"Let's try," she said.

"Goodbye, Becca. I'll see you soon."

"Goodbye, Daddy. I love you." She said it just like Becca used to say goodnight. And then, without a disappearing pop or a fade, Jesse stopped noticing her.

After a moment to savor the extraordinary exchange, he reached for the phone to report to Jerry.

Alexandra and the boys were concerned about the tests that Jerry was running but they understood he was experiencing "visual artifacts" without any pain, so they weren't beside themselves with worry. He couldn't believe how large his lie to Alexandra was becoming. The deception was completely incongruous with the powerful love he felt toward her, and with any of his past behavior. Yet somehow he was living with it, all to prevent Alexandra from finding out that he was deriving a feeling of worshipful wonder in part through dwelling on images of their daughter being tortured, murdered, buried, neglected, and every other thing they most feared.

The neuropsychological testing he did on the quiet, with Jerry. Jesse met him at Jerry's clinic to review the results.

"Okay, what's the story?" Jesse asked him. "Keep it simple."

"Simple it is. No detectable tumor, no sign of stroke or aneurism, no abnormal cerebrospinal fluid pressure, no sign of physical trauma. The brain looks fine, structurally. So do both the psych tests and the neuropsych tests. I'd say it's schizophrenia but you seem so selective with your symptoms and you never experienced any hiccup in your ability to function at your usual high level, apart from that one time you were hospitalized briefly. The same problem applies to delayed PTSD attacks—they should look more like disabling panic attacks, like the first time Becca appeared, and less like highly selective psychosis. So we'll call it stress-induced idiopathic psychosis, complicated or maybe enhanced by a strange brain with an unusual capacity for simulation and visual control, intensified by your genuinely odd meditation practice." Jerry paused to laugh incredulously. "I'll be the first to admit that's thin as diagnoses go…so really you can think of this condition however you want."

They both laughed. "Fair enough," Jesse said. "But bottom line, I don't need to break bad news to Alexandra about my imminent death."

"That's right," said Jerry. "But sometimes tiny growths are difficult to detect, so we do need to keep an eye on that ugly mug of yours."

"What does that mean, practically?"

"For now, six-monthly MRI scans and neuropsych evals, which I can coordinate from here after you return to Boston."

"Any need for medication?" asked Jesse.

"Not at this point. Also, medications would almost certainly destroy the hallucination, which would mess with our little experiment here, so we have an additional reason to avoid them."

"My thoughts exactly," Jesse said. "All right, Jerry, thank you. I can cross a bunch of things off my worry list."

"Just remember this is a dynamic situation, and definitely atypical, so we are taking nothing for granted, okay?"

"Okay. And one more thing: What are the chances that this—let's call it an illness—could get out of control and render me non-functional?"

"Jess, that's the right question, okay?" said Jerry. "But we can't know the answer because it's such a strange situation. I've never seen or read anything like it. The mental training you're so intent on pursuing is almost certainly a triggering factor, so the safest way forward is for you to abandon those exercises."

That, Jesse admitted, was exactly what Lily had advised.

"I really don't want to give up my visualization practice," he said. "But I don't want to wreck my life, either... and I really don't want to endanger my relationship with Alexandra. I'm already lying to her about this."

"Well, let's just resolve to keep a close eye on things and see how they develop."

"Deal," Jesse replied. Though even as he said it he was wondering if he was being foolish. He very well could be putting his health and his relationship with his family at risk.

"Okay, let's get back to the fun part," Jerry said.

Jesse grinned. Jerry was a careful physician and psychiatrist, but research was the love of his life.

Over the next weeks, Jerry and Jesse collaborated on a genuinely unusual paper called "Cultivating Hallucinations," which anonymously documented Jesse's experiences with the Becca apparition. Meanwhile, Jesse was treasuring his moments with Becca. Sometimes she'd appear unbidden, right in the middle of conversations with others. She and Jesse would exchange glances and non-vocalized comments. Sometimes she'd tease him. Sometimes she'd comment on his conversation partners. She spoke in a weird mix of his own thoughts and words and what he imagined an eleven-year-old girl would sound like. Jesse was still working on keeping a straight face during Becca's tirades, as she mercilessly skewered some annoying person, giving wicked voice to the juvenile aspects of his own personality.

This was particularly dangerous in meetings with faculty colleagues.

"Daddy," Becca would say, "you and your colleagues are as boring and useless as lumps of chewed bubblegum. All you do is say inane things in needlessly complicated ways. The guy talking right now is a pompous windbag and you're just sitting there listening politely as if this situation weren't absurd. You're no better when you talk. I'm losing my respect for you, Daddy."

"Maybe you shouldn't come to these meetings, then," he'd thought-reply to her.

"That's a great idea. If only I could stop you dragging me along with you. Look, that crazy dude with the weird teeth is about to say something again. Every time he opens his mouth, everyone in the room has to stop themselves from rolling their eyes."

And then he'd have to stop himself from snorting with laughter.

When Jesse slipped up and asked Becca about her life, as if she were his real daughter, she'd go fuzzy, flicker, and disappear. Jerry said this was because it was too stressful a subject for him, and laughed when Jesse told him that Becca concurred with his expert opinion.

Jesse also felt weird speaking to her as if she were really Becca and alive, so he resolved not to do it. He was afraid that would spell the beginning of the end for him: he might become overly absorbed into the hallucination if he wandered too far down that dark path, treating her like the ghost of his daughter. It's not that he believed in ghosts—he adamantly did not—and he wasn't given to supernatural beliefs. But he could see the dangers of her becoming "realer and realer," as he said with a sad laugh to Jerry, as well as the dangers of becoming increasingly dependent upon the presence of the Becca hallucination.

He was already so attached to it that he'd started to feel afraid that she'd one day disappear. Jerry told him there was not a lot he could do about that so he should enjoy Becca while he could. The irony of having his own advice—viparinama dukkha—given back to him was not lost on Jesse.

Becca joined in. "Viparinama dukkha, Daddy," she'd sometimes whisper to him, the same way he used to whisper those words to Matt. "Viparinama dukkha, Daddy," she'd say until he felt his grip loosen, and he'd breathe and she'd smile and he'd think-say "I love you sweetheart" and she'd say "I love you Daddy," and he'd let her go again.

And again and again and again.

THE WHOLE POINT OF LIVING
AWAY FROM HOME

During the Princeton year, they went home for Thanksgiving break. Jesse was reading in his office recliner when Alexandra came in and plopped into his lap. Early in his marriage he would have complained about the intrusion, but he had long ago figured out that this was the good stuff, the experiences he wanted to treasure, and the memories he'd want to savor on his deathbed. He set his book aside and wrapped his arms about his beloved.

"You're happy!" he remarked.

"I am. The boys will be here soon. I'm so excited!" she said, as she thrust her hand underneath his shirt to caress his chest.

"We've been through a lot of Thanksgivings together," he said. "I don't remember you being quite this excited before."

"I've missed the kids. I want to hear about Matt's law-school experiences. And Josh's applications for grad school—they're due soon and I want to know if he's really going to go through with it. And we know almost nothing about their dating lives!"

"Ah, interrogation time," Jesse said, and caressed Alexandra's hair as her head lay on his shoulder. She slapped his chest in fun and then resumed running her fingers through the forest of hair there.

"Becca would be almost fourteen," said Alexandra. "A teenager, for heaven's sake. It's hard to imagine, isn't it?"

"It is," he lied, and felt such a sharp pang of guilt his heart skipped a beat. "Well, hey, we're with Meg & Co as usual for Thanksgiving, right?"

"Yep," Alexandra said. "It'll be fun." She grabbed his free hand and shoved it under her shirt.

"No bra?" he asked.

"Don't need one for what I have in mind," she said, leaning in to kiss him.

"I see where this is going," he said, and carried her down the stairs to their bedroom.

The four of them spent the Wednesday evening before Thanksgiving Day catching up over a splendid roast lamb dinner. Becca had shown up for part of the time. Jesse had become so used to her commentary that he could handle his simulation of her feelings and his own native feelings at the same time. Mostly it was parallel emotional play; she happily went her way while he went his—separate but in tune, reflecting the complexity of his states of mind. On this occasion, Becca expressed enormous affection for Alexandra and the boys. Sometimes she'd rest her hand on one of their heads and say something to Jesse about how she was feeling.

Matt was full of stories about his second year at law school, made more amusing because of his angular, autistic perspective on human sociality. He didn't like the competitive atmosphere because it made the cooperative study routines seem cynical and exploitative. But he was practical about it. Entire careers depended on law school reputation and class ranking, so it was no wonder the competition was so fierce. He knew he wouldn't be top of his class and he knew he wouldn't crash and burn, so he just dug in and kept at it. He loved living in the Big Apple. He'd found all kinds of cheap graduate-student ways to amuse himself. He'd made a few good friends of both sexes. He'd become a better judge of beer and wine. He was working out again, had lost weight and put on muscle, and had returned to martial arts to stay fit and keep his large body under control.

At one point, Matt smoothly introduced his friend Jennifer into the conversation as someone who worked in advertising in Manhattan. Becca jumped in and informed Jesse that Jennifer was more important to Matt than he was letting on. Jesse enjoyed for the hundredth time the way he used Becca to formulate subconscious perceptions with clarity and speed.

"Matt," Jesse began, "Jennifer sounds nice. If Becca were around, I bet she'd be interested in your friends. What do you think she'd say about Jennifer?"

"Becca would love her, Dad. They'd get on great."

Becca let Jesse know this was very probably correct.

Matt looked very pleased with himself.

"Any chance we can meet her?" hinted Alexandra.

"Mom, the whole point of living away from home is to give me space to develop my own life in my own way. I'll decide if and when to introduce you to my friends," declared Matt in his most patronizing lawyer-to-be voice.

Everyone was suddenly quiet, tensely watching Matt, trying to decide if he was being serious. He almost imperceptibly smiled and they all burst out laughing.

"Anyway," he added, "I need to protect my friends from this crazy family as much as possible or I won't have any friends at all."

Obviously something was afoot with Matt and Jennifer, but they weren't going to find out any more tonight. Unfortunately, Becca was of no use for that sort of information, which Jesse made a point of silently communicating to her. She poked her tongue out at him. "I didn't know you could do that," he thought-told her, and she did it again.

Josh, meanwhile, started telling stories from his bartending work, which were always entertaining. Jesse had been worried about this job, but so far, no relapses. Josh was biding his time, saving money and contemplating a Master's in social work, and dating here and there. Several relationships had come and gone, and at the moment he was staying away from women, as he put it, to cut down on the drama in his life.

He seemed okay for now, but everyone knew he did better with a structured schedule, Josh himself most of all. Too much time on his hands and he only ever seemed to get into mischief, even at nearly twenty-four years old. His alcohol problem was easier to manage when he was busy, even if that meant being busy working in a bar. Jesse sighed. This wasn't the path he or Alexandra would've chosen for their son, but they never stopped believing that Josh's capacity for mischief was a sign of creativity and would someday transmute from self-destructive pointlessness into something Josh found truly beautiful and genuinely satisfying.

Becca placed her hand on Josh's head. "I broke him, Daddy. He loves me so much, and I completely smashed his heart. He needed me."

Jesse acknowledged the truth in what she was saying. Josh started out taking care of his older brother, who no longer needed protection, and then he'd lost the kid sister for whom he was a godlike presence. Ever since, he'd been struggling to find his bearings.

"He's going to make it," Jesse thought-said to Becca. "One day he'll give his life to something larger than himself and all of that energy, intelligence, and compassion will come into focus."

Becca looked at Jesse with tear-rimmed eyes.

The next morning, as the time drew near to leave for Thanksgiving lunch with Meg and her family, Alexandra began shouting from the kitchen. "Where are the keys?" she said. "They were *right here!*"

Jesse and the boys hurried in, where Alexandra was frantically burrowing through piles of paper on the kitchen desk.

"Mom, chill, it's all right," said Josh.

"I thought you always put them in the same place," said Matt.

"I do! Right here!" she yelled, stabbing her finger on the countertop.

"Well, they're not there now," said Matt.

"Matt! Seriously?" said Josh.

"Sweetheart, when did you last use them?" Jesse asked.

"This morning," said Alexandra. "Last minute shopping. Stuffing. Extra beans."

Josh went to the fridge and poked around.

"Eureka!" he declared, holding up the keys.

"I left them in the fridge?" said Alexandra.

Matt and Josh snickered. "Mom that's *weird*," said Matt.

"I must be losing my mind," she said.

"Nah, Mom, you're just stressed from all you have to do," Josh said. "Come on, let's get you over to Meg's and you can relax."

"Right," she said. "That sounds great, actually."

Jesse exchanged a glance with her, and he could see she was sad and afraid. "Your son has an excellent idea," he said. "Let's go have a good time."

He flashed on an image from the Alexandra stack, of his beloved skillfully walking a tightrope of cognitive performance yet constantly looking down, afraid of falling. These little incidents deepened her longstanding anxiety about dementia. They both knew that memory lapses were increasingly common as people aged. But Alexandra was only fifty-eight and she thought it was too early for the kind of lapses that led to keys in the fridge or milk spoiling in the car or pausing in a room with no idea why she had gone there. All of which had happened, though they had not disclosed any of this to Matt or Josh.

"We should get you one of those find-your-keys thingys for Christmas," said Matt. "Works with an app on your phone, like a Geiger counter, apparently."

"Sounds like fun," said Josh. "But right now I'm ready for Thanksgiving. Let's go!"

Matt and Josh had grown up with Meg's three children in church and in the local school system.

Everyone was home for the holiday and everything felt right. Almost. Nobody mentioned it, but Becca was on all nine minds.

Becca popped in from time to time, on and off through the latter part of the afternoon.

"I used to love Thanksgiving here, didn't I, Daddy?"

"You were everyone's darling," he thought-said to her, "and we all still miss you terribly."

"Is Mommy going to forget me?" she asked.

Jesse's heart rate spiked as he absorbed this manifestation of his own anxiety about Alexandra's cognitive powers.

"I reckon you're the last thing she'd forget," he said, pointlessly trying to comfort his daughter as a way of comforting himself.

The day after Thanksgiving, the boys and Jesse headed out for a long-overdue breakfast while Alexandra caught up on sleep.

It was at this breakfast that Matt made a creative suggestion.

"We all miss Boys' Breakfast," he said. "We should try doing it remotely."

"What do you mean?" asked Josh.

"If two people are together, bring the third one in on a mobile device," said Matt. "Then we can all eat together. Sort of together."

"That could work," Josh said. "Dad and I are together fairly often, so we can just set up a time with you and make it happen. Dad, you game?"

"You bet I am," said Jesse, touched more than he was willing to admit that his sons wanted to keep up the tradition.

Thus began another transformation of Boys' Breakfast. Doing breakfast remotely wasn't ideal but in some ways it made the conversations more intense because they needed to pay closer attention to one another. And as it turned out, that transformation was exactly what they needed to keep the tradition going.

TRYING NOT TO TRY

With the boys living their own lives, and Alexandra busy with her educational consulting work, Jesse had more free time. How to spend it was obvious: he wrote more and ramped up his meditation training. The meditation felt good and it was helping him write more effortless, compelling prose. He was now meditating about two hours each day, six days a week.

Sometimes he'd do compassion meditation, sometimes insight meditation, and sometimes simple relaxation meditation, just to keep up those skills. But most of the time he focused on his spiritual goal for visualization meditation: to see reality in all its complexity, at all levels, from all disciplinary perspectives, with all its wonders and ambiguities, simultaneously, consistently with the best knowledge of the world, and with no invidious oversimplifications or supernatural fictions. This was how he engaged ultimate reality, as he'd come to understand it. It was his own kind of naturalistic and mystical spiritual worship. It was how he made sense of Becca's life and gave it meaning. It was how he coped.

When animals or shiny beings or Dead Grandpa would try to communicate with him, or when Chester the plucked-chicken power animal appeared unbidden, Jesse could ignore them because he knew there was little of value in those delusional experiences. When Becca intruded on his meditation sessions he usually ignored her, too, either trying to eject her from the mental state he was working on or treating her as a silent companion. Sometimes she talked to him while he was meditating. If he felt like listening, he discovered that she could actually be useful, occasionally interpreting his mental processes more quickly and clearly than he could otherwise. With time, she became more integrated into the meditations, as a neutral or helpful presence rather than a distraction.

His visualization method remained the same: he'd pull out two images from an image stack and meditate sequentially on them. He'd then try to move from one to the other, trilling faster and faster without losing any details. The problem was all he got was a mental blur. It felt good, a kind of blissful haze, but it seemed useless except for feeling good for a few minutes, and the insight he craved was still out of reach.

Still, his spiritual quest continued to pay off and it felt great, so it was worth it to him even though his ultimate spiritual goal remained elusive.

One evening Jesse resurfaced after a frustrating session in which he'd been attempting to juxtapose the socio-economic realities of whale hunting with the fixity of the speed of light for observers in inertial frames of reference. He was in one of the recliners in his office and opened his eyes to find Becca sitting beside him in the matching recliner.

"You were just in there with me," he thought-said, "and now you're out here. You certainly get around."

She just smiled.

"Answer a question for me, would you?" he said. "If I'm at a dinner party and you appear, these days I can communicate with the people around me while also thought-speaking with you. Right?"

"Right."

"Sometimes it seems like I'm doing both at the same time, but if I slow down to think about it, I'm really just flitting back and forth between two conversational contexts, one with the people at the table and one with you. Right?"

"Right," she said again.

"And that's exactly what's happening when I meditate. I'm flitting between two simulated processes, trying to do it faster and faster, but never really experiencing both at once. Right?"

"Right," she said, obviously amused at his frustrated recounting of the obvious.

"But now think about my simulation of you," said Jesse. "At this moment I'm mentally simulating this room, thanks to sensory input, and I'm simultaneously simulating you, thanks to God only knows what, and I'm doing both seamlessly and effortlessly. Right?"

"Right," she said. "But there's a difference. In the dinner-party setting you're trying to have two conversations at the same time, whereas with me you're merging images. It's probably easier to double up on visual processing than language processing."

"Wow. That's not bad for a fifteen-year-old," he said.

"Well, you've been dragging me through your dreams, your meditation exercises, and your waking consciousness for four years now, so I've had a chance to watch you," she said.

"So that's what's happening, is it? I'm dragging you places? You're not rudely intruding?"

"It's your brain, Daddy. I'm pretty sure you're doing everything. You never leave me alone."

"Well, I'm too tired to try another approach tonight," he said. "Maybe I'll focus on a non-verbal visualization process tomorrow."

The next day, Jesse did exactly that.

He first returned to work on a mental simulation of the sport of curling, focusing on the physics of the interface between ice and stone, which impacts pretty much all the rules and equipment in the game. He tried to eliminate words and concepts, leaving only a visual simulation of the physical interactions. He then revisited a visual simulation of the amazing protein chains embedded in mitochondria that create the cellular fuel ATP by passing high-energy electrons and pumping protons across a membrane.

He dropped in, savoring each visual simulation individually. Both were intensely beautiful, so ordinary at one level and yet packed with glorious dynamic processes that unfolded lightning fast. When he started verbalizing the wonder of the process—"that ATP-Synthase protein assembly is spinning so fast!"—he'd release the words and focus on the simulated image, watching the embedded proteins studded in the mitochondrial membrane waving and vibrating, driving up the energy hump needed to catalyze the reaction between ADP and a lonesome phosphate group. When he found himself estimating the thickness of the layer of unbound water molecules that allowed the stone to drift on the ice, he'd refocus his attention on the dynamics of hydrogen bonds snapping under pressure and liberating partially electrically polarized water molecules into the space below the rock to create a transitory plasma that was reclaimed by the ice as soon as the rock passed.

Jesse could feel the beauty as a kind of longing, like the wistful pain of being in love. The translation to emotions helped: he could retain the visual representation with no loss of insight and yet he was not dependent on words and concepts to express the beauty and complexity of the process.

When he sensed that he'd internalized both visual simulations, free of words and full of imagistic detail, he started his usual procedure of flipping back and forth between the two. He needn't have bothered. It was immediately obvious that the second visual simulation could overlay the first. He could feel both at the same time, vividly, without loss of detail, without loss of understanding, and with a marked increase in the intensity of his appreciation.

He'd done it.

The combined state felt extremely good: intense, clear, valid, emotionally rich, continuous with the best extant wisdom about reality, free of delusional fantasies about special revelations, and absolutely devoid of any new information. It was an intimation of what he longed to feel: the world as it is, in all its richness and ambiguity, unburdened by the self-protective fantasies so common in spiritual practices—the very world in which Becca could come to be and all too soon disappear without explanation.

It was shockingly easy to do—much easier than the hard-grinding effort of flipping between conceptually voiced simulations he was used to. In fact, he didn't even have to try to achieve the merging of visual models. It was the difference between vainly pushing two north-pole ends of magnets together versus effortlessly watching a north-pole and a south-pole leap toward one another. As with so many meditation techniques, the key was figuring out how not to try.

Jesse could sense Becca's delight as she watched the two visual simulations coexisting in his consciousness without a hint of degradation or interference. Then he became aware that she'd said something, but he couldn't understand it. As he sought to grasp what she was trying to communicate, he eased out of the merged state. He gave up the linguistic effort and elastically zoomed right back in again. Becca laughed as he felt in his body the difference between the linearity of language and the bypassing of language altogether.

Jesse played around in the merged state for a while, exploring its edges, until he was convinced he knew how to get back to that precious place. He discovered that he couldn't move any more than he could verbalize if the merged state was to persist. Apparently both the motor and language centers of the brain had to be isolated or commandeered for the merged state to arise.

He resurfaced, smiling from ear to ear. "Now we're getting somewhere!" he said aloud. At long last, he felt he'd graduated from kindergarten in his journey of spiritual self-education.

NOT-SO-SWEET SIXTEEN

On what would have been Becca's sixteenth birthday, Alexandra was visiting friends in San Francisco. Matt was pulling down a new lawyer's salary in Sydney with a multi-national firm, while training to get his Australian legal credentials in place to match his US credentials. He was also engaged to Jenny, who'd traveled to Australia with him briefly before returning to New York to continue working with her advertising firm. Josh was back at school in Boston, half-way through a master's degree in social work. He was dating Olivia, whom everyone called Oli.

It was a cold Tuesday in January and Jesse was nestled in his home office, spending the day writing.

"Hi Daddy," said Becca.

"Hi kiddo." He was speaking out loud because nobody was in the house. "Happy birthday. Sit down and chat with me for a while."

She'd become superb at sitting. The simulation was extraordinary: she could move parts of her body independently of others, use her hands to talk, cast the correct shadow. Also, she didn't just float on top of the chair like she used to; now she seemed to sink down in a physics-appropriate way, though the chair itself never changed shape or moved.

She looked like a young woman now. She still had the flawless skin and the piercing blue eyes, though her face was more angular, and her gaze reflected a bit more wisdom. Today her bright blonde hair fell loosely around her shoulders and she was dressed in black jeans and a white blouse.

"I've never seen you with acne, or with holes in your jeans, not even for the sake of fashion," he mused.

"I suspect you don't like pimples or air-conditioned clothing," she replied.

"Makes sense," he said. "Hey, I want to talk seriously today. Are you willing to do that?"

"It's kind of up to you, isn't it?"

"Just play along will you?"

"So you think you can control me, is that it?" she teased.

"What's the use of a first-rate hallucination if I can't actually use it to simulate anything that matters to me?"

"Okay Daddy," she said. "I'll play along, no problem."

"I want to discuss Becca's and my relationship," he said.

He had resolved several years ago not to talk to her as if she were his actual daughter, but something about the sixteenth birthday was driving him.

"When you were little, your Mom and I were afraid of what would happen to you in your teenage years. You loved being the center of attention and you were gorgeous to the point that strangers couldn't take their eyes off you. It seemed like a dangerous combination and we were pretty confident we were going to feel completely out of our depth. So here's the first thing that's on my mind. Would we have been able to help you make it through the teenage years without any major disasters, and without too many minor traumas?"

"You and Mommy always took beautiful care of me. You'd have found a way."

"But something tells me we wouldn't have been enough for you, that we'd have lost you no matter what we did."

"I don't think so, Daddy. You and Mommy would have found a way to let me go, and trust me and love me, so I'd always come back. I'd have been a pain in the ass for a while but eventually I'd have settled down. Josh would have helped me make sense of everything. Ultimately, I'd have stayed very close to the whole family."

"I'd like to think so." Jesse hesitated. "I have a second question."

"Go on," she said.

"If you're still alive, what are you doing on your sixteenth birthday?"

Becca paused at this, as if Jesse himself were deciding how much he really wanted to go down that particular rabbit hole. Then she took a slow breath, her chest rising, her eyes piercing, and started speaking the most devastating words.

"My 45-year-old fake husband would bring home a lame birthday cake and give it to me and my son, where we live locked in an attic. I'd pretend to be happy and thankful, which would have become a serious survival skill. My son and I would eat some of the cake after the fake father left us alone, and I'd read him a book. I'd have almost no memories of my childhood with you and Mommy but on this particular day I'd be able to remember my sixth birthday party, a decade earlier. I'd cry because I just knew that the absent family loves me even though I can't remember much about them. I'd cry because of my miserable situation, as I wonder whether anything good and pure and beautiful will ever happen to me, the way I imagine those things used to happen to me all the time. I'd cry because nobody had rescued me. Because even if I escaped I wouldn't know how to get home. Because I'd been abandoned by the people who were supposed to take care of me."

Tears welled up in Jesse's eyes. That really was about the size of it. If Becca were alive, that was very likely the kind of life she was living every day, and those were very likely the thoughts she harbored. He was overwhelmed with sorrow.

"Sweetheart I'm so sorry I couldn't protect you. I'm so sorry this happened to you. I was determined to make your life happy and healthy and I failed, utterly." He was sobbing as he finally realized why he wanted to have this conversation.

"It's okay, Daddy," she said. "You couldn't have stopped this. It's just a part of life. This thing happened to me, to you and Mommy, and to Matt and Josh. It just happened. That's all."

"I know, sweetheart." He paused a moment. "Thank you for listening. Thank you for telling me the truth."

"I love you, Daddy."

"I love you, Becca." And she was gone.

Jesse felt horrible—partly because Becca had helped him surface still-unresolved guilt, partly because he'd coerced his hallucinated companion into speaking as if she were the ghost of his daughter, and partly because Becca really might still be alive, living in circumstances like those, and thinking about him in that way.

A couple of days later, with Alexandra still away, Jesse checked in with Jerry on a video call. He walked his friend through what he'd done and explained how stupid and guilty he felt. Jerry took it in stride.

"Here's the thing, Jess," he said. "You've been enhancing this simulation for several years now. I'm surprised you haven't tried something like this before. I'm sure I would have. It looks just like Rebecca, after all. Who wouldn't want to try to recreate a ghost-daughter from a hi-fi hallucination? And listen, for what it's worth, I'm not worried. I don't see signs of you losing yourself in the simulation. Your neuropsych tests and brain scans continue to show no functional or structural impairments. I think this was an inevitable thought experiment, and it was illuminating. You surfaced some pretty strong feelings and lived to tell the tale."

"Thanks, Jerry," said Jesse. "I didn't mention one thing before: Becca left after that exchange and she hasn't appeared since."

"It's just been a couple of days, right?"

"Yes, two days," said Jesse, "but before that I saw her almost every evening."

"Well, a change is as good as a holiday," Jerry said, and Jesse could see his grin on the screen matching his jovial voice.

That night Jesse had one of the most stunning dreams of his life.

He was wandering through a mannequin factory, lost. In the half-light he could see that he was surrounded by mannequin faces that were exact copies of how he imagined Becca at sixteen. The figures began moving, slowly picking up speed. Then they started darting toward him and away again, trying to scare him, to send him into a panic. It was working.

He begged Becca to stop but the wild movements continued more violently, with mannequins zooming through the air, dive bombing him like angry crows. He tried to grab one to use it for cover but it turned to sand in his grasp, dissolving into a pile on the floor. The same happened to each one he touched: he was destroying all the Beccas, one by one, until the last zooming Becca hovered above him with a fearsome grimacing face and accused him of killing them all.

Jesse woke up, shaking, heart pounding, gasping for breath. It came to him once more how guilty he felt, whether for Becca's death, or for her miserable ongoing life. He realized how irrational he was being, but he felt powerless to stop the self-accusation.

He closed his eyes in the moonlit room and let his thoughts tumble together for a while as he settled down. He opened his eyes again and saw Becca hovering above the bed, dark and brooding, but liquid now instead of mannequin-like. He spoke to her, out loud.

"Becca, I'm so truly sorry for what happened to you, and for my failure to protect you. But I mustn't allow myself to get this attached to my sorrow and self-recrimination. So I won't apologize again. I won't nurture these guilty feelings or my shame at being an inadequate father any longer. I love you, Becca. If you're alive, I hope you're finding some moments of happiness, and that one day you'll find your way back to us."

The liquid floating image of Becca hovering above him dissolved and a human-looking Becca sat on the foot of his bed, the moonlight illuminating her features. She smiled gently, exactly the way she did the first time Jesse saw her four-and-a-half years earlier, perched on the rail fence of the diner parking lot.

Part V
Safe Haven

THE 1,515TH BOYS' BREAKFAST

"Hi Matt," said Jesse as Matt came on the screen.

"Hey, who've you got there?" asked Josh, grinning.

"Little Jake!" Matt said. "He's restless, so I've got him for Boys' Breakfast while Jenny tries to get some sleep. He's fed and changed. I think he just needs some company." The baby seemed fascinated with watching his uncle and grandfather eating breakfast on the screen.

"I seem to remember that you never felt comfortable holding Becca," Jesse said. "But look at you now, baby number four in one arm, wrangling coffee and breakfast with the other."

"Nothing like practice, I guess," Matt said. "Where are you guys? I don't recognize the place."

"It's a diner out my way," answered Josh.

"Who's that little darlin'?" asked their waitress, who'd stopped to refill Josh's coffee.

"This is Jake, grandkid number six!" Jesse answered.

"Such a cutie!" she exclaimed before heading back into the melee that was Dave's Diner on Sunday morning at 9am.

Matt was thirty-four and moving between the two sides of the Pacific as a corporate attorney for a firm with offices in Sydney and San Francisco, among other places—the same firm that first hired him out of law school. He was married to Jenny and living in San Francisco. They had a boy, identical twin girls, and ten-week-old Jake. He and Jenny swore there would be no more.

Josh was thirty-two and working as a social worker in Boston. He'd completed extensive training in supporting families dealing with missing children. Between that and his personal experience, he was exceptionally good at his job. He, too, was married, though that had seemed to be an afterthought in their case. He and Oli had been raising two of their children when they decided to marry the previous summer. Their third child would arrive in about three weeks.

The boys had started their families about the same time, so both couples were in the frantic years of childrearing, complicated in Matt and Jenny's case by the facts that their middle two were twins, and Matt was traveling so much. Nanny Dora helped. The boys exchanged news about their families. Jesse absorbed the details, relishing the fact that his beautiful men were so into sharing the fatherhood process with one another.

"Any news in your life?" asked Matt, redirecting the conversation Jesse's way.

"A new book just appeared," Jesse said.

"Is this the one that'll make you famous?" teased Josh.

"Quite probably, yes," Jesse answered. "Among the half dozen people who'll read it and the other half dozen who'll say they did."

"Well, thank God for university professors," exclaimed Matt. "What would the world do without them?" The boys loved having something to tease the old man about, and his utter irrelevance to the world as they knew it was fertile ground for mockery.

"I still find it difficult to believe that you can get paid for doing whatever it is that you do," added Josh.

"It got you two through college, so it was worth something," said Jesse.

"How's Mom?" asked Matt. Jesse deferred to Josh, who saw Alexandra a lot, as she had retired and was helping Josh and Oli with childcare. Alexandra would also occasionally fly out to San Francisco to help Matt and Jenny with their kids when Matt was traveling.

"She's good," Josh said. "A huge help with the kids. Dad knows more about her day to day, though."

"She's still volunteering at the homeless shelter," Jesse said. "And she's looking into a new gym. Better equipment, nicer pool, but a bit further from home. She says it's a toss-up, convenience versus quality."

It occurred to Jesse then how stable and predictable Alexandra's and his lives had become. If Becca had been around, she would have just finished college, and he and Alexandra would be poised to launch another young adult into the world, excited to see the path she'd forge for herself.

But of course, that wasn't the case. It was a fact that still had the power to shock him.

Josh looked at his Dad oddly.

"What?" asked Jesse.

"Well, Mom's memory isn't what it used to be," said Josh. "At least it seems that way to Oli and me. Maybe we're a bit oversensitive to it because of her own mother's dementia."

"Actually Jenny and I have talked about it, too," said Matt. "It isn't a huge change but she's definitely forgetting to follow through on things she used to remember with no problem."

"I don't know, boys," said Jesse. "I've seen what you're talking about. But memory changes with age, for all of us."

"But Grandma had Alzheimer's," said Matt. "Did Mom ever do genetic testing for it?"

"She hasn't done genetic testing of any kind," said Jesse.

"Maybe she should," said Josh.

"How would that help?" asked Jesse.

"Well, at least you'd have some idea of what *might* be in store for her, and then you can take preventive measures," said Josh.

"What preventative measures?" asked Jesse sharply. "She's already doing everything possible to fend off memory problems." There was an awkward pause. "Good lord, look at me. I'm sorry boys. Look, I hear you, okay?"

UKULELE STRINGS

A few days later, in the summer of the year Becca would have turned twenty-two, just before the sixteenth anniversary of her disappearance, a pair of detectives showed up. Alexandra led the police to the dining room, where the four of them took seats around the table.

"What's this all about?" asked Alexandra.

"We've found a young woman who's been held prisoner in a Rhode Island farmhouse for a long time—longer than she can remember," one of the detectives said. Alexandra and Jesse both gasped and Jesse reached for her hand. "We don't yet have a reliable identification, and there are several missing persons she could match. Unfortunately, the young woman can only remember bits and pieces of her life before she was abducted, and nothing about her family of origin—she was abducted when she was only five, maybe six. She's blonde-haired, blue-eyed, and about the right age, so your Rebecca is one of the possibilities. We need to run DNA tests, obviously. But our policy is to reach out to families that might be affected because hearing information like this through the media can be very upsetting."

"Do you have a photograph?" Alexandra asked, voice trembling.

"We do," replied the other detective, and handed them a photo. They saw a gaunt but potentially beautiful young woman, pregnant, with a child standing on either side, holding her hands.

"It could be her," Alexandra said. "Is she alright?"

"She calls herself Madeline, or Maddy for short," said the detective. "She's malnourished and has been abused for a long, long time, but yes, she's basically healthy."

"What do we do in the meantime?" Jesse asked.

"Maddy and her kids are in protective custody in Providence for now. You can wait until we know more, or you can go to Providence to be close by in case the DNA results tell us that she's Rebecca. Either way, you won't be able to see her unless and until we determine that she's your daughter."

"The children in the photo—they're hers?" asked Alexandra.

"Yes."

"Who's the father?" Jesse asked.

"We don't know for certain. Four men lived in the house where Maddy was found, a father and his three adult sons. Maddy says any of the four could be the father of either child, or of the baby on the way."

"Dear lord," Alexandra said.

"Where are those men now?" Jesse asked, skidding along the edge of fury.

"The father and one of the sons were killed in a shootout with the police," the first detective said. "It will be all over the news within hours. A second son was critically wounded and we don't know whether he'll make it. The third son is in custody and cooperating, so we're learning something about what was going on in the house. That son shot and killed a police officer during the firefight. I think that's a measure of the kind of severe conditions Maddy's been forced to endure."

"Oh no," Alexandra said, shaking her head. "This is all so terrible. But thank God you got this young woman and her children out of there."

Jesse heard Becca's voice before he saw her. "It's not me, Daddy."

He studied the photo and thought-asked why she'd say that.

"The hair is too wavy, the blue eyes aren't bright enough, and the face is heart-shaped whereas mine would be longer."

"It sounds as though things could be complicated in Providence while you sort this out," Jesse said. "Since it's so close, I wonder if it might be best to wait it out here, and keep our lives and yours as simple as possible."

Jesse could see that Alexandra wasn't at all sure about that, but one of the detectives spoke up before she could protest.

"Honestly, I think that's a wise decision," he said. "It would be different if you lived on the other side of the country but you're only an hour or so away. Still, you should do whatever makes you feel most comfortable."

The detectives left them with contact information and the photograph. As soon as they were gone Alexandra and Jesse collapsed into each other's arms and then sat down to study the photo.

"You don't think it's her, do you?" Alexandra said.

"Look at her hair," said Jesse. "It might be the right color but shouldn't it be completely straight? Her eyes don't seem the right piercing shade of blue. And her face is rounder than all of the aged pictures of Becca we've seen."

"Maybe," Alexandra said. "But couldn't those sorts of things change as someone grows up?"

"Possibly," Jesse replied.

He thought-told Becca that Alexandra had made a good point, and Becca, standing with her hand on Alexandra's shoulder, agreed.

"Jesse, what if it *is* her?" Alexandra asked, her hand on his arm, and turned her teary face to look at him.

"I have no idea, sweetheart," he said, "except that it would be life-changing for all of us. Speaking of that, we should let the boys know what's happening. We should also call Meg and a couple of other friends to head off heart attacks in case they see this on the news."

"Good idea," she said. "Let's call the boys first."

Despite being local, Josh was the harder child to reach because he was always scrambling from one human disaster to another for work. By contrast, Matt's schedule was quite predictable, so long as they knew which country he was in. On this occasion he was in San Francisco and answered immediately. His face filled the screen.

"Hi Dad!" he said. "Oh, and Mom too. How are you guys?"

"We're okay," Alexandra said. "But right now we have something to talk about."

"What's going on?" Matt asked.

"Do you mind if I put you on hold while I try to track Josh down?" Jesse asked.

"Good luck with that," Matt said. Jesse caught Josh on the way out.

"Dad, I can only talk briefly," Josh said. "I've just been called to assist the police on an abduction, so I'm about to drive to Charlestown."

"Josh, this is important," Jesse said. "Can you spare five minutes?"

"Sure. What's going on?"

Jesse brought Matt back and after all four of them finished quick greetings, he caught Josh and Matt up on the detectives' stunning news.

Josh was the first to react. "Holy *shit*," he said. "Holy shit!"

Matt was all business. "Have you seen a photo?"

"We have," Jesse said. "Have a look." He held the picture up to the screen. "I'll send a hi-res version shortly. My gut reaction is that it's not Becca. We're sitting tight here in Boston until we hear back from the DNA tests. If it is Becca, we'll drive down to Providence right away."

"This is a lot to take in," said Josh. "What can we do at this point?"

"I don't think there's anything we can do except wait," Jesse said. "You guys should let Jenny and Oli know in case they hear something on the news."

"Makes sense," said Matt. "Should I come out there? Seems like we should all be together."

"Not at this point, Matt," Jesse replied. "Let's wait a couple of days to find out more, okay?"

"Are you guys doing okay?" asked Josh.

"I don't know how I feel," answered Alexandra. "I'm still trying to take it all in. I'm afraid to let my hopes get too high, and equally afraid that this poor, brutalized girl is in fact Becca."

"Same for me," Jesse added. "Mostly we just wanted to make sure that you guys weren't caught off guard by a news report."

"Well, I guess I should go," said Josh. "They'll be waiting for me. I'll check in later, okay?"

They said their goodbyes. Alexandra went to her office to place calls to close friends. Jesse climbed the stairs to his study.

Jesse slumped into his leather recliner and noticed Becca nestled into her usual spot in the matching chair.

"Twice in one morning," he said. "You don't normally show up before lunch."

"Special circumstances," she noted, and then Jesse thought he saw her turn her chair a fraction to face him more directly.

"Holy Moses! Did you just turn that chair?!"

"Settle down," she said. "I just turned in the chair; I didn't move the chair."

"I must be losing my mind," Jesse said. "I could have sworn the chair moved." He closed his eyes, trying to get a grip on himself. Becca said nothing. Chester appeared, his single feather drooping as he struggled for his dignity. Jesse opened his eyes to dispel the ridiculous chicken power animal.

"What happens if Maddy is you?" he asked. "I mean what happens to you?"

"Good question," Becca replied. "I've no idea. I'm a figment of your imagination so I suppose it's up to you."

He turned to stare directly at her, and got a second shock. Her hair was slightly wavy now, her blue eyes less bright, her face more rounded, and she was obviously pregnant.

"Whoaaa, you're freaking me out today!"

"You're doing this to me, you nitwit. The photo didn't show all the details. But this is probably what Maddy would look like, if she were sitting here beside you."

"It really could be Becca," he said. "Even if Maddy is Becca, I'd be sad to see you go."

"I don't see how Becca reappearing would end your hallucinations. They come with your bizarre brain at this point. At most, I might change to be a different pseudo-person."

Jesse closed his eyes and pondered his indirect, Becca-delivered self-diagnosis. When he opened his eyes again, Becca was a slender twenty-two-year-old woman with dead-straight blonde hair, sparkling blue eyes, a lean and long face, and belly-bump-free, as usual.

"How have I aged you in the precise way I have?" he asked. "How likely is Becca to look like you, if she's still alive?"

"You're probably relying on the algorithms in the automatic aging software the police use," said Becca, "at least up until the last time you saw an age-progressed image. I guess you've been doing it by yourself since then."

"Maybe I've been doing it wrong."

"Could be," Becca allowed. "The aging algorithms aren't perfect. And nutrition makes a difference to things like hair and eyes and faces."

Jesse reached for the photo of Maddy and studied it. "I'm going to try to morph you," he said.

"Whatever floats your boat, nut job."

He tried but couldn't get the morphing to work smoothly. He could see her as Becca or as Maddy but he couldn't produce a smooth transition between the two.

"You should tell Jerry about this," Becca said.

"It'd be a nice distraction," he agreed. "Anyway, he needs to know about this new source of stress in my life."

"Tell him I say hello," Becca said.

Jesse dialed Jerry, who was still his sole confidante and case manager for all things neuropsychological and hallucinatory. Jesse was sixty-four and had now been living with this condition, whatever it was, for over a decade.

Jesse explained about Maddy in Providence, Becca's shape shifting in Boston, his sense that Becca's chair had moved, and his failed attempt to morph Becca into Maddy and back again.

"Oh, and Becca says hello," he concluded.

Jerry laughed. "Well my friend, you never disappoint," he said. "That is a *lot*. How're you holding up?"

"I'm a little shaky, to be honest," Jesse said.

"Perfectly normal reaction," Jerry said. "To a very abnormal situation. Hey, is Becca still there with you now?"

"She is."

"Ask her to stand up. Put her in the same position as Maddy in the photo and then try that morphing thing again."

"Good idea," Jesse said. Becca was already standing in front of him, looking like Maddy in the photo. And then he was able to ease her back and forth between the familiar Becca and the pregnant Maddy.

"I can do it," Jesse reported. "I think I can even focus on the face changes, though not when we're talking. Hang on a sec." In the quiet, he stared at Becca's face as it changed into Maddy's and back again.

"Tell him it's not me," Becca said.

Jesse relayed Becca's message with a wry smile.

"But I might have been aging Becca incorrectly, so maybe I can't trust anything I learn from staring at the morphing face of my favorite hallucination," Jesse noted.

He and Jerry talked for a few minutes about sources of information Jesse might have used to simulate Becca at age twenty-two, and they were forced to acknowledge that just about anything might have impacted his mental extrapolation.

"I'm just going to have to wait and see what the DNA tests show," Jesse finally said.

"Right," Jerry said. "And that's enough experimenting for now anyway. I hope the next period of time isn't too crazy for you and Ali and the boys. I'm here when you need me, as always."

They said goodbye and Jesse turned to face Becca, now nestled back into her leather chair. He just stared at her for a minute. She stared back, a gentle smile on her perfect face.

"I think I might feel lost without you," he thought-said to her, and she nodded, blue eyes gleaming.

The story was all over the news that evening, and the media made the most of it. Every account seemed a bit more lurid than the last, with reporters dramatically recounting the shootout and emphasizing the young girl's years of physical, emotional, and sexual abuse while being held prisoner, chained up in a concrete basement. Soon enough the story was picked up all over the country.

The critically wounded son died from his injuries overnight, so now there was only one survivor besides Maddy and her children from the perverse family setup. Twenty-five-year-old Charlie, the youngest of the three sons, had shot and killed a policeman, and wounded another in the gunfire. He was cooperating in an attempt to win leniency from the justice system. Rhode Island had abolished the death penalty decades ago but, if crossing state lines was involved, the case could go federal, where the death penalty was still an option, so he had something at stake in helping the police with the investigation.

According to Charlie's account, as relayed in the news reports, his mother had died when he was young and soon after his father had abducted Maddy, when Charlie was ten or eleven. Maddy had been used and abused right from the start, first by the father, then by the older boys, and eventually by Charlie. Charlie had no idea who'd fathered the two children or the soon-to-arrive baby but he claimed it wasn't him because his father had required him to use condoms.

Maddy's life had been brutal, with no school, no health care, and only the twisted companionship of her captors for human company, at least until her children were born. She'd become fiercely protective of them, an older boy and a younger girl, then aged about five and two, though nobody knew their exact ages.

She was always chained up, but she'd convinced her captors not to chain the children, so they'd be free to run around in the locked cellar.

Ultimately, that's how they escaped. Maddy had squeezed her five-year-old son through a boarded-up basement window, after prying some of the boards off. He'd followed her instructions, running through the woods until he found another house, where he asked for help. After that, the horrific situation was unmasked to the world.

That's as much as the news hounds could get out of the police and medical staff taking care of the survivors. And that's the story that cycled for several days, with only tiny crumbs of new information.

Jesse and Alexandra fielded a couple of calls from people who saw the report but hadn't received the warning Alexandra had sent around. Anna Feld reached out, promising to share any news that came across her desk. Mrs. Buxton, their old social worker, also contacted them. She was retired but had never forgotten their family, and offered any help they might want. They were all waiting.

With Alexandra, Jesse, and the boys stressed like ukulele strings, three days later the detectives returned.

Alexandra pounced. "It's not Becca, is it?" she said. "If it had been her, you'd have asked us to come to Providence."

"That's right," one of them said. "I'm sorry—sorry it wasn't her, and sorry you lost her in the first place."

"Thank you," Alexandra said. "So what's the story with Maddy's real family?"

"She has no surviving family, as it turns out. She was from the Boston area originally, but she was an only child of only children and both of her parents are dead. The father committed suicide within a few years of Maddy's abduction, and the mother died of cancer a couple of years ago. Both sets of grandparents are dead so Maddy is entirely alone in the world, apart from her children and the surviving gunman who helped hold her captive."

"And he'll soon be going to jail for life without parole," said the other detective.

"What'll happen to Maddy, then?" asked Jesse. "And is that her real name?"

"Maddy was not her original name," said the first detective. "I suppose she has to decide what to call herself. She's now in the care of the Massachusetts Children and Families people. That's all the information we have for now. Again, we're very sorry to have raised your hopes."

"Is there anything we can do to help her?" Alexandra asked.

"Just keep her and her kids in your thoughts," said the detective.

After showing them out, Alexandra and Jesse stared at one another with heavy hearts. Then Jesse reached for the phone to begin the process of conveying the news to the boys and their friends. He had a sinking feeling that they'd all feel depressed for months.

"Thanks for the update, Dad," Josh said. "So let me tell you both the weird thing of the week."

"What's that?" Alexandra asked.

"I've actually been roped into Maddy's case," said Josh.

"You're kidding!" they exclaimed, simultaneously.

"Nope," said Josh. "Once they figured out her identity they knew they had to move her and the kids up to Boston, since it's our problem to resolve. The transfer happened this morning. I've just finished a meeting between the Providence people and our people, who're trying to figure out what to do."

"That's amazing, Josh," Alexandra said. "What will your role be?"

"I'll be the lead social worker, heading up every aspect of the case," he said. "They're pulling me off other work for now, so this will be my full-time assignment."

"Well I'm not surprised," Alexandra said. "You're the best person for it. Maddy and the kids must be terribly traumatized, and Maddy probably has virtually no education, I assume."

"That's about the size of it, Mom. I've been told that she can read, though I'm not yet sure how that happened, or how good her reading is. She can draw brilliantly, as well. There are some physical problems, especially related to eyesight, but I'll know more tomorrow."

"How's this new assignment going to work with Oli so close to delivering baby number three?" Jesse asked.

"Same as always, I guess," Josh said. "We'll muddle through somehow."

"We're proud of you, Josh," Jesse said.

"Thanks, Dad. I feel like helping Maddy gives me a chance to do something for Becca, indirectly. I'll do my best."

As soon as they hung up, Alexandra said what Jesse was thinking.

"Jesse, do you think we could actually get involved? Maybe Josh could set us up as a foster family? Or something like that."

They immediately called Josh back.

Josh said that he'd been thinking about it as well, but warned them he could make no promises, and there'd be multiple hoops to jump. He also pointed out that Maddy was over eighteen and would almost certainly be given guardianship of her children, so it mightn't be a standard fostering arrangement. The state normally arranged fostering only for minors, though an adult fostering system did exist for rare cases.

"We're up for jumping hoops, Josh," Jesse reassured him, "and we don't care what the arrangement is called."

"Well all right then!" Josh said. "I'll see what I can do."

HOW DO YOU KNOW ABOUT STOCKHOLM SYNDROME?

When Jerry came to Boston for a conference, Jesse went into the city to see him.

"Want to sit down somewhere and have a drink?" asked Jesse.

"Actually, I was thinking of a nice long walk," said Jerry.

Jesse led him down to the Charles River, which they crossed on the Massachusetts Avenue bridge before setting out westwards along the Cambridge side. As they walked, Jesse told Jerry about their hopes of getting involved in Maddy's life and Jerry caught Jesse up on his family.

"I also have some news about our pair of cultivating hallucinations papers," said Jerry.

"Do tell," said Jesse.

"There's been a bit of chatter," said Jerry. "Right before we met up today, I was presenting on a panel about hallucinations, and someone in the audience brought up that pair of papers. Mind you, they weren't the topic of the panel. But she took the opportunity in public to flat-out deny that what's described in the papers is possible. She reckons nobody can train themselves into psychotic states and that it's impossible to cultivate high-fidelity hallucinations. I couldn't very well produce the evidence for her to examine, so there may be some trust issues involved." They chuckled at the side effects of keeping Jesse's identity secret. "She was very confident," Jerry added.

"I suppose you were your usual calm self," said Jesse.

"Of course," said Jerry. "It was a nice opportunity to get the word out, actually."

"She might be right," said Jesse. "I could be controlling psychosis that has psychiatric roots rather than creating hallucinations that look like psychosis."

"If you really had schizophrenia or something similar, I don't see how the symptoms could be so selective," said Jerry. "Whoever heard of just anxiety and hallucinations, and staying high functioning, otherwise? But you could be right. That's the thing with your situation: we probably won't ever know."

"Becca says I'm *definitely* a lunatic," said Jesse.

"When did she say that?" asked Jerry, laughing.

"Just now," answered Jesse. "She's right here."

"Oh wow, that's so cool," said Jerry. "Hey, I've always wanted to have a conversation with her, without you interpreting. Is that possible?"

"That's... weird," said Jesse.

"C'mon. Just say whatever she says, no changing any words, no commentary. You can be like a medium for listening to a ghost."

Jesse laughed. "Okay, I'm not sure this is a good idea, but Becca says she wants to do it."

"Brilliant," said Jerry. "Let's go. How are you today, Rebecca?"

"Seriously?"

"Is that you or Rebecca saying that?" asked Jerry.

"That's Becca. And me, too, actually," said Jesse. "Look, this is going to be impossible if you keep wondering which of us is talking. I promise: it'll be just Becca."

"Okay, good. Rebecca, is your Dad controlling psychotic states with his visualization practice or is he inducing hallucinations because of all that meditation training?"

"You're the psychiatrist," said Becca. "Why are you asking me?"

"I thought you might have privileged access to your Dad's brain, somehow," Jerry said. "People with high image-control capabilities can picture things with a degree of vividness that would shock regular people, but normally, what they picture doesn't merge with sensory input or appear in their visual and auditory fields."

"I don't know why or how I'm here," said Becca. "Daddy's really ly good at combining visual things, though. Like in his meditation, he figured out how to see multiple visualizations at the same time. That's the way it is with me. He sees me and he sees the ordinary world and they merge perfectly. That's not a part of what psychologists mean by image control is it?"

"No," said Jerry. "But maybe it should be. Maybe we just haven't recognized that this sort of thing is possible for human minds."

"You know about his memory playback thing, right?"

"Maybe not," said Jerry. "Explain."

"Daddy can see memories like movies. Multisensory movies. If he wants."

"That is part of image control, like lucid dreaming," said Jerry. "Except for the multisensory part."

"What about crossing senses? Hearing what he's seeing and feeling what he's hearing and all that?" asked Becca.

"Who's interviewing whom here?" asked Jerry, laughing. "Your dad's experiences of synesthesia have been documented in other people but not in ordinary remembering. He can control that, though, right?"

"Yeah, Daddy can control the cross-sensory stuff," said Becca. "But there's other things he can't control. If he's seeing multiple visualizations at the same time, he can sense emotions and he can even cross senses but he can't talk or move."

"Fascinating. Hey, you call Jesse Daddy. Around here, most twenty-somethings would be saying Dad. What's that about?"

"Well, I've been here for more than a decade, from a girl to a twenty-two-year old. I guess I've earned the equivalent of a college degree directly from Daddy. But part of me still feels like a little girl, probably because that's the last time he knew anything about me for sure. Also, I just like it—calling him Daddy makes me feel close to him."

"So it's your choice," said Jerry.

"Jerry," said Becca, "of course it's my choice. I do what I want. Just because I know what Daddy likes doesn't mean I always do that. I do what I want and sometimes he likes it and sometimes he doesn't."

"Okay," said Jerry, shaking his head. "Let's go back to your Dad's visualizations. How many can he see at the same time now?"

"Too many to count," said Becca, "and the number is higher all the time. There are almost two hundred images just in my stack. The Maddy stack already has a couple of dozen, and that just got started. I get to see all that stuff for free while he does all the hard work."

"What makes your Dad's work on those images so hard?" asked Jerry. "Can't he just see them?"

"He can see images one at a time without effort," Becca said. "But if he wants to merge images, he has to get rid of ideas and words, and focus on pictures and feelings. That's really hard to do. He also has to get super familiar with image stacks and that takes a lot of effort."

"So words and concepts prevent the merging of visualizations," said Jerry.

"Yeah," said Becca. "Any language, even just in Daddy's head, stops the merging. Body movement stops it, too."

"I see," said Jerry. "You must have feelings about some of the images. For example, how do you feel about the tough images in the Becca stack? Oh, wait, is it okay for me to ask?"

"It's okay to ask," said Becca. "Daddy does something to keep me at a distance from those. For the scary stuff, he's imagining possibilities, not remembering, so I don't get too frightened. I watch them like he does, kind of wondering."

"What about the Maddy stack?" asked Jerry. "There's a lot less guessing in that case."

"The images of her life before she was abducted come from Daddy's imagination but they make me feel happy and warm," Becca said. "The images of Maddy being stolen and what her captors did to her are horrifying. They make me angry and scared. He has some less explicit ones that are somehow even more terrifying, like this simulation of the start of Maddy's trauma, a cloud of dark blood billowing under water. Then there are images about lost memory and Stockholm-Syndrome, which make me feel helpless. I hate hate *hate* Daddy's visualization of her kidnappers' motivations, their values, their feelings—it's like he's trying way too hard to empathize with those assholes. I wish I could punch him when he does that. Then images of Maddy's kids arrive and I feel this surge of joy and even a kind of vengeance, because cruelty can't kill that kind of love. And I love the visualization of Maddy as a mother. That's where her greatest joy came from."

"How do you know about Stockholm Syndrome?" asked Jerry.

"Seriously?!" exclaimed Becca. "Jerry, wake up already. I live inside this dude who's like a walking encyclopedia."

"Touché!" Jerry said. "Okay, how about emotion? Do you feel your own emotions, no matter what your Dad's feeling?"

"What do you take me for, Jerry? I'm no second-rate hallucination!" Becca laughed. "Of course I've got my own feelings. About everything, not just about what Daddy is visualizing at the time."

"Those feelings are other aspects of your Dad's complex emotional field, though, right?"

"I don't know. I mean it's all his brain," said Becca. "But I just feel what I feel."

"So what do you feel about *him*?"

"That's complicated," she said. "I know I come from Daddy but to me he feels like an extension of *me*. He's a bit strange. A bit wordy. He thinks a lot. He gets anxious. None of that's me, but I feel those things as bits of me stretched out to create something different, kind of the opposite of me as an extension of him. Mostly I adore him. And a lot of that is because he loves me so much he made me. He made me *twice*, Jerry, and the second time was a lot more work than the first!"

"How do you feel about your Mom?"

"I miss her so much," said Becca. "But it's like there's this bullet-proof glass between Mommy and me. I can see everything Daddy can see and think and feel. But I only feel things between them secondhand. I love how much Daddy loves her and she loves him—those two have a real love story going on! I get pissed if he does something thoughtless toward her, but that doesn't happen often. I worry about her memory, like Daddy does. The closest I feel to her is through their physical affection. I know that's super weird. But that's how I feel her physical touch, through him. It's the best I can do."

"What about private things, like making love?" inquired Jerry. "Can I ask about that?"

"Sure," said Becca. "At the start I never experienced any of that. It's like Daddy kept me out of any private stuff. But I've been with him so long that I know everything about him. I guess in that way I'm not at all like a real daughter. And I'm an adult now, too. Put those things together and the whole ick factor doesn't really apply anymore. It's not weird to me, and Daddy's not aware of it, so it's not weird for him."

"That glass-separation thing with your Mom, and the distance thing from the Becca stack, those things interest me," said Jerry. "Do you ever get lonely?"

"Yeah, I get lonely," she admitted. "I'm not always present in Daddy's world and I barely exist in those times, like a shadow within his under-consciousness, time barely passing. I miss everyone then—Daddy, Mommy, Matt, Josh. I *really* don't like the shadow waiting state."

"Rebecca, I want to talk to Jesse for a sec. Is that okay?" asked Jerry.

"Whatever you say, doc," said Becca.

"Hey Jesse," Jerry said. "Dude—you've been holding out on me!"

"Really? I didn't think so," said Jesse.

"*Definitely* holding out," said Jerry. "She's a *lot* more independent of you than I realized. The way time passes for her, the way her feelings work, the way she senses her Mom... You've created something that's much more complex than a high-res projection. It's more like an independent AI housed in your mind. With a college degree! And not particularly compliant! Why didn't you explain all that to me?"

"I thought I did," said Jesse.

"No way, Jess. I think you take this for granted so much that you aren't explaining the details. Becca has a sense of time! She has a kind of awareness even when she's not in your consciousness. She gets lonely, for Pete's sake!"

"Okay, okay," said Jesse. "Look, I'm not trying to hide anything. I guess I didn't realize what would be important to you."

"Jeez!" said Jerry. "Listen, Jesse, Becca's not just a hallucination anymore. She's a nearly separate being. I mean obviously it's still your mind doing the work..."

Jerry paced quietly for a while, trying to wrap his mind around what he'd heard.

"I just can't think of *any* examples in the clinical literature of hallucinations like this," he finally said.

"Okay, whatever," said Jesse. "She's getting impatient and wants to talk to you again."

"Let's go then," said Jerry.

"I'm back," said Becca.

"Do you have any more revelations, Rebecca?" said Jerry.

"Not really," said Becca. "I just don't get to talk to other people and I didn't want to stop. You're the only person who knows about me so it's you or nothing... even though you keep insulting me."

Jerry shook his head. "It's amazing how you've got your own wants, separately from your Dad. I wasn't expecting that."

"It's just normal to me," said Becca.

"Do you remember the early days, when you were more like a regular hallucination?" Jerry suddenly laughed. "I'm asking a hallucination about her memories! Jeez!"

"I remember a bit," answered Becca, "but those things feel like second-hand memories, like I see them through a story Daddy told me and not by directly remembering. I guess it took me a while to grow into myself."

"Fair enough," said Jerry. "But now you have your own preferences and desires."

"Yes, and I don't always agree with Daddy about what to do or what's good."

"Do you have favorite visualizations? For instance, do you like the Becca stack?"

"I like it well enough," she said. "But my favorite, by far, is the love stack."

"What's that?" asked Jerry.

"Daddy made a whole bunch of stacks for people he loves," she said. "The family, for sure, but also for good friends like you."

"I'm honored," he said.

"You should be," she said. "A lot of work goes into each image, and into stacking them. But the most complicated part of the love stack is all the stacks about love itself. It took him years to build. He's got visual simulations for family affection, love between friends, sexual attraction, you name it. We've both got our own sexual fantasies in there."

"Wait, you have sexual fantasies?!" asked Jerry.

"Jerry, you're doing it again," said Becca. "What healthy girl wouldn't have sexual fantasies?"

"Good lord," he said. "Okay. Carry on."

"He's got infatuation images, too, with desperate longing," Becca continued. "Those make me feel like I'm getting to experience things the abduction robbed from me, you know, things I would have felt as a teenager when I fell in love."

"Have you ever fallen in love?" asked Jerry.

"I'm kinda in love with you," said Becca.

"Oh. Um…," said Jerry.

Becca snorted. "I'm teasing, dummy."

"Oh, teasing," said Jerry. "That's your thing, isn't it? You're good at it."

"Thank you!" said Becca. "I get that from Daddy. Anyway, the love stack also has bonding love, like Daddy and Mommy have; it's calming, with quiet closeness and cuddling and loyalty and trust."

"I guess the biochemistry is in there, too," said Jerry. "Testosterone, dopamine, oxytocin…"

"Yeah," said Becca, "but that's Daddy's weird thing. I focus more on the people stuff. He's got all these images of cooperation. There are stories about the boundary between the safe zone of friends and family and partners, and the danger zone of strangers. But there are also stories of how we break through that boundary, making friends with strangers and even connecting to people long dead and not yet born. Daddy's compassion meditation obsession takes him even further, out to living beings of all kinds, and even to ecological systems. He's been doing that for longer than I've been around. Of course, his version is full of science and history. There are simulations of the way love gets twisted, too. He gets riled up about the way the fashion and pornography industries exploit our love-hungry brains, the way infatuated people have really bad judgment, the way people are wary of strangers, and the way people who don't feel empathy can be brutal if they want. There's a lot to it. But it hangs together in one gigantic superstack. I watched Daddy build it, piece by piece for years, and now he can bring the entire thing into his meditation states whenever he wants."

"It sounds amazing," said Jerry.

"I love it," she said. "When all the pieces are fitted together, all the horror and happiness, the wonder and joy, the awesomeness of it all—we can feel it all *at the same time*. It's not just a fuzz of feelings, either. It's extremely detailed and intense. It's so beautiful and so true that it hurts. Like a bright light that stings but shows us the way things really are if we can stand to look. And it sparkles with cross-cutting sensory stuff, too. It leaves Daddy and me aching with longing for this poor, broken world, and fills us with gratitude for every moment of kindness that ever appeared in the universe. It's addictive. Sometimes he might be working on some other visualization thing and I'll practically beg him to do the love stack so we can feel that feeling again. Sometimes he tells me to go away but other times he gives in because he loves it as much as I do. It's our drug of choice."

Jerry laughed. "I think I can see why," he said.

"That's just the love stack, Jerry," said Becca. "Daddy has these visualizations of the entire cosmos, its history and the way it works, from physics and biology to evolution and economics. Tiny little things and great big things, physical things and social things. There are hundreds of them. Put that with the love stack and you get this picture of everything the way it really is. That's how Daddy and I make sense of what happened to me. And to Maddy.

It's like the best we can do is see it for what it is, accepting it. And you know that Daddy takes it even further. He reveres it. Worships it. If things just are that way, and if he can accept it, then what happened to me and to my family doesn't hurt so much."

"I don't get the worship bit," said Jerry. "To me that implies churches and synagogues and mosques and temples, and a deity wanting deference from lowly human beings."

"I'm with you on that," said Becca. "He'll probably have to explain it to you."

"I'd like to hear it from you," said Jerry.

"I don't really have the words for it," Becca said. "It's all philosophical."

"But you have a Jesse-style education."

"I have a PhD in Daddy," she said. "But I still don't see things like him. And he has all this technical language for talking about complicated topics. It's just not my thing."

"Can't you borrow some words from your dad?"

"I'll try, ok?" said Becca. "Daddy's idea of reality is that there's a hidden part, like the parts of the ocean that are too deep for us to see. We can find out about it slowly and carefully, through science and mathematics and poetry and music and art and meditation and whatnot. He calls it the depth dimension. Or he calls it ultimate reality compared to the conventional reality of everyday experience. The deep stuff is wonderful but it's also scary because it doesn't really fit what human beings like. It's not conscious like us; it doesn't feel or plan. It's more like patterns and chances. The trying and doing and thinking and feeling part is up to us. Anyway, Daddy senses that deep part just like he senses the ordinary world. He feels both, conventional reality and ultimate reality, all the time. But he had to work for years to do that. It's the depth of everything that he's learning to love, even when it doesn't suit him and even when it almost destroys him, like when I was abducted."

"So the worship is really about accepting everything the way it is," Jerry said.

"Yes," said Becca, "but there's more to it."

"Always," Jerry said.

"Yeah. He's studied everything about this way of thinking, how it shows up all over the world but constantly gets twisted. The deep part can be pretty hard to swallow so people make up a lot of stuff about it, pretending that it's like a loving person, which it obviously isn't, or that it has a super-meaningful plan, which it obviously doesn't. Most people invent invisible meanings and pretend stories, which feel real because they do it all in groups where everyone around them seems to believe the same stuff. Those stories make people feel special—their group is super special or their own life is super special or whatever. And you can control other people with those stories, too, so they can help groups feel safe. To most people, Daddy's love of the deep parts has nothing to offer. It's terrifying to see the world that way and they can't even imagine being drawn to it or loving it. To them it's like running to hug an angry and hungry tiger. Better to shoot it and stay safe. Daddy isn't out to change anybody's minds. He just wants to worship everything the way it is. He wants to let it be."

"Is that a Beatles reference?" asked Jerry.

"You keep half-insulting me, Jerry."

"Ha! Sorry about that," he said.

"The complicated bit about letting it be," continued Becca, "is that Daddy's way of worshipping reality as it really is means that everyone else is delusional, making up invisible beings and controlling each other with them. Of course, their way of worshipping implies that *he's* nuts, so I guess that's just the way it goes. But there's so much pain in the world and Daddy cares more about people managing their pain than making sure everyone believes the right things, so he lets that be, too. Some people don't really believe the fancy stories and invisible beings, though. They want to go another way but they have no idea how. So Daddy thinks we should talk with each other about the way nature has this wonderful, terrifying deep part that's even more beautiful than all the delusional stories. He sees his books and lectures like breadcrumbs helping people find their way out of the maze of delusional, controlling stories, heading in a new direction, into the deep parts, where they can explore for themselves."

Jerry could only shake his head and smile. "I just can't get terribly excited about reality as a whole, or reality as it is most profoundly, in its stunning depths and dynamics, or ultimate reality, or whatever, like your Dad."

"I know what you mean," said Becca. "You and me, we're the same way. We're mostly happy, usually at peace with the world. Maybe that's why we're so in love."

"Ah… teasing, right?" said Jerry.

"Hey, you're getting good at this," said Becca. "Daddy's a thinker, you know? He's calling it like he sees it, same as you are."

"Well," said Jerry, "it's incredibly cool to be talking like this with you, Rebecca. I hope we can do it again sometime."

"Fewer insults next time, though, okay?" said Becca.

"Yeah, sure. I know better now. Bye, Rebecca."

"Bye, Jerry."

"You guys done?" asked Jesse.

"Yep," said Jerry. "For now. That was amazing. And it's not just Becca's independence from you. I hadn't known how far you've come with your meditation tricks. You must be merging more than a thousand visualizations by now through stack-merging. Seems like I have to talk to Rebecca to get the straight story."

"Well, she's up for it, I think," said Jesse, as they ambled onwards.

"Your worship thing is weird, though," said Jerry, pacing slowly along the riverside.

"Loving what is, without any distortions and delusions—it's my thing, Jerry. It's how I tell myself the truth about Becca. And I want—no, I *need*—to accept it, to surrender to it, to revere it. It's suchness. So yes, worship."

"You're a strange one, in so *many* ways," Jerry replied.

Their friendship, especially because of the chasm of difference, was priceless.

A MALNOURISHED
SAY-IT-LIKE-IT-IS TEXAN

It was safe to say that Maddy had been on their minds every waking hour from the moment they learned of her existence, but since Josh had called with the news that they could be considered for being her foster family, Jesse and Alexandra could talk of nothing else. Jesse found that Maddy was often in his dreams as well, but none of them were nightmarish. He took this as a good sign, internally rolling his eyes at this uncharacteristic display of superstition.

After a battery of interviews and background checks, they were cleared to begin preparing to meet Maddy.

It helped enormously that Josh was her primary social worker—though that almost hadn't happened. After Maddy and her children were settled in the temporary housing assigned by the state, they were closely supervised by three staff members at any given time in shifts—one each for her and her two children—and visited by an endless stream of medical specialists, psychotherapists, and educational evaluators. It had quickly become obvious that all visitors and resident minders had to be women. Maddy would tense up or become aggressive when a man approached her, and completely freak out if a man touched her. But rather than excuse himself from the case, Josh argued that Maddy needed to have different and positive experiences with men, and that hiding from them indefinitely couldn't be the solution to managing her trauma. Maddy's head clinician agreed, so the team came up with a plan that was not unlike exposure therapy to get Maddy accustomed to Josh's presence.

Josh told Alexandra and Jesse how it unfolded. He continued to organize services for Maddy and the kids, but he made a point to drop in a few days a week, remaining by the door at first, and gradually staying longer and moving closer. At first he was completely silent, offering nothing more than warm smiles. While Maddy remained standoffish, the kids had taken to him right away, and would've played with Josh if Maddy had permitted it. Finally, one day, Maddy looked at him and nodded, and after that it was like opening a dam: the kids were all over him, play fighting, climbing, and tumbling, while Maddy watched from the other side of the room. Eventually he had conversations with the oldest child, sometimes holding the younger child on his lap while everyone was on the floor. Soon enough Maddy came to understand Josh's vital role in her life, and seemed to believe that Josh was different from the men she'd known in the past. She started speaking to him, telling him what she and the kids needed.

The speed with which this constructive response took shape was a sign of profound resilience, Josh said. But so far, Maddy wasn't saying anything about her experiences in the farm house, not to him, not to the police, not to her small army of therapists and case workers. She wouldn't talk about the future, either. Her focus was exclusively on the present moment, especially on her children's needs.

"So," Josh said, "given all that, you guys sure you're still up for this?"

"I'd say we've spent years preparing," Alexandra said. "I'm determined to make this work. I keep thinking this might be what Becca would be like, if she were rescued from such a horrible situation. I already feel flooded with love for Maddy, and I can't explain how, but I know with certainty that this love is unbreakable and ultimately irresistible."

Jesse stared at his wife. She could still take his breath away, after all these years.

With the preliminary hoops jumped and with Maddy's consent given, Josh prepared them the day before their first meeting.

"She's still pretty gaunt, she wears dark glasses because even indoor light gives her eye pain, she cusses like a sailor, she's shockingly blunt, and she's *totally* intolerant of insincerity," Josh said. "So you're going to need to be very plainspoken and straightforward. No jokes or innuendo."

"Got it," Jesse said.

"Just think of her as a malnourished say-it-like-it-is Texan, and you'll have a good idea of what you'll be facing," joked Josh. "In fact, think of her as a malnourished say-it-like-it-is Texan you can't touch, who knows nothing about culture or current events, whose existence is totally focused on her children, who's been tortured, raped, and abused for fifteen years, who possesses a very limited vocabulary and emotional range, and who has fiery intelligence and fierce maternal instincts."

"We can do that, Josh," Alexandra said. "How is she being prepared to meet us? Especially Jesse?"

"She knows you're my parents, and that you're safe, good people," Josh said. "I told her you want to help take care of her and her children, if she feels she wants help. She said she takes care of her children, and I agreed, and then she asked me whether I trust you both. I told her I trust you with my life. Then she looked me in the eyes, which she hardly ever does. I think that's when she made the decision to let her world get a tiny bit bigger."

On the day of the meeting, Josh met Alexandra and Jesse at the curb. He gave them a few last-minute reminders, especially about simple words and no touching, hugged them both, then led them into the living room of the small transitional home.

Maddy was sitting on the floor playing with her children, in bare feet and a light summer dress. She was painfully thin, and obviously pregnant. They could see the scarring on one ankle, where she'd been chained up. Her blonde hair was clean but lifeless. Despite the window shades being closed, she was wearing wraparound sunglasses, and her son and daughter were also, to help manage the vision problems they'd acquired from living for so long in a poorly illuminated basement.

Jesse remained by the door, while Alexandra drew a few steps closer. Maddy stood up and very deliberately dipped her head at Alexandra and then Jesse, a no-touching greeting ritual she'd been taught. They nodded back. Josh made introductions, finishing with Michael, who seemed about five, and Jamie, who might have been two.

Alexandra smiled warmly at each of them. "Maddy, we're so happy to meet you," she said. "Would it be okay if I played on the floor with you and your children?"

"Yes," Maddy said.

"Maddy," Jesse said, "if it's okay I'll sit over here with Josh."

"Yes," she said again, and Jesse joined Josh on the couch while Alexandra settled in on the floor. Michael and Jamie weren't hypersensitive about touch the way Maddy was. But Maddy vigilantly monitored their personal space. Alexandra was careful not to touch either child.

The four of them formed a loose circle on the floor and played with wooden blocks and little plastic people. It was in this way that Jesse's beautiful wife began the long process of winning Maddy over through ever-so-patient, ever-so-gentle, ever-so-powerful love. She was right, Jesse thought: her love was unbreakable, and it was irresistible.

That first visit was less than an hour. Maddy said nothing as they left, not even goodbye. She didn't get up from the floor and she didn't look at them. In fact, apart from the rehearsed greeting and the two "yes" answers to questions put to her, she'd said nothing the entire visit.

"That was good," said Josh, as we made our way outside to the car.

"Really?" asked Alexandra.

"Yes, Mom, really. Maddy was content the whole time and the kids were totally into you. Dad kept his distance. It was perfect."

"Good to know," said Alexandra. "When can we do it again?"

"I'll talk with Maddy about that and call you tonight, okay?"

"This is important to me, Josh," Alexandra added.

"Don't worry, Mom. I'll call you. You guys did great today."

As Jesse hugged Josh goodbye, he saw the window shades in the house move and Maddy's sunglasses-clad face looking down at the three of them. He mentioned it to Josh.

"I think she's fascinated by you guys," he said. "I mean just think—this is the first normal, loving relationship she's seen between two adults."

In the car, Alexandra gave Jesse a pointed look. "This is going to work out," she said. She moved the car into the street and said nothing more.

That evening, Josh called as promised.

"Maddy said—and I quote—'It was a good fuckin' visit. Bring 'em back.'"

Jesse chuckled. "So I guess things went well!"

"Very well," Josh said. "Would you like to visit again tomorrow?"

"Oh Josh we'd love that," Alexandra said.

She was beaming. Jesse hadn't seen her engaged in anything with this degree of energy and personal investment since the boys left home—not even in the volunteer work. He noted that her weird little slips of memory had all but disappeared, lending credence to the theory that this was no more than normal aging coupled with episodes of acute stress. Certainly it helped that she had a purpose to throw her energy behind. And she wasn't leaving him out of it either. As soon as she'd made arrangements with Josh for the next visit, she threw herself at him with as much passion as he'd seen in years.

The next day they drove back to Maddy's temporary housing. Jesse wasn't teaching or in meetings at the university during the summer months so he was as free as a bird and glad for this grand new life adventure, which served to break up long days of writing and meditating.

Maddy greeted them with the same rehearsed nod she'd used the previous day.

"Okay if I join you again?" Alexandra asked.

"Yes," said Maddy.

"How are you feeling today?" asked Alexandra, as she joined the children on the floor. Michael was engrossed with Legos, while Jamie sat quietly eating Cheerios from a plastic bowl.

"My back really fuckin' hurts," said Maddy. She looked all around the room when she spoke, never making eye contact with anyone but her kids.

"Do you think it's the pregnancy that's making your back hurt?" asked Alexandra.

"Yes," said Maddy.

Alexandra offered some blocks to nearby Jamie, and following Maddy's lead, directed her gaze to the children or toward the floor. "When I was pregnant with Josh," she began, and pointed at him, "my back hurt all the time. He was a gigantic baby."

"What's that?" asked Maddy.

"What do you mean?" asked Alexandra.

"What kind of baby?"

"Oh, I see. Big. He was a very big baby. And very fat. With a very big head."

"Big babies must really fuckin' hurt," said Maddy.

"Yes," said Alexandra. "With Josh, I had to have a Caesarian section because he wouldn't fit. Have you heard about those?"

"No," said Maddy.

"It's when doctors help get a baby out. So they won't get stuck."

"My babies were small and didn't get stuck," Maddy said. "Still hurt like a bitch, though."

Michael looked up at her and Maddy reached over and brushed his hair back, face impassive.

"When my back hurt when I was pregnant," Alexandra said, "I'd put a heating pad on it, or Jesse would rub my back to help relax the tight muscles. That helped me feel better."

"Heating pad?"

"Yes. It's like a piece of cloth that you can plug into an electrical outlet, and it warms up."

"Plug-in cloth?"

Jesse suppressed a grin, and he suspected Alexandra and Josh were, too. It really was a bizarre thing, if you thought about it.

"Yes," said Alexandra. "I'll show you some time, if you like."

"Yes," said Maddy.

The conversation ended there and Alexandra turned to Michael and Jamie.

"What've you built there?" she asked Michael.

"A big fuckin' house!" he replied.

"It's beautiful," she said, and then encouraged him to share the intricate details. She was mind-melding with Michael the same way she once did with Matt and Josh, the same way she did with her grandchildren and every child she spent time with.

The expletives, from Maddy and Michael, were so frequent and so matter-of-fact that they stopped hearing them after a while.

After playing for an hour, with Maddy almost completely silent, Jamie walked over to Maddy and sat on her lap, where Maddy breastfed her. Breastfeeding a two-year-old made perfect sense in basement-lifestyle logic.

Alexandra turned to Josh and asked, "Should we go now? It's getting close to lunch time."

"You fuckin' stay," said Maddy. "Him too." She pointed at Jesse.

"Is it okay if we stay for lunch, Josh?" asked Alexandra.

"Don't ask him!" Maddy said. "Just fuckin' stay."

"Okay," said Alexandra, smiling. "We'll stay."

Josh started laughing gently and, for the very first time, they witnessed Maddy's smile. It was a half-smile, and it was fleeting, but they all caught it.

Jesse also caught Alexandra's face. She was deeply happy, and thoroughly captivated by this extraordinary young woman. As was he.

A BIT MORE LIKE A
NORMAL HUMAN

"You must be Jesse and Alexandra," said the police officer.

"Great to meet you, Helena. We're so sorry for your loss," Jesse said.

"Nice to see you in person, Helena," said Josh, as they shook hands.

"You too. I've got a conference room ready for us," she said. "Come on back."

They followed her through the corridors of the police station and settled at a table.

"So," said Helena. "You're the foster family. That's very generous of you."

"It's really no trouble," said Alexandra. "We have plenty of room and plenty of time. We're glad to do it."

"Still—mighty generous!"

"So Helena," Josh said, "we'd like to hear details about the night Maddy was rescued—anything you're comfortable sharing. "We've got all sorts of clinical info on her, but only the barest of outlines about how Maddy and her kids were living and what happened the night you and your partner rescued her."

"Any insight you have can guide us as we figure out how best to help them," Jesse added.

"I'm willing to talk about it," Helena said. "The therapists here have forced me to talk about that night over and over again so I've gotten used to it. It'll be nice to focus on the kid and his mother instead of on me and my partner for a change."

"Thank you so much," said Josh.

"So what should I do? Just walk you through the timeline?"

"Sure," said Josh. "Whatever feels right."

"Okay," she said, "so my partner Phil and I are on patrol, night-shift. Around 2am, we get a call about a disturbance at a house on the edge of town. We're told there's a little kid on the back porch of this house banging on the door and screaming 'Get help! Get help!' over and over again. The homeowners think it might be some kind of home-invasion scam so they don't open the door. Wouldn't be the first time. They call us instead.

"Anyway, Phil and I get there in under ten and as soon as we're out of the vehicle we can hear the ruckus. The homeowners are at a front window, and they're waving at us to go around back. Sure enough, there's a little boy back there, still pounding the door and screaming. We do a quick scan of the property with the Maglites, and it looks clear, so Phil holsters his gun and starts trying to get the kid's attention. The kid can see us both, but he won't stop banging on the door and screaming. Phil starts to walk toward him and the kid completely freaks. I don't mean he runs away—he just cowers in the corner and screams even louder. I ask him if he's hurt but he won't say anything except 'Get help! Get help!' I shine the light on him and we see he's barefoot and his feet are bloody, and his face and clothes are scratched to hell. Phil is starting to lose his patience so I say let me try. I take off my belt and my hat, trying to look a bit more like a normal human, and I say, as loud as I can, "We will help!" And that does it—he goes quiet for the first time. He's still scared as hell though, watching us like a nervous squirrel. I walk over very, very slowly, and just keep saying, "We will help," until I sit down on the porch stairs, about eight feet away from him. I tell him my name and I ask him his, and he says Michael, but he doesn't seem to know his last name. I ask him his mother's name, and he says, 'Maddy said to get help.' I ask him if Maddy is his mom, his sister, his aunt? But he won't say a thing. So I ask him if I can talk to Maddy. No answer. So I say, 'Michael, where is Maddy?' Then he points to the woods.

"I look over at Phil. He nods and radios for backup. I ask Michael if he'll take me to Maddy, and he says yes. I hold out my hand to him but he won't budge. I realize he's scared of Phil, so I say, 'This is Phil. He's my partner, and he will help, too.' Phil backs up, and then Michael comes toward the steps. He won't let me touch him. He leads us through the woods in the dark for a solid fifteen minutes. I know his feet must be in such pain, but he still won't let me touch him. Phil keeps his distance, and he keeps HQ updated on our location. Anyway, eventually Michael stops and points at a house. He won't go one step further. Phil calls in our location and asks the dispatcher to send backup there. I ask Michael if that house is where Maddy is, and he says yes."

Helena paused to dab the corners of her eyes. "He was pitiful," she said. "I've never seen anything like it."

"I can't imagine," Alexandra said. "And it sounds like you handled it so perfectly."

Helena shook her head. "I don't know," she said quietly. "I don't know."

"Anyway, Phil tells me to stay back with the kid until they check out the house and secure it. He meets another unit out front, and one of those officers, Officer Tran, and Phil go up and bang on the door. After a minute lights came on and a guy opens the door. I hear Phil ask about Maddy and the guy tells him to wait a sec. Next thing I know—oh God—next thing, there's a shotgun blast and Phil just goes flying backward off that porch. Then everything happens at once. I duck and yell for Michael to get down and he copies me and drops to the ground, Officer Tran raises his weapon and that's when he gets shot too and flies over the side railing into the garden. Tran's partner starts firing, and I report two officers down and request more backup, and then I grab Michael's hand and I guess he's so shocked or terrified or something that he doesn't resist at all, and we run to a tree and take cover.

"Backup gets there, and then we're in a standoff. At that point I don't know how many shooters are inside but they seem to have plenty of ammo, and a dozen officers are outside, plus a couple of ambulances and before long the SWAT team. A team gets to Phil and the other officer who's down. Phil's already gone, but they get the other guy out. Anyway, inside an hour, we've got sharpshooters in place. The people inside are not willing to communicate, let alone negotiate, and nobody knows if Maddy is okay, whoever she is, wherever she is, so a SWAT team storms the house, front and back simultaneously. Two of the suspects go down and two others are injured and surrender. No more injuries on our side. One of the suspects died later but the other one, the guy who killed Phil and shot Officer Tran, recovered.

"Once it's all over, I try to get Michael to move but he won't budge. I don't want to force him. He won't even let me get close enough to give him my jacket to keep him warm. He just stands behind his tree, watching the house. Once it's cleared, there's a lot of shouting, then someone runs in with bulk cutters and a few minutes later, what do you know—there's Maddy, just like Michael said, and she's carrying a little girl. Michael takes off for her, and I run after him. He's shouting, 'Maddy! Maddy!' and she kneels down and the three of them hug. EMTs try to treat them but let me tell you, Maddy was not having one *minute* of that! So now, believe it or not, we're in another kind of standoff, with this little trio refusing to let anyone get close to them!"

Josh laughed a little. "Oh I can believe it."

"We call for a social worker but I know that will take hours," Helena said. "So I go over and sit on the ground about six feet in front of Maddy. She's got her hands in front of her eyes, and the kids have their faces tucked into her neck. I yell at everyone to kill their flashers. Maddy takes her hand away from her face and stares daggers at me.

"'Michael,' I say, 'is this Maddy?' He nods. So I say, 'Maddy, Michael led me right to you—he was very, very brave, and he did a perfect job. You are safe now, okay? You are safe now.' She says okay and I ask if she's cold. She says yes and an EMT brings me three emergency blankets. I toss them in their direction and Michael spreads them over Maddy, the girl, and himself. Then I say, 'Maddy, look at Michael's face and his feet. He needs medical help.' I have no idea whether she understands but then she says, 'You help Michael.' So I bring over Pauline, one of the EMTs, and Maddy lets Pauline help Michael.

"And that's how it got started. Maddy believed she really was safe and she could get help from us. I was stunned that neither she nor Michael seemed to know anything about police or ambulances. Maddy wouldn't even get into an ambulance unless both Pauline and I were with them. And she wouldn't let men near her or the kids."

"Amazing. I am so sorry you had to go through this, Helena," said Josh. "I guess you don't expect this kind of thing out here."

"Let's just say it was a strange beginning to my career in law enforcement. Two months in and I've already lost a partner. My superstitious colleagues don't want to ride with me."

"Did you get a chance to go inside the house?" asked Josh.

"Yeah, I came back the next day. It was pretty grim. A lot of bullet holes, obviously. But Maddy and the kids had been locked in a concrete basement. I went down there and saw where she had somehow pried off a couple of boards screwed down over a window high in the foundation wall, enough to push Michael out the hole and through the little window. There was a heavy-duty chain still attached to an iron column. There was laundry equipment in one corner, and a couple of crappy beds, like camp cots. There was an open toilet. There was a little box of toys and a couple of books on a wooden table in a corner and a tiny wooden chair. And that was it. Oh and it was really dim, even with the lights on." Helena paused. "It was horrifying. I have more nightmares about that basement than I do about Phil getting the life blasted out of him by those assholes."

"I can only imagine," said Josh. "I hope you're getting the support you need."

"I'll be all right," said Helena. "Y'all take care of that family."

"We'll do our best," Jesse said, though he felt slightly sick, and burning with fury.

"Do you have any questions?" Josh directed the query to Jesse, who shook his head. Alexandra shook her head quickly, tears flowing.

"Thank you, Helena," said Josh. "Walking us through that night is going above and beyond. Hang in there, ok?"

They said their farewells.

They drove out of town in silence until Josh said, "One more stop, okay?" Jesse just stared straight ahead, not looking forward to the second phase of this trip to Rhode Island. Alexandra, in the back seat, had continued to cry quietly.

Ten minutes later, they had threaded their way through police tape and were standing in the accursed basement that had been Maddy's prison since she was a little girl. They took in details Helena hadn't mentioned. Exposed beams with heavy-duty hooks and eye bolts. Pencils and paper. Two wooden chairs, not one. A large sink near the washing machine with a bucket. A large cabinet with a jimmied lock containing ropes and chains and cuffs and whips and various other devices.

As tears flowed over Jesse's and Alexandra's cheeks, Jesse's mind filled with a kaleidoscopic array of horrors: torture, rape, malnourishment, deprivation, disease, despair. And cold. A little girl had been stolen from her family when she was younger than Becca had been at the time of her disappearance and wound up in this place. Here that little girl grew up, in a certain sense, chained to an iron post, knowing almost nothing about the world. Here she gave birth to two children and became pregnant with a third. Here she learned to understand what the world was and who people were. Who men were.

Is this what had happened to Becca? If she were still alive, it would probably be in circumstances like this. Maybe she was better off dead.

Battling nausea, Jesse turned on his heel and ran up the stairs and out to the car. A few minutes later, Alexandra appeared, followed by Josh, carrying a few of Maddy's drawings, which he tucked into his briefcase. Jesse didn't want to talk. No one said anything on the trip back to Boston, not even when Josh dropped them off home. Jesse just stood on the front porch and watched Josh drive away. Alexandra disappeared immediately, slamming her office door behind her.

Jesse collapsed on the step. He had no idea what to do with himself, and set off on a long walk into the woods. Every step was accompanied by another horrific visualization of Maddy's life. It wasn't that he couldn't shut this one down; it's that he couldn't bring himself to end it. Loyalty to Maddy demanded that he let it all pour through him, no matter how painful. And pour through him it did, like molten iron through glass, reshaping him utterly. He was irrevocably bound to that young woman and her children.

I'M GLAD WE HAD
THAT LITTLE CHAT

Alexandra and Jesse looked good to the state officials who needed to make the final determination about fostering. After all, Alexandra was a trained expert in families and children with special needs, she had almost fifteen years of experience dealing with traumatized single mothers through her shelter volunteer position, and they both had empathy to burn on this particular issue. They could also comfortably support Maddy and her two, soon-to-be-three children, and their supervised visits with Maddy, Michael, and Jamie, at her home as well as theirs, had gone far better than anyone expected. Maddy could speak to Jesse without a problem now, and her vocabulary and social skills were blossoming rapidly. And, of course, Jesse hadn't mentioned his invisible companions in the required psychological evaluations.

Crucially, Maddy had said that she'd like to live with them, at least on a trial basis. Neither their relationship with Josh nor Maddy's similarity in appearance to Becca were ultimately judged to be impediments, and the emerging consensus was to support the fostering plan.

The fact that fostering was being considered at all was a consequence of the unusual situation. The state was responsible for Maddy's young children, and Maddy knew virtually nothing about the everyday world, so the officials were making an exception and offering services despite Maddy being an adult. Moreover, it was a high-profile case, so the state wanted to be seen doing a good job. They would only fully fund a foster arrangement for the children but they'd make other resources available to help Maddy within an adult fostering framework.

The only fly in the ointment was Matt. When Alexandra and Jesse told him what they were planning, he launched into a legal-style argument.

"You can't be serious!" he said. "Consider your age. You should be enjoying the fruits of a long life lived well, not tying yourselves down to child rearing for a young family. And surely Maddy needs more help than she can ever get from you, no matter how much you care for her."

"Matt, you've got a point," Jesse began, intending to build a counter-case for their decision, as lawyer-like as he could muster, but Alexandra jumped in.

"What Maddy needs is love and we love her."

The way she said it brooked no contradiction, as Matt and Jesse both immediately recognized. But it also cut off a conversation that they needed to have with their protective eldest son.

Mid-August of that year, just after Alexandra's sixty-seventh birthday, Maddy, twenty years old, seven months pregnant, with Michael and Jamie, moved in.

They arrived in a van. Josh was there with his assistant manager who was part-time on the case, and their driver. The six of them piled out and met Alexandra and Jesse on the driveway. Maddy and Michael were wearing sunglasses again. Little Jamie's face was buried in her mother's shoulder. From their previous visits to the house, they knew where they'd sleep and roughly how they'd live, so a tour was not necessary.

After moving the tiny amount of luggage inside, along with a box of the kids' favorite toys from their first post-captivity house, they sat down for an official meeting. Josh's assistant handled the kids while he and Maddy sat at the table with Alexandra and Jesse. Josh ran through a checklist of discussion items.

There was to be a heavy schedule of expert interventions at the outset, as determined through the educational, psychological, and physical evaluations of the past several weeks. The medical checks had been all clear, save for the eyesight problems, some scarring on Maddy, and a sexually transmitted infection for which Maddy had been treated. Expert educational assistance was needed, for Michael and for Maddy. Maddy needed life skills training. Maddy and Michael both needed counseling. Alexandra and Jesse were also assigned a state-funded consultant to help them with their role.

Home schooling and home visits for all specialists except the therapists and doctors was the way forward. Josh drew up plans to integrate expert help into daily life in the house. The state funded the specialist care.

Maddy had decided to retain the name her abductors had given her, both because her former name meant nothing to her and because her kids called her Maddy. The police had told her what her birthday was, but she didn't have much idea about the birthdays of her children.

Alexandra was quietly ecstatic. She was a powerhouse, infinitely gentle, staggeringly potent, and incredibly perceptive, tirelessly generating an unending supply of transformative love. Jesse was in awe of her. He could no more do what she was doing than fly to the moon. For her it seemed effortless. He could scarcely believe how lucky he was to witness it, to be with her, to love her, to be loved by her.

He sensed that finally Alexandra had found a way to fight for healing. It was a characteristically practical path. He couldn't help smiling at the difference between them. Where he'd turn inward and meditate in search of healing, his beloved would turn outward and try to help others. She had done that at the homeless shelter for most of the years since Becca disappeared, and now she was doing it with Maddy and her children.

After Josh and the other social services people drove off in their van, Alexandra and Jesse showed Maddy to what had seemed during previous visits to be her favorite place, the back deck. They all sat down with cups of fruit juice, Jamie on Maddy's lap and Michael next to her, eyeing an unfamiliar toy truck that Alexandra had put on the deck for him. It was overcast but all three wore their wraparound sunglasses.

Jesse wanted to start a gentle conversation but was unsure what to say. Alexandra seemed to be in the same place. Becca tried to help.

"Daddy, tell her you won't lock the deck door. She can come out here whenever she wants, day or night."

"Maddy," Jesse began, "I know it will take a while for you and Michael and Jamie to feel completely at home anywhere, including in this house. You have two bedrooms to spread out in when you feel ready, but your room is set up so that all three of you can sleep together if you want. Eventually, I hope you'll feel comfortable in the laundry and kitchen whenever you like. As for this deck, I was thinking we might leave the deck door unlocked so you can come out here any time, day or night. The outside of this house is yours just as much as the inside is."

"Yes," said Maddy.

Michael slipped out of his chair and retrieved the toy truck, bringing it close to Maddy's chair, which he sat partly behind and partly underneath. He played quietly with no vocalized truck noises. Jesse imagined that playing quietly might have been a critical survival skill in their former life, and Michael probably didn't know what trucks sounded like, anyway.

Jesse looked over at Maddy. She was as vigilant as ever—it would be a big day when she could relax. But she'd get there. At that moment, she looked comfortable in her body, her face was smiling, and she was gently stroking Jamie's hair with her left hand.

"What do I have to do to live here?" Maddy asked. Jesse's mind spun about imagining what she meant, especially given that this had already been discussed in detail with Josh. He realized that this was Maddy's way of making a contract with the two of them.

"Make sure she knows there's a cost," warned Becca. "Be specific." But Alexandra jumped in before Jesse could say anything.

"Maddy, living here will be a lot different than what you and Michael and Jamie have been used to," she said. "For one thing, you can come and go when you want. This is a place for you to learn to live and to choose what kind of a person you want to be, and you'll have as much time as you need to do that. But we're also a family, so we care for each other. That means being kind and trying to help each other. Houses are a lot of work so we all care for the house. We all cook and clean, we keep our bodies clean and our rooms neat. We have to tidy up when we make a mess, be honest when we break something, say sorry when we hurt someone, and have as much fun as we can."

"Talk about sex, Daddy, just be matter-of-fact about it," interjected Becca. "She'll be thinking about it and you can't be subtle if you want her to relax."

"Maddy, there's one more thing," Jesse said. "If I understand your old life correctly, you were forced to take care of the family who kept you captive by having sex with them. We don't live that way. Being kind and thoughtful, being happy and learning, staying clean and healthy, caring for each other and for our house—those things are part of the deal. Sex has nothing to do with it. Okay?"

"Yes, Josh told me," she said.

"Well, I'm glad we had that little chat," Jesse thought-said to Becca.

"It was wise to be straightforward about it, Daddy," Becca said.

A loud motorcycle screamed by and Maddy spun around. Her grip on Jamie tightened and her other hand instinctively reached for Michael.

"It's okay, Maddy," Alexandra said. "That was a motorcycle out on the road."

Jesse thought how quiet that farm-house basement must have been and how strange city noises must seem to Maddy. He'd add that new perspective into his Maddy stack.

⁜

That night, after their very first day with their new family in their new home, both the children and Maddy were exhausted. After they were ready for bed, Alexandra and Jesse visited their bedroom, Becca's old room. All three were in Maddy's bed and Alexandra sat on the edge with a storybook. Jesse sat in the rocking chair in the corner while Alexandra read the book to them and showed them the pictures. His mind was full of memories of their bedtime routine with Becca.

By the end, Jamie was asleep but Michael wanted another book. Alexandra pointed to the bookcase, filled with wonderful picture books, and promised that she'd read as many of them as he wanted, one each night, and maybe some during the day as well. She leaned over and kissed each of them on the forehead, and, after asking if it was okay, Jesse did the same.

"Good night sweethearts," Alexandra said. "Sleep soundly. Tomorrow is another wonderful day."

It was the birth of their nighttime ritual with Maddy and her kids. Jesse couldn't believe he got to do this all over again.

I'M NOT ANGRY AT YOUR FICTIONAL GOD!

Over the next few weeks they became acquainted with the kinds of challenges Maddy would be facing. Her emotional range was polarized into fearful flashing protectiveness on the one side, and simple, uncomplicated happiness on the other. It seemed that sustained trauma had compressed the normal range of human emotions into a single, simple question: Are we safe right now? Yet she was wide open to new experiences and seemingly impossible to intimidate.

Her friendship with Alexandra was the single most important factor in helping her find a quiet, protected space where she started to feel that she had nothing to fear. They were together virtually all the time: fifteen hours each day, broken only by classes for Maddy. They were silent a lot in the first few days but Maddy talked to Alexandra more and more with time. Jesse would come home from the university and find them sitting together on the long couch chatting while the kids played on the floor.

The two women didn't tell Jesse a lot about their conversations but he came to understand that Maddy was asking questions and checking her interpretations of the world with Alexandra. Alexandra was teaching her about children, parenting, and family life; about people, culture, and social conventions; about bodies, sex, and illness; about politics, economics, and international relations; about food, farming, and cooking; about technology, communication, and manufacturing; about entertainment, music, and movies.

All of this happened at Maddy's pace. Eventually, Alexandra started telling Maddy about her own life, her profession, her parents and siblings, her children and grandchildren, her loves and hates. She'd do that in little snippets, and expand on a point only if Maddy asked questions. She also started to tell Maddy about Jesse and his life, which helped to consolidate Maddy's trust in him.

Josh and Oli visited with their kids at least once each week. All the kids got along well. When Oli was in the house, the three women were inseparable. They talked quietly, seriously, and non-stop, though Maddy continued to avoid eye contact.

Maddy was scrupulously clean and tidy. Their bathroom and bedroom never seemed to need any cleaning. Alexandra found a stash of cans and bagged food that Maddy had hidden under her bed. Alexandra never commented on that but instead showed Maddy all the cupboards in the house, and emphasized that they and everything in them were all for Maddy as well as her and Jesse. Within a few weeks, the stash disappeared.

Maddy was eager to learn. She especially loved geography and social studies, and would soak in everything she could, perpetually amazed that the world contained so many fascinating places and people. She was a quick study in life-skills training, and took especially to cooking. She already knew how to wash clothes because that was the one skill she'd been forced to acquire in captivity.

Her motor skills were distressingly limited aside from drawing, however. She couldn't catch or throw, she couldn't run naturally, and her eye-hand coordination in areas other than pencil and paper was sorely limited. She learned the basics of how to write and was learning how to type, picking it up quickly. But she moved her whole body awkwardly, as though her major joints were stiff.

Her language abilities were impressive but strange. Maddy knew how to get what she wanted but didn't know how to say what she was feeling. She'd been taught reading basics by the oldest son in the basement family so she could handle simple children's books. But she was a halting and hesitant vocalizer of any text, and she had difficulty understanding news reports, novels, and textbooks. Her swearing and Michael's declined as they found another language system to copy.

One evening, Jesse came home from a day of lectures and meetings with a new batch of students to find Maddy and Alexandra sitting together on the couch, talking quietly, as usual. Michael and Jamie were playing nearby.

"Hello everyone," he said.

"Hello everyone," Maddy echoed, imitating his voice and accent perfectly. For the next few minutes she repeated everything he said in her Jesse voice, until Alexandra brought it to an end by erupting in laughter. Soon all of them were laughing, even Maddy. It was the first time they'd seen her laugh heartily, her arms wrapped around her pregnant belly.

It had been a mere six weeks since she moved in, and already she was comfortable enough to tease. It felt like a minor miracle to Jesse—his kind of miracle, not Father Jimmy's sort, though Jesse suspected that the church would be happy to have their God take credit for the changes in Maddy's life. That realization left Jesse feeling uneasy, so he made an appointment to speak with his favorite delusional priest.

A few days later, the two men sat in their usual chairs, angled toward the playing fields and the woods beyond.

"I appreciate everything you and the church are doing, Jimmy," began Jesse. "The food, the toys, the clothes... we're truly grateful. We haven't told Maddy where all these things come from because we're worried she'll freak out if she knows all these people are aware of her situation. She probably thinks this is just the way life works, things magically appearing on the front porch."

"Thank you, Jesse," said Jimmy, "but you're stalling. If we're talking it's because you want to get all philosophical on my ass, so let's dig in." They both laughed, Jimmy's bright broad smile sharply contrasting with his dark face.

"You pray for Maddy and her kids regularly in church and you probably pray for her privately as well, right?" asked Jesse. Jimmy nodded. "And ever since Becca disappeared, you've been praying for her and us and for other missing children. You're asking God to do something in all of these prayers, right?" Jimmy nodded again. "That means you think your God *could* do something. And that means that your God is *allowing* things to be the way they are."

Jesse was suddenly almost boiling over with rage. Where did that come from? It took all his prodigious self-discipline to stay calm as Father Jimmy absorbed his fury. Jesse closed his eyes and breathed deeply to relax. Jimmy closed his eyes, too, his chin perched upon templed fingers.

"Why would you be angry at a God you don't believe in?" asked Jimmy, as gently as he could.

"I'm not angry at your fictional God!" yelled Jesse. "I'm angry at *you*. You worship and pray to a being who allowed Becca and Maddy to be raped and tortured, and in Becca's case probably murdered. And then you offer solace to me and my family in the form of prayers to change this deity's mind about what to do. As if that's supposed to make any of us feel better! Can't you see? You're commending a God whose behavior and decisions are so utterly appalling, so completely opposed to the good as I understand it, that I would devote my life to morally resisting this God's depravity if I thought there was any reality to your ideas. How can you do this to me? How can you abandon me to this darkness in such a spectacularly cruel way?!"

Jesse finished his complaint with a roar and then they both lapsed into a long silence. They stared at one another, one pair of eyes in agony, the other brimming with compassion. Soon both pairs of eyes yielded up tears.

Jesse knew he was being unfair, and that there was no rational answer to his question. But there were Jimmy's tears of love, pleading with Jesse for forgiveness and understanding, yet conveying compassion and confidence borne up by his faith. Jesse lowered his gaze and wiped his eyes. Dammit if Jimmy hadn't found the perfect way to respond, to demonstrate that Jesse wasn't alone in his anguish.

"So. How is Maddy?" Jimmy finally asked, as gently as a summer breeze. Just like that the outburst was behind them, and never needed to be spoken of again. Another precious gift from Jimmy.

"She's amazing," said Jesse. "Funny, too. She's extremely direct. It'd be rude in any other setting but at home it's sweet. No please or thank you. No small talk. At dinner yesterday, she announced 'water' and pointed at the jug of water on the table. This morning I was making a shopping list with Alexandra. Maddy jumped in and said, 'Get milk.' Not 'We need milk' or 'We're out of milk' or 'Add milk to the list, please.' In the last several weeks she's learned about politeness conventions. She's a quick study and could conform if she wanted. But she's so averse to insincerity that she stubbornly refuses to say please and thank you, even when Michael is starting to do that.

"With her kids she almost never talks. If she wants Michael to pack away some toys, she just points and Michael leaps into action. If one of the kids is upset, she touches but says nothing. Her face remains almost impassive in her interactions with them. There's none of the exaggerated facial movements that most parents employ with their children. Yet their bond, especially between Maddy and Michael, is extremely strong. They all bathe together, use the bathroom together, sleep together, and move about the house together—unselfconsciously naked when upstairs around their bedrooms. It is a tiny alien subculture living, protected, in our home."

"She can read, right? How's her education going? And Michael's?" asked Jimmy.

"She can read a little. But she didn't know how to write and knew no arithmetic, so her teachers have been focusing on the basics with her and Michael. They both learn fast. There's no pride, none of the cultural linkages between learning and self-esteem that are pervasive in American schooling. Once the teachers figured that out, their colored stick-on stars went out the window and the teaching became as straightforward as the learning was. So they're getting there, in their own way."

"How about her mental health?" asked Jimmy. "Does she suffer from nightmares like you?"

"As far as I know, no nightmares. It's hard to give an overall assessment of her mental health. In some ways she's emotionally damaged to such an extreme degree that healing is almost impossible to imagine. In other ways she's resilient and occasionally quite happy. She's an extraordinary mimic, with dead-on imitations of everyone she meets, including me and the professionals who come and go from the house. And she's an incredibly talented sketch artist. I guess there weren't a lot of options, stuck in that basement for a decade and a half, so all her intelligence and effort went into the things she could do: mimicry, drawing, and loving her kids. Of course, all of that was punctuated by monstrous moments..."

The movie images from Jesse's Maddy stack flashed through his mind.

"She's cooking up a storm, too," he continued. "She's a creative cook, with a perfect memory of everything she's ever tried—and absolutely no ego about the outcome. She just wants to get it right. Yesterday she tried lasagna for the first time, and a lot of the pasta near the top came out burnt and crispy. She asked us what we thought, and Alexandra let me put my foot in it. I said, 'I really appreciate the effort, Maddy. Did you enjoy figuring out how to do this?' And Maddy let me have it. 'Stop lying! Say what you fucking think!' Alexandra had tears in her eyes from laughing so hard. Anyway I told Maddy what I thought, in very plain language, and she just rolled with it. 'Yes,' she said. 'It's not good. But I know how to fix it.' She couldn't care less about being criticized but she hates insincerity with a fiery passion. Alexandra says her anger is a sign of health because it means her emotional range is decompressing. Her life isn't just about safety now and she can have other goals and other emotions to go along with them."

"Sounds like a sign of mental health to me," said Jimmy.

"Yes," acknowledged Jesse, "but it's still early, and she leaves the house as little as possible, only to the eye doc, the psychotherapist, and the ob-gyn. She's gone to the grocery store a couple of times with Alexandra. Maddy and Michael love the supermarket, despite their discomfort with the bright lights. To them it's a wonderland. She'll go outside but she won't leave the safety of the deck even to play in the back yard with the children. Everything else is indoors, from education to exercise. Alexandra handles clothes shopping for Maddy and the kids online. She won't even take short walks."

"That's transitional, surely," said Jimmy.

"I guess so," said Jesse. "I hope so."

"She's learning so much, so quickly," said Jimmy. "She's feeling safe for the first time in many years. It must be tempting to focus on the worrying aspects but there's a lot to celebrate."

"You're absolutely right," said Jesse. "I actually think I'm more worried about Michael than Maddy."

"How so?"

"Well, Maddy had five-and-a-half years of love and security before she was abducted. Alexandra keeps telling me how vital those early formational years are, so we figure Maddy has a solid foundation underneath the horror of what's happened since. But Michael was born into that misery. He saw everything that happened to Maddy. His first encounter with the wider world was running away in the middle of the night through the woods to find help. Can you imagine? He'd never even seen a tree or the sky or a house or anything other than what was in that dingy basement."

Jimmy sighed heavily. "No," he said. "I really can't imagine."

"And there's something really different about his behavior," Jesse continued. "I don't know what it is. He's definitely not like any five-year-old boy I ever knew."

"Do you think he's dangerous somehow? Unstable?" asked Jimmy.

"No, at least not to us. It's more that he seems more like a mature adult than a child. I have never seen him be selfish for instance, which would be totally developmentally appropriate for a kid that age. His whole being is organized around keeping Maddy and Jamie safe and happy—and lately Alexandra and me, and Josh and Oli and their kids. He's freakishly disciplined, too. He never gets restless during his lessons. And he watches his family like a hawk. Especially Maddy. The other day Maddy was sitting out on the deck with Alexandra while the kids were playing inside. I was in the kitchen watching Michael constantly glancing quickly at his mother. At one point he must have seen something because he picked up a blanket and took it to her out on the deck. Maddy accepted it with a simple touch but not a word was exchanged. And then he was back with Jamie, still keeping watch over his mom."

"Michael has spent his formative years trying in vain to keep the only adult he loved safe from harm," Jimmy said. "And nothing he did would have protected her. God only knows what he went through."

"Seriously Jimmy?" said Jesse, smiling. "After our earlier conversation, you want me to think that your blessed deity had a clear view of what was going on in that basement."

"Sorry," said Jimmy. "But you know where I'm coming from."

"You're right, though," said Jesse. "We don't know any details. Neither Maddy nor Michael has said anything about what happened in the basement. I'd just be guessing except that I've seen the place and I know about the damage to Maddy's body."

"That is Michael's first world," said Jimmy, awe-struck.

"Was," said Jesse.

"Was and is," corrected Jimmy. "He'll be carrying that world with him his whole life."

"True," acknowledged Jesse. "The psychologists tell us that it's so extremely rare a situation that they're merely guessing at what would even count as healthy for Michael's development."

"Fodder for prayers, my friend," said Jimmy. "I appreciate the insight."

"Hey," Jesse said, "you're coming to Maddy's twenty-first birthday party this Saturday, right?"

"I'd be happy to attend if I can, but I haven't received an invitation," said Jimmy.

"Oh, that's right," said Jesse. "We can't invite men, only women. Sorry, I momentarily forgot about that. Aside from Josh and me, there are no men in her life. All of her teachers, doctors, and therapists are women."

"Totally understandable," said Jimmy. "I'll be glad for another update, though, when you feel ready for another conversation." He said this with the warmest and most caring smile, leaving Jesse feeling both loved and lucky. But he was also more convinced than ever about the lunacy of Father Jimmy's worldview.

SOCIAL SITUATIONS LIKE THIS MAKE ME A BIT NERVOUS

Maddy's twenty-first birthday arrived less than two months after she moved in, just as the maple leaves were giving colorful evidence of sensing the cooling weather. They had a party planned for Saturday. Maddy had already spent a lot of time with Josh, Oli, and their three kids, including new-born Kate. But this time Matt and Jenny and their four young children were coming from San Francisco to meet Maddy for the first time.

"Matt seems convinced we're making a serious mistake," said Jesse as they lay in bed, limbs tangled, staring at the trees.

"He'll adjust," said Alexandra.

"I get the feeling there's more going on than just concern for us," said Jesse. "D'ya reckon he might be worried about sharing our affection with a new sibling?"

Alexandra didn't answer immediately. Jesse turned to look at her face in profile.

"Maybe," she said. "Doesn't matter. He'll adjust."

Maddy was due to give birth within two weeks of the party. Michael and Jamie had adapted to the new life routine and were almost as comfortable with Alexandra and Jesse as they were with Maddy. The nighttime routine Alexandra had devised was rock solid and a source of security and loving warmth for everyone. Michael and Jamie were starting each night in their own beds in Maddy's room, though by morning, both children were usually in bed with their mother. The kids' love of story books was insatiable and Alexandra or Jesse read to them multiple times during the day, as well as one book each night when going to sleep.

Each day they saw new evidence of Maddy's artistic gifts as she created black-and-white pencil sketches of people and places around the house, routinely achieving a kind of photo-realism. She'd often draw while chatting with Alexandra, able to concentrate on both activities at the same time. Pictures of Michael and Jamie, of Alexandra and Jesse, and also of Josh, Oli, and their children, were in one or another of Maddy's large sketch pads, along with scenes from the back deck.

Jesse was still at work three or four long days each week but Alexandra had retired, including from her volunteer position at the shelter. Caring for Maddy and the children had become her full-time occupation. Josh had returned to his regular round of social-work duties, though he remained the lead on Maddy's case, checking in with her at least once each week and managing her services.

That was the extent of Maddy's social contacts. Almost all those people, including those delivering services in the home, were planning to attend the birthday party. It was to be a celebration of Maddy's wonderful existence with almost everyone she'd discovered in her new life.

On the Friday morning of her actual birthday, the day before the party, Alexandra and Jesse introduced Maddy to their family birthday tradition. Everyone gathered in the family room and presented her with a box of colorfully wrapped presents.

"Maddy," Alexandra said, "birthdays are moments to celebrate someone's existence. We bought some gifts for you and wrapped them in colorful paper and ribbons. Because it's your birthday, you're the one who gets to unwrap the presents and keep them. Giving gifts is our way of showing you that we love you, that we're very happy you exist, and that we're grateful to have you as a part of our lives. Now we sing the Happy Birthday song and then you unwrap your presents."

Alexandra and Jesse were the only ones who knew the song, so the singing part wasn't pretty. The kids wanted to help unwrap and Maddy happily let them. Jamie tore the colored paper into shreds and threw it in the air like confetti, whereas Michael was extremely slow and careful, trying to preserve the wrapping paper—personalities in formation, thought Jesse. Among other little gifts, Maddy received a beautifully illustrated cookbook, a new sketch pad, and high-quality graphite pencils.

At the end of the frenzy, Alexandra handed Maddy a small box, which Maddy unwrapped herself. Inside she found a diamond necklace and matching clip-on diamond earrings, which Alexandra explained would look wonderful with the black maternity dress they'd purchased the previous week for the birthday party. Maddy launched herself across the room, as quickly as a woman that pregnant can, and hugged Alexandra. They had been very careful about physical contact with Maddy, limiting it to good-night kisses on the forehead, so this took everyone by surprise. Alexandra looked at Maddy then Jesse, tears in her eyes.

The next day was party day and Maddy was cooking up a storm. She'd learned about birthday parties and she'd planned this one carefully. She'd already tried out the dishes on her new family, discarding the failures. She was even planning to bake her own birthday cake. Alexandra explained that people usually let others prepare their birthday parties but Maddy was adamant. She'd recruited Josh and Oli to help on the morning of the big day while Alexandra and Jesse looked after the children.

Matt and Jenny were the first to arrive, around nine in the morning. They'd flown in overnight and rented a van, complete with four car seats for Walt, who was four, the two-year-old twins Abby and Millie, and six-month-old Jake. They were planning to stay for nine days, two weekends. Everyone scrambled outside to welcome them.

Jesse watched the arrival with a vague sense of anxiety, wondering how Matt's opposition to the arrangement might express itself, and how Jenny might be feeling about it. Maybe getting to know Maddy would help.

Maddy was standing with Michael on the edge of the driveway, Jamie on her hip, as Matt and Jenny began unloading the kids. Jesse watched with surprise as Maddy introduced herself to the new arrivals, hugged Jenny, walked over with Michael and Jamie to meet Walt, then held Walt's hand, walking both boys away from the car and up onto the front porch. They all sat down in a circle, with Jamie in Maddy's lap, and Michael started talking with Walt.

While that was still going on, Josh drove up with Oli and three more children. Jesse was worried Maddy would be overwhelmed and retreat, but it never happened. She jumped up and said hello to everyone and hugged Oli before collecting their oldest, Rebecca, and sitting down on the porch with her and the two older boys, Jamie again in her lap. Without a lot of words, Maddy just behaved as though they should be together and that's how Walt and Rebecca responded. It was as easy as if she'd been just another kid. It dawned on Jesse then that in some ways that's exactly what she was, a child who still had a lot of developing to do, and that Maddy felt completely at home with children—all children, not just her own—because she didn't need to feel afraid of them. She was extremely attentive to them without a trace of over-indulgent fawning, idiosyncratic but deeply intelligent in the way she cared for them.

Alexandra had arranged for childcare all day, beginning at ten o'clock. Four high-school girls, all children of her church friends, would soon arrive to spread the burden and free up parents. Until they came, all nine kids and seven adults gathered in the family room.

Maddy sat between Alexandra and Oli, her usual position when Oli was visiting, and Jenny sat beside Oli, the four women chatting away. Jenny was a firecracker, ideal for the advertising industry, though now she only occasionally consulted on projects and devoted most of her time to raising children. She handed Jake to Maddy while they talked.

Matt was sitting beside Jesse across the room, both of them watching the chaos in the aptly named family room. Jesse could sense his son's unease.

"You know," Matt whispered, "she really could be Becca."

"Mmm," Jesse replied. "But remember that she doesn't know anything about Becca's disappearance. She's seen Becca's baby photo on the wall, but she's never asked about it. And given her live-and-let-live nature, she's not likely to. So we're just letting things lie at the moment. If Maddy asks, we'll tell her the situation."

"I hope you know what you're doing, Dad."

As Matt said these words, Jesse saw Becca appear, and float around the room. Floating was her method of staying out of the way and keeping the simulation simple for Jesse's busy brain. He wondered what his oldest son would think if he knew that Jesse was hallucinating a twenty-two-year-old version of his missing sister at that very moment. Jesse set that concern aside and sank into the wonderful moment of ingathering, hoping the frown on Matt's face would eventually dissolve.

When the high-school girls arrived to take up their childcare duties, Maddy leapt into action. She dragged Josh and Oli into the kitchen and directed food-production activities like the head chef of a restaurant.

Matt and Jenny joined Alexandra and Jesse on the back deck to enjoy what was proving to be an unseasonably warm day for early October. Jake woke and Jenny fed him while they all enjoyed the colorful woods, ablaze with maple orange and yellow. The dirty orange of the oaks would appear later.

Jesse was wary, concerned about what would transpire in the four-way conversation. Becca was looking on, obviously worried.

"Brilliant idea to hire sitters," said Matt, trying to be positive.

"Actually, we're planning to do it every day, after the girls get out of school, and all day on the two weekends you're here with us," said Alexandra. "And I think I can get some help from my friends during some weekdays."

"That'd be amazing, Mom," said Jenny.

"We want to make the most of the time with you guys," Jesse said.

"We'll cover the cost, Dad," Matt said, but he saw Jesse's "like that's going to happen" face and quickly added, "Okay, okay," while Jenny and Alexandra laughed.

"Jenny, how are things at home?" asked Jesse. "It must be crazy with Matt's travel schedule and four kids under five."

"Things are pretty good, actually," answered Jenny. "Our nanny Dora is a life-saver. She moved in right after the twins arrived and she's become part of the family. I don't know how we'd manage without her."

"She sounds like a great addition to the family," said Alexandra.

"I loved meeting Maddy," said Jenny. "She's fun to talk to and fabulous with the kids. If she starts thinking about employment, maybe childcare would be an option to consider."

"That or cooking," Alexandra said. "She's a creative and determined cook. And she draws amazingly well—I think she could earn money as a portrait artist. But all of that seems a long way off, especially with a baby about to arrive."

"Does Maddy ever talk about what happened to her?" asked Jenny.

"No, and we don't ask," replied Alexandra. "She may never talk about it and I wouldn't blame her. We hear different things from therapists about whether she needs to learn to talk about it or to put it behind her. Honestly, I don't think they really know what's healthiest for a person like Maddy. But we've grown confident in her judgment about what she needs so we find it easy to let her decide how to handle her past."

"There but for the grace of God..." said Matt.

"Matt, did you just invoke a deity?!" Jesse asked.

"Just a figure of speech, Dad. The thought of a deity who could let Becca disappear without a trace and allow Maddy to spend most of her life caged and at the mercy of monsters is too appalling to contemplate. But Becca and Maddy do get me thinking about our kids, especially the twins. You know the story: possibly futile parental hyper-vigilance and all that."

"Yes, I do know that story," Jesse said, and they lapsed into silence. Becca had her hand on Matt's head and was staring at Jesse intensely.

"How are you two dealing with all this?" asked Matt.

Here we go, Jesse thought, hoping that Alexandra's fury wouldn't be triggered.

Alexandra looked at her eldest son. "We're doing great." She said it flatly, essentially daring Matt to get into it with her. Jesse watched Matt calculating the cost of voicing his concerns about Maddy. He seemed to conclude that discretion was the better part of valor.

The guests started arriving at five. It was already almost dark at that time of year so Maddy could do without her sunglasses, as long as the lights were dimmed. All five specialists were there, along with the social worker who was assisting Josh on Maddy's case, Maddy's therapist, and Dr. Amy Parsons, her obstetrician, who brought a gift box that dwarfed everything else.

Becca was also there, hovering off to the side. "This is Maddy's entire world, Daddy," she said.

Jesse went to the kitchen to compliment the chef.

"Here she is!" he said, with Josh and Oli watching. "Congratulations, Maddy. This is a first-rate event. Everyone is here to celebrate you. If things are under control in here, would you like to come say hi to everyone?"

Maddy looked unsure.

"Tell her how you feel," Becca said.

"To be honest," Jesse said, "social situations like this make me a bit nervous. I feel like withdrawing, I mean running away. So Alexandra grabs my arm and we move around the room together. Would you like to hold my arm and navigate, I mean move around the room with me?"

"Okay," Maddy said. "But I have to change these shitty clothes first. Oli, will you help me?"

Maddy waddled off with Oli. A few minutes later, Maddy returned wearing her new black maternity dress and the diamond necklace Alexandra had given her the previous day. Her long blonde hair was pulled back into a ponytail and she was wearing the matching diamond earrings.

"You look wonderful!" Jesse declared and gallantly offered his arm, which she took. As they ventured into the madness, he leaned toward her and said, quietly, "You're a very special person, Maddy, and all of us here love you and admire you. Happy birthday, sweetheart."

She sideways hugged him and kissed him on the cheek—two more firsts—and then they joined the party. As they entered the big family room, everyone stopped their conversations to offer "happy birthday" greetings mixed with "you look lovely!" comments in a cacophony of welcome. Maddy's grip on Jesse's arm tightened. As they made their way around the room, she gradually relaxed. She didn't say much but she graciously received everyone's birthday best wishes and Jesse guided her onwards before it was possible to experience any awkward moments.

It was a triumph for a geek-professor psychiatric patient and a recently escaped prisoner with no experience of ordinary human adults. Jesse could tell that Becca approved, from where she hovered above the crowd.

Everyone dug into Maddy's amazing food and scattered around the house and outside on the deck to eat and chat. During dinner, a mostly silent Maddy sat at the dining room table, flanked by Alexandra and Jesse. She was more comfortable in the kitchen and went there a couple of times to help Oli with dessert. But each time she came back and resumed her position of relative safety between Alexandra and Jesse, smiling and listening. A couple of times she reached for Alexandra's hand and squeezed it for a few moments, apparently sufficiently reassured to be able to continue. It was a brilliant performance.

After dinner, it was time to open presents, which Maddy did with the help of the three older children. Dr. Parsons's huge box contained a double stroller that had room both for Jamie and a click-in baby carrier.

Right in the middle of inspecting it, Maddy turned to Alexandra and said, "Where do we go with the stroller?"

"Anywhere you want, sweetheart," Alexandra replied. Maddy stared at Alexandra for a moment, maintaining eye contact longer than usual, and then smiled and shook her head.

The day after the party was Sunday, which meant in-person Boys' Breakfast for the first time since mid-July on the sixteenth anniversary of Becca's disappearance. They all felt the same way: eating together in person was so much better than Josh and Jesse sitting on one side of a table while staring at a screen showing Matt chomping on an early breakfast in San Francisco, or Josh and Jesse enjoying an early Sunday breakfast while watching Matt eat a late dinner in Sydney.

On this occasion, they also had the two older boys, Matt's Walt and Maddy's Michael. They'd never been included before so there was a lot of energy as everyone bundled into a large booth at a local breakfast place and sorted through the menu.

The highs and lows ritual had to be explained to the young boys. "When you tell us a high and a low," Matt said, "you're opening a window into the house of your life, letting the rest of us boys peek in so we can see what you're like on the inside. It's pretty cool."

Michael was the last to speak, and his sharing caught them all off guard. "My high is that Maddy is so happy about her birthday," he said. "We never had a birthday party before. My low is I don't know when my fuckin' birthday is."

Matt's eyes widened but Josh snickered. "Well, well, well!" he said. "That certainly is a problem. We can't have a birthday party if we don't know when to hold it. So let's see. Normally a birthday happens on the day someone was born. What do we know about the day you were born, Michael?"

"All I know is Maddy says she was happy when I was born and it was super fuckin' cold."

"But that's quite a lot to know," said Josh, and Michael brightened. "If it was really, really cold, we can bet you were born in December, January, or February. How about we choose a winter birthday for you? Maybe we can pick the very middle of those three months, which is January fifteenth. Then you wouldn't be far away from whatever your real birthday is. How's that sound?"

"Okay," said Michael, shyly.

Matt and Jesse and Josh exchanged a meaningful look. January fifteenth was Becca's birthday.

"Well it's settled, then!" said Josh. "Your sixth birthday will be on January fifteenth, 2026. Congratulations Michael!"

The kid was beaming. Walt gave Josh a high five and everyone copied the youngsters.

"That's fuckin' great!" said Walt, making Matt wince.

Back home after breakfast, Matt dragged Jesse outside on the pretext of going for a walk.

"Everyone likes Maddy," he began.

"Mm-hmm," said Jesse. "What about you?"

"I like her well enough," Matt said. "I'm going to have a hell of a time getting Walt to stop swearing, though. It's spreading like an infection."

Jesse couldn't help but laugh, and Matt allowed a grin. "But Dad," he continued, "how much I like Maddy isn't relevant here. I know you're invested in her recovery and her well-being, which is really great, but I have to tell you, I think this whole thing is a giant mistake, for you and for Mom. It's like you're infatuated and can't see how crazy this situation is and how it's ultimately going to hurt you both. Mom is in so deep at this point I can't even talk to her about it."

Jesse paused in their pacing and turned to face Matt.

"So let's talk this through," he said. "Be specific. What dangers do you see?"

"You're both mid-late sixties," said Matt. "You're about to have a newborn in the house, not to mention a toddler and a cussing kindergartner and a traumatized torture victim...I mean Dad, this is crazy! And do the math on how old you'll be when Maddy's baby graduates high school. In the meantime there'll be three kids to raise, which takes a ton of energy even with well-adjusted kids. The stress on you both will hit you at exactly the wrong time of life. You need to focus on your health and relaxing." Jesse knew Matt wanted to say something about his Mom's memory but he stopped himself.

"Maddy's raising her children, not us," Jesse said.

"C'mon, Dad, they're in the house," said Matt. "It's not like Maddy's renting space from you. You're helping to raise her kids. And you're raising Maddy, too, for that matter."

Matt was right, of course, about everything, though Jesse didn't want to admit it.

"And Dad, don't kid yourself: taking care of Maddy is not going to bring Becca back." He stared at his father intensely, seeming to believe that he had unmasked his parents' true motivation.

"You have good points, Matt," Jesse said. "But could taking care of Maddy be a way for your Mom and me to honor your sister? Maybe even eventually for you?"

Matt shook his head. "So your minds are made up."

"They are," said Jesse. "This is going to be our life until Maddy is able to take care of herself and her family all on her own."

Matt shook his head again, but he reached out and pulled Jesse into a hug. An awkward hug, as usual.

"You're a silly old man," he said. "But I love you."

"I love you too, Matt. Shall we resume our walk?"

"Are you kidding?" said Matt. "I hate walking in the cold. Let's go home."

AT LEAST ONE OTHER
PERSON KNEW

Exactly two weeks after Maddy's birthday, a few days after Matt and Jenny and the kids returned to San Francisco, Maddy delivered a baby girl. Maddy named her Jessie Alexandra after her two guardians.

Alexandra had been with her during the delivery. Jesse, Josh, and Oli visited in the recovery room, while Meg stayed home with Michael and Jamie.

"How was it?" asked Oli, an old hand on both sides of the delivery process.

"Not too bad," said Maddy. "Way better than the first one when I was with a complete stranger, chained up in the old basement, with no idea what was happening to me."

There was a stunned silence as they all realized that Maddy had uttered the first words about her time in captivity. Maddy, too, seemed shocked at what she'd said.

"Well, Jessie looks so sweet and she's got a good set of lungs on her," said Josh, easing everyone past the weird moment.

"She's healthy and feeding well," Alexandra added, "and Maddy was fabulously brave through the entire delivery."

Jesse and Josh spoke in the corridor a few minutes later.

"What just happened?" asked Jesse.

"I don't know for sure, Dad. Victims of sustained trauma handle their situations very differently. But I think Maddy might be starting to put some of these traumatic experiences into a new frame of reference, where maybe she can talk about some of them."

"Is it okay to ask about things she says about her past? For instance, who was the complete stranger with her when Michael was born?"

"I think it's okay to ask about something she brings up," said Josh. "But no pushing, obviously."

"Okay," said Jesse. "But she just told us there was another person who knew she was locked up in that basement! Wouldn't that be critical information for law enforcement?"

"I get it, Dad," said Josh, "but the police already questioned Maddy. She chose to say nothing and the psychologists have advised the police not to pursue it unless she starts talking of her own accord. Everything has to go at her speed."

Jesse groaned. "I get that too, but Josh, there's something so wrong here! *At least one other person knew.* How can we just let that go?"

"I'm not saying you should ignore it," said Josh. "You can ask about it, gently, if the opportunity presents itself. And you can encourage her to talk with her therapist about any incidents like that. Just don't force anything."

Jesse's eyes blazed. "We should be going after every single one of those fuckers," he said.

Josh gaped, astonished to hear his father swear.

"Yes," Josh said. "We should. But at Maddy's pace."

Alexandra and Jesse stood in the kitchen looking into the next room and watching the little family reforming around the new arrival, Jamie in Maddy's lap and the baby in Michael's arms. They found it strange to watch Michael interacting with Jessie in a way only a much older child would normally have done, handling her easily, gently rocking her, talking quietly to her, and even including two-year-old Jamie, as a parent might have.

"Shockingly incongruous," whispered Jesse.

"Trauma under transformation," said Alexandra. "It can sometimes be converted to a positive character trait in the right circumstances."

"But it's so weird," said Jesse. "He never acts like a five-year-old boy. Shouldn't we be worried?"

Alexandra frowned but didn't answer. They watched Jamie try to breastfeed but Maddy gently stopped her.

"If you drink, there won't be enough for Jessie," she said. Maddy grabbed a sippy cup of water and fed Jamie as if it were a bottle, with Jamie lying back in her arms, her hand on Maddy's breast.

"When you came," Michael said to Jamie, "I had to stop feeding to make sure you had enough milk to drink. Now you can take care of Jessie the same way."

"Seriously?" whispered Jesse. "What five-year old talks like that? He's more of a father than a brother."

"It is what it is," said Alexandra. "Stop worrying so much. They're all adapting."

With the baby awake half the night, Maddy was determined to get Jamie sleeping in her own cot and Michael sleeping in his own bed, both of them in the second bedroom. She always kept the interconnecting door open, no matter how noisy Jessie was at night. Michael usually woke when Jessie did, and if Jamie woke then Michael almost always woke too. Michael would lift Jamie out of the cot and the older children would be with Maddy for a few minutes while she changed and fed Jessie, everyone cuddling in Maddy's bed. But then Maddy would say, "Back to bed," and Michael would lead the way, helping Jamie get back into her cot and then putting himself back under the covers of his little bed.

Maddy was gentle yet definite. She did what she felt was best, guided perhaps but certainly not dictated by what she was learning in her day-time lessons about parenting. Alexandra encouraged her to learn everything she could about child development, and taught her a lot, but then insisted that Maddy trust her own judgment about the welfare of her children.

Jessie's first bath was almost like a party. Maddy had only ever had a bucket for cleaning herself and her children so she loved baths with the kids. There was always playing and splashing, with Alexandra and sometimes Jesse getting soaked as they knelt on the floor beside the bath and leaned over the edge to play with boats and buckets. Jesse had made sure the entire bathroom floor was a watertight basin to avoid damaging the house. Alexandra would make up stories about the bath toys and the kids would be enthralled. Maddy was like a child in those moments, loving the fun and the stories, and she was never self-conscious about being naked. Whatever modesty Maddy had developed by the time she was abducted at age five had been thoroughly erased in the subsequent years.

Naturally, Maddy wanted to include Jessie in the fun. Alexandra had explained that it was safer to bathe newborns in special containers where there's virtually zero risk of drowning, but Maddy insisted. She sat at one end of the tub opposite the older kids. She told Michael and Jamie not to splash and Alexandra handed the baby over. Maddy washed Jessie carefully and then passed her back to Alexandra. While Alexandra dried the baby, Jesse took over the story-telling duties, explaining how the tugboat lost the ship it was supposed to be tugging, and had to go searching for it. Michael would hide the cargo ship while Jamie would move the tugboat around looking for it. Alexandra sat on a chair in the corner with Jessie wrapped in a fluffy towel, the little girl watching her family laughing and splashing.

A few weeks after Thanksgiving, Alexandra and Jesse met with Josh and Shondra, the lead on education services in their home, to take stock of Maddy and Michael's progress. In Michael's case the main challenge was finding a pathway to get him into school, though perhaps home-schooling was the better option, given his atypical behavior. In Maddy's case, the issue was achieving personal and financial independence.

"Let's start with Maddy," said Shondra, who had become a good friend of the family. "Her handwriting is still barely legible, but she's learned to type lightning fast. She's still refusing to try creative writing, though she's not saying why. She seems happy to be a sponge, soaking up information about the world. She never forgets anything she's learned, including facts about social studies. That's her favorite thing, actually. She's typing up reports on burial practices in China, cuisine in Peru, and a hundred other topics—it's all amazing to her, as you can imagine. She still can't believe how many people and places are in the world." Shondra grinned. "Her reports are always to the point—information only, no frills—and totally accurate. I'm sure you've noticed her vocabulary is expanding rapidly, she's stopped swearing almost entirely, and she can understand most of what she hears on the internet, radio, or television. She's started reading middle-school chapter books on her own, which is showing her a lot about the way children are socialized. She often says that some aspect or another of teenage life is stupid."

They all laughed.

"She'll ask about something she doesn't understand," Shondra continued, "but she never asks about the same thing twice. She's just fine at arithmetic because she can see how to use it to analyze grocery store prices. But none of us has been able to get her interested in geometry; she says she just doesn't see the point. Obviously, you know how good her drawing skills are, simply stunning. So that's what I'm seeing. What about you?"

"Have you tried introducing geometry through perspective drawing?" asked Jesse.

"Good idea," said Shondra. "We'll give that a go."

"I've noticed some weirdness around reading," Alexandra said. "Her reading to the children, I mean. She's started reading aloud to them here and there, and doesn't seem self-conscious about the halting way she reads. But a couple of days ago, Jamie was adamant that she didn't want Maddy to read to her—she insisted it be me instead." Alexandra paused. "So I'm wondering, might Jamie come to regard her mother as somehow inadequate because she can't do certain things, such as leave the house or read fluently?"

"It's a good question, Ali," said Shondra. "But don't all kids have to come to terms with their parents' limitations, as they learn who they are and what they can and can't do?"

"Sure," said Alexandra, "but that kind of unmasking doesn't usually begin when the child is two years old. After everything Maddy has been through, I hate to think that the children she has so fiercely protected could ever look down on her."

"We'll keep working on reading but, honestly, it might be too late to improve her fluency much beyond where it is now. I think we have to handle the interpersonal issues between Maddy and her kids some other way."

"There's another thing," said Alexandra. "Maddy has become fascinated with human anatomy. As a person exposed to extremely complex anatomical processes at a shockingly young age, I was worried about how this part of her schooling would go."

"We all were," said Shondra. "But she's surprised us by jumping right in, learning faster than we're ready to teach. She seems fine with it."

"I agree," said Alexandra. "But she's stumbling onto things online that worry me."

"You mean porn?" said Shondra.

"Exactly," said Alexandra. "The other day, she was looking for information about human anatomy and she landed on a porn site. And we know this because she asked Jesse and me about it— utterly unselfconscious, as usual, and not disturbed in the slightest. I would've thought she'd be shocked or have horrible flashbacks or at least want to know why people would do that. But she seemed to assume it was all perfectly normal."

"Wow," said Shondra. "So what did she say?"

"The conversation actually went in a direction I never would've expected. 'It must feel so different to have a different body,' she said. 'Big boobs would wobble all the time. Big balls would bang on your legs when you walk. Pointy nipples would always rub on things. Having no hair down there would feel weird.' It was so uncomplicated and straightforward—and an amazing exercise in empathy. I told her I hadn't really thought about it but she was right—people probably do feel different in their own bodies. I said I'd heard it was tiring to be fat because you have to carry a lot of extra weight around with you. Then she asked both of us what it felt like to be in our bodies. I said we are getting older so we move more slowly, our skin is a bit more saggy and wrinkly, and our joints and muscles ache sometimes."

Everyone chuckled at that plain description of aging before Alexandra resumed her story.

"Then I asked whether she was okay with seeing sex acts on the internet. She said she was fine with it. Then she said something like, 'I've done all that stuff and it's like seeing it from the outside, the way Michael and Jamie saw it.'"

Alexandra paused, tears coming to her eyes, and Jesse reached for her hand.

"She was so matter-of-fact about it, about what the kids saw, and we know it was torture and rape. How are she and the kids supposed to get past that? Especially Michael, who spent the most formative years of his life watching that unfold in front of him."

Nobody could speak for a while. There was nothing to say.

"There was another strange moment in that conversation," Jesse said.

"That's right," said Alexandra. "I explained that some people choose to participate in pornographic films and photo shoots because they like it, but other people are forced to do it, maybe because they're desperate for money or drugs, or maybe because they'd been tricked into it. And *that* is what shocked Maddy. She said, 'So some of these women might not want their pictures on the internet?' 'Some of the men, too,' I said, 'and you can't easily tell which ones.' Maddy wanted to know whether someone would rescue them. I had to explain that some of the coercion wasn't illegal and that there would probably be few rescues. Then Maddy just stared at the computer screen in horror. It was the same pattern we've seen before: she handles bodies in an open, matter-of-fact way, but she's appalled by the violation of bodies in every form, and by the way violations are culturally accepted."

There was nothing to say about that, either.

Josh finally broke the silence. "Okay, let's be sure and keep all this on the radar, and I can follow up with Maddy's therapist, if she's okay with that. Shondra, what about Michael?"

"That's more straightforward," answered Shondra. "He's already caught up with a kindergarten level of schooling. The home-schooling routine is working perfectly and he can switch over to regular school anytime he and Maddy want that. Or he can keep doing what he's doing at home."

"I'm worried about school for him," said Jesse. "He's really not like any five-year-old boy I've ever known. He'll stick out like a sore thumb."

"I appreciate your protectiveness, Jesse," said Shondra, "and you're right about his weirdly mature behavior. I've never met a kid so able to concentrate. And there's got to be profound effects from the way he grew up and what he saw. Maybe he would seem strange to his peers. But school would also help him socialize and learn the way other children tend to behave."

"Let's just keep an eye on this as we go along, too," said Josh.

Jesse was grateful for Josh's intervention. His own response wouldn't have been so diplomatic.

Maddy's drawing had progressed in a few short months from exceptional to truly stunning. The main stairway and upstairs hall had become her personal gallery, filled with sketches of the people she loved and the scenes she could see from the back deck. She always used eighteen-by-twenty-four-inch sketch paper, which she framed using black-plastic-and-glass, clip-in frames. She had many dozens of pictures to choose from, and she took responsibility for cycling the display of thirty pictures on the crowded walls. They looked like monochrome photographs from a few feet away.

One early December afternoon, Maddy was feeding Jessie in the family room, staring at the woods under a brooding sky that threatened snow.

"Maddy," Jesse said, "do you know how to draw snow falling?"

"Not yet," she said. "I've seen it snow online but I'd like to see it for real before I try. If I saw snow when I was little I don't remember it."

"Looks like you'll get your chance today," he said. "This will be a big moment!"

"Yes."

"There's something on my mind," Jesse added.

"There always is," she teased. Alexandra chuckled. It was the first time they'd heard Maddy utter anything resembling a wisecrack. A miffed Chester appeared to Jesse.

"You know about money now," he said. "And how independence is tied up with being able to earn money, right?"

"Yes," she answered.

"I've been thinking about ways you might become independent by earning your own money. Have you been thinking about that?"

"No."

Jesse was suddenly worried that he was raising a topic for which Maddy wasn't ready. He pressed on, gently. "I reckon there are several things you could do that would earn you money and that you'd enjoy. They're quite different. Would you like to hear some ideas?"

"Yes," she replied.

Maddy unlatched Jessie from one breast and switched her to the other side, not bothering to cover up. Jesse realized that Maddy had been breastfeeding continually for six years at that time, which was almost a third of her life, only weaning one child when a new baby arrived. In fact, it was probably only the birth-control effects of breastfeeding that had prevented Maddy from conceiving even more children.

"So here's one idea," Jesse said. "You're good with children, and people pay for childcare. There are several ways that happens. You know about Dora, who takes care of Matt and Jenny's kids. That's the nanny way, but you can't have your own young children and do that. That might be something to consider when your children are grown. Another way is day-time work in a childcare center. You'd need someone to take care of your children while you were working, but we could do that, and you could earn money. You wouldn't earn much money, though, because early childhood educators aren't highly respected." Alexandra grimaced; this was a sore point for her. "And you couldn't do it until Jessie was weaned anyway. But you'd develop a community of friends where you work and you'd be involved in the lives of dozens of children."

Maddy said nothing.

"Here's another idea. You love cooking. You might work as a cook in a restaurant. It'd be more difficult to get a job because the training is more specialized, but I think it would be doable, with a bit of patience. The same thing applies with the kids: it's a job that would require someone else to care for them while you're working."

"I don't want to leave the kids," she said.

"Makes sense," responded Jesse. "So here's a third idea, one that doesn't involve leaving the kids. I'm not sure if you know this, but parents love sketches of their children at various ages, and around here they have the means to pay a lot of money for them. A single sketch of the size and quality of yours could fetch about a week's pay working in a childcare center. This would be a much more solitary occupation but you could start it whenever you wanted and control the work flow easily. I think you could earn a lot of money doing this, as people passed the word about the quality of your work."

"I'll need more money than I can get from being a childcare worker," Maddy said. "How much money for a good portrait?"

"I've been looking into it and I think you could charge $450 for an unframed picture," said Jesse. "A lot of people beginning in the market would charge about a third of that, around $150, and gradually raise prices as they became better known. But your initial target market would be right around here, with people who know something about your situation and want to support you. You'd have great difficulty raising prices later without making newer people feel you were treating them unfairly. I reckon you might start out at $450 for people in our local network, and then you won't need to worry about raising prices later."

"And Maddy," Alexandra said. "Please know that we're talking about future plans. We can take care of you for a long time."

Jessie had fallen asleep and unlatched. Maddy put the baby over her shoulder to burp her, smoothly doing what she'd done thousands of times before as she pondered this new information.

"The drawing sounds better," she said. "I could do five of those a week if enough people want them."

"You may also be able to sell drawings using a website," Jesse added. "You'll have to learn about running a business, which is complicated. You'd need to know about taxes and bank accounts, advertising and invoicing. We could point your life-skills lessons in that direction if you want."

"Yes. I want to do it," she declared, as if it were the simplest thing in the world to start a business.

The snow had started. Maddy put Jessie in her carrier, reassembled her top, and walked with Jesse and Alexandra to the window. Jesse opened the door to the deck and they stepped outside. It was one of those snowfalls with gigantic lumps of snowflakes, falling silently with no wind. Maddy caught some in her hands and watched it melt. She copied Alexandra and poked out her tongue and caught some in her mouth.

It was an extraordinary moment, and Maddy started crying. There were no heaves or sobs, just tears, running down her face. Jesse looked at Alexandra, uncertain about whether they should feel alarmed. Up to that point they weren't even sure she was able to cry. Were these tears of joy? Tears from the grief of lost years? Alexandra gave him a reassuring smile and shook her head slightly. *Just let her be*, his beloved was communicating to him. *She's doing the work of healing.*

"Dad! Glad I caught you," Josh said. "Is this a good time to talk?"

Jesse had just climbed the stairs to his office, where he was going to add the image of Maddy's reaction to snow to his Maddy stack.

"It's perfect, Josh. What's up?"

"Well I had this idea of tracking down information about the disposition of Maddy's mother's estate."

"Huh! Very interesting. What did you find out?"

"Well, when Maddy's mother died a few years back, there were no close relatives, and she left her entire estate to a non-profit dedicated to finding missing children. No distant relatives surfaced to challenge it. Our people tracked down the lawyer involved and he told us there was no provision made for Maddy in the will—everyone assumed she was dead."

"Was Maddy mentioned at all?" asked Jesse.

"Only as the mother's motivation for giving the entire estate to the non-profit. But she wasn't explicitly excluded, either, which may give us a promising basis for negotiating with the probate court for a redistribution of the estate, or with the non-profit organization itself."

"Brilliant."

"But Dad, we really have no legal standing to pursue the matter with either party, and there's a host of legal intricacies to navigate. Do you know a lawyer who might be willing to pursue this on Maddy's behalf?"

"I think I can find someone to take it up," said Jesse. "I'll connect you as soon as I can. How much money are we talking about, anyway?"

"It was a decent middle-class estate, dominated by the sale of a suburban house, with a pretty sizable retirement fund due to the mother's early death," said Josh. "After expenses, a bit over two million went to the non-profit. It was a windfall for them but it would be a life-changing amount of money for Maddy."

"Thanks, Josh. Maddy's lucky to have you looking out for her. Love you."

"Love you too, Dad. See you Sunday for breakfast."

The following Sunday, Alexandra and Jesse were surrounded by friends at coffee hour after church. As usual, many wanted updates on Maddy and the kids. Jesse's mind flashed on a set of images from the Maddy stack depicting a supportive community who had their family's back when Becca disappeared and now stood ready to do anything at a moment's notice to help Maddy. Everyone felt honored to be a part of the network of love and expertise that was drawing Maddy into a new life, even though only a few of the high-school girls and some of their mothers had even met her. Maddy had no idea that an entire array of support was standing by.

Today Jesse had an agenda of his own. Their old friend Peter was an experienced probate attorney, and already knew Maddy's story. When Jesse took him aside and described what he was looking for, Peter was eager to take on Maddy's case. He also wouldn't hear of being paid.

Typical. Church might drive him nuts, but the network of caring it could give rise to was community at its very best.

AMBIGUOUS ADVENT

"Jesse!"

It was Alexandra, standing on the front porch in her dressing gown, silhouetted against the porch light. Jesse was slowly shoveling snow from a late autumn storm, clearing the driveway in the near darkness so he could drive to work. He walked over to her.

"Hey," he said, "it's really early. What're you doing up?"

"It's going to snow," she said.

Jesse looked around at the snow on the ground and back up at her, leaning on his shovel.

"It already snowed, sweetheart. What do you mean?"

She looked around and finally realized that he was shoveling snow.

"I meant that you should get up early and shovel so you aren't late for work," she said, a no-less confusing attempt to finesse an awkward moment.

Jesse walked to the porch and leaned the shovel against the house.

"It's cold, Alexandra. You only have socks and a robe on. Come inside and let's get warm." They walked inside, arms around each other. She sat down in the kitchen and stared at Jesse as he put on the kettle to make her some tea. While the water was heating, he sat opposite her and they looked into each other's faces.

"Jesse," she began. He waited. She reached for his hand and squeezed it, saying nothing. He gently touched her cheek and sadly smiled.

"It's like this, Jerry," began Jesse. "Alexandra has had rock-solid temperament her whole life, but lately her mood is more free-wheeling, and occasionally she's irritable for no good reason, though mostly with me and never with Maddy or the kids. She can't argue coherently, as she once could, though she gracefully deflects, making it difficult for most people to tell that anything is amiss. She might ask the same question several times over a couple of hours. The habits she's cultivated to make sure she doesn't forget little things are starting to break down. I find the car keys or her phone in weird places, for example, and groceries spoiling in the car."

"Has anyone else noticed?" asked Jerry.

"Josh and Matt have both seen it but they don't know how worried to be. Maddy has seen it too, and she knows something is wrong. A few days ago she and Alexandra were at the supermarket and Maddy said Alexandra was confused about where things were and twice she forgot that she already picked up items on the shopping list. I told her I'd been seeing similar things and that we'd make an appointment with a specialist to find out what's happening."

"I agree there's reason for concern, Jesse," said Jerry. "I'll give you a few names of good people up your way who specialize in neurodegenerative disorders."

"I have this yawning feeling, like I'm falling, or about to throw up," said Jesse.

"Well, don't make up your mind about this too quickly," said Jerry. "Be patient. See the specialist."

The doctor whose office was closest was booked up but Jerry got them in to see her. Alexandra then ran the gauntlet of neuropsychological and imaging tests. Just before the Winter solstice that year, they met with the neurologist to receive the verdict. Alexandra cut off the doctor's polite preliminaries in a snippy tone and asked for the results in plain language.

"Okay," the doctor said. "I can't explain your symptoms in any other way, so my conclusion is that you do indeed have Alzheimer's Disease. The neuroimaging scans show the kind of damage we'd expect in Alzheimer's. It's not curable, but medication can sometimes slow the advance of symptoms for a while." She reached for Alexandra's hand. "I'm sorry to have to give you this bad news. I'd like to help you manage this condition if you'll let me."

Alexandra looked at Jesse darkly. So did Becca, who was standing beside Alexandra, her hand on her mother's head.

Everyone was together again for Christmas, the first in living memory for Maddy. The anticipation was intense, not only for Michael and Jamie but for Maddy, too, and for everyone who cared about them and was privileged to see Christmas through their gleaming eyes. Alexandra was mistress of the gifts, which were mostly reserved for children in their family. She had designated everyone under twenty-five as a child for the purposes of Christmas presents, which made Maddy happy.

Maddy was planning a Christmas feast, spread over several days because she had too many ideas for one meal. She spent every spare minute in the kitchen, experimenting and perfecting recipes. She occasionally had Alexandra or Oli help, but mostly, the kitchen was her domain. She'd listen to digital books while she worked, often with Jessie nestled against her back in a baby sling.

They had decorated a Christmas tree right after Thanksgiving, with Josh's family joining in the fun, and hung the traditional Advent calendar. This involved removing a tiny cloth representation of a wrapped gift from one of twenty-four numbered pockets corresponding to each day before Christmas, and sticking it on a white Velcro Christmas tree. Decorating that tiny tree was Michael's job and he did it first thing every morning, without fail and without reminders.

During one visit, Jesse and Josh watched Jamie "help" Michael with the advent tree. He let her do what she wanted without trying to control her, returning the tree to its proper condition as soon as the little girl lost interest.

"It weirds me out watching Michael behave like this," whispered Jesse. "Why doesn't he yell at Jamie not to wreck the tree? Why doesn't he slap her hands or tell her to go away? And why does he never need reminders?"

"I know you're worried about it, Dad," said Josh, "and I do see what you see. But can't it be a positive thing? His ability to suppress his natural instincts and take care of the people he loves is really impressive."

"It's impressive, sure, but I sense an explosion coming," said Jesse. "I think people can't behave from sheer force of will without ultimately breaking." A new candidate image for the ever-growing Michael stack came to Jesse's mind: a pipe carrying water uphill and springing leaks under the pressure.

The evening before Matt and his family were due to arrive, with Maddy and the kids getting ready for bed, Becca joined Jesse for a stroll along the upstairs hallway, admiring Maddy's latest sketches. Jesse saw something that almost gave him a heart attack.

It was a sketch of Becca as a young teenager.

"Holy Moses. That's you, isn't it?" he exclaimed out loud to his equally shocked hallucinatory life companion. Jesse quickly looked around to make sure nobody had heard him.

"It looks exactly like the last age-advanced images from the police," Becca said.

"Holy Mother of God." Jesse went to see where things were at with bedtime preparations and caught Maddy in between the two bedrooms.

"How are things going?" he inquired, neutrally.

"Good. I'm glad we could stay in these two rooms even while Matt and Jenny are here with their kids," Maddy said.

"It's nice to have a big house when you have lots of grandkids," Jesse replied. "Hey, can I show you something? Down here?"

"Yes," Maddy said, and followed him down the hall.

"I haven't seen this one before. Who is it?"

"That's Christina," Maddy said. "She's the girl they brought in to help me when Michael was born."

Jesse tried to remain calm. "Did you see her any other times?"

"No. They brought in an old lady for Jamie's birth. She had a huge lump on her nose, long grey hair, and horrible breath, just like a storybook witch. But Christina was kind. She was chained up like me."

"I see," Jesse said, still trying to stay calm. "Well, it's a lovely sketch. It looks like she has blonde hair."

"Yes. And shining blue eyes. She was so beautiful. I thought we'd be friends but they took her away right after Michael was out and she'd cleaned me up."

"Thanks, Maddy. Sorry to disturb you," Jesse said, and she went back to running the evening routine.

"Holy Moses," Jesse said once more, out loud, to Becca.

Jesse sat restlessly through the bedtime ritual as Alexandra read to Maddy, Michael, and Jamie. Becca was staring at Jesse, in the form of a scared-looking little girl hunched into a corner of the room. Jesse's head was quietly exploding. He calmed himself enough to kiss all four of them on the forehead and allowed Alexandra to complete the ritual.

"Good night, sweethearts," she finally said. "Sleep soundly. Tomorrow is another wonderful day."

Jesse practically sprinted down the hall to take a photo of the Christina picture, and then ran to his office to call Josh.

"Holy crap," Josh exclaimed. "It sounds like there was a network of abducted kids, including Maddy and Becca, or Christina, or whatever her name was. And the older woman helping with the second pregnancy suggests there was at least one other family involved."

They both paused.

"Holy crap," Josh said again.

"Do you know what to do, Josh?"

"Hell, yes, I know exactly what to do. And Dad, think carefully before telling Mom about this, okay?"

"I'll keep it to myself for now," said Jesse. "Let's see how things develop. Maddy might be confused, or nothing may come of it."

Jesse felt incredibly restless. Matt would be traveling shortly and they would meet in person the next day so there was no point in reaching out to him now. Becca was scrunched into a corner of the office.

"Hey kiddo, let's sit down, okay?" he suggested.

"You're doing this to me, you big dope," she said. "How about *you* sit down and relax? We'll see what happens to me."

Jesse sat in the recliner and closed his eyes to try and relax. When he opened them again, Becca was leaning back in the matching recliner, staring at him. He couldn't help thinking about the possibility that she might be alive after all, and that they might find her, just as Maddy had been found. And he couldn't help thinking how difficult that might be as well. Becca the apparition was gorgeous, model-like in her appearance and build, but who knew what Becca their daughter would look like after years of abuse? And her mind…

Jesse smiled at Becca and closed his eyes again, breathing deeply and trying to relax. But he didn't sleep a wink that night.

Matt and Jenny and the kids arrived in their usual rental van about nine the next morning. After the kids ran off to play, Jesse pulled Matt aside. He felt the urge to tell his oldest son about his mother's Alzheimer's, but kept his promise to Alexandra and said nothing. But he did tell Matt about the photograph in the hallway and that Josh was investigating. Without a word, Matt marched upstairs. Jesse watched him staring at the sketch, not daring to intrude on his thoughts. After a minute of quiet staring, he turned to face Jesse, his eyes red and damp.

"Dad," he said, "I…"

This child had almost never been without a complete sentence since he was a toddler.

"I know, son. We just have to wait and see what Josh turns up. It'll be easier for me knowing that there's someone in the house who's aware of all this. I'm going bananas."

Neither one of them slept that night.

After Josh and family arrived the next day, the boys and their dad stole off to Jesse's office at the first possible moment.

"What's the story, Josh?" asked Matt. "Dad and I are going nuts."

"Here's what I know so far, and it's not a lot," Josh said. "I contacted my boss and the Providence police who recovered Maddy. I relayed what Maddy said and sent them the photo of Maddy's sketch and passed along her description of Christina and the old woman. I told them interviewing Maddy about this had to be a last resort. They told me that phone and computer records from Maddy's captors had never been analyzed, so that might shed some light. Another interview with Charlie might turn up something new, too—he never said anything about other imprisoned kids or a network of families, but nobody ever asked him about that, either. Maybe he can help them identify a second family that might be involved in abductions. They said it's a new angle and they'd pursue it. I have no more information than that."

"Why weren't phone and digital records investigated after the shootout?" asked Matt.

"I don't know for sure," said Josh. "But at the time everyone said it was cut and dried with three perps dead and the fourth up on murder charges. My bet is that they saw no loose ends to pull on, and nothing Maddy said at the time led them to think there was something larger going on."

"Dammit!" Jesse said. "This is what happens when you let Maddy set the pace of uncovering what went on in that house. We could be finding out so much more right now."

"Dad, we've been through this," said Josh.

"There could be lives at stake!" said Jesse. "Maybe even Becca's life!"

"I know, Dad, I know," said Josh. "We're trying to balance a lot of considerations here."

"So it's just wait and see?" said Matt.

"That's about the shape of it," replied Josh.

"We're always fucking waiting!" Matt shouted.

Jesse noticed Becca hovering over them menacingly, and he felt like he was about to drop off the deep end. He held it together just enough to say, "Well, you boys had better check on those kids of yours or there'll be hell to pay. The babysitters don't arrive until eleven. I'll stay here for a few minutes. I need to make a call."

When they left, Jesse called Jerry.

"Jess. You don't sound so good," said Jerry. "What's up?"

Jesse looked over at Becca, now partially merged with the wall in front of him, looking weirdly distorted. He laid out the details of what had happened and ended by saying, "Right now, I feel more like I'm about to lose my sanity than at any time since this thing hit me over a decade ago. I'm feeling nauseous and disoriented, I can't think straight, I haven't slept the last two nights, and Becca is looking truly bizarre. I need some fast help here, Jerry."

"Okay, Okay. Look, this sounds like the beginning of a panic attack, like you had after the first time you saw the apparition."

"Yeah," said Jesse. "No paralysis or treacle-thinking this time, not yet anyway, but that didn't hit me immediately last time, either."

"So you know what to do," said Jerry. "One of your meditation routines should do the trick."

"I think I need your help, Jerry."

"Okay," he said. "Turn off all the lights and sit somewhere comfortable."

"All the lights are off and I'm in a recliner," said Jesse. "Becca is dark and liquid and swooping all around the room right now."

"Ignore that for a minute," said Jerry. "Lie all the way back. Close your eyes. Listen to my voice."

Jerry walked him through a mindfulness meditation routine, focusing on breath-awareness. Ten minutes later, with Jesse's heart rate closer to normal, he opened his eyes, and saw Becca sitting in her usual place in the companion recliner.

"Thank God," he said out loud. "I thought you were going to go liquid zombie on me again."

"I'm still here," Jerry reminded him.

"Sorry, Jerry. That helped. Becca's back to normal. She says to thank you for bringing me back to her," and they both chuckled.

"Seriously, Jess, if this new source of stress is going to throw you off, you're going to have to use medication. And you need to sleep. Stay in touch about this, okay? I mean it. Call me tomorrow, first thing."

"Will do," Jesse said.

"And good luck with this whole situation concerning Rebecca," said Jerry. "Keep me updated."

"Okay," Jesse answered, and they said their goodbyes.

"A person with a psychiatric disorder can't afford to have one sleepless night, let alone two," said Becca, suddenly all school-marmish.

"Got it," Jesse said. "I'll take something tonight."

ANCIENT HISTORY

After a few minutes to gather his wits, Jesse rejoined the family. The four women were still sitting around with the three babies, chatting, while the boys were down in the basement keeping an eye on the other children.

"Here's the professor," Alexandra said. "He should be able to sort this out."

Jesse collapsed on the sofa beside her and leaned into her comforting body and tried to focus.

"Apparently Maddy has been learning about Christmas," Jenny said, "and she has some questions about Jesus and Mary and the Bible and that sort of thing."

"We figured you'd know what to say," said Oli. "Maddy is running rings around us."

"Maddy is turning into such an intellectual!" Jenny said. Everyone laughed, and Maddy smiled at the praise.

Jesse knew he couldn't handle anything strenuous at that moment, but he was curious. "Do you know how to play Twenty Questions?" he asked. Maddy didn't, so he explained that they'd play a version of the game. Maddy got to ask as many as twenty questions and he was confined to answering Yes, No, Maybe, Probably, Probably Not, or Don't Know.

"But I want information you can't give with those answers," Maddy said.

"Give it a try, anyway," Jesse said. "We can always go deeper later. Girls, help Maddy come up with her twenty questions."

The three of them began consulting in whispers.

"Hey," Alexandra said. "You seem tired. You okay?"

"I'm fine, sweetheart." An outright lie. But there would be time enough for updates if any actual news about Becca materialized. He thought about his decision to talk to the boys but not to Alexandra. It seemed condescending, disrespectful... and necessary.

"Okay!" said Oli. "She's ready."

"First," said Jesse, "are you looking for my personal opinion, the consensus of relevant experts, or my interpretation of traditional beliefs?"

"You're an expert," said Maddy. "I want to know what you think."

"Okay," he said. "Shoot."

"That's a weird saying," said Maddy.

"Another keen observation from our budding intellectual," he said.

"You keep count, Oli," said Maddy. "Question one. Was Jesus a real person?"

"Probably."

"Was Jesus born on December 25?"

"Probably not."

"Was Jesus' mother a virgin?"

"No."

"Was Jesus' father God?"

"No."

"Was Jesus' father Joseph?"

"Probably."

"Were there angels singing to shepherds?"

"No."

"Were there wise men traveling to see the baby Jesus?"

"No."

"Was there a special star when Jesus was born?"

"No."

"Was there a mass killing of babies?"

"Probably not."

"Was Jesus born in Bethlehem?"

"Probably not."

"So Jesus was this ordinary baby born to ordinary parents in the ordinary way, right?"

"Yes."

"How many is that, Oli?" asked Maddy.

"Eleven," Oli replied, "if you don't count the question you just asked me." They exchanged a smile. "Nine to go." The women quietly conferred for a minute before Maddy continued.

"Your answers have thrown me off track," said Maddy, "so now I want to ask different kinds of questions, Okay?"

"Anything is fine, Maddy," said Jesse.

"Question twelve. The Christmas pageant we're going to see on Wednesday, that's all made up, right?"

"Yes."

"Lots of people believe it really happened like that, though, right?"

"Probably not."

"But a few people really believe it, right?"

"Yes."

"And most people don't really believe it but they like the story because Jesus is important to them, right?"

"Yes."

"Do most church leaders know that the Christmas story is all or mostly made up?"

"Yes."

"Wow," exclaimed Maddy. "I'm getting this picture of a whole big thing based on a fairy tale that works because the message matters to people. Is that right?"

"Yes."

"And the message is that God sent Jesus to rescue people from... I don't know, from all the bad shit that happens and all the bad things people do."

"Yes."

"Did God really send Jesus to do that saving?"

"No."

"But most people think God really did send Jesus, right?"

"Yes."

"So your picture of Christmas is that the story of Jesus' birth is a fairy tale that lots of people love because of the meaning behind the fairy tale, and you also think that the meaning behind the fairy tale is *another* fairy tale that lots of people love because they really want it to be true. Right?"

Jesse grinned. "Yes."

"But you love Christmas despite all of that, right?"

"Yes. How many is that, Oli?"

"Four to go," replied Oli, making Jesse roll his eyes skeptically.

"Okay, four more," said Maddy. "You love it because there's another meaning behind the God-sent-Jesus-to-save-us fairy tale, and that meaning is actually true and not a fairy tale, right?"

"Yes." This girl was sharp.

"I want to know what that other meaning is but I don't know how to guess so I'll ask you about that later... Why do people want to believe in a fairy tale? Is it because they're in pain and they don't know how to stop hurting?"

"Yes," Jesse replied, quietly now, as he beheld this amazing young woman analyze a world she was only just discovering.

"Believing in fake rescues actually helps ease the pain, right?"

"Yes."

"It'd be cruel to take away something that helps people in pain when they have no other solution, right?"

"Yes."

"And that's why you don't protest Christmas and say it's a stupid fairy tale, because you care about all the people in pain who're trying to feel better, right?"

"Yes."

"Okay then! So now I've figured it out. The other meaning, the one behind the God-sent-Jesus-to-rescue-us fairy tale, is that we can care for each other and stop our pain together."

"Yes, you've got it exactly," Jesse replied. Everybody was silent, staring at Maddy in wonder.

"Maddy," Jenny finally said, "how did you work all this out? How is it possible?"

Maddy said nothing for a moment, as if she was deciding whether to speak.

"I learned two things chained up in that basement," she eventually said. "One is that I could love people, I mean really love them, which I learned from my children. The other is that people lie to themselves all the time about pain and love, which I learned from the people who imprisoned me, and from watching myself. I know how to recognize a big lie about love."

Jenny leaned in and kissed Maddy on the forehead. Oli gave her a hug. Jesse closed his eyes and immersed himself in the moment, enjoying his wife beside him, worrying about the disintegration of her mind, yet feeling surrounded by love, wishing it would never end, hoping they would find Becca and reunite their family. Then he heard Becca, without seeing her.

"You need some sleep, Daddy," she said.

Jesse dragged himself from the comfort that was deepening his delirium, kissed each of his four girls, and went to attempt a nap.

THE 1,540ᵀᴴ BOYS' BREAKFAST

The following day was Sunday. Jesse checked in with Jerry, as promised, and vowed to report to him each day until his sleep was normalized.

With the blessing of their wives, Jesse, Matt, and Josh made their way to a nearby diner. It was a grim car ride, and they remained grim as they ordered food.

"This is a crazy situation," said Matt. "I hate being so helpless—all we can do is wait."

"That's the way it is," agreed Josh.

"How about a distraction?" Jesse asked.

"Sure," said Josh. "But what?"

"Let's stick to the routine," said Matt. "Highs and lows."

"Excellent idea," Jesse said. "Josh, why don't you start? But nothing about Becca today, okay?"

"Okay," said Josh. "My high is clear-cut: it's so good to have everyone together again. Our family is so different from the disasters I deal with on a daily basis. Even with Maddy and her traumatic past, everyone seems basically healthy and happy. The whole thing feels like a miracle of good fortune...like we have no right to expect to be this happy."

Jesse smiled. How often he'd had those same thoughts... his tainted with images of the cackling deities who'd haunted him when Becca disappeared.

"My low is about Oli's mother," Josh went on. "She's gotten to the point that she doesn't recognize Oli sometimes, which is hard for both of us. Oli's trying to figure out how to care for someone who doesn't even know who she is."

They paused to absorb what it would be like to go through what Oli was going through, and then Matt volunteered to go next.

"My low has to do with Mom. Her memory seems worse than when I was here in October, and she seems emotionally more frag-ile as well. I'm worried that we'll be dealing with Oli's situation soon. What's the diagnostic situation, Dad?"

That put Jesse in an awkward situation, given his promise to Alexandra that she'd be the one to talk about it. But his boys were obviously worried, and there was no deflection at Boys' Breakfast.

"It's not good," said Jesse. "The testing has ruled out every reversible source of dementia that's currently known. It looks like untreatable Alzheimer's disease, and hitting pretty early. She made me promise to let her tell you but I've gone ahead and broken that promise now, so please be discreet. I'm so sorry about this, boys. It's going to be a long road from here, I'm afraid."

"Especially for you, Dad," said Josh.

"It isn't going to be a lot of fun for Alexandra or Maddy, either," Jesse added, with more force than he intended. He apologized to Josh with his eyes and then asked Matt to cheer them up with a high.

"My high," Matt mused. "Well it's kind of similar to what Josh said. Can you believe my life? I have a beautiful wife who's a brilliant mother to four adorable children, an amazing nanny, a challenging and satisfying job, and I regularly see two of my favor-ite cities in the world. I'm shockingly happy. Maybe all the misery lies ahead but I'm making the most of the good times right now."

Again they paused, absorbing Matt's feelings, as was their habit.

"Okay, Dad," said Josh, "assuming your low is Mom's health situation, you owe us a high. Make it a good one."

"It's Maddy," he said. "She constantly leaves me awestruck. How can anyone bounce back from what she went through?"

"Not everyone does," said Josh.

"And that makes it even more special," Jesse said. "Her resil-ience, her cooking, her drawing, and most of all her fiercely loving nature—it's difficult to take in. Lately she's been offering acute observations and her intelligence is shining through. Yesterday she even spoke about insights gleaned from her long captivity. Alexandra and I are so grateful to have her in our lives, and so glad to be able to offer her a home."

"You and Mom are doing a great job with her," said Josh. "If you aren't careful, you'll soon be getting requests to host other lost souls."

"Well, actually," said Matt, "I guess Mom's condition rules out that possibility."

A somber mood settled over them once more, as they contemplated the fate of their beloved Alexandra and wondered whether Becca might still be alive.

SOME OF IT IS LOVELY

On Christmas Eve the family went to the mid-afternoon church Christmas pageant. It was the first social event Maddy had ever attended outside the house. Alexandra and Jesse were never far from her side. Though practically everyone in the church knew who Maddy was, few had ever met her in person, and their friends were careful not to draw attention to her. It helped that Jesse located their clan up in the balcony, out of the way of the worst of the people traffic.

From Jesse's perspective, the pageant itself was the usual thoughtless merging of multiple ancient legendary traditions into a single incoherent and slightly annoying story, but he enjoyed watching everyone playing their roles. The lawyer working on Maddy's case, Peter, was one of the three wise men and sung about frankincense in his deep bass voice. The church was absolutely packed, as always.

Maddy couldn't remember ever having been in a church, and it was definitely the first time her kids had been in one. She stayed home when Alexandra and Jesse went to church, which was most weeks. On the way back to the cars, Jesse asked her what she thought.

"I loved the Christmas music," she said. "Maybe we can listen to some at home."

"Sure, we can do that," he said, realizing that they hadn't played any Christmas music since they set up the tree several weeks earlier. "It didn't occur to me that you wouldn't know any Christmas music," he said. "I should've thought of that. Some of it is lovely."

"It's interesting to hear the story after our twenty-questions game," said Maddy. "I like the super-special baby thing. The angels announce the birth and everyone visits and gives gifts. It's nice, especially with the animals and the star, like everything in nature knows the baby is special even though most of the stupid humans don't get it. But I couldn't understand *why* the baby is special. I mean, I know why from our talk, but they don't say in the pageant. It's a hole in the story, or it's a story mainly for people who already know it."

"That sounds about right," Jesse said, surprised that he hadn't noticed that himself.

Jesse saw Josh take a phone call, two-year-old John in his arms. He told himself to calm down; that call could be from anyone.

After recovering some sleep he felt less fragile, but Jesse was still in a high pitch of anxiety, desperately trying not to bug Josh for updates. Rather than resorting to medication, he was meditating a couple of times each day to stay steady, though nothing special, just relaxation and mindfulness.

Before dinner that evening, he called Jerry to check in.

"You're late," said Jerry.

"Yeah, sorry," said Jesse. "Crazy day."

"Any news on Becca?"

"Nothing," said Jesse. "Still waiting."

"How's the sleep?" asked Jerry.

"Good, last night anyway," answered Jesse. "I still have a big debt to pay off, though. I'm having trouble believing that I'm so emotionally vulnerable, having had such refined control over this damned anxiety condition for so many years. It'd be humiliating for me if my loved ones had to learn about this part of my life by means of a hospitalization at this juncture, the way Alexandra and I learned about it."

"I guess that's powerful motivation to stay calm," said Jerry. Chester the one-feathered, prideful, power-animal chicken was stalking the phone and determined to help Jesse do exactly that.

"Becca isn't helping much beyond the usual reminders," said Jesse. "Her appearance is regularly shifting in tone, which is a freaky measure of how close to the edge I am. Honestly, I'm angry at myself for such weakness of mind."

"Sounds like you," said Jerry. "But you know those self-accusations only further complicate matters. What you need most is reduction of external stress and increase in internal calm. There's not a lot you can do about the former so you have to focus on staying calm and keeping self-recriminations to the absolute minimum."

Jesse wondered what that absolute minimum might be, given his Chester-style pride.

Christmas Eve bedtime was no small thing with their crew of seven adults and ten kids who were beside themselves with excitement. Josh and Oli's family were staying over, so everything was more complicated than usual. Alexandra and Jesse said goodnight to Matt's and Josh's five older kids, who were piled into the basement. Then they helped get Maddy and her kids down. Even knowing that the other kids were in the basement, Michael and Jamie wanted to go to bed with Maddy as they always did.

When everyone was finally settled, and Alexandra retired to the bedroom to work on the Christmas stockings, Jesse retreated to his office to meditate quietly.

A few minutes into the meditation state, feeling momentarily relaxed, and enjoying Becca's quiet company, Matt and Jenny, Josh and Oli crept up the stairs to join him, with two sleeping babies in the mothers' arms.

"Dad, we wanted to tell you how sad and sorry we all are," said Jenny. "Matt told me about the diagnosis this evening and we all wanted to reach out to you, and to get your advice about whether and how to speak with Mom about it."

"That's sweet of you, Jenny, and all of you, thank you," Jesse replied. "I don't know precisely how to broach this because your Mom wants to control the announcement herself. Alexandra and

I are worried about Maddy's reaction, too. I think I need to have a quiet word with Maddy after Christmas, and then Alexandra might choose to have a family meeting among the adults before you guys leave for San Francisco. But it's up to her."

"Okay," said Matt. "I'm afraid we're going to feel a long way from you guys and not very useful in a day-to-day way."

"But we'd love to help if there's anything we can do," Jenny said.

"It looks like what's ahead of us is a painful downward spiral," Jesse said. "So I think making the most of the moments we have together should be the highest priority."

"Mom seems to be bearing up well," Matt observed.

"You know her, Matt," Jesse said. "She always makes the best of everything. But she's scared."

"Dad, this is precisely why—" began Matt but Jenny interrupted him.

"Now's not the time, okay?" she said.

"Matt," said Jesse, "I think you might have this the wrong way around."

"What do you mean?" asked Matt.

"Maddy and her kids are going to be a huge comfort to me in the years to come," said Jesse. "I thank my lucky stars each day they're in our lives now."

"It looks like a piece of great good fortune to me, too," said Josh. "Maddy is good company and she can help take care of Mom."

Matt raised his eyebrows, but said nothing more.

The five of them trekked downstairs with the babies to check on Alexandra. Jesse poked his head around the corner to warn her that she was about to be invaded by eager helpers. She told him to wait while she covered everything up.

"It's safe now. Come in!" she declared, and they filed in with questions about how to assist with Christmas morning preparations. "I'm doing the stockings. I already wrapped the presents and some of them are under the tree, but you can take the rest downstairs now," she said, gesturing to the pile in the corner. "Then you can sit down with a cup of cider and listen to Christmas music while I finish up here."

She was pleased with herself and they were happy to leave her to complete her self-appointed task of stuffing stockings. She even stuffed her own stocking, as she'd done every year, not even once allowing Jesse to do it for her. He'd given up offering. It was her thing.

"I'll see you shortly, sweetheart," Jesse said, and kissed the top of her head. She laughed crazily, and Jesse knew she was picturing the fun her grandchildren would have in the morning.

COSMICALLY BAD TIMING

Just before seven, the parents crept downstairs to await the basement storm troopers. Maddy sent Michael and Jamie down to the basement so they could all come up together. Walt poked his head around the corner and asked if it was time. Matt gave him the green light and everyone came charging into the family room, eyes wide at the decorated tree and the colorfully wrapped gifts.

Alexandra handed out the stockings. Jesse took the baby from Maddy so she could receive her stocking. The parents watched the kids, absorbing the unbridled joy. The two grandparents watched the parents, lost in wonder at the beauty of families.

And they all unobtrusively watched Maddy, Michael, and Jamie. Michael and Maddy were observing rather than unwrapping. Maddy seemed paralyzed, holding her stocking in her lap while watching her children participate in the family Christmas ritual. She turned to look at Jesse, with tears in her eyes. She kissed him on the cheek and said, simply, "Thank you."

It was the first time Jesse had heard her utter those words, or anything like them. He put his arm around her shoulders, with Jessie in his other arm, and kissed her on top of her blonde head, as she leaned her head on his shoulder and ran her hands over the intriguing bumps in her stocking.

"Are you going to dig into that, Maddy?" he asked.

"I think I want to leave it just like this, to remember the moment," she said.

"Well, it'll keep, I reckon," he said.

From across the room Alexandra looked over at Maddy and Jesse, obviously happy. But as she stared into her husband's eyes, she breathed in that slightly shuddering way that let him know she was also scared, wondering if moments like these would soon be lost to her forever.

Jesse held fast to Maddy and little Jessie, gently staring back at Alexandra, and he watched as she steadied her breathing by copying his, for the thousandth time. Josh noticed the exchange—noticing people was his gift. He smiled sadly at them and then turned his attention back to the young ones.

After the stockings, it was breakfast time, then getting ready for the day. Then it was games and talking. Early in the afternoon, still before lunch, they started the ritual of unwrapping the presents under the tree.

For some reason long forgotten, handing out those gifts had become Josh's responsibility, which he carried out that year dressed in a Santa suit, ordered especially for the occasion. He always exercised superb judgment in the order of the gifts, doing his best to keep the little ones calm and happy. He also knew just when to interrupt proceedings for the mid-afternoon lunch, which was Maddy's greatest feast of the week.

Maddy, being under Alexandra's cut-off age of twenty-five, had presents under the tree like the children. In fact, she received the most of anyone because everyone wanted this first Christmas to be special for her.

Jenny and Oli had been full of compliments about how rapidly Maddy had regained her slender figure after Jessie's delivery, and they were driving the point home with their gifts of a form-fitting dress, tight jeans, and a couple of simple, flattering blouses.

Oli had forewarned Josh to get Maddy's clothes gifts opened in the first shift of unwrapping. As a result, when her cooking duties were completed and the afternoon feast was ready, Maddy ran upstairs with Jenny and Oli and changed into a lovely knee-length black dress, arranged her hair the way they said she should, and put on her diamond earrings and necklace. Everyone was already sitting at the big tables when the three ladies returned, and they all clapped and cheered for Maddy, who looked simply stunning. She smiled to acknowledge the welcome.

In some ways it is such a simple thing to give love, thought Jesse, and Maddy was good at giving her love to those close to her. It is more difficult to accept love, because resentment and regret make us long for something other than love unadorned. Despite everything, Maddy was utterly free of self-pity, and she accepted love as easily as she gave it.

Partway through the Christmas luncheon, Jesse dinged his glass with a fork to get everyone's attention. Because Matt was a Christmas baby, it was easy to forget about celebrating his special existence. When he was little, they used to celebrate his birthday on the other side of the year, June twenty-fifth, to make sure he got the attention he deserved. After presents and parties stopped mattering so much, Alexandra and Jesse got in the habit of specially noting his birthday on Christmas day itself.

"As you all know," Jesse began, "your Uncle Matt—also known as Daddy, son, bro, darling, sweetheart, and Matty Boy—is a Christmas baby. As a result of this cosmically bad timing, he's felt neglected his entire life."

Matt and Josh cracked up.

"I kept telling him that it's better to be a Christmas baby than to be born near Christmas but not on the very day, because those unfortunates both are neglected and have nothing special to show for it. Unsurprisingly, Matt never found this line of reasoning persuasive, or if he did, it didn't stop him from complaining about the poor timing of his birth."

"That argument wouldn't hold up in court," Matt interjected.

"I further pointed out that his birth was ten days overdue, and that if he'd been a well-behaved, considerate child, he'd have arrived as scheduled on December fifteenth. But thus far he has been unwilling to take any responsibility for the bad timing."

"Nothing to do with me," Matt said.

"Therefore, on this special day, I want to do what Matt has desired all along. I'd like, finally, after many long years, to apologize to him for the fact that he's a Christmas baby. I admit it: this has been a gross injustice."

"About time!" Matt declared.

"Unfortunately, it's too grave an injustice to be rectified. Compensation of any kind would be insulting when compared to the terrible suffering he's had to endure. My lame apology will have to do. So suck it up, Matt."

When the laughter died down, Jesse continued.

"Seriously, Matt, we love you, we're amazed by you, and we count ourselves extraordinarily fortunate to have you in our lives." Jesse raised his glass. "Happy Birthday, Matt!"

Everyone echoed the toast, and then Alexandra appeared carrying a birthday cake. The cake was decorated with two giant candles: a three and a five, indicating Matt's age. They sang "happy birthday" to him, he blew out the candles, and all was right with the world, at least for one fleeting moment.

Jesse couldn't help wondering what Becca might have been doing at that very moment, were she still alive somewhere.

The next morning, Jesse found a quiet moment to take Maddy aside. She carried the baby up the stairs to Jesse's office. They sat in the recliners and Jesse told her about Alexandra's Alzheimer's diagnosis. It turned out that she'd learned a little about neurodegenerative diseases in her anatomy classes, prompted by talking with Oli about her mother, and of course she'd noticed Alexandra's symptoms herself. But she didn't really know what that meant practically.

"One day," Jesse said, "Alexandra mightn't recognize Matt or Jenny, Josh or Oli, you, or her grandchildren. Eventually she might no longer recognize even me. And she will probably be increasingly emotionally unsteady, confused, irritable, and unable to take care of herself."

Maddy gently bounced Jessie on her knee as she absorbed this.

"How fast does this happen?" she asked.

"We don't know," said Jesse. "It's different for everyone. We just have to take it step by step. But it seems to have been a rapid decline so far."

"Can I talk with Ali about it?"

"Not yet. Alexandra wants to tell everyone together, and I'm not sure when she'll choose to do that. I'm trying to convince her to talk with everyone later today, after the babysitter brigade arrives."

Maddy didn't seem upset. Jesse couldn't discern whether that was because she didn't really understand dementia or because she had some special perspective on Alexandra's unfolding life reality.

Alexandra did agree to Jesse's suggestion about timing. Right before lunch, with the kids in the basement enjoying the attention of high-school girls, the seven adults with the three babies gathered in the family room.

Alexandra got straight to the point. "It turns out that I have Alzheimer's disease," she said. "It runs in my family so it was always a possibility." She started to get upset and paused to calm down. "I think I slowed its onset as much as possible through diet and exercise. But it's clear I'm losing the battle.

"Oli," she said, "I know your mother has dementia. Between that and your medical background, I hope you'll be able to share with me what you know as we go along. I have a lot to learn about this condition."

She paused, looking around the room at her beloved family.

"I'd like us to be able to talk about this, to the extent that you want. I'll try to be open to whatever you want to say to me. And I'll try to answer your questions completely and honestly, whenever you want to ask me something."

Alexandra was silent, and Jesse asked whether anyone had anything to say. To everyone's shock, Maddy spoke.

"Ali, life has brought you this terrible thing. But life also brought you wonderful gifts, which you used to become the most beautiful, most loving woman I can imagine. You saved my life, and my children's lives. You have an amazing family, which your love created. You're my model for being a good person, a mother, and a woman. I can't picture a fuller life than yours, a better life, or a more loving life. I hope my life is half as happy as yours."

"Well," said Josh, "I guess that settles it. Tomorrow we have a party to celebrate Mom!"

The hugs that followed were teary but they were shot through with gratitude and joy. Jesse just sat there, once more, staring at Maddy in amazement. He caught Matt's eye. He seemed to be silently apologizing and Jesse gave him a little wink. He then gave Maddy a big hug and whispered his thanks to her.

CLOSE

Matt drove Jesse through light snow to the diner Josh had nominated. They found him already inside, at a booth. Before they even got their jackets off, Matt demanded to hear the news.

"Sit down first," said Josh, and they settled themselves across the table. He waved away a waitress and then launched into the story.

"Late last night I got a call from my contact in Providence. It turns out the trafficking over state lines did draw in the FBI. They've been pursuing Maddy's lead. It paid off, at least from a law enforcement perspective. They analyzed phone records, email, and social-media networks, and uncovered an entire sex-slave ring, based mostly in Rhode Island. It's built partly from kidnapped American children and partly from foreigners, all girls. Different ages and races. Last night the FBI conducted more than a dozen raids simultaneously. Almost two dozen girls were found, including some kids like Maddy who were taken when they were very young and have no memories of another life. They discovered about the same number of children born in captivity. And they dug up a bunch of bodies."

Matt's mouth gaped in horror. Jesse felt like he'd crawl out of his skin with anxiety.

"And no—they didn't find Becca, alive or dead," Josh said. "But listen, some of the girls remembered a Christina with straight blonde hair and bright blue eyes. The key might be the old woman who helped Maddy with the second birth—maybe she's the one who imprisoned Becca. But nobody has been able to identify a woman with the characteristics Maddy described. They say Charlie, the kid in jail, would help if he could but he has no memories of either person, and says he knew nothing about the ring, though he did know about outsiders visiting the basement. It's tempting to suppose there's more to the ring than the FBI has been able to identify at this point. And if that's the case, the natural worry is that people holding these girls might attempt to dispose of them quietly."

"*Wow*," Matt said.

"I know," said Josh. "It's a lot to take in."

"It is, and it also sounds like there are still a lot of loose ends," said Matt. "How long will it take to run them all down?"

"Well, I don't know about the loose ends," said Josh. "My informant says this cancer had clean boundaries so the FBI are confident they cut out the whole mass in one operation."

"That's what they thought last time!" said Matt.

"There are reports of a few other women not matching anybody who's been recovered," Josh said, "but they're from several years ago, as with Maddy's testimony about Christina, and there's nothing more recent. Those children may already have died or been sold to other people, outside this ring."

"What's the next step, Josh?" Jesse asked.

"The next step is more systematic interviews with everyone involved. Hopefully they can turn up witnesses who can fill in more details. There's also further grave-hunting to do. There's still a chance that something relevant to Becca will turn up. It's also possible that she was never involved. I mean think about it: a lot of the girls are blonde and blue-eyed—it seems to have been a prized type—so Christina might not even be Becca."

"Maddy's picture of Christina sure fits the bill, though," Matt said.

"Yes it does," said Josh. "Hopefully something breaks and they can find out more about this mysterious Christina character and the fairy-tale-witch lady. Anyway, that's all I know at this point."

They were quiet, absorbed in their own dark thoughts, until Jesse broke the silence.

"Thanks, Josh. We're lucky to have you as a connection. I wish things were otherwise but it looks as though we're back to playing the waiting game."

"We're back to waiting, yes," said Josh. "But at least there are a few leads for the FBI to follow now."

"This is so damn frustrating!" exclaimed Matt. "We seemed so close."

They decided not to say anything to Alexandra or to Maddy about the bizarre wild goose chase that had gotten their hopes up, only to dash them again. The same principle applied, given Alexandra's state of mind and Maddy's history: the right time for news of that type was when there was real news to share. But Maddy and Alexandra needed to know about the slave ring. That had been the context for the great majority of Maddy's life, after all, and telling her about it would probably involve telling Maddy something about Becca.

Later that day, Josh and Jesse sat down with Alexandra and Maddy. Jesse explained that he'd passed along Maddy's information about the two people who'd helped with her deliveries to Josh, and that Josh had contacted the police. Josh took over the story at that point and described the extensive slave ring of which Maddy had been a victim.

"And Maddy, you need to know that you made all this possible," Josh said. "Thanks to you, almost four dozen girls and young children are free, and there are a lot of families who finally have some answers and some peace of mind."

Alexandra's face had registered increasing shock as Josh told the story. "But what about Becca?" she said. "Did they find Becca?"

Jesse reached for both her hands. "No sweetheart," he said, "They didn't." The look of fresh pain on his beloved's face was more than he could bear. Without letting go of Alexandra's hands, he quickly turned to Maddy to explain. "Maddy, you know that we have a daughter; you've seen photos of her on the wall downstairs. Becca disappeared when she was six and we've never heard from her again. When we learned about other people involved in your captivity, we wondered whether this might have been something that affected Becca, too. As it turns out, there are no signs of Becca anywhere in this mess, dead or alive. But that's a side story. The main point is that so many people are now free, and the remains of many others have been found, bringing some sort of closure to their families."

There was a long pause before Maddy spoke. "So all those men who… visited… they might have had chained-up slaves like me?"

"Maybe," said Jesse. "Or your captors might have been doling out favors or making money from doing that. We just don't know."

"Do you have more photos of Becca?" asked Maddy.

"Yes," Jesse replied, "and some home movies. You're welcome to look at them if you want."

"Yes, that's good," Maddy said. "I'm sorry you and Ali lost your daughter. I hope you find her alive one day."

"We hope that, too, Maddy," Jesse said. "But the waiting and the uncertainty have been incredibly painful for our family. What really gives us hope is you and your ability to reconstruct your life with integrity and courage. You remind me that sometimes people can come back from these brutal situations, that they can answer evil with love and kindness."

Alexandra asked whether it'd be a good time to watch one or two of those old home videos. Josh jumped up to organize the event. Michael, Walt, and Rebecca might be old enough to appreciate seeing their grandparents, aunt, and uncles as much younger versions of themselves.

Later that day, Jesse handed Maddy their special Becca photograph album. He and Alexandra sat down either side of her as she moved through the pictures.

"She was only a year and a half older than you, Maddy," said Alexandra. "I think the two of you would have been good friends."

Maddy smiled and squeezed Alexandra's hand. "I think so too, Ali."

Jesse took a deep breath and decided to break his earlier resolution not to involve Maddy too closely in their Becca troubles.

"Maddy, when I saw your sketch of Christina," he said, "I wondered whether it might be Becca. Of course, we never knew exactly what Becca would look like at age sixteen or seventeen, when Michael was born. Blonde-haired, blue-eyed girls seem to have been a favorite target of the group that stole you, so we really had no way of knowing whether Christina was Becca. But I do want you to know that several people rescued in the FBI raids recalled meeting a few people who hadn't been recovered, and one of them was a girl named Christina. Unfortunately, the last report of Christina being alive was from more than two years ago, and nobody has been able to dig up any more information about her. I know she was special to you and I was hopeful that she'd be found, but that hasn't happened, at least not yet."

"The police could find out more, though, right?" Maddy asked.

"Josh seems to think so, and it makes sense to me. The FBI might also recover Christina or Becca from their search of grave sites. But it's difficult to know where else to look without cooperation from the perpetrators, so the interviews are probably quite important."

They looked at the picture album together. Maddy reached out her hands and took theirs.

The following day, eleven people gathered on the porch to wave goodbye to the six who were leaving. Matt and Jenny, with Walt, Abby, Millie, and Jake, made their way to the airport, and then home to San Francisco. Their visit had been a slice of life, with amazing highs and terrible lows.

Josh didn't have to go back to work until the day after New Year's Day so they'd enjoy one another's company for a little longer.

Maddy and Oli had been hatching big plans for a New Year's Day feast. It was so heartwarming to see them bustling around the kitchen, often with babies in slings, chatting away. Despite the almost ten-year age difference, they had become fast friends.

Meanwhile, Alexandra and Jesse bore the double burden of waiting in agony for Becca to come back to them, and the encroaching darkness of disease, hoping against hope that it would close in slowly.

Neither was to happen. Their agony of waiting continued all too slowly and Alexandra plunged all too quickly into the inky abyss.

Part VI
The Winding Way Home

THE 1,542ND BOYS' BREAKFAST

For the first breakfast of the New Year, Josh drove Jesse to a local hotel overlooking the Charles River. They sat down and connected with Matt back in San Francisco.

"Dad, Matt, I've got an agenda today," announced Josh.

"Do you need to return that ridiculous Santa Suit you bought?" cracked Matt.

"That gorgeous Santa suit is just fine, thank you very much," replied Josh. There was an awkward pause, then Josh suddenly cradled his face in both hands.

"Hey Josh, what's up?" asked Matt.

"Where's the damn coffee?" muttered Josh, looking up restlessly.

Jesse put his arm around his son's shoulders.

"Here's the thing," Josh began. "I'm not happy with Oli and I think we need to separate."

"What the fuck?" exclaimed Matt. "We were just with you! I didn't see anything wrong."

"I haven't talked to Oli about this," said Josh, "and I'm sure she doesn't suspect a thing. I'm doing what I'm supposed to do but the whole marriage thing feels wrong somehow."

"You've only been married a year and a half, for God's sake!" shouted Matt. "What could have gone wrong in that time?" Jesse looked around to see if anyone was staring at them and turned down the volume on the tablet.

"We've been together a while, Matt. Rebecca is four now. And you both know how I feel about marriage; it took me ages to pull the trigger with Oli."

"This makes no sense," declared Matt. "None whatsoever."

Jesse's mind was flooded with Matt-stack images of his oldest son trying to control his life, and he was reminded again of how closely Matt must be bonded with Josh to experience his little brother's family troubles as a threat to the stability of his world.

"Steady on, Matty," Jesse said. "Let's back up, okay? Josh, what's going on?"

Josh explained what sounded to Jesse like a premature mid-life crisis. Already at thirty-two, he was feeling trapped, his life options narrowed by the everyday routines of a family with three small children. He didn't say anything much about Oli; his focus was almost exclusively on his own state of mind. That was better than blaming her, Jesse thought. Josh went on a while until he became aware that he was talking in circles and suddenly lapsed into silence, shaking his head, disgusted with himself.

"Little Bro," said Matt, "what you're describing as a fate worse than death is something that most people prize as the height of life satisfaction. You've completely lost it."

Harsh. True, but harsh. Matt probably saw Jesse wincing because he added, "Sorry Josh. I know you're in pain. But you're driving me nuts here. Are you really gonna throw all this away?"

Jesse pondered how Matt delivered feedback to co-workers, Jenny, or his kids. He tried a different approach. "Josh, why haven't you tried talking to Oli about this?"

"How can I? She's damn near perfect. She never gets tired of loving everyone and taking care of me and the kids. If I tell her this, she'll despise me as a moral weakling." Jesse winced internally, hearing words that could have come from his own mouth about Alexandra. "She's my best friend and I can't even talk to her about this," Josh went on. "I'm so fucking lonely at home."

"Don't do anything stupid, Josh," said Matt.

Jesse waved away an approaching waitress.

"Oli loves you, Josh, right?" Jesse said.

Josh nodded, his eyes full of tears.

"Talk to her, son. Find a way. She'll be there for you. If you can fake it, she might be hiding frustrations, too. Be there for each other. Then do two things. First, get some professional help. Matt's right that you shouldn't want to throw away a hard-won life on an impulse. I suspect Oli will be totally there for you. She'll want to go on this journey of uncertainty with you. Trust your love for her and her love for you. Second, everyone goes nuts with young children. Let's figure out a way for you and Oli to get away – say, once a month. Your mom and I can take care of the kids for a weekend and you two can bust out and remember what it's like to be young and carefree."

Josh half-smiled, grimly, eyes shining with tears. He squeezed his father's hand.

"Josh," Matt said, "how about coming out here one weekend and the four of us can go away somewhere? I can get the nanny to take care of the kids."

Josh didn't reply. Jesse watched Matt spiraling into the painful chasm of belated self-awareness—one more time.

"Hey, I'm sorry, ok?" Matt said. "I'm sorry."

Josh nodded. "It's okay, Big Bro. I know."

IT'S A GOOD QUESTION

Shortly after Josh's revelation, it was Michael's first real birthday. The date was January fifteenth, Becca's birthday, as determined at Boys' Breakfast the previous October. Since that time Josh had arranged a birth certificate for Michael as part of the state services to Maddy's family.

Little Jamie had also been assigned a birthday, based on Maddy's memory of her having been born in the warm part of the year. She'd be deemed three years old in the world of officialdom on the anniversary of Becca's disappearance, July sixteenth, 2025.

While browsing the Michael stack in meditation, working on adding a visualization of Michael's first real birthday celebration, Becca showed up.

"We should celebrate my birthday too," Becca said. "We can do a double birthday, Michael and me together."

"We never celebrate your birthday," Jesse said.

"It'll be okay, now," she said.

Becca wasn't the only one who thought that way. When Jesse raised it, everyone liked the idea. Somehow, involving Michael made all the difference. Maddy, who was fascinated by Becca, was especially enthusiastic.

Josh and Oli and their kids came over for the party. They were joined by Shondra, Michael's main teacher. They set up a video call with Matt and Jenny and the kids in San Francisco. They'd pulled Walt out of kindergarten at lunchtime so he could participate because Walt was Michael's closest friend in the world.

Jesse was relieved that Maddy and her kids now knew about Becca. The new transparency allowed everyone to resume the matter-of-fact inclusion of Becca in their daily living and talking. But transparency only went so far. Jesse still wasn't telling any of them about the Becca apparition that kept him company most evenings. Chester the Chicken certainly wouldn't have approved if he had.

Michael was pleased to be the birthday boy. He loved receiving presents, which he opened in the same cautious manner that had been evident at Christmas and at Maddy's birthday. Maddy had to restrain Jamie from speeding up the unwrapping process. Michael enjoyed the way they talked about the strange beginning of his life, calling him the winter child, and downplaying the artificial, yet now official, date of birth.

Becca came up, in passing. Josh and Jesse told a couple of stories about her but they kept it brief and then switched the attention back to the winter child who was actually with them. The cake and the presents were all about Michael. Maddy had baked the cake and Michael blew out the six candles precisely, one at a time.

Not long after, Shondra convened a meeting to revisit the question about whether Maddy should send Michael to public school in September. Shondra assured everyone that Michael was ready for first grade, so the question came down to whether he was willing to leave the family for part of the day and whether Maddy was prepared to expose him to socialization processes about which she harbored serious reservations.

"We've been hiding here," Maddy said. "It's impossible for Michael and me to decide about school unless we get out of the house and explore."

"Sounds right," said Shondra. "We can do outings if you want. Like school outings."

"We can help," said Alexandra. "What do you have in mind?"

"We should go on walks with the big stroller the doctor gave us," said Maddy.

"That should be fine in good weather," said Shondra.

"You told us about the Children's Museum and the Science Museum," Maddy said to Shondra. "We should go to those places, too."

"That's no problem. We can do that in almost any weather," Shondra said.

"You two have been focused on me and my kids, and your own children," Maddy said to Jesse and Alexandra. "You can invite your friends over and we can meet them and get used to new people."

Alexandra looked at Jesse, stunned. But that's what they did. Maddy and her family got to know Alexandra and Jesse's friends, their neighborhood, and two of the most wonderful museums for children anywhere. They went slowly at first, always at Maddy's pace. By the summer, approaching the first anniversary of their escape, she and Michael had made their decision. The world was strange and sometimes scary. But Michael would attend public school beginning in September.

As expected, friends of the family were extremely supportive of Maddy's art business, and nobody blinked at the $450 price tag for a first-rate eighteen-by-twenty-four-inch sketch of a child. Sometimes they had sketches of themselves done, too. There was a huge backlog of work as soon as Maddy launched her business.

Her life-skills lessons on running a small business were paying off. She learned how to use a finance program to track income and expenses relative to a simple budget, and she also figured out how to calculate projected revenue, expenses, and profit using a spreadsheet program. She set up personal and business bank accounts. She obtained her own business and personal credit cards, with Jesse as co-signer. A friend of Jesse's set up a web site for her. Another friend donated accounting services and yet another business cards and letterhead design.

Through dinner parties and portraits, Maddy's silent watchers, her dedicated supporters, could meet her and get to know her at last. Nobody explained to Maddy how these ordinary, wonderful people felt towards her and her children, how vigilant they were, how compassionate and prayerful. But Maddy started to catch on to how welcome she was in that little community. Her dawning awareness was included into Jesse's Maddy-stack visualization of a dynamic support network, flexible and skillful, graceful and non-intrusive, an entire village silently arrayed around Maddy and her family, invisible, fiercely protecting their little household.

Most of Maddy's portraits were with live subjects at first. But as Maddy's web site displayed more of her work, people also took advantage of her ability to create sketches based on photographs. She asked for several photographs from different angles and in different lighting conditions, and she also requested a photo that showed the particular pose her clients wanted. Quite a few family friends soon had sketches of their children both when they were younger, based on photographs, and at their current ages.

Maddy's built-in childcare arrangement allowed her to maintain an average weekly pace of four sketches during the first part-year, from March to December. Those 170 works of art brought in about $70,000, allowing for discounts to repeat customers. She had almost no business or personal expenses. She was sharply aware of this but she was not interested in changing the arrangement. She understood that the point was security for her and her children, and that Alexandra and Jesse were as committed to that goal as she was.

It was with survival in mind that, in June of that first year of the business, after three months of producing sketches for clients, Maddy worked with her life-skills teacher to calculate a realistic family budget, as if she were living on her own. She assumed normal expenses for a single mother with three young children, renting in a cheaper part of Boston, funded solely by projected business revenue, with business expenses held to a skimpy, probably unrealistic, 30% of revenue. She factored in saving for college and retirement. She then sat Jesse down and showed him the result.

The numbers were sobering, and Maddy knew it.

"When the kids get older, I can take on more commissions," she concluded. "But sooner or later I'll have to advertise to get new clients, which will increase my expenses. There's not enough money to survive. The only solution is more commissions and charging higher prices. But I've been learning about the market and I really don't think I can charge more than I'm already charging. So how the fuck do artists make a living?"

Jesse hadn't heard her cuss in a while. "As I understand the art world," he answered, "most artists don't make anywhere near as much as you're making. They survive because they have other sources of income, such as spouses with professional careers. Or they don't have children to support and can live with very low expenses." Jesse wanted to tell her about Josh's inquiries into her mother's estate but he still wasn't sure how much of a long shot that was. He hadn't received an update from Josh or Peter in several months.

"So one solution is to find a rich husband," she said. "Like that's going to happen."

"Maddy," Jesse ventured, "I really don't think finding a wealthy husband who'd be willing to support you and your children would be that much of a challenge for you. The problem is more likely to be that you mightn't be happy."

She looked right at his face, which was unnerving because it was rare.

"The problem is that I never want a man to touch me as long as I live."

"Maddy, have you talked to your therapist about this?"

"I told her what I just told you."

"Are you open to a conversation about it now, with me?"

"Yes."

"Okay, then. I have a question. I think it's an important question but I'm not sure if I know how to express it clearly so it might take me a couple of tries. The thought of a man touching you is repellant, right?"

"What's that?"

"Disgusting, horrible."

"Yes," she said.

"In your mind, can you separate sex in general from sex with a man who forces you?"

"What do you mean?"

"I'm asking whether you have any sexual feelings or thoughts or desires at all, separately from your memories and experiences of sex at the hands of the men who enslaved you. I'm trying to help you think about whether your sexual feelings have completely shut down or whether they're still active but complicated by your experiences and memories. My understanding is that people can react to your kind of trauma in either of those ways."

"I get it," she said. "It's a good question."

Jesse marveled at how practical she could be under intense psychic pressure. "You don't actually need to tell me the answer," he said. "My point is that you might want to think about it, and maybe talk with your therapist about it."

"I'll tell you the answer," she declared. "It's that I don't know. I haven't had sexual feelings that weren't forced on me. Ever. Not in that basement and not since. I felt horrible about feeling anything when I was forced to feel things, until I realized that it was all about bodies and nothing to do with who I really am. I hated the pain, too, and I found it harder to distance myself from the forced pain than from the forced pleasure. Most of all I hated Michael and Jamie watching. I had to pretend not to be upset to reassure them both. Near the end, Michael tried to protect me by jumping on one of the men, but he beat Michael and threw him into a corner."

She was breathing fast and now paused.

"I don't think I'll know the answer to your question until I actually feel something sexually that isn't forced on me. I suppose I might still be able to feel things but I might not. At the moment, though, I don't care about finding out. I just want to take care of the kids and stay safe."

"Right. That makes sense. And for the record, I'm not recommending that you embark on a quest for a wealthy husband, or a wealthy wife, for that matter. Just to be clear."

They chuckled, wryly.

Jesse felt crushingly aware of the fact that Maddy had chosen to talk about this with him and not with Alexandra, who was playing with Jamie in another room while Jessie slept. The entire family structure was reconfiguring around Alexandra's horrible disease, like a body healing around a bullet that couldn't be surgically removed.

Jesse found Alexandra on the floor with Jamie and sat down behind her. She leaned against him and carried on chatting with her young charge. He wrapped his arms around her waist, pulling her back into his chest and hanging his chin on her shoulder, watching Jamie. Alexandra held his enclosing arms tightly.

He synced his breathing with hers, closed his eyes, and visualized the biochemical devastation occurring in her brain at that very moment, mere inches from his own. He scooted along the surface of an intimately familiar meditation state, dominated by the Alexandra stack, his mind filled with memories of their life together, tracking one another through the meandering pathways of personal development. He pictured the relentless disassembly of those memories in Alexandra's mind, and was flooded with loneliness.

He felt empty, abandoned.

Late in the afternoon, Jesse called Josh about Peter's work on Maddy's inheritance case.

"I'd hoped to have definitive news for you in about ten days," Josh began. "Here's where things stand, as of a few days ago. Peter has all the documents from the estate and from the non-profit sole beneficiary of Maddy's mother's will. He says the non-profit put the $2.1 million into operating expenses and fairly liquid investments, not into a permanent endowment fund; the group has no endowment, by policy, and their operations expand and contract depending on their revenue. Peter's spoken with their legal representative repeatedly and at length. He says the non-profit feels caught in a terrible bind. They argue that helping a rescued person isn't part of their remit; their job is to help find people who're still missing. At the same time they know that Peter has them over a barrel in the world of public relations. We could go to the press with this story and close them down because nobody would ever donate to them again, knowing what they had, or hadn't, done. But Peter insists that making that threat explicit would be counterproductive, possibly destroying any chance we have of reaching a settlement."

"I see," said Jesse. "What about going to probate court?"

"That's an option," said Josh. "But it's complicated. Let me see if I can conference Peter in."

Peter happened to be available, and explained the challenges surrounding taking Maddy's case to court.

"The first problem is the timing," he began. "We're way past the statute of limitations for contesting a will, which is very short in Massachusetts. Even so, under these extraordinary circumstances, I think it likely that a judge would recognize as valid our reason for a late filing to contest the will. But there's a very great risk associated with contesting the mother's will because the grounds for contestation are complicated, and once we go to court we probably lose the chance to negotiate a friendly settlement with the non-profit."

"The grounds for contesting the will seem pretty obvious to me," Jesse said.

"Not so, Jesse," Peter replied. "Current state law doesn't envisage this situation and there's no existing case law for guidance. What does exist is a very strict rule about what kinds of complaints are allowed. The only admissible complaint in Maddy's case is probably that the mother was not of sound mind when she wrote the will, in the very specific sense that she assumed her daughter was dead, contrary to fact. That's easy for us to prove, obviously, but it isn't obvious that a judge could accept our evidence under the existing statute. We might argue that the mother's lawyer misled her by not making allowance in the will for the possibility that her daughter would reappear, but that would probably take us right out of probate court and into a malpractice lawsuit against the lawyer involved. If I'd been able to uncover any relationship between the lawyer and the non-profit suggesting that the lawyer proceeded improperly in advising the mother to leave Maddy out of her will, then we'd have another possible approach to contest the will before the court. But that hasn't worked out, either."

"Okay, bottom-line it for me. What's the best strategy?" Jesse asked.

"I think we're initially best off using non-binding mediation both with the non-profit and with the lawyer who drafted the will. Our aim would be to recover the entire $2.1 million from both sources combined, without laying formal blame at anyone's doorstep. If that doesn't work, or produces too low a settlement, then we have to gamble on taking the matter to the court, hoping they'll accept a very late complaint against the will, agree with our argument about the mother's state of mind that led to the unintentional exclusion of her daughter, and help us recover as much of the money as possible. I have a three-way meeting scheduled, which includes representation from the lawyer's malpractice insurance company. Jesse, the reason I think this is the best way to proceed is that there's such good will toward Maddy. Nobody wants to exacerbate the difficulty of her situation."

"Okay. You're keeping Maddy out of it as much as possible, right?" asked Jesse.

"Yes, Josh has stressed that point with me," said Peter. "If things go to plan, Maddy will only need to be involved at the point when we approve the settlement, if one ultimately emerges from this tangle."

After Peter left the conference call, Jesse asked Josh whether he thought the plan would work.

"Dad, I think he's approaching this in the best possible way, and our people here agree. Maddy has a real chance of getting something from a settlement without going to court."

Jesse thanked him for taking such good care of Maddy and then switched gears.

"How's the marriage counseling going? It's approaching six months, right?"

"It's good," said Josh. "Oli has totally been in my corner. It's become the two of us battling something together instead of me feeling as though my marriage is falling apart."

"It's important to know where the problem really lies," said Jesse.

"Matt was right, too," said Josh. "About not throwing away something as wonderful as a loving wife and three young children. I don't know what I was thinking."

"It's easy to panic when things feel wrong," said Jesse. "I'm glad you and Oli are together in this now. Okay, sorry to jump around, but back on Maddy... Do you think I should be speaking with her about the estate case? I'm worried she might be angry that we're all attempting to help her without her knowledge. But I'm also concerned about adding to her stress."

"I don't think you have to worry," Josh said. "Maddy trusts us and knows we have her best interests close to our hearts."

"It does seem that way," Jesse said. "Anyway, we'll know more soon so I might as well leave things as they stand for now."

"You worry too much," Becca said, in a teasing voice, suddenly intruding as Jesse ended the call. "Lighten up!"

"Easy for you to say," Jesse thought-said. "You can float any time you want to."

"Anytime you want me to, you mean," she said.

"Let's see," he said, playfully, and sure enough, off she floated.

"You've still got the knack," she giggled, flying around the room.

I DON'T REMEMBER THEM

Jesse hadn't planned to retire but Alexandra's health situation and the need to care for Maddy and her family had forced the issue. The family was arranging a family-and-friends retirement party for the weekend following July sixteenth, 2026, which was Jamie's first proper birthday on her specially assigned summer-child date, and also the seventeenth anniversary of Becca's disappearance. Matt and Jenny were coming across the country with their kids again. They were also inviting a few of Jesse's close friends to one meal within the party weekend, at Maddy's insistence.

Jesse's colleagues were shocked that he was retiring because he was productive in terms of teaching, publication, and administration, and he had a lot of doctoral students. They didn't know about Alexandra's situation but word had spread about their new family structure and everyone assumed that was the reason for the decision.

Thankfully, Jesse had been awarded emeritus status, which meant he retained certain privileges in the university, including library access and the right to teach more or less whenever he wanted. He'd continue to take care of his existing doctoral students; he just wouldn't take on any new ones.

Jesse was resolved to enjoy this new phase of his academic career. He'd have no distracting administrative responsibilities and he wouldn't teach classes. He could focus on writing. He could also invest in his personal spiritual quest. His meditation practice was deepening, and he was constantly expanding his skills in visual simulation building, simulation stacking, and stack merging. He was making progress and it was paying off for him. He felt more centered and purposeful, more peaceful and joyful.

Anna Feld called in June, earlier in the year than her traditional anniversary-of-Becca's-disappearance call around mid-July.

"I heard that the first woman recovered from the Rhode Island sex-slave ring, Madeline, is living with you," she said.

"Is that so?"

"Jesse, the state has blocked information about Madeline to protect her privacy, and I fully understand. But this information just dropped into my lap and, given that I know you, I thought I'd reach out. I'd love to do a story on her and her recovery. You know me well enough to be confident that I'd handle it sensitively."

Jesse was silent, feeling incredibly worried and frustrated all at once. He decided to throw all his cards on the table.

"Anna, please don't do this. Maddy is extremely fragile. She needs space and privacy. Please, Anna."

"I hear you, Jesse. But think about this. There could be a lot of money in this for Maddy and her children. She'd care about that, right?"

"She doesn't have concerns about money, Anna," he lied. "She's worried about safety and survival. Can you let this one go?"

"I can let it go, at least for now," she said. "But think about what I'm proposing, will you? Anything might be possible, from a book deal to high-priced interviews on television news magazine programs."

"I'll think about it," he said. "And I promise I'll discuss it with Maddy. But trust me: now isn't the time, okay? And please don't attempt to track her down. It will freak her out."

"Okay," she said. "I'm sorry for intruding. By the way, Jesse, I'm also sorry that nothing about Rebecca has come to light through all of this. I'd been hoping there'd be some resolution for you and your family."

"Thanks, Anna," said Jesse, wondering if she'd been fishing for information about Becca under the guise of an apology. He chided himself, recalling that Anna's good deeds warranted a high degree of trust. "If things change with Maddy, I'll let you know, okay?"

"That's good enough for me," she replied.

╬

A few days before the grand party weekend, Jesse received a call from Josh, with Peter already on the line.

"Dad," said Josh, "it's all over. We don't need to take this to court. We got everything we wanted."

"Josh, that's amazing! Peter, how did you do it?"

"Basically," Peter said, "the two other parties decided to split the $2.1 million evenly. I thought the non-profit was going to push for more from the lawyer's side but I think they really grasped that they never should have received any of the money in the first place, so keeping half of it was a pretty good outcome for them. The non-profit will pay a bit over a million, in three installments, with the first payment of $500,000 due by the end of June this year, and the following two installments splitting the remainder due at the end of June in the next two years. The lawyer's insurance company will pay its million and a bit immediately, which in practice probably means a couple of months from now. The lawyer who drafted the will is probably in a bit of trouble. Nobody wanted this story to go to the media before it was resolved, and I didn't even need to make the threat explicit. It was a fast and congenial negotiation process because there had been some behind-the-scenes haggling between the non-profit and the lawyer's malpractice insurance representatives."

"You've got to meet Maddy and tell her this news yourself," Jesse told Peter.

"I'd love to do that," said Peter. "I've been staring at nothing but paper and other lawyers for months. I need her to sign some documents, anyway. I have them drafted already and I can come over today, if she's available. I take it she still doesn't know about this."

"Right," Jesse confirmed.

"Okay!" said Peter. "This should be a very interesting conversation. I'll see you soon."

When Peter arrived, Alexandra pulled Maddy away from her lessons and Jesse made introductions.

"Maddy, I'd like you to meet Peter, a good friend of mine, and indirectly of yours. Peter is a lawyer. I've been unsure whether or when to speak to you about this, sweetheart, and please forgive me if I've handled it poorly. But your mother had a will, and Josh asked Peter to investigate. It turns out she gave her entire estate— that's what was left after she died—to a non-profit organization dedicated to finding missing children, and she did this in memory of you, believing you had died. That was a mistake, obviously, and the lawyer who advised her is partly to blame for it. Peter has been trying to sort this out. Josh and I haven't been keeping you up to date because recovering any of the money seemed like such a long shot and we didn't want to get your hopes up."

Jesse nodded toward Peter.

"Maddy, we have great news for you," Peter said. "The lawyer and the non-profit are going to share the cost of paying back all of your mother's estate to you, the rightful heir. It's going to take a couple of years to recover the full amount, but I'll make sure that it all arrives eventually. The first payment will come in a few days, the lawyer's payment a few weeks after that, and then two more payments this time next year and the year after. All we need to make this real is for you to sign the settlement agreement."

Maddy was speechless.

"Tell her how much it is, Peter," Jesse said.

"It's $2.1 million," Peter said.

Maddy started to cry into Alexandra's shoulder, not the just-tears crying Jesse had seen before but a new kind of crying, complete with heaves and sobs and shakes.

When she'd calmed down, Peter added a few details, including that signing meant she couldn't talk about this settlement to anyone. She tried to read the document but couldn't understand it. Eventually, with Peter's assurances, she just signed it, with Alexandra and Jesse as witnesses.

"Peter," Maddy said, "do you have children?"

"Sure do," Peter replied "Three kids, all under seven."

"Can I create sketches of them for you?" asked Maddy.

"I've heard about your portraits, Maddy, and I'd be honored! And listen, there's something else. I worked hard with Josh and your mother's lawyer to locate anything that might have survived your mother's death—anything at all to help you remember her or your father. I'm now virtually certain that all her personal effects were destroyed because there was no family to receive them and because nobody else was interested in photographs and mementos, or thought to keep them for you. All we found was a single photograph of you as a baby with your mother and father. It had been given to the non-profit with your mother's bequest and they'd mounted it with a plaque in their offices. It was their suggestion to reproduce the photograph for themselves and to give you the original."

Peter reached into his briefcase and handed Maddy a package. Maddy carefully unwrapped it and stared at the elegantly framed photograph.

"I don't remember them." She said it so quietly.

Peter stood to leave and held out his hand to shake Maddy's. Jesse suddenly realized he hadn't coached Peter about not initiating contact with her, the way he did with their dinner-party guests. After a slightly awkward pause, and possibly recalling her life-skills training, Maddy reciprocated.

Later that day, while Alexandra was playing with Michael and Jamie before bed, Maddy tracked Jesse down in his office. She sat in the leather recliner while Becca floated away and settled on another chair.

"This changes everything," she said. "Now I don't need to worry. Instead I need to plan."

"That's exactly right, Maddy," he replied. "I checked with your life-skills people and they don't have expertise in investment decisions and long-term financial planning, which is what you need now. But I have a friend from church who's a certified investment advisor and also a certified financial planner. I haven't spoken to her about your new situation but I know she'd be willing to help you."

"Okay," Maddy replied.

They lapsed into a comfortable silence again. Becca was smiling happily at them and Jesse wondered whether Maddy would still trust him if she knew he was hallucinating the woman who might very well be her Christina. Eventually, Maddy turned to look at him.

"You did this," she said, matter-of-factly.

"Actually," Jesse replied, "Josh and Peter did it. Josh used his connections to figure out what had happened originally, and I brought Peter on board, which he did at no cost. So it was all Josh and Peter."

Maddy looked right at him, with a half-smile.

"I want to keep doing my art," she said. "And now I don't need to worry about my revenue flow. I think I'll enjoy it more. I can also expand my product line."

"Listen to you!" he teased. "Using all those fancy business phrases. What's happened to you in the last few months?!"

She smiled and placed her feet on the recliner's matching footstool, settling in for a longer conversation. But she was quiet for a while, leaning back in the chair.

After a couple of minutes, Maddy turned to face Jesse. Her eyes were filled with tears and what she said next came tumbling out quickly.

"Would you adopt me?" she asked. "I want you to be my father and I want Ali to be my mother. I want Matt and Josh to be my brothers and Jenny and Oli to be my sisters. I want to be an aunt to their children and I want my children to have a family." She paused before continuing.

"I stared at that photo of my mother and father and me. I have no memory of them. They didn't even call me Madeline. And now they're dead. It made me feel so alone, all over again. The only family I know is yours. I want to belong to you and Ali and your boys and everyone, and I want you all to belong to me."

Jesse's eyes filled with tears. They looked at one another, smiling with simple affection.

"Alexandra and I would be honored to adopt you, Maddy," he said.

She burst into tears. "Can I call you Mom and Dad?" she said.

"Of course, sweetheart," said Jesse. "That'd be very special for us."

She rose from her recliner and knelt beside Jesse's, leaning over the arm rest to hug him. It was a long, tight hug, and she was still sobbing, but gradually she calmed down as she allowed him to caress her hair.

"It's going to take a while to get used to calling you Dad," she said with an uncertain laugh as they disentangled. Jesse chuckled gently and she returned to her seat.

"Can I switch the conversation in a new direction?" he asked.

"Yes," she replied.

"I noticed that you shook Peter's hand when he offered it today. That's a first for you, right?"

"Yes."

"There was a bit of a pause before you took his hand," said Jesse. "In the moment, I wondered whether I should have handled the situation differently."

"It was okay. I need to figure this stuff out. It takes me a while to trust a man, as you know... When I do feel trust I can shake hands or even hug, like I do with Josh and Matt... I've gotten to know that feeling of trust; it's like relaxing inside, like the feeling I have when I'm breastfeeding... I didn't feel that today but somehow I was able to shake hands by thinking about the situation and the nice man who'd done so much to help me... But I know that nice men who I want to trust can be horrible. They start out friendly and then they turn somehow. I saw that lots of times, when my farmhouse family let strangers visit me in the cellar… It's hard to know what a man is really thinking, or what he'd really do if he could act without being seen… So I don't feel that relaxing trust with a man until he proves himself to me."

She looked at him, perplexity scrawled on her face.

"My therapist says lots of women can trust when they first meet a man and only become cautious if they have to. I'd be happier if I could be that way. But I don't have control over it. I just feel tight and tense and scared around men, all the time, until that relaxing feeling happens. And it's only happened with three men so far—you, Matt, and Josh."

Jesse smiled, in a broken-hearted way, and looked at her tenderly. He could feel a new image readying itself for the Maddy stack: the hateful men of the human species, too dangerous to trust by default. He wished Maddy would draw pictures of everyone who ever abused her so the police could nail the bastards. But he remembered Josh's warning: that had to be up to her.

"Well," Jesse said, "we have two additional reasons to celebrate this weekend. Not only do we have Jamie's summer-child birthday, the traditional family gathering around Becca's disappearance, and my retirement, we also have your settlement and your adoption. I think this might be the party weekend to end all party weekends!"

"I have big plans in the kitchen with Oli," Maddy said.

"That sounds wonderful," Jesse said. "I can't wait. I'd like to switch gears again, though, if I may. We seem to have a lot to talk about today."

"Okay," said Maddy.

Jesse told her about Anna Feld, her role in their lives after Becca's disappearance, her offer to help take Maddy's story to the world, and what that might mean in terms of money.

"I don't know how she found out that you were here," said Jesse, "but something like this had to happen sooner or later. Fortunately, Anna is discreet, and her knowing where you are won't lead to reporters on our doorstep. Or at least I hope not."

"I don't need to worry about money anymore. So the only reason to talk to Anna would be if I want to get my story out, right?" Maddy asked.

"Right," answered Jesse. "And now that a couple of dozen girls from the slave ring have been recovered alive, thanks to you, it's likely that some of them will go the publicity route, helping people understand what happened."

"I have to protect my children," said Maddy. "I don't want to turn them into a news story."

"Fair enough," said Jesse.

"Tell Anna no," Maddy said. "I don't want to talk to her, or anyone."

"Okay. I'll do as you say," Jesse replied. "Now, let's go tell Alexandra about the adoption. This will be so special for her. You can practice calling her Mom."

As they went to find Alexandra, Jesse was painfully aware that Maddy had asked him about the adoption, and they were about to inform Alexandra of their decision. It had only been a year since they first met Maddy and in that time Alexandra had gone through a precipitous decline. The person with whom Maddy had shared so many intimate conversations during her early days living with them was gone. Maddy still spent much more time with Alexandra, but now substantive conversation was mostly with Jesse. They gave Alexandra information but didn't expect her to participate in complex decisions. She took care of the kids but the adults monitored her closely because she would often get confused doing even simple tasks. Jesse sighed under the weight of creeping, accumulating, anticipatory grief.

Matt and Jenny and the children flew out on the Wednesday before the big party weekend, the very day of Maddy's windfall and the adoption decision. They arrived early on Thursday morning, July sixteenth, the anniversary of Becca's disappearance. Josh had arranged for the next two days off. They'd canceled Maddy's and Michael's classes for Thursday and Friday so everyone would have four delicious days together, with a lot to celebrate.

Alexandra had organized childcare for all four days. Arranging childcare was now a cognitively challenging task for her, and it was her only responsibility for the entire visit. She managed it with lists on paper taped to a kitchen cupboard.

After Matt and Jenny were settled in, and when Josh arrived, Jesse took the two men out for a late Boys' Breakfast.

He first shared the news about Maddy's adoption, which would shortly be underway with Peter's help. Josh was thrilled. They both looked at Matt to assess his view of the news.

"Well, what difference does it make?" he said. "My concerns are the same whether she's my adopted sister or not. I'm getting to love her, too, so I'm glad about this, okay? And stop staring at me." He half-smiled. "You're all bananas."

Josh brought Matt up to speed on the settlement, and then gave everyone an update about the FBI investigation. It was short and severe: there was no news. The hot trail they'd so hoped would lead to Becca had turned stone cold. The FBI had discovered nothing new about the old woman.

Several people recalled the woman that Maddy called Christina, but nobody had seen her for almost three years at that time. None of the captured ring members knew or were willing to say anything about her. The FBI agents on the case assumed that she'd been sold onwards in a way they couldn't trace or else had died and was either incinerated or in a grave somewhere yet to be found. None of the remains they'd found matched Becca's DNA.

Josh reported a new twist. He'd pursued the question of the biological father of Maddy's three children. It turned out that all three children had the same father: the oldest brother, now dead. They didn't know why this was, but it simplified matters somewhat that the surviving brother was the biological uncle and not the biological father of Maddy's children.

All three men were infuriated that these promising leads in Becca's disappearance had led nowhere. They were forced to keep living with her presence-absence, and they all felt it especially acutely on that anniversary day.

The penultimate topic for discussion was Alexandra's health. It had been half a year since she'd shared the news about her diagnosis with everyone in the family but even in that time the deterioration was obvious. She couldn't keep her grandkids straight, though it didn't help that they were tightly clustered in age. She could no longer drive safely and she'd get lost or confused doing things she used to do routinely. Living at home made her happy, but she was not reliable about turning off the stove and cooking was becoming cognitively challenging for her. Fortunately, at this point Jesse could take care of her and she was still a trustworthy care-giver for Maddy's children when someone else was in the house, so staying at home remained a feasible solution.

"There will come a time, though," Jesse said, "not long from now, when I'm not going to be able to care for her and when it won't be safe for her to take care of Maddy's children. You have to be ready for the moment when I'll need help finding an institutional setting for her."

"Understood, Dad," said Matt. "Can you afford to keep Mom at home if Maddy's kids might be at risk? And can you carry the financial burden of housing her in an assisted living facility or a nursing home?"

"They're the right questions, Matt," Jesse replied. "We're okay on finances, thanks in part to a very good long-term-care insurance policy that covers dementia. It won't cover all expenses, but it does ease the burden."

"Have you started looking for assisted living facilities that can handle dementia?" asked Josh.

"I haven't, no. Can you help me with that?" Jesse asked.

"I sure can," Josh said. "And we should start sooner rather than later. There's usually a long waiting list."

Jesse sighed. "She seems so young to me," he mused. "I'm awestruck at this disease and the way it takes people from us in one way while leaving them still with us in another."

Jesse's visual simulation of the progression of Alzheimer's disease was appalling. It featured the growth of amyloid plaques containing miscellaneous brain debris; clumping tau proteins inside neurons leading to neurofibrillary tangles; breakdown of synaptic communication due to decreasing production of key neurotransmitters such as acetylcholine, norepinephrine, and serotonin; the consequent isolation of neurons and cell death from that isolation; atrophy of affected brain regions; and the unstoppable evisceration of cognitive and emotional function. It gave him the creeps but he had incorporated it into his Alexandra stack. Love what is, he told himself. It was his faith: love what is.

The final topic was a check-in with Josh about his marriage. In previous check-ins, Jess and Matt had learned that Josh had talked to Oli, almost immediately after the January breakfast revelation. Unsurprisingly, Oli had noticed subtle ways in which Josh had seemed unhappy, and she'd been relieved that Josh was finally communicating. She had her own feelings of being trapped and desperate, which Josh had failed to notice, so a much-needed conversation began. From time to time at Boy's Breakfast, he'd shared insights gained from their marriage counselor. And that day he seemed back to normal. "I can truthfully say we're stronger than ever," Josh concluded.

"Despite you being an idiot," declared Matt.

Josh shook his head. "Dude," he said, "whatever you do, don't ever become a marriage counselor, okay?"

Jenny and Oli practically hugged the life out of Maddy when they learned the news of Maddy's adoption. There was a special warmth and excitement among the women as they worked in the kitchen. The three sisters had claimed the space as their own.

Alexandra and Jesse watched through the serving window as the women bustled about, the much younger Maddy not hesitating to give instructions—matter-of-factly, without any bossiness. She was doing her job and Jenny and Oli were happy to defer.

Alexandra squeezed Jesse tight as they watched. He could feel her desperately trying to record the moment, fighting the rising fear that such simple joys would soon be stolen from her. He kissed the top of her head while she watched and then she relaxed, laying her head on his shoulder. Already her life was becoming so simple that what she was feeling was rarely difficult for him to sense.

The meal was a joyful ruckus. The high-school babysitters had the children at one table, attempting to control proceedings. Jake had turned one a couple of weeks earlier and Kate was four days away from doing so. Both were walking in that zombie way young toddlers do, with arms up high, body weight tossed from one foot to the other. Jessie was almost nine months old and crawling. The three babies were great fun for the teenaged sitters, and they handled them in highchairs along with the older children. The grownups made the most of their much quieter table.

Everyone could feel Alexandra becoming less and less at the functional center of the network, and Jesse more and more. But she still ruled without ordering, set the finest imaginable example of kindness and devotion, and handled the degeneration of her mind with dignity and openness. She was utterly free of the kind of misplaced pride that might have made things awkward for the rest of them. She was equally free of self-pity. In both respects she was the precise opposite of Chester the pride-obsessed chicken, and thus of Jesse. She invited her family into her experience and they loved her all the more for it.

Alexandra was also the one who'd made everything happen in their family, while Jesse was off building an academic career. She was the one everyone would consult about schedules, the decision-maker and designer, the hub for the family spokes. Jesse funded it all but was not great with organizing things, unless it was a research project or a faculty committee process. He just had to hope they could all figure out a new family structure, together.

Despite his complicated feelings of inadequacy, and his despair about Alexandra, Jesse was also very happy. He watched Becca flitting around as if she were so full of joy that she couldn't decide where to focus her attention, a reflection of his internally giddy state of mind.

ETERNAL-NOW

A few short years later, just before their forty-fifth wedding anniversary, the whole family gathered for Christmas and made plans to stay together into the new year. This would be a big year: January marked Alexandra and Jesse's wedding anniversary, Becca's twenty-eighth birthday, and Michael the winter-child's eleventh birthday.

It was a momentous time of life for Jesse, not that his family would really grasp why. The final part of his multi-volume magnum opus had just been published and, about to turn seventy, he finally felt that he'd finished the bulk of his academic labors. All his scholarly training and the accrued effects of his long intellectual effort had been poured into those volumes. Now he was at peace. Anything from here would be a bonus.

Alexandra was seventy-two. She'd been housed in a nearby assisted living facility for the last few years. She often confused Matt and Josh, she often called Maddy by Becca's name, and sometimes she didn't even recognize her children. She didn't know her grandchildren anymore, but she tried to be kind when they were introduced, usually as if it were the first time. She was still fairly healthy but her mind was failing badly. She couldn't do much to take care of herself. She was sometimes testy, suffering from erratic behavior, though she never behaved that way around strangers, which often enough was the way she regarded her own family. Jesse didn't mind her mood swings, even on the occasions when she directed her hostility at him. He just waited a few minutes and it passed, and usually she didn't even realize what had happened.

The worst times were when Alexandra remembered bits of her life, when she recognized saying something nasty, or when she was capable of picturing how complicated her condition was making things for Jesse and their children. Her lucidity left her collapsed by fear to the point of panic. If she could get past that, tears would flow and she would press mournful but needless apologies on her husband. Jesse would reassure her of his love and they would hold hands and kiss and stare at one another. Sometimes Jesse would join her in weeping. Other times he would smile gently, trying to help her transform her sudden pain into a moment of joy. If the blessedly agonizing state lasted long enough, they might talk about the children. They might recall precious moments from Becca's life. Then it would end. Alexandra would never notice when clarity was lost to her, which was a kind of mercy. But the aftermath of lucidity was sheer torture for Jesse. It felt like losing her all over again, and he could bear neither staying with her nor leaving her.

He would cling to Becca in those moments. She would weep with him as they tried to absorb the lancing pain. He couldn't fathom how lifelong lovers handled the cruel dissolution of the fabric of memory without someone like Becca to ease the burden. Becca felt the same way: Jesse helped ease her grief. But Becca was also his coach, helping him adjust emotionally to conversations thinned out and curled up by dementia. Such conversations were less agonizing than the increasingly rare episodes of lucidity but they were pervaded by nauseating isolation as Jesse sought to honor their mutual love by carrying the burden and blessing of it for them both.

It was lunchtime and Jesse was sitting opposite Alexandra in the facility's dining room. She started complaining about the food and then shouted at one of the workers. Jesse apologized to the man who was trying to help. Alexandra then looked at Jesse harshly and said, "You're completely useless." Thirty seconds later she'd recovered a calmer mood and seemed not to recall what she'd said.

"You have to learn to switch as fast as she does," said Becca.

"But I have a functioning memory," thought-said Jesse. "How am I supposed to switch?"

"It's non-attachment, viparinama dukkha to the max," she said. "You need to learn to be non-attached even to things that happened one minute ago."

Jesse was unconvinced.

"Look," his beloved apparition said, "if you can simulate me, surely you can learn to simulate lack of short-term memory."

Shondra was still tutoring Maddy. The family used her as an educational consultant for Michael, who had been attending public school since first grade, and Jamie, who was in second grade. Jesse had also hired Elizabeth, a PhD student in clinical psychology, as another way for him and Maddy to understand trauma and the process of healing in her and her older children, especially Michael. On this occasion, Maddy was meeting with Elizabeth and Shondra as well as Josh and Jesse, as they did once each month.

Jamie seemed completely normal in terms of her emotional and intellectual development, seemingly with no memories of basement life, and no hidden undercurrents of anxiety. But Michael continued to be a puzzle, as well as a point of tension between Shondra and Maddy.

"Is Michael still avoiding after-school events?" asked Shondra.

"Yes," said Maddy. "But it's fine."

Shondra glanced at the men across the table and ventured once more to help Maddy see things differently.

"Do you remember when Michael started in first grade?" she asked Maddy.

"Yes," she said.

"Lots of times he would run away from school and walk the mile back home. You'd call the school to let them know everything was alright and you'd just focus on him and cuddle. Maybe read a story."

"Yes," Maddy said again.

"You handled that brilliantly," said Shondra. "But that was then. He's in fifth grade now. He has no friends, apparently he's being bullied despite the fact that the staff is trying to protect him, and he's missing out on amazing experiences with sports and music and volunteering."

"He *wants* to come straight home after school," said Maddy.

"But look at Jamie," said Shondra. "She has friends and participates in the usual activities. That's good for her, right?"

"Yes," said Maddy. "But Michael is different. And they both do what they want."

"Okay," said Shondra with a sigh. "How are his piano lessons going? And the ping-pong?"

"He's a natural," said Josh. "I've taught him almost everything I know about both. We'll have to get a better teacher soon."

"You're a good teacher, Josh," said Maddy.

"He's still as fiercely focused as ever," added Josh. "And he's vigilant, making sure everybody is safe, at least when he's home. I've never seen a single instance of selfishness the entire time I've known him. I'm not sure what puberty will do but I suspect we're about to find out because his voice is starting to break."

Elizabeth had taught them a lot about the different ways children handle a traumatic past, especially during the period when adolescence forces upon them powerful sexual feelings and confusing identity questions. The practical bottom line was that they were doing all they could to help Michael heal. Most importantly, Maddy's own fearless example of healing was right there for Michael to behold and emulate. Even so, his future was difficult to predict.

"There's nothing wrong with Michael," said Maddy.

In the ensuing silence, Jesse's mind filled with a recent memory that had since made its way into the Maddy stack. He was taking Maddy and the family to an end-of-year Christmas concert at which Jamie and the other second-grade children were showing off their talents for doting parents. Nobody would call Maddy doting. Nevertheless, she was accompanying Jesse, along with Michael and Jessie, trying to do her parental duty in what she believed to be a socially deranged practice of building up children's egos.

They walked away from the car with Michael instinctively walking directly in front of Maddy to give her cover and holding

Jessie's hand. Maddy was clinging to Jesse's arm. As they exited the parking lot and came into open view, the gathered families turned to look at her—the stunning twenty-six-year-old blonde on the arm of an old man who was probably her father or grand-father. Her grip on Jesse's arm tightened, as it always did, and Michael slowed down, as he always did, creating less space behind him back to his mother. This formation appeared spontaneously when they were in public, without any planning: Michael in front, Jesse at Maddy's side, and the girls on the periphery. When Josh's family was present, Oli was always on the other side of Maddy, and Josh walked behind.

Jesse patted Maddy's hand. "Easy, girl. Breathe," he said.

In Jesse's simulated extension of the memory, Maddy actually did what he was afraid she might do in real life. She leapt away from him and clawed the eyes out of the most egregiously ogling man while screaming at him to stop staring at her. Michael was right behind her, attacking whatever made his mother afraid. So far she'd never lost it. Instead, she steeled herself and walked the gauntlet of eyes.

Unlike many people, perhaps, Maddy's anxiety wasn't actually about her body, or being seen. She wasn't a modest person. In fact, she might have enjoyed walking naked to confront the gawking men more directly with their own fundamentally depraved char-acter. The idea that she wasn't safe, that she didn't have *control* over her body, was what upset her. The ogling felt like violation. She had seen the thin veneer of civilized decency that separated ogling from violence and rape erased time and time again. And Michael sensed everything.

Whatever happened to chastity of the eyes? Jesse wondered, and then dragged himself back to the stalled conversation.

"You're right, Maddy," said Elizabeth. "Michael can be loyal and private and come home after school if he wants. But what if he also wants to play a sport or perform in a music concert? Would he even allow himself to feel that desire given how protective he is toward his family?"

There was another silence.

"You're saying he might not know what he wants because he's so protective of me?" said Maddy.

All four adults with her at the table nodded quietly.

"I'll talk to him," said Maddy.

Jesse kept picturing a little boy being thrown through the air into a basement corner after being beaten for attempting to stop a dangerous man from raping his chained-up mother. He pictured an undernourished five-year-old who'd never been outdoors squeezing through a tiny gap in a boarded-up basement window hole and running through the night in bare feet to find help. Maddy thought of her son in precisely those ways. So she never forced him to go to school and she never scolded him for returning home, not in first grade and not in fifth grade.

Jesse could barely take into his sorry old soul the bond between these two people. They'd looked horror in the eye for years, often side by side, trying in vain to protect one another, yet they'd survived. And they were still surviving.

The one sign of individuality Jesse had seen was the way Michael took to his piano lessons with his uncle Josh. At the keyboard he seemed to relax. He'd improvise, sometimes for hours, headphones plugged into Jesse's aging electric keyboard, on which Josh had learned to play many years earlier. Michael would practice diligently, possessing the mental discipline to stare tedium in the face and back it down, subordinating his immediate feelings to his chosen longer-term goals. His favorite subject at school was music and he was just as good at the theory aspects as he was at performance. At that time, however, he'd never performed for anyone outside of the home, not even in school bands. He avoided any activity that kept him away from his family.

Michael's over-developed sense of loyalty was even more obvious in other ways. This child simply never complained, never fought with his mother or sisters, and never failed to notice when Maddy needed something. A lot of eleven-year-old boys are good natured, thought Jesse, but there was something unnerving about Michael's goodness.

In conversations with Elizabeth, Jesse had become concerned that there was something inside Michael that limited his behavioral choices and drove the over-responsible, hyper-controlling approach to every part of his life. Despite the sweetness that charmed almost everyone he met, to Jesse he seemed in grave danger of being consumed by a dark necessity that coerced him. "Maybe it's my imagination and he's actually a saint," thought Jesse. "But I doubt it."

Michael had been in therapy for as long as Maddy, an ever-so-gentle process of conversation built around play. His therapist had given them no indication that Michael had concrete memories of basement life, though they'd discovered that he remembered events surrounding the escape.

The basement in Alexandra's and Jesse's home was light, with doors and windows opening to the outdoors, nothing like the basement of Michael's birth. Michael never hesitated to go down there—just as well because that's where the workout room, the pool table, and the table-tennis table were, Michael's only physical activities beyond compulsory physical education at school. He was already better than all of them at pool. He could beat everyone except his uncle Josh at table tennis. Michael had even started exercising, but at that age Josh wouldn't let him do anything more strenuous than dumbbells and stretching. Jesse and Josh found it weird and worrying to see an almost-eleven-year-old behaving with such focus and discipline. Maddy saw it as boy doing what he wanted to do, what he liked.

"Maddy, here's a thought," said Josh. "It's a kind of compromise. When you talk with Michael, you could suggest that he take Matt's advice and learn a martial art. That wouldn't be a school activity, which he probably wouldn't want, but it would be physical exercise, and it'd be a fun way to explore something outside the house."

"That's what Mom did, right?" said Maddy.

"Yes," said Josh. "She and Matt worked on their belts together for years, and Matt still keeps it up."

"I'll talk to Michael," she repeated, this time definitively, bringing the conversation to a close.

Almost everything was wonderful about having everyone in the house again. The only element out of place, besides Becca, was Alexandra. The family could visit her but it wasn't safe to bring her home. They arranged an indoor post-Christmas picnic for the entire family at her facility and invited her caretakers to attend as well.

The picnic was in the middle of a gentle storm, with snow falling just beyond the glass, and the assigned party room was decorated for Christmas, giving everything a festive mood. Josh and Michael played Christmas carols and songs on the piano while everyone sang along. It was the first time Michael had played for strangers, if Alexandra's nurses counted as such. Alexandra unwrapped a few small gifts they'd stuffed into a colorful stocking.

She was confused about the event but also entranced. She was socially graceful, with lots of smiles, but almost no conversation. At one point she beckoned Jesse over. He knelt in front of her wheelchair, to which she had been confined for a couple of months, though she could still walk a few steps if she absolutely needed to.

"Who are all these people?" she asked, searching his eyes.

"People who love you," he replied, laughing and standing and twirling, bringing a beaming smile to her beautiful face. She momentarily forgot her confusion. But a few minutes later she told Jesse she was tired and he arranged for her to go back to her room.

They all knew not to crowd her with goodbyes because it frightened her. But Jessie ran over to her as one of the nurses rolled Alexandra's chair away. The nurse stopped and Jessie hugged her adoptive grandmother over the arm of the chair. She reached up and placed her tiny five-year-old hands on either side of Alexandra's face.

"I love you, Grandma," she said, smiling and staring into Alexandra's eyes, as if trying to sear the moment into Alexandra's memory.

Alexandra smiled, touched the little girl's cheek, and said, "I love you, too, sweetheart."

Jessie was delighted and ran back to Maddy, leaping into her arms.

"Grandma remembers me!" Maddy lifted her up and gave her a big hug.

It was the delusion of childhood, but a sacred delusion, a holy thing.

Maddy smiled at Jesse over her daughter's tiny shoulder. Jesse smiled grimly back, turned away, and walked to the window, staring at the snow falling outside. A few seconds later he felt the strong arms of his beautiful boys around him and he started sobbing, with them.

When the men had calmed down, they turned around to find that the three women were hugging as well. True to form, Michael had herded his cousins and sisters away from the adult melee and was doling out cookies and punch while the grownups returned to their senses.

The six adults sat in a tight circle of chairs, emotionally drained, while the kids played. They briefly took stock of the day's events, concluded that things had gone very well, and reminded themselves that there was no easy way through this kind of disease.

"She was happy the whole time," Jesse said.

"Jenny and I have some news," Matt said. He looked at Jenny and she picked up the thread.

"Matt and I are moving the family back to Boston!" she said, and everyone gasped.

"How is this possible?" asked Oli.

"I landed a job with a new firm in Boston," answered Jenny. "With Jake in kindergarten I think we can swing the childcare side of things, with a new nanny obviously."

"My company is starting a Boston office and they want me to head it up," Matt said. "I'll still be traveling a lot. But I'll be based here."

"We miss you guys," added Jenny, "and our kids miss their cousins. It's time for me to return to my career and we want to be near you all."

"When is this going to happen?" asked Josh.

Matt and Jenny looked at one another and replied together, "It's complicated," making everyone laugh. But they were all going to be together again. Becca was beaming as she walked around the circle of chairs.

Right then Jesse was hit by the most extraordinary feeling of zooming outwards from that blessed moment until he was taking into his consciousness wider and wider spans of time. First his whole life with Alexandra up until that point fell open before him, followed by the lives of his loved ones; then outwards to his ancestors, to the history of his inherited cultures, and to the whole of human civilization; then further outwards to the vast swathes of evolutionary time in the planetary ecosystem; and then still further, to the cosmos unfurling within an endless multiverse. These varied perspectives were individually familiar states of mind for Jesse. He'd constructed intricate visual simulations for all of them and worked hard over the years to integrate them into his writings about the meaning of human life. He'd always found the cosmic and evolutionary framing of the personal realm to be comforting: it relativized the intensities of his little life, reminded him of the miracle of meaning in a universe hostile to its emergence through vast stretches of space and time, and sparked undirected gratitude for the islands of ecological fecundity that permit the full richness of value to emerge in the chancy orderliness of biological and cultural evolution. On this occasion, Jesse experienced the zooming feeling from the local to the cosmic in a bodily way, in his bones and in his whole being, and all of these time scales were luminously present in his mind simultaneously. It was utterly mind-blowing.

After he'd fully entered this state of awareness, cosmic reality merging with personal meaning, he elastically rebounded, zooming inwards to another odd sensory state, watching the happiness unfold before him as if in slow motion, complete with incredible detail and distorted voices getting slower and deeper. He was invaded by a vivid sense of the roaring metabolism in every cell and the ferocious pace of the biochemical world, hearing and seeing every molecular collision and every chemical reaction. Those perspectives were also deeply familiar, as he'd fought with all his intellectual might over the decades to visualize the human quest for meaning in a bodily perspective. But he felt this new state in his body, once again. It was sweeping him inwards and slowing the world down until he could trace the ribosomal machinery that sucked in mRNA and pumped out amino acid chains for other biochemical machines to fold into the protein workhorses of life. The intensity of particularity, of these special lives, of the individual creative genius of each person forcefully flooded his awareness along with the natural grace of each body and the natural miracle of metabolic pathways and living tissue and reliable organs and stunning brains.

The feeling of bodily zooming continued even deeper to the quantum landscape of possibilities, first as it governed the probabilities of chemical interactions and then as it formed the backdrop for sub-atomic interactions in the fundamental particle zoo. As he zoomed deeper, he moved smoothly from the fitful order of the subatomic underpinnings of biology to the mathematically precise chaos of the quantum vacuum that gives birth to rippling cascades of independent universes. Then he rushed through some veil and found himself back at the cosmic perspective, and on his way back in again, to the personal timescale, and further inwards to the biological and quantum perspectives, then back out and in, out and in—breathing through a gigantic cycle of wondrous, severe, tender, glorious, complex beauty. All these states of mind with all their varied time scales were co-present in a dizzying juxtaposition, testifying to the miracle of meaning and the awesome vista of its quantum-cosmic conditions. Every stack of visual simulations Jesse had ever created was there, everything overlaid, co-present, undimmed.

He felt god-like, or at least the way he imagined a being unconstrained by temporal awareness might feel. Time became a mere marker of change, effortlessly transcended. Every moment became tangible, sensible, visceral. The intensity of meaning was just the flip side of the coin of life, chaotically tumbling between a random walk through a vast possibility space and the focused achievement of love.

Jesse saw Becca flying around the room in a kind of blissful haze, her long blonde hair streaming and a long white dress flowing in some untraceable cosmic wind. As he eased out of that bizarre state of mind, he recognized that it felt right, as if he were seeing the way things truly were. Also, Becca wasn't terrifying or distorted; she was surrendering to it. It was *ananda*, bliss. He was seeing the real, the normal, in a more spectacularly intense way than ever before.

He realized at the time that he was opening up the next stage in his meditation journey. He'd learned to create potent visual simulations, to stack them without mutual interference, and to merge those stacks without loss of detail. Now he'd suddenly stumbled on a way to see processes on all time scales in a monumentally intense awareness of the present moment.

He felt as if he'd finally graduated meditation high school.

It only lasted a minute. But he knew that, from then on, he'd be able to recover the exact same "eternal-now" way of perceiving reality. He could only hope that this comforting vision of blissful surrender would accompany him at the moment of his death.

Amidst the hubbub Matt caught his eye, grinning because of the splendid gift he and Jenny were giving all of them. Jesse looked back, smiling.

"Welcome home, son," he said.

YOUR GOD IS ON ALL SIDES OF
THIS LITTLE DRAMA

Jesse was at home, asleep, when Alexandra died. The house was ready for the fiftieth wedding anniversary party later that day, which was going to take place without her. He was woken by a phone call conveying the news.

He dragged his creaky seventy-four-year-old body out of bed and sat on the edge, shaking his head. It had been a long journey, suddenly ended by a deadly heart attack. He was crying and he knew why. Alexandra had been released from her living hell at last. He was so relieved.

He dressed and went to wake Maddy. He called Matt and Josh. While the boys were driving over, in the middle of a cold winter night, Maddy sat with Jesse on the couch, her head nestled into his shoulder.

He'd always hesitated to share his personal misfortunes with people for fear that they'd say something so agonizingly stupid, so painfully insulting that he'd destroy the holy moment, and ruin friendships, through a vengeful reaction toward the insipid spiritualities of comfort. He never needed to worry about that with Maddy. She knew extreme suffering from the inside, she knew the uselessness of words, and she was fearless about silent presence. So they sat there, quietly, waiting through the confusing fog that always arises when grief is blended with relief.

In the last years before Alexandra died, the only person she recognized was Jesse. Her behavior was more frequently disturbing and she became virtually immobile. The grandchildren hadn't seen her in a while and their children couldn't visit unless Jesse was present because she became irascible.

He'd visited her at least seven times each week for the better part of a decade. He'd always share a meal with her and they'd talk about her life, now so constricted in scope. It was risky to speak about the children because it frightened her, inviting the panic of transitory lucidity. Eventually she stopped asking about Jesse. So they just chatted about her little world, often in tightly repetitive circles of conversation.

These visits were often not a lot of fun for Jesse. He was always glad to see her but she was a mere husk of the woman with whom he was still so deeply in love. It was too exhausting to allow his heart to break each time they were together so he created a routine to manage the stress. Becca would coach him through the circling conversations that result when perseveration meets ravaged memory.

On the very last occasion, the day before she died, Becca was advising him as usual.

"See how she's thinking about her hair? It's on her mind today," Becca pointed out. "Remember to flutter past the theme a hundred times, like a playful butterfly, with no intentions and no plans, just flitting, full of love."

He closed his eyes and absorbed his apparition's reminders of what he knew. He opened them and smiled at his sweetheart, the love of his life, as he was forced to watch nature have its brutal way with the beauty that nature itself had created.

"Thank God there's no God to have to weave into my narrative of this little life drama," he thought-said to Becca, drily, and she chuckled at the irony.

"Your God is on all sides of this little drama," she reminded him.

Jesse relaxed for the thousandth time as he felt the confidence of his faith buoying up within him. It was such a relief that there was no deity standing by to watch this oh-so-familiar agony unfold in appallingly slow motion. There were no invisible beings to make excuses for, no Gods to resent for allowing this to happen to his beloved, no omnipotent deities whose neglect he had to explain to his grandchildren who wisely trusted their parents more than any God, no fantasies of a better life after this one because that imagined deity didn't see fit to give the best version of life in the first place.

Still sitting beside Alexandra's bed, Jesse had slipped into his eternal-now state, which he did easily at that point. He could feel the entire sweep of the quantum-cosmic story co-penetrating the intensity of love in that little room. Becca started floating in bliss, as she always did in those moments. While in this state, he couldn't talk or move. So he eased out of it and described to Alexandra how our lives are so sublimely beautiful when their intensity takes its rise from cosmic indifference, which presses toward and against profound meaning, in all directions at once, sometimes savage and sometimes gentle, but always, always holy. He described the end of life as the dewdrop slipping silently into the shining sea. He looked deeply into her eyes, searching for traces of their shared intensity, while she looked at him politely.

"Do you like my hair?" she asked. Jesse chuckled and ran his fingers through her hair. Nobody else could touch her now, except the nurses who took care of her every day.

"Your hair is lovely, sweetheart," he said. And so their conversation ambled onwards, like a gentle stream filled with tiny eddies, while Becca helped him find the freedom he needed to drift along, aimlessly, out of endless love.

Now she was gone, her horrific spiral into nothingness over at last. Her Alzheimer's seemed like perfectly indifferent professional torture to Jesse, the torturer all business, taking no pleasure in the deconstruction of a precious personal identity, and the decline just slow enough so Alexandra could periodically feel the disintegration happening, thereby maximizing terror. He was so relieved—scared to say how relieved for fear someone would accuse him of not loving his wife, or not missing her enough.

"That'd be someone who doesn't grasp how love can long for death," Becca said.

"Soon I'll be crushed with grief," he thought-told her. "My love is dead. I'll never love another. But right now it's all about relief. And our children."

Josh met Jesse on the front porch and gave him an especially intense version of his usual warm embrace, just as Matt drove up. Maddy and the boys and Jesse hugged against the cold and then made their way inside. Jesse made coffee for the three children and they sat around the kitchen table at three o'clock in the morning. His fourth child was with them, unbeknownst to the others.

Matt asked whether they should delay the golden anniversary celebration a few days.

"No, let's do it today, just as we planned it," Josh said. "It can do double duty as a family wake."

Maddy reached out her hand across the table to touch Josh's in gratitude, smiling tenderly at her big brother. Josh grasped her hand. "How are you doing with this, Maddy?"

"I've missed Mom for a long time already," she said. "Today I'm mostly happy for her and for Dad and for all of us." She paused and started again, tears forming in her eyes. "I felt so honored when she confused me with Becca, like the two of us were merging somehow. It was my accidental gift to her. It helped ease her pain until she forgot everything. Everything except Dad." And she leaned over and hugged Jesse, still holding Josh's hand across the table.

"What about you, Dad?" asked Matt. "This has been a long time coming but everything is different when it finally happens."

"I'm relieved," he said. "Yesterday's visit was well over the three thousandth time I sat with your mother in that place, watching the disease dissolve the fabric of our life together until only the slenderest threads remained. The last thing we talked about was her hair, over and over and over again. Her beautiful hair. She let me run my fingers through it. And then we said goodbye." He choked up.

They held hands across the table and somehow there in the silence, they solidified their new family identity, the one toward which they'd been moving for over ten long years, ever since Maddy arrived and Alexandra's mind started to leave.

After the boys had left, while Maddy was preparing a light lunch for the kids, Michael tracked Jesse down in his office. He'd just turned sixteen. He was tall, dark, handsome, and blessed with a deep and resonant voice. In fact, he looked and sounded eerily like his imprisoned biological uncle, and thus probably a lot like his dead biological father. Michael knew about the physical resemblance but it didn't seem to trouble him.

He was a hardworking sophomore at the local public high school, a jazz pianist who could also play classical and maybe had the chops to go professional. He was still preternaturally self-disciplined. He was extremely strong from working out and athlete-fit both from the high-school wrestling team, which he'd joined the previous year as a freshman, and from martial-arts training, which he'd started four years earlier. He'd raced through the levels and was preparing to test for his second-degree black belt while helping to teach in his local dojo to earn spending money. He was a formidable force on the wrestling mat, which had helped transform him from the target of middle-school bullying to a high-school hero. Jesse was teaching him to drive and was pretty sure he could already handle a car better than his Grandpa could at seventy-four. Michael could now even hold his own on the table-tennis table with his uncle Josh.

The boy and his Grandpa sat on the two black leather recliners and put their feet up. They'd become used to entering and leaving one another's presence quietly, sometimes saying nothing at all. Michael was more comfortable with silence than with talking, and Jesse appreciated the change of pace. Their relationship had become the suburban equivalent of the going-fishing-with-Grandpa relationship that they might have had if they'd lived near water. That day Michael wanted to talk.

"Grandpa," he began, "I want to ask you something… something potentially awkward."

"Go ahead, Michael. I have a potentially awkward question for you, too, if you're up for it."

"Okay. I've watched you and Grandma for years, how you loved each other, took care of each other, and made each other happy. I want Maddy to be happy like that but I don't know how to tell her, or even how to talk about, well, love."

"You understand Maddy pretty well, right?" Jesse asked.

"I think so," he answered.

"Why do you think she hasn't tried to develop an intimate relationship?"

"That's pretty obvious," he said.

"I mean why hasn't she got past all of that? She's been so successful in changing herself, getting an education, starting a business, raising three beautiful children, and all the rest. It seems like she could do anything she put her mind to. So why can't she be in an intimate relationship?"

"She doesn't want to," Michael answered.

"That's right," Jesse said. "And does she seem happy anyway?"

"She's happy," Michael said.

"So why do you want her to pursue an intimate relationship?" Jesse asked.

"So she can be happier. Complete, maybe." He then added, "So there can be someone to care for her the way you cared for Grandma, so she'd never feel alone."

They were silent for a while. Jesse tacked in a new direction.

"I used to worry about you, a lot," he said. "You were wound pretty tightly when you were younger. We thought you might snap under the pressure you put on yourself to control your life and protect everyone you love."

"It could still happen," Michael said with a half-laugh.

"Maybe, but I'm not so worried anymore. Your self-control seems more relaxed now, flowing downhill like a river rather than pumping uphill in a pipe that's springing leaks under the pressure." They both chuckled at the image, which was still a part of Jesse's Michael stack.

"So here's my question," said Jesse. "What about you—do *you* want an intimate relationship?"

"I think I do now, Grandpa," answered Michael. "I never felt this way before but some of the girls at school seem really nice."

"Anyone in particular?" Jesse inquired.

"Maybe, yes. Catie."

"Same name as your cousin?" asked Jesse.

"Different spelling," said Michael. "And she's my age. And we're not related."

"Do you know how to talk with her, how to ask her out, what to do when you're out, and all the rest?"

"I listen to the guys on the wrestling team talk about girls and it pisses me off. So I guess I know more about what I don't want to do than what I do want to do."

"You know some of that's probably boasting and exaggeration, right?" Jesse asked.

"I guess," said Michael.

"Young men often pretend to be heartless cads toward women when they're talking with other men. They speak as if they treat women as conquests rather than as real people. It's a kind of peer pressure. Most aren't like that but some young men actually are horrible to women."

"That's just it," Michael said. "I'm afraid to ask Catie out. I'm scared I won't be any good for her. Like, I'm scared I could hurt her."

There, he'd said it. He'd given voice to one of Jesse's deepest fears. It was what they were all worried about: seriously disordered sexuality after early years of sustained abuse. It was a topic Michael might well have difficulty broaching with Maddy.

"Michael," Jesse said, "have you talked with your therapist about this fear?"

"No," he answered.

"Try to do it, okay? Your therapist knows you very well and has excellent judgment about what you're likely to do and what you're not likely to do. Does that sound right?"

"Yes, that's right," said Michael.

"You know, if there's any real chance that you could become a monster with Catie, you can't date her, right? You have to sort yourself out first."

"I know," Michael said. Jesse could tell his grandson wanted more from him. He searched the boy's face for clues as to where to go next.

"Michael, from my conversations with Elizabeth, I've learned that sometimes people who grow up like you did before you came here are afraid that they'll do what they saw other people do, even though they'd never actually do those things. The fear they feel is a part of caring for the person they like."

"The monster-fear and that caring-fear seem similar. How do I know what kind of fear I'm feeling?" Michael asked.

"I'm not sure," said Jesse, "and that's why it's important to talk with your therapist. But here's my guess. I reckon the first kind of fear, the fear that means you're not ready to care for Catie, feels like an unstoppable urge inside, a kind of brutal monster waiting to get out. I think you used to have such a monster in you but only you can decide whether you've tamed it. The second kind of fear has a different source; it feels more like a desire to protect the thing you care about, the thing you love, like the way you feel toward Maddy, your sisters, and me."

"I do have this monster in me and I think I've been taming it," said Michael. "But I'm not sure how tame it is right now. It comes out when I'm wrestling. I'll talk to my therapist and then decide what to do."

"That's smart, Michael," said Jesse. "Remember that most men have inside them something predatory toward other people, including women. The difference in your case is that you and Maddy had very little control over the first five years of your life, so your monster will be differently shaped than the monsters of most other boys. Maybe your monster gets its power from different sources. Does that make sense?"

"I guess," said Michael. "How do I know when I'll be safe around Catie?

"I don't know, Michael," said Jesse. "But it isn't smart to go out alone with a girl until you feel sure you can protect her the way you protect your family. Maybe going out in groups at first is a good way to go."

"Yeah," he said. "That's not a bad idea." Suddenly he grinned. "Grandpa, I really came up here to tell you that I love you, that I miss Grandma, that I admire your relationship, and that I hope you won't be too lonely without her."

"Thank you, Michael," said Jesse. "That's kind of you to say."

"I guess all this other stuff was just ready to come out," he added.

⁜

After Michael left, Becca struck up a conversation.

"He's popular at school now," she said. "Better than being bullied."

"It must be partly because he's a physically powerful and attractive young man," said Jesse.

"There's more to it than that," said Becca. "The deeper part of his attractiveness is that he's culturally alien. He stands out from the crowd at high school."

"Maddy's girls seem like all the other girls," said Jesse. "They fight with each other and with Maddy, they're interested in what other girls care about, they're vulnerable to peer pressure, their values match those of the surrounding social environment."

"The same thing that makes Michael broken, and potentially dangerous, creates fascination in his peers," said Becca. "The question is whether the way Maddy has raised him is enough to give him control over the consequences of sustained early abuse."

"That's the question alright," said Jesse. "Unfortunately, none of us knows the answer to that, not even Michael."

EVERYWHERE-HERE

The mid-afternoon arrival of the rest of the family was as lovely as ever and more orderly than it used to be when the kids were little. Matt's Jake and Josh's Kate were now ten years old, only a little older than Maddy's Jessie, who was also ten. Josh's John and Matt's twins Abby and Millie were twelve, like Maddy's Jamie, and all four were in puberty with rapidly changing bodies and hormone-pickled brains. Josh's Rebecca and Matt's Walt were fourteen and well on their way to being young adults.

Michael, the winter child who turned sixteen on his artificial birthday three days earlier, looked like a muscular giant beside his seven cousins and two sisters. All the grandkids looked up to him and it wouldn't be an exaggeration to say that they adored him. Michael and Walt were still best friends, despite the eighteen-month age difference and the huge difference in size.

Maddy and Jesse had organized simple snacks and drinks for the sit-down wake. They all gathered in the living room, scattered on couches, chairs, and the floor. Matt and Josh explained to their kids that they'd all be sharing stories about Grandma. There was a feeling of anticipation, of something new and strange.

It was starting to darken outside, as it did in Boston at that time of day in the winter. Jesse soaked in the memories, falling into a deep silence as the stories washed over him. He had his precious memories, and would share them on other days, but on this occasion, nobody pressured him for Alexandra stories. Instead, they let him be, bathing him in their own blessed recollections, relieving him of any obligation to perform.

The laughter was healing. It intensified and purified their shared grief, bringing it to a slow boil and keeping it there, allowing them to feel it fully. They drank of their grief deeply, blended with the sweetness of laughter, and steadied themselves together above the abysmal chasm of nothingness that Alexandra's disease and her passing had opened beneath them.

Becca was there. "My brothers are brilliant!" she said at one point and Jesse could only agree. In complete harmony with one another, Matt and Josh guided the entire family through the afternoon. From time to time they'd glance at Jesse, reading him, wordlessly comforting him. It was a mostly hidden emotional transaction, potent and graceful. The boys' wives and Maddy occasionally hugged when one of them was overcome by sadness. They'd become so close over the years.

Jesse was so sad and so happy all at once. He'd have given almost anything to have had this moment as a guiding, centering goal from the time he was young, a memory to which he might have aspired. But memory doesn't work forwards like that. His life had unfolded haphazardly, without such an aspirational vision of aged bliss. Yet he was blessed that the natural grace of circumstance brought him to this place, underserving, ready to savor its sweet pain.

As the stories and laughter continued, Jesse felt awareness of his old body's boundaries slowly dissolving and his body-mind merging into the surrounding environment. He was sensing each of these fifteen wonderful people, the details of their lives, so familiar from his meditation routines, pressing into his consciousness without any crowding or rushing. His bodily awareness was spreading out, pervading everything and everyone around him. He was flooded with recognition of himself in the other, which sparked potent compassion. Even inanimate objects felt as though they were a part of the ambit of his compassionate attention, part of his being.

Jesse was practiced at this, especially because of his compassion meditation, the advanced stages of which were all about identifying with other beings and processes in just this way. But there was also something new happening. His Tantric pseudo-synesthesia meditation training was making a spectacular contribution. His senses were cross-linked in a sparkling kind of way: he'd hear textures for a few seconds and then he'd smell-taste them or feel them as touches, even while he could still see them. This rippling multi-channel awareness glistened away, deepening his awareness of the blooming, buzzing confusion that infants experience before neural pruning peels apart the sensory channels.

As this everywhere-here synesthetic state blossomed in Jesse's consciousness, the oh-so-familiar eternal-now state joined forces with it. The incredible cosmic conditions of this simple moment of meaning flooded through him, displacing nothing and intensifying his sensitivity to every little detail. Becca started floating, face toward the sky, hands open, palms up, shimmering hair flowing, long white dress billowing as she drifted like a leaf on the wind, perfect. Through all of this, every word spoken, every nuance of voice, every facial muscle in that room was emotionally vivid, even though he wasn't processing language or moving. Jesse was entranced.

Then Alexandra joined this symphony of sensory awareness. She was young again, the way she looked when Jesse first fell in love with her, the way she'd been seared into his memory his whole long life. She stood in the corner of the room opposite him, behind their daughters, softly smiling and staring into his face. He stared back lovingly without losing any of his feeling for what was happening in the room. While he stared, Becca floated downwards the way a feather does, growing younger until at last she was six, the age they'd last seen her and held her. She stood beside Alexandra, the two of them holding hands just as Jesse had seen them do a hundred times. Both mother and child were relaxed, as if it weren't a reunion but a normal thing to be with one another.

Jesse's tears were flowing. Jenny was standing beside Matt, listening to Walt tell a story. Oli and Maddy were arm-in-arm on the couch. The laughter came and went like lapping waves on a lake. The infinitely quiet roar of the quantum vacuum, the mathematically precise cascading chaos of the Big Bang, the unassimilable organization of every living cell in the universe, the relentless logic of order and randomness in the evolutionary process—all of it washed over and through Jesse, along with beautifully crafted images from poems, the shapes and textures of art and architecture, the moral and spiritual exemplars who inspired him, and every detail of the lives of these people he knew so well. Alexandra was in the middle of all of it. Everything was together, all time with now, all space with here, and all meaning in them, in Jesse's family.

Alexandra and Becca smiled as he ever-so-politely lost his own mind in the merging of time and space, of perspective and meaning. He was all of this, and nothing at all, all at once.

The astonishing state of awareness must have lasted twenty minutes. Alexandra eventually released Becca like a dove. Jesse's wife dissolved away while Jesse's oldest daughter became thirty-three again, dressed in jeans and a white blouse, watching proceedings from the side of the room, relaxed, leaning against the wall, her hands tucked into her pockets.

Oli was perched on the arm of Jesse's sofa chair when the ecstatic state yielded to normal consciousness. She seemed unaware of anything out of the ordinary. She rose and kissed the top of his head before retreating to the kitchen to refill her coffee mug. Jesse looked around and everyone seemed fine except Maddy, who was staring at him, confused.

Jesse was feeling very strange, a little frightened due to this new state of mind, and shocked by seeing Alexandra.

"You're okay," Becca reassured him.

"Are you sure?" Jesse thought-asked.

"Seems to me like one of those compassion meditation states in which self merges with world," she answered, "but you combined it with synesthesia, your eternal-now trick, and some weird grief-relief thing. How do you feel now?"

Jesse paused to take stock.

"Pretty normal," he thought-said. "Holy Moses, that was weird, though." After a moment, he added, "Do you reckon we can do it again?" and Becca's rippling laughter echoed in his mind, just as if he were hearing it from across the room.

When Becca calmed down, her face gleaming with joy, she said, "Worth a call to Jerry, eh?"

"Yes," Jesse thought-said. "Tomorrow. Do you think I'll see Alexandra again?"

"You're the expert in the post-death appearance of loved ones, you big dummy," she said. "What do you think?"

Jesse didn't know. But he hoped he would.

Maddy made her way over to Jesse and sat beside him on the arm of the big chair, where Oli had just been, her arm around his shoulders.

"Are you okay, Dad?" she whispered. "I felt like something really strange was happening. To you, I mean."

Jesse held her free hand and quietly replied, "I did feel a bit strange there for a few minutes but I think I'm fine now." She looked at him, her face full of concern. "Actually, it was good strange, not bad strange, so I really am fine," he added, smiling at her as most of the worry dissolved from her face.

GRANDPA'S ONLY GOOD AT
IDEA STUFF

Later the next day, Jesse took Michael aside and asked if now was a good time to have "the talk" with Maddy. Michael's eyes widened, but then he shrugged and said, "Sure. I guess now's as good a time as any."

"Good man," said Jesse. "Go find your mother and meet me in my office."

They joined him moments later.

"What's up?" Maddy asked.

"Maddy," Jesse began, "Michael asked for my help to start a conversation with you about something he finds difficult to discuss." He paused but Michael was not ready to pick up the ball. "He loves you and worries about you, same as you do him. You're both so proud of one another, the way you've healed and grown. But Michael wants to tell you one thing he worries about more than anything else." Jesse looked at the young man and he swallowed, apparently ready to go.

"Maddy," said Michael, "I'm worried about what'll happen to you when I move out and can't... can't protect you. I... I don't want you to be lonely. Grandma and Grandpa were a good team, and Grandpa took such good care of her when she couldn't take care of herself. I want you to be happy and safe, just like that." He swallowed hard.

"Do you want me to get partnered up, Michael?" asked Maddy.

"Maybe," he said. "I want you to be safe and happy and I think you're safest and happiest when you're with people who love you for your whole life."

"Michael," she said, "how long have you been worried about this?"

"A while," he said. "Since I started thinking about dating, I guess, and now more because Grandma died."

Jesse offered to leave at that point, but Maddy told him to stay, saying with a smile that he should finish what he started. Then she turned to Michael. "You're always trying to protect me, aren't you?"

"Yes," he said.

"Michael," she said, "we've never talked about this but what exactly do you remember from the cellar?"

Michael hesitated, without ever taking his eyes away from Maddy.

"It's time, Michael. Let's talk about it," she said, her voice quiet.

Michael's face shifted subtly, yielding to her in trust, in a way he did with nobody else. It was as if the tension dissolved and his entire big body relaxed.

"I remember you chained up and your ankle bleeding," he began. "I remember you being attacked and your face and you trying to take care of me with your eyes even in the middle of it. I remember the sounds...and you being tied up and whipped." He paused and started to sob quietly, never taking his eyes away from hers. "I remember them forcing me to touch you when you were tied up. I remember them hitting me when I tried to stop them hurting you. And I remember you pushing me up through the window hole and then running away from the house into the night, hurting my feet, thinking I might never see you and Jamie again."

She was out of her chair and they were in each other's arms, Michael still sobbing, and Maddy eerily quiet, looking at Jesse over Michael's shoulder, her eyes alight with fury. Jesse looked at her with all the love he possessed, absorbing her anger, tears rimming his sad eyes, until the fire in her eyes was extinguished by her own tears, the silent non-sobbing kind, running down her face. She closed her eyes then and leant into Michael. Once he calmed, she returned to her seat.

"Okay," she said, "now we talk. But move your chair over here so we can hold hands." When they were resettled, holding hands, Maddy said, "I didn't know you remembered all of that. I'm glad you told me."

He nodded.

"You're right to be worried about me," she said. "I really am broken in a way, in a different way than you are. I don't want physical intimacy, I'm not interested in sex, and I can't trust many men, or even many women. It's been more than ten years and I'm still almost a shut-in here. I depend on my therapist and our family, Grandpa and Oli especially, for emotional support. When your Grandpa dies I really don't know what I'll do, even though I know the rest of the family will take care of me. Michael, you're right—I face a big problem in my future and I don't have a clue how to solve it. You can see that problem coming because you love me, and because you love your Grandma who always had what I don't have. I'm proud of you for finding a way to tell me how worried you've been. I'm glad you're trying to protect me."

Michael just nodded again, still looking at her face and holding her hands. His huge hands made hers look incongruously small given the extraordinarily powerful role she played in his life.

"The problem might not be quite what you think it is, though," she said. "People can be happy living alone, without a partner. My problem is partly that it will be hard for me to be happy without Grandpa and you kids, whether I'm alone or not. The other part is that my body is broken somehow, and I can't really choose to be alone in a healthy way until I get my body back from the people who stole it from me."

She paused for a moment.

"Here's what I'm going to do. I'm going to start fighting to get my body back. Maybe doing that will change my ability to trust people. Maybe it will help me feel interested in a romantic relationship. I don't know how to do it but my therapist would be glad to advise me if I'd let her. She's been trying to get me to budge on this for years. Maybe what I needed was a push from you."

Michael reached out and hugged Maddy. Part-way through the hug, she held him at arm's length and said, "Those memories of yours—the way they were training you to be like them, the way they'd beat you if you didn't go along—all of that can mess a man up, you know that, right?"

"They *have* messed me up, Maddy," he said. "I can feel the messed-up parts of me inside, even though I try hard to control them."

"And you're going to talk about that with your therapist, right?"

"Yes," he said.

"Okay. Come here!" she exclaimed, and pulled him into another close hug.

Jesse was in awe of these two people. Maddy could traverse emotionally complicated terrain with extraordinary speed and wisdom, and Michael's compassion and care were seemingly boundless.

"Well done, Michael," Maddy said, taking the words out of Jesse's mouth. "I know that was hard, but you did it. Thank you. Now—go have some fun!"

Michael beamed at both of them and went downstairs to find his cousins.

Maddy sank into the recliner and looked at Jesse. "Well, that seemed important," she said, with a cock-eyed smile.

"You think?" he replied.

They burst into laughter borne of relief, and then Maddy took a huge, shuddering breath.

"It was when they started trying to train Michael that I got really desperate to escape," she said. "If he'd been chained up like me, I don't think we ever would have gotten out of that hell hole, and he'd have become exactly like them, probably much worse. And Jamie…"

There was a long silence while Jesse absorbed this new revelation, which would soon appear within the Michael stack. Maddy switched gears.

"I seem to have taken on some challenging homework," she said.

"Yes indeed! Are you ready for this?" Jesse asked.

"Not at all," she replied. "But Michael is right to push me. I know I've been stupid and lazy about this."

"Hey, steady on!" he said. "That's my daughter you're talking about."

"You know what I mean," she said. "I've learned to be happy. You and Mom and Josh have helped me solve the problems of survival and safety for my children. Until now that's felt like enough. So I keep putting off the whole reclaiming-my-body thing, as my therapist keeps calling it—the sex thing, the intimacy thing, the trust thing, whatever."

"Maddy, you're an instinctive emotional genius," Jesse said. "I'm amazed at how quickly you saw the real meaning of Michael's concern, how decisively you connected it to his traumatic memories, how you absorbed his point without a trace of defensiveness, and how you gave him the only reassurance that would really work: your promise to try to deal with the deepest part of the problem. You astonish me. I can barely fathom how your sort of being is even possible."

"Dad," she said, sighing, "the truth is that I can't do that with everyone. Just Michael."

They heard thumping and laughter on the stairs and Abby and Millie appeared. They were dressed differently but their faces and bodies were almost indistinguishable.

"Aunt Maddy, John and Jamie and Millie and I want you to give us a drawing lesson," said Abby.

"What about Grandpa? Can't he give you a lesson?" teased Maddy.

"Grandpa's only good at idea stuff and nobody cares about that. We want to draw," said Millie, giggling.

"And Grandpa can't draw to save his life," added Abby.

"Well then looks like I'm on deck!" she said.

She sprang up, kissed Jesse on the head, grabbed the twins' hands, and descended the stairs.

Becca took Maddy's place in the recliner. "What are Maddy's chances of actually regaining sexual feelings and wanting an intimate relationship?" she asked.

"Don't know," Jesse thought-responded. "Seems like a long shot to me. But she's come a long way and she's an extremely determined woman. I guess we'll see."

"I wouldn't mind having sex," Becca said. "It seems beautiful and fun."

Jesse was flabbergasted. "I have no idea how to respond to that," he said.

"You shouldn't be surprised," she laughed. "You simulated a complex AI companion and I've been doing my own thing for quite a while now. I'm more interesting than even you know."

"Jerry's gonna love this," said Jesse. "Let's organize another chat and you can explain it all to him directly."

"Deal," she said.

As Jesse went to rejoin the family, he wondered what Alexandra would have said to Maddy about this, had she been alive and still in full possession of her faculties. He paused in the hallway in front of Maddy's beautiful sketch of Alexandra, made ten years earlier.

"You'd be proud of your girls," he said to the picture.

"Grandpa, are you talking to that picture?" asked Jake, watching him from the foot of the stairs.

"Why yes," he answered. "I often stop for a chat with Grandma here, or with one of the other sketches Maddy has hung in the hallway."

"Do the pictures ever talk back?" Jake asked.

"Not usually," Jesse answered, "but it's fun when they do."

Jake laughed and ran off to play. Becca giggled, too, standing beside Jesse watching her mother's beautiful face.

THE FAKING THING WORKED

Later that year, on her thirty-second birthday, the day before her Saturday party, with autumn colors everywhere, Maddy asked Jesse to go for a post-lunch walk beside the woods near their house. Jesse used to walk through the woods but one of his concessions to being seventy-five years on this spinning planetary rock was that he limited himself to walking on smooth paths, free of roots and stones and mud.

"We'll enjoy the leaves while we celebrate your existence," he told his youngest daughter, delighted. With jackets closed against the chilly air and Maddy on his arm, they walked toward the forest, beside which they could amble for several miles if they wanted to go that far.

"It's time for an update on the reclaiming-my-body project," said Maddy.

"That would be splendid, Maddy," he said.

"It's not all good news, I'm afraid, and some of it has been really weird for me," she said.

"Well, I'm too old to be shocked by much," Jesse said, "and I know you too well to believe that you're doing anything other than following your heart's path."

Maddy squeezed his arm. "Okay, do you remember our spring fling, when Jenny took Oli and me to a spa?"

"Sure."

"Well that was part of the get-my-body-back project," she said.

"Ah! Ulterior motives," teased Jesse.

"It was Oli's idea," said Maddy. "She thought the three of us could work on it together so I wouldn't feel alone. The spa was part of it. We had a massage each day. All three of us were in the same room. Oli and Jenny loved it, but I was way too nervous… a bit frozen. A lot frozen. Anyway, on the last day, they convinced me to get a massage from a man."

"Wow," said Jesse. "You really went for it, didn't you?"

"I did! I never could relax…but I didn't run away screaming, either," she said, smiling.

"Was there any part of it you did enjoy?"

"I loved the manicure-pedicure! Jenny set the three of us up beside one another, and we got the whole deal—massage, exfoliation, nails, everything. The touch was so gentle and I actually felt tingly. There was one weird moment when a girl asked about my ankle scarring, and all five of the other technicians looked over to stare, but Oli jumped in and said I was her slave and that's where she'd chained me up. For a second everyone just stared but then Oli and Jenny lost it, and then I did, too. Oli is crazy! After that, I could relax. I closed my eyes and just enjoyed it."

"I'm proud of you, Maddy," said Jesse.

"What I've realized, through therapy and a bunch of other things, is that I'm totally at ease with bodies, so long as nobody is being forced. My issue is with *feeling* things—feeling pleasure. I just feel… kind of dead inside."

Jesse didn't know what to say and just put his arm around her shoulder as they walked.

"This is all Michael's fault," she said, "forcing me to confront my demons."

She laughed a little. "So here's the next part. I've been round and round with my therapist on all this so many times, but I was just stuck—and so frustrated to have nothing to show for all that effort. Nothing at all has made me want an intimate relationship with another person. So my therapist suggested a sex surrogate. She recommended a woman, Angela, and it turned out that Oli knows about her as well, and respects her, so I decided to give it a try. This started a couple of weeks after the spa weekend. I've been meeting weekly with Angie."

"Wow!" Jesse said.

"Yeah," Maddy said. "It's pretty unusual, but my situation is, too." She paused and then added, with a sheepish smile, "She says I'm the most determined patient she's ever had."

"I don't doubt it," Jesse said, and they laughed.

"Things have gotten pretty intense with Angie," Maddy went on. "I've gotten upset a bunch of times. I mean big-time upset. Memories sometimes hit me, and leave me breathless and panicky. I actually had a full-blown panic attack early on, but Angie helped me through it."

"I've had some of those," Jesse confided. "Not a lot of fun. One time a friend of mine led me away from the edge, maybe like Angie did with you, except my friend was on the other end of a phone line."

"I wouldn't have guessed that you ever had a panic attack!" she said. "What happened?"

It was a reasonable question and Jesse was tempted to answer it, but he held back.

"I was doing this meditation routine and got into some bizarre emotional territory. I might tell you more about it sometime, but I don't want to distract us from your story."

"Fair enough," Maddy replied. "Angie and I have met about a dozen times now. We've tried all kinds of things. Right at the beginning, Angie discovered that easing me into things or warming me up isn't the issue, like it is for many of her female clients. She could do anything she wanted and I'd do anything she asked with no fancy buildup, no resistance, no convincing. I think that's why she says I'm all determination. The issue in my case is just responsiveness—and also some weird wiring that connects me up all wrong. That's how she puts it: my brain is wired so that pleasure is linked up differently in me than it is in most people."

Silence took over again for a few minutes, as they watched the squirrels desperately scrambling for nuts before the cold closed in.

"This next bit is going to be hard to talk about, Dad," she said. "But I have to say it. It's really important."

"It's okay, sweetheart," Jesse said. "Say only what you're comfortable saying."

Maddy took a deep breath. "Angie helped me remember the way I used to long for sexual contact from the men who held me prisoner, even when I was really young. I felt so horrible when I recalled that, but Angie said it was perfectly normal, even inevitable, because it was the only human contact I could get. She also helped me remember the terror of being attacked in the early part of my captivity, before they had me properly trained. I was only five and the father was doing everything imaginable to me, sometimes with his sons watching. I didn't need help remembering the times when they'd switch from rape to torture, or when they'd give me to a stranger, but we explored all those memories as well."

After a minute, Maddy resumed, with a fierce resolve in her voice.

"And now we come to the big discovery. I'd learned to be a cooperative, enthusiastic slave to all four men, and to the men they invited into the basement. But all of that changed when I was fourteen and got pregnant with Michael. He saved me, even before he was born, because he showed me that there was someone worthy of my love. Every day in that basement from the time I knew I was pregnant with Michael became this steadily intensifying mix of protective love and increasing horror at the way my child would be growing up. Somehow, having a baby flipped me out of my submissive, compliant slave mind and into a fierce and protective *mother*, someone who now had to fake everything just to stay alive and keep my child safe. That weird mixture of feelings just got more intense when Jamie came. That last five or six years was all about shutting down my natural bodily feelings, faking compliance and pleasure, and focusing on the kids."

"The faking thing worked," Jesse said. "You lived long enough to escape. A lot of other girls in the ring didn't survive."

"It worked in one way, yes," Maddy said. "But I think it also did a lot of damage. It's in those years that my ability to respond sexually somehow shut down. Angie says the survival-faking thing went on for so long that I rewired myself in a big way."

"That's staggering!" Jesse exclaimed. "Talk about bodies being spectacular systems. I'd guess all of that yields really important insights into your reaction to physical intimacy."

"Yes," she said. "Exactly. So anyway here's where things stand with Angie after three months. The good news is that I can enjoy intimate contact and I can feel intense pleasure again. The bad news is I can only do it when I'm bound and helpless. The plan is to teach me how to get there in other ways. Angie says she thinks she knows how to rewire things through a kind of cognitive-behavioral sex therapy. And she believes there's a way for me to be intimate with someone, but not yet."

Jesse pulled them both to a stop. He placed his hands on her cold cheeks, looked into her blue eyes, and kissed her on her forehead. "I'm so proud of you, Maddy," he said. "I can't even express how much."

"I'm going to get there, Dad. I think I know how to do it now. I'm going to do it for Michael, and I'm going to do it for me."

"I don't doubt it for a second," he said.

They resumed their walk, Jesse wondering about what the future could hold for his extraordinary daughter.

GIFT CORPSES

Jamie was in ninth grade in the same high school where Michael was in his senior year. She told her Mom and Grandpa about Michael's reputation—handsome, athletic, a musical genius, chivalrous—and how popular he'd become. "The girls say he's like some old-school knight in shining armor!" Jamie said, giggling.

Michael was captain of the wrestling team, which had won the state championship in his junior year. He'd just achieved his third-degree black belt in kung fu, having completed six years of rigorous training, moving through the ranks at the maximum speed permitted in his dojo. He was still teaching classes and earning money doing it, which gave him more independence.

Everything was going well, until six weeks into the school year. Maddy got a call from the school asking her to meet with the principal. She and Jesse drove over right away.

"What's this about?" Maddy asked.

"I'm afraid Michael got into a physical altercation with another student," said the principal.

"What? What happened?" asked Maddy.

"The reports I have from several sources, including Michael, tell the same story. Another student confronted Michael during a volleyball game in gym class and was talking about your daughter Jamie. This boy was taunting Michael with various... things he was going to do to Jamie as soon as he got the chance."

"What things?" asked Maddy.

"He threatened to... abuse her," said Principal Betts.

"What *kind* of abuse?" asked Maddy.

"Ah... sexual abuse."

"Are you saying this bully told Michael he was going to rape Jamie?" Maddy said, her tone ice-cold.

"Ah, yes, that's right. Michael apparently remained calm at first, while this student continued talking about Jamie—"

"You mean, Michael remained calm as this student continued to talk about *raping* Jamie," said Maddy.

"...until suddenly a switch flipped," the principal said. "The gym teacher said—"

"Wait a minute," Maddy said. "The gym teacher was right there and just allowed this other boy to threaten to rape my daughter?"

"I don't have information on that," Principal Betts said. She picked up a piece of paper. "But here's what he reported: Michael swept the legs out from under this kid and, while the boy was still falling backwards, thrust his back and head into the gym floor. He then elbowed his solar plexus to paralyze his diaphragm and gripped his throat with one hand as the boy struggled for air. He then leaned down to the student and said so everyone around could hear: 'Talk about her again and I'll spend longer than two seconds taking your body apart. Touch her and I'll hunt you down and present your corpse in sections as a gift to my sister.'"

Jesse covered his face with his hand. So that's what it was like on the inside of the sealed-up pressure cooker that was Michael's ravaged psyche.

The principal resumed her narrative. "This was witnessed by a dozen other boys as well as the gym teacher. And Michael himself confirmed it. He was upset with himself for losing control, but he told me he didn't regret what he did. Students are not allowed to make death threats so I have no choice but to suspend Michael for one week."

"Are students allowed to make rape threats?" asked Maddy, just barely calm.

"No," said the principal, "and the other student has been suspended as well."

"You're lying!" Maddy roared. "There is no way this bully would have been suspended if Michael had merely reported him rather than taking care of it himself."

Jesse reached for Maddy's arm. "Steady on," he whispered.

Privately, Jesse thought Maddy was dead right—the rape threat would have been dismissed as boys' locker-room talk and the kid would have been slapped on the wrist, if anything. Jesse sensed that Principal Betts knew Maddy was right, too, but she delicately slid by Maddy's accusation and moved the conversation forward.

"I'm sorry all of this happened," she said. "Let's be grateful it didn't turn out worse. Michael is ready to leave now. You have to keep him home for one week."

"Your school's morals are twisted," said Maddy. "I'll take Michael out of school to celebrate his courage, his loyalty, and his self-control in not permanently hurting the bully who threatened to rape a fourteen-year-old girl. You think it's okay to allow a student to threaten rape, and it only crosses a line when someone intervenes to stop it. You bring Jamie to me too. Right now. She's not safe here."

Principal Betts picked up the phone to summon Jamie and then showed Maddy and Jesse out of her office.

A few minutes later, Jamie arrived, wanting to know what was going on, and the school secretary retrieved Michael from a nearby room.

Maddy addressed the secretary. "Jamie wants to know why I'm taking her home. Principal Betts should explain."

"Isn't it your decision to take Jamie out of school?" asked the secretary. "She's not suspended."

"Principal Betts needs to explain what happened herself," said Maddy.

The secretary hesitated but knocked on the principal's door, exchanged a few words, and then invited the four of them in.

"What can I do for you?" asked the principal warily.

"Explain to Jamie," said Maddy.

"Ah... Jamie, I'm sorry to say that a student has threatened you," Principal Betts said.

"What?" said Jamie, suddenly worried and looking at her mother.

"Say what you mean," demanded Maddy.

"A student threatened to... ah... assault..."

"Say what you mean!" shouted Maddy.

"I'm so very sorry, Jamie," said the principal. "But a student threatened to rape you today. He said it to Michael, who defended you, but threatened to kill the student if he touched you. Michael and the other student have both been suspended for one week."

Jamie started crying and Michael and Maddy both hugged her.

"Your mother wants to take you out of school, too," said the principal.

"No," said Maddy. "Her mother *needs* to take her out of school, because it's not safe here."

Maddy led her children, still in a huddle, out of the room. Jesse looked at the principal and quietly added, "We'll be expecting a full report on why a student was allowed to threaten rape without censure by a teacher who evidently witnessed the entire, prolonged exchange, and only intervened when Michael lost his cool. We'll need that report in four days so we can decide whether it's safe for Jamie to return and what other measures we'll be taking."

"Listen, this is a terribly regrettable situation, but I really don't think—"

"Would you prefer to get lawyers involved right now?" asked Jesse. "You deal with the rot that led to this situation or we'll organize some very public, very unwelcome motivational assistance for you."

The principal nodded. "I understand," she said.

A week later Michael returned to school with Jamie at his side. They were both showered with hallway applause. Everyone had heard the story, everyone knew the two boys, and everyone knew which way the moral compass was pointing.

Jamie didn't realize it at first, but Michael had organized a network of guardians for his little sister, with the two wrestling teams at its core. He explained this to Maddy, which helped her believe that Jamie would to be safe when she returned. When Jamie saw people constantly watching her from a distance, she was freaked out at first. Eventually one of her friends explained that the monitoring eyes were Michael's watchers, and she was able to relax.

The gym teacher was disciplined after a rapid investigation but the Principal refused to allow Maddy and Michael to meet with him. He left the school soon after, and the message was received by the other teachers loud and clear. The student who threatened Jamie was reduced to slinking around hallways, giving Michael and Jamie a wide berth, avoiding both wrestling teams and everyone else who felt any sense of loyalty to Michael, which was a lot of people in that high school.

SOUNDS LIKE A MINEFIELD

Michael's mixed feelings about the suspension yielded a fascinating college-application essay explaining high-school disciplinary actions. He was applying for music schools. His classical and jazz piano was first-rate, especially for a high-school kid. He had grown out of his hesitancy about performing in public and participated in several concerts both in bands and as a soloist. He wasn't as good in other subjects as in music but he maintained grades around the B-plus level, had decent standardized testing scores, and later that year succeeded in getting admission offers from music programs at a variety of excellent colleges and universities.

Michael told Maddy and Jesse that he knew music was a tough business, competitive and political, but he wanted to give it a shot. Keyboard performance was his focus but he'd also started to write music for keyboards and instrumental groups, and he wanted to get training in composing and arranging to keep his employment options open.

After exploring his options, Michael decided to attend Berklee College of Music, right there in Boston. It was world-famous, and he didn't want to move far away from Maddy and his sisters and the rest of the family. But he also decided to move out and go for the "full college experience," and Maddy agreed. Even without any concrete understanding of what was involved, Maddy saw the wisdom in encouraging Michael to take advantage of dorm living, learning to take care of himself.

Michael already had a gig playing cocktail piano in a high-end restaurant within easy walking distance from Berklee. The plan was to keep that job going while he studied, generating spending money and maybe the beginnings of some personal savings.

Michael had started dating in groups half-way through his junior year, but he didn't ask a girl out for a solo date until near the end of high school. Michael was doing homework in Jesse's office, comfortably tucked into one of the black recliners, when Jesse broached the subject.

"So this is the big moment, Michael," he said Jesse. "First one-on-one date tonight, right?"

"That's right!" said Michael, setting his book aside. "I guess I should feel nervous about it, but I feel okay, mostly because of the girl I'm taking out. I still have this background worry that it'll get all serious and I'll end up hurting her feelings, but I think tonight will be fine."

"Explain something to me," said Jesse. "The girls you've dated over the last couple of years must have expectations, even though you've been dating in groups. How have you managed all that?"

"It doesn't really come up in the group," said Michael. "I'm also super clear right up front. You know: I'm not looking for anything serious but it would be cool to get to know you better, so would you come with me and this other couple to a movie on Friday? or whatever. So there's always something going on, and before you know it, we're dropping the girls off home. Nothing too emotionally intense."

"But don't girls who want more get angry when you don't ask them out again, or when you ask out one of their friends?" Jesse asked. "I guess I don't understand why some of them don't hate you."

"Maybe some of them do!"

"That's not what Jamie reports," Jesse said. "She says all of the girls like you and respect you. She says nobody says nasty things about you."

"They don't say nasty things about me to *her*," Michael said.

"Point taken," Jesse said.

"There might be one other thing," Michael added. "Everyone found out a couple of years ago about my...you know, background. So I think they cut me some slack and let me do things my own way. But that's just a guess."

"Mmmm... Well, tonight's a proper date," said Jesse. "Does that mean you've changed your mind about getting serious?"

"Well, I like Willa a lot," Michael said. "I think I feel safe with her because she's not gossipy, she's down-to-earth, she's skeptical about romantic love, she's wickedly funny, she's absolutely gorgeous, and she likes me but doesn't seem infatuated with me. I guess I'm just not as worried about her expectations getting out of control, or about me getting out of control with her."

"She sounds wonderful and I hope you have fun," Jesse said. "I'll be glad for a report. I feel like I'm reliving my far-off youthful years when I listen to you talk about the high-school dating scene! We're almost the same, you know, except for the muscles and the musical skills. And the wrestling and the state championship. And the black belt and the popularity. And the high-paying part-time employment gig and the enormous array of friends."

Michael laughed.

"I bet you were wicked smart, though," said Michael.

"True, but that's not honey to bears when it comes to romance," said Jesse.

"It was attractive to Grandma," said Michael.

"Yes, but not in high school," said Jesse, thinking fondly of his early years with Alexandra and noticing Becca suddenly appear, smiling with him at the memory. "Speaking of high-school, what're you going to do about the prom? From what Jamie tells me, a couple dozen girls would love you to invite them. It sounds like a minefield to me."

"If you're exclusive with someone, the prom-date thing is easy," said Michael. "But I'm just not into that while I'm in high school. I'm not ready—if I get close to someone I'm almost positive that I'll fall totally in love and never want to leave that person for the rest of my life. Because I'm built with this 'massively over-developed sense of loyalty,' as you call it, I need to be super careful about the whole exclusive dating thing. Anyway, yeah, if you aren't exclusive with anyone at prom time, the date thing is tricky, just like you say. I might go stag or I might ask someone like Willa, a good friend who isn't that into me."

"You sound so strategic and in-control about all of this. At your age, I was a total muddle when it came to romance. I could've used your perspective," Jesse said.

"I don't think that's right, Grandpa. It's more like I can feel how close I am to losing control and just falling in love with the first girl I date more than a few times. That relationship might be a total disaster and I wouldn't be able to tell because all that loyalty machinery would have kicked in. I think I'm sorta skating on the surface because I can get away with it and because I'm afraid of what'll happen when the ice cracks and I fall through."

Jesse looked carefully at Michael after that extraordinarily insightful self-appraisal. His grandson really had come a long way in therapy.

"You're exactly right, Michael," he said, "but I still wish I had your self-awareness when I was your age. They say 'wisdom is wasted on the old' precisely because of moments like these. It's when we're young that we really need wisdom, and you have more than your share of it."

"Thanks, Grandpa," said Michael. "A lot of that's because you and Maddy keep pounding it into my stubborn head."

In the end, Michael invited Willa to the prom. They never formally decided to go steady, probably because Willa thought that was stupid. But they stopped going out with other people and spent a lot of time together. Maddy and Jesse and the girls enjoyed getting to know Willa, who often studied with Michael at their house and shared meals with the family.

Michael's assessment of Willa's character seemed to be on the money: they were safe for one another. Neither demanded things the other wasn't ready to give. Michael knew why he functioned that way and Willa no doubt got to that point in her life along a very different route. But they were well matched.

Willa was skeptical about the prom, but Michael talked her into it. The clinching argument was Michael's simple observation that vigorously protesting prom seemed to take it all too seriously. Willa paused and something reconfigured in her mind.

"You're right," she said simply. "Let's go."

So they went. Maddy and Jesse didn't see the formal meeting of the couple, which took place at Willa's home. But they did come by the house on the way to prom so that Maddy and the girls and Jesse could see them together. Jesse took a few photographs like the proud grandfather he was.

Four days later, on a Wednesday after school, Willa was once again in the home. There wasn't a lot of studying to do at that point in the year and Michael and Willa were hanging out almost all the time.

As everyone settled down for the evening meal, Maddy presented the young couple with two large sketches of them together on the front porch in their prom regalia. One was framed so that the entire length of Willa's gown and her shoes could be seen, alongside Michael in his tux. The other was closer in, showing them from the waist up, and focusing on their faces. Maddy had set the large sketches in proper wooden frames and had affixed identical descriptions on the back: "Michael and Willa, Prom Night, 2038."

Maddy had spent even longer than usual on those sketches and they were incredibly detailed. Her artistic skills having widened, their photorealism took shape in a different way than in her early portraits. Up close, the pencil markings were more impressionistic, but from a short distance away it was like looking at a black-and-white photograph. Every detail of the faces and hands, the beautiful clothes and shoes, Willa's bouquet and Michael's boutonniere, was perfect.

Willa was speechless.

"They're gorgeous," Michael said. Then to Willa: "Pick one."

Willa's mouth and eyes were still wide in shock. "I can't choose!" she finally said.

"They're both amazing," said Michael. "But maybe you'd prefer the picture that shows your whole dress?"

"That'd be great," said Willa, who then spontaneously gave Maddy a huge hug.

Jesse was worried for one nanosecond, but Maddy hugged her right back.

"Two peas in a pod," said Becca, who was taking in the lovely scene. "Neither one says 'thank you' but both sure know how to express gratitude."

LOOK WHAT LOVE CAN DO

High-school Graduation Monday was a family affair. Matt and Jenny and Josh and Oli took the day off work and pulled their kids from school so they could witness the first cousin to escape from high school—the same high school Matt and Josh had graduated from years earlier. Walt and Rebecca were taking mental notes, knowing that they'd be doing the same thing in their own schools the following year. Jesse was seventy-seven and glad to be around to witness his oldest grandchild graduating from twelfth grade.

The kids knew some of Michael's friends from watching his wrestling matches, and of course they'd met Willa on many occasions. They excitedly pointed out people they knew as the students processed in, dressed in cap and gown, and later as they came forward to collect their diplomas.

Josh, a serious amateur photographer, took care of photos. Even Matt was walking around snapping pictures. Maddy and Jesse sat beside one another in folding chairs on the grassy hill, watching it all.

"Look what you've done," Jesse said, as Michael's row stood up and started filing toward the stage. "You've raised a wonderful man, Maddy."

"You and Mom, too. We did this together," she answered. Maddy was right: Alexandra was the first human being aside from Maddy to show Michael what love was, what it could accomplish, how it transforms.

"Alexandra would have loved this moment," Jesse said, happily squeezing Maddy close for a moment.

When it was Michael's turn to shake hands with the principal and take his diploma, the cheers of fifteen rowdy family members were easy to pick out, even amongst the cheers from the students.

"Look what love can do," Jesse whispered to Maddy when the noise quietened down. She grasped his hand and looked at him happily.

Holding on to Maddy's hand, Jesse leaned back in his chair and allowed himself to slip into the everywhere-here, eternal-now state. Only a thin veil separated him from that state by then and he could slip into it and out of it effortlessly. When he entered, Becca always appeared, floating face up, hands open to the sky, long hair and long dress flowing.

Jesse's bodily boundaries dissolved and he felt Michael resume his seat as if it were him. At the same time, he sensed the two-hundred-some annual graduation processions that had taken place on that hill, all overlaid on top of one another, Matt's and Josh's included. The intricate meaning of each precious life exploded in his mind as thousands of blooms falling upwards toward the sky, some already scarred by poor decisions, some destined for greatness, each linked to a formidably complex array of influences and journeying into a staggering richness of possibilities.

The vision swung outwards to the planetary ecosystem that miraculously underwrites these lives and at the same time inwards to the beating heart of every young person who ever strove to realize his or her potential. The hearts beat and the planet pulsed and the blood pumped and the energy flowed and the neurotransmitters flooded and the electromagnetic force fluxed and axons fired and stars exploded.

Alexandra appeared while Becca still floated. Her healthy young body with its smiling face was set against a dramatic cosmic background. The universe's constant dynamism was massively accelerated, its centerlessness offset by the intensity of meaning in Alexandra's life of love.

Jesse slowly regained his ordinary senses, still suffused with accruing memories of these regular cosmic journeys into the mind-blowing meaning of possibility and the miraculous possibility of meaning. His hand still in Maddy's, he cast his eye over his children and grandchildren, scattered about him, his heart full of longing for each one of them. His old soul was sad that he wouldn't be around to witness the fullness of their lives, as they realized and failed to realize their own possibilities and created holy meanings that were distinctively theirs.

As he settled into normal consciousness, he heard Becca's voice.

"It's okay to tell them now. They'll understand."

Jesse was shocked. Then he turned to face Maddy beside him, her face lit up with questions.

"What just happened to you?" she asked. "Was that the good-strange thing you've been feeling lately?"

"Yes it was, and I'm okay," he said.

"What's going on, Dad?"

"I promise I'll tell you about it, soon," he answered, surrendering to Becca's advice.

He gave Maddy's hand a squeeze. He was unsure whether telling his children about his internal world would be received as the gift he intended it to be. He hoped Chester wouldn't be too devastated since not sharing that information was that ridiculous chicken's reason for existing in Jesse's mental menagerie.

Michael and Willa left with friends for a post-graduation party, but before the evening meal, the two new graduates were back.

"Willa said the party was lame," Michael said. "So we left."

"Well, it *was* lame," Willa said, punching Michael's gigantic arm. "It's more fun here anyway."

Jessie appeared in the kitchen and saw the new arrivals. She shouted to let everyone know that Michael and Willa had arrived, and ran over and gave Willa a big hug.

"Hey!" joked Michael. "What about me?"

"You're always here," said Jessie. "Willa is special."

"I'm only going to be living here a few more months," he said. "So come on, give me a hug, too."

Jessie gave her big brother a hug as the rest of the children appeared with noisy greetings. Walt and Rebecca offered their sincere congratulations.

"Alright!" declared Michael. "Run-around-the-table ping pong downstairs in two minutes. You're all going to perish!" The other kids ran off happily, leaving Michael and Willa with the six adults.

"It was a great day," said Matt.

"I'm proud of you, Michael," said Josh. "You too, Willa."

"So glad you came back," said Jenny. "We don't feel the same without you."

"Did you see Rebecca taking notes?" asked Oli. "You're both inspirations. Anyway, go keep those rowdy kids in line. Dinner will be in thirty minutes."

Maddy stood in the corner, leaning against a counter, smiling happily. Jesse sat in another corner, perched on a stool, taking it all in. So normal. So beautiful.

Michael walked over to Maddy and wordlessly lifted her off her feet and spun her around in a glorious embrace. He put her down, they smiled at one another, he touched her face and she touched his, all without a word being spoken. Then he left with Willa.

Becca was floating and watching the proceedings.

"Isn't thirty-five too old to be floating around the kitchen?" Jesse thought-asked his apparition.

"Isn't being north of seventy too old to be a nutjob?" she said in reply, smiling. "Telling them about me and all the rest will work, Daddy. The mystical experiences will help. You can fold Mom's and my appearances into those experiences. And you won't need to say anything about the more explicit and terrifying aspects of your visualizations. They won't freak out. All five of them are ready."

Jesse could feel his anxiety easing.

"And Chester told me you have his permission," she added, grinning.

The day after graduation, as soon as the kids had left for school and with Michael still asleep, Maddy found Jesse in his office. They leaned back in the recliners, put their feet up, and sank into one another's presence. Jesse closed his eyes and breathed deeply. His mystical home beckoned him from the other side of the gossamer veil, but he gently declined, opened his eyes, and turned his head to take in his darling daughter.

Maddy was thirty-three, and in some ways at the height of her beauty. At that moment, she was barefoot, wearing a simple, brightly colored floral spring dress with spaghetti straps. Her long blonde hair cascaded around her shoulders. Her small frame was slender but she was fit and strong, and stronger still in mind than in body.

There was almost no trace of the emaciated body and twisted mind she'd had when she escaped her captors at the age of twenty. Her face was ruddy, her skin was clear, her mind was unburdened, her intelligence shone, and after almost two years of sustained mind-body retraining, her body now did more or less exactly what she wanted it to do. Love did it. Love and nothing but love transformed Maddy into the luminous woman she was on that day.

"Sweetheart," Jesse said. He watched her turn her gorgeous heart-shaped face toward his. He was about to start speaking but the words seemed burdensome. He put the burden down and just smiled. She smiled back and started the conversation.

"When Mom died, you changed," she began. "It was small at first but now the contrast is obvious. You're quieter than ever. You're more joyful and more peaceful and more content. Your ambitions and goals seem to have disappeared. Sometimes you go to some strange mental place. It happened yesterday but I've seen, or felt, that happen a bunch of other times as well. You're like the Hindu sannyasi Shondra told me about one time. The old man who lives in the forest after his family and community duties are finished so he can meditate and focus on enlightenment."

Maddy stated it all, just like that. She didn't ask for confirmation and she didn't seem uncertain.

"That sounds about right," Jesse said, smiling gently. He was going to say that Matt and Josh had also noticed some of those changes, but talking still felt burdensome and Maddy didn't seem to need any reassurance. He let those words go, too.

"You tell me you're okay and I believe you," she continued. "But I'm not only concerned. I'm also curious because you seem to be affecting me, too. It's like you're a radio transmitter and I'm picking up your signal."

"I've noticed that, Maddy," said Jesse. "Every now and then you seem to know that I'm having a strange experience even though my outward behavior doesn't change in any significant way."

"Your body does show when you're in the midst of whatever it is you're experiencing," she said. "You get really still and your face muscles relax. It's not obvious. But I can see it. I can also feel it. It's not like I'm reading your mind; it's more like watching somebody I love go through something important. And I get this sense that you are…"

"Go on," he urged.

"I don't know how to say it," she said. "Flying, maybe. It feels like you're lifting off and flying around without moving a muscle. I don't feel like you're leaving me; it isn't a sad feeling. It's more like you're so extremely joyful. No, blissful."

They were silent until Maddy finally said, "Dad, don't leave me hanging here!"

"Oh Maddy, I'm sorry sweetheart," he said. "I was lost in my thoughts there for a moment. Yes, you're right: the thing that happens to me, the thing that happened to me during the graduation ceremony yesterday, is a bit like flying. An old friend of mine used to call it Riding the Windhorse."

"Are you sure you're okay, medically?" she asked

"I'm truly fine, I think. I do talk to someone about these states of mind and he's not too concerned. In fact, he's rather happy for me. Basically, I've spent my entire life cultivating the ability to do strange things with my mind, and in recent years I appear to be reaping some of the fruit of that peculiar form of self-discipline."

They were quiet, then, for a long time, before Jesse broke the silence.

"Maddy, I think I should talk with Matt and Jenny, with Josh and Oli, and with you about this. It isn't something for grandchildren but I'd like to explain it to my children, if only to ease your concern. Also, something in me is longing to share these hard-won states of mind with the people I love most in the world. I feel a little nervous doing that because I don't want to be misunderstood. But I do want to share my experiences with you all."

"I'd love to hear about them, Dad," said Maddy, "and I'm sure the others would, too."

"We'll see, I guess," he mused.

IT'LL BE DIFFERENT, ANYWAY,
I CAN PROMISE YOU THAT

Jesse chose the July fourth weekend to open up his strange internal world to his beloved family. The older grandchildren were going to wrangle the younger grandchildren at Matt and Jenny's house, with the nanny there for back-up, and all of the kids were excited about this new adventure. Jesse had arranged for Jerry to spend a few hours with them on Saturday.

Jesse had been emotionally preparing himself, battling a persistent trace of anxiety, worried that one or more of his children couldn't or wouldn't recognize the beauty in what he wanted to tell them. But Becca's constant refrain was that everything would be okay, that Chester agreed with her, and he surrendered in trust to that side of his mind.

It was decompression time for the boys and their wives. All four were leaving behind complicated work weeks and crashing into the long weekend, exhausted and ready to unwind. Maddy took the lead in prepping the food and the house. When everyone arrived there was nothing for anyone to do except relax.

Jesse smiled gratefully at Maddy, who was sitting at the opposite end of the table from him, flanked by her big brothers. She smiled back at him. Oli launched into a hilarious story about a woman who'd just delivered a baby and momentarily forgot that she was having twins. Becca laughed along. Having actually delivered twins, Jenny said that was easier to do than you might think.

Jesse heard the siren call through the midst of the laughter and drew near to it. Becca floated upwards as the eternal-everywhere joined the meaning-rich here and now. Jesse hovered near the edge of the state, enough to enhance the feeling of intense connection to his children. It was another trick he'd discovered, and it allowed him to process language better.

Maddy looked at her Dad cock-eyed, recognizing the reappearance of this strange state of mind, about which she still knew almost nothing beyond its similarity to flying. He smiled in acknowledgement and, almost imperceptibly, she shook her head.

Jesse had learned that, when he was skating on the edge like that, he could move his eyes and facial muscles to engage those around him. But he couldn't talk. If he went any deeper, he couldn't move, either, not even his eyes. As soon as he started to use language, he'd ease right out of the state, but he could reenter it quickly if he lapsed back into silence. Something about the linearity of language interfered with the neurological requirements of the mystical state: the ability to feel and visualize a thousand luminous dynamic images at the same time. But he could dip in and out, combining a mild version of ecstatic awareness with an ordinary conversation.

This shallow state was akin to crossing the wall of a vast dam, with a mountainous drop back into ordinary consciousness on one side and the dark watery depths of the full-blown mystical state on the other. He'd figured out how to keep himself balanced on the dam wall, sensing everything in an intensified way without becoming totally immobile.

The boys and their wives retired early, Maddy shooing them out of the kitchen before they could switch into helper mode. Maddy and Jesse pottered about, cleaning up the kitchen and preparing for the morning's breakfast, which Jesse would be cooking, as was his custom.

When they were done, they sat on the stools at the kitchen island. Jesse thanked Maddy for a wonderful evening and described what he'd noticed about her thoughtful touches.

"I love these people," she said "It'll be strange going to bed without the children in the house."

"It's good practice," he said. "They'll all leave eventually."

She smiled, slightly grimly. "I figured something out today," she said.

"Do tell."

"Jessie's a few months from turning thirteen and officially being a teenager," she began. "Five years from now, she'll probably be headed to college, Jamie will be in college, and Michael will be off working somewhere on his music career and living his own life. That means, in just a few more years, most of my parenting obligations will be completed, hopefully all three kids will be independent, and I'll be on my own, at least quite a lot of the time. I've been a mother practically since the beginning of my remembered life. Becoming a mother saved me and helped me fight my way to health. The prospect of not having daily mothering tasks feels... well... confusing, and a little sad, and scary.

"Anyway, I've been thinking through what I'll do. I have my art and I can dig more deeply into that. Five years from now I'll be thirty-eight. I'll still be young enough to immerse myself in the art world. I have all these ideas on the abstract side of my portfolio and maybe I could do some exhibitions. Art has come to me through books and online but maybe I could travel and visit art museums. Apart from my childhood detour to Rhode Island, I've never left Boston."

"That sounds wonderful, sweetheart," Jesse said. "And you should do all of those things, maybe even let yourself fall in love. You're young and beautiful and full of passion. It's rare for someone to raise three children to independence before the age of fifty, let alone thirty-eight, so in five years you'll have all this experience while you're still young with plenty of time to enjoy wonderful life adventures. And you don't need to wait five years before this new kind of life begins. It might be wise to ease into it, beginning now. Take a few trips. Rent a proper studio. Join an artists' group. Make some friends and try being intimate with someone."

"I won't leave you," she said.

"Taking your children to Paris to see the Louvre, or skipping down to New York for a few days to visit the Met isn't leaving me, sweetheart," said Jesse. "Neither is working in a studio around the corner or going on a date."

She laughed. "True."

"Do you remember when you couldn't hold anyone's gaze, even for a second?" he asked.

"Yes," she said, with uncharacteristic shyness.

"You could win a staring contest with a statue now," he said, and they both laughed.

At breakfast the following morning, over pancakes and sausages, crispy hash-browns and made-to-order omelets, Jesse made an announcement.

"I invited an old friend of mine to visit after lunch today. I want to have a conversation with all of you and I think my friend's presence will help me do that. I don't want to make anyone anxious so let me say up front that everything is okay and there's no need to worry. I hope it will be a fascinating afternoon for all of us. So please reserve a couple of hours after lunch."

Everyone except Maddy looked a bit shocked.

"You didn't think we could have an entire weekend like this without a meeting of some sort, did you?" Jesse joked, which got some laughter, but not much.

"This is why you set this whole weekend up, isn't it, Dad?" asked Josh, half-smiling.

"That's part of the story, yes," Jesse acknowledged. "But I also wanted to try a different family rhythm for a few days. The conspiracy isn't as deep as you might think."

"Okay," Josh said. "Sounds like fun."

"Well, it'll be different, anyway, I can promise you that," Jesse said.

MY WORK HERE IS DONE

Jerry showed up at one o-clock in the afternoon. Everyone slowly organized themselves with coffee and tea in the family room. Becca was present and Jesse quietly mentioned that to Jerry, much to his amusement. Jerry still didn't know about Chester, who was also present, perched on Becca's shoulder, his single feather sticking up proudly.

Jesse began by thanking everyone for setting aside a couple of hours, and especially Jerry for traveling up from Princeton.

"Jerry is a psychiatrist and scientist who conducts research on the neurology of psychiatric conditions," Jesse began. "We've published some things together in the past and we've been good friends for a long time."

"I'm recently retired," added Jerry, "so I've hung up my neuro-spurs and am concentrating on writing things I never had the time to write when I was trying to survive in a grant-driven industry. Your father has been a fascinating and loyal friend and I'm thrilled to meet you all. He's told me a lot about you over the years."

"Matt and Josh know this, I think," Jesse said, "but I'm not sure about you girls. I've spent my whole life learning as much as I can about, well, everything really. I've written a lot of books in which I try to knit what I've learned into a seamless garment. Some scholars focus on one area and dig deep, mastering the nearby details in all directions. My academic career has followed a different path. For almost sixty years I've been training myself quite deliberately to think and feel everything I've learned all at the same time, using one field of knowledge to put pressure on others, encouraging these competing interpretations of reality to jostle against one another and settle into an optimal model. I know this is a bit strange as a life calling but I've loved it.

"I think of this as a kind of rigorous brain training. This model I've created lives in my own mind more than in my books. The books necessarily line up my thoughts in an orderly sequence and explain them one by one. But in my mind, these thoughts and feelings fit together in something more like a network. This mental model is like the internet: there's a lot of information present all at once. But it's also different from the web in that I feel my way emotionally around the mental model of reality that I've created as much as I think my way around. It's full of color and emotion as well as arguments and evidence and information. At any moment, I can dip into my mental model and feel the ideas and think the feelings and navigate it in a state of wonder. It's like having a fascinating companion always with me. I can just switch gears and move into that world, exploring it, tasting it, feeling my way through it. In short, my mind has become host for a complex simulation of reality, or at least the bits of it that I've been able to understand and internalize."

Jesse looked around and everyone seemed to be following so he just pressed on.

"Here's the thing. Something happened toward the end of Alexandra's life, as I finished my big book series. I discovered that I could enter my simulated world differently than I'd been able to do previously. I'd already learned how to think of several things in great detail at the same time, without loss of nuance, and that was wonderfully satisfying, even thrilling. But in that period, instead of just thinking and feeling a stack of things simultaneously, sensing the way each thing was tinged by every other thing I knew and felt, I found myself able to think about pretty much everything at once. It was the difference between looking at a hundred web pages, thinking about them in relation to one another, and seeing all one hundred web pages at the very same moment and truly understanding all of them. This was an unnerving state of mind at first, but it was also an incredible high. I'd float through my simulated world mentally, feeling and understanding the most amazing things all together, while my body remained completely relaxed. I couldn't speak while it was going on and even moving wrecked this precious state of mind. I'd spent enough time studying meditation states to know that something quite like this can occur under special circumstances."

"That sounds totally amazing, Dad," said Matt.

"It is really, really cool, Matt. Those mystical states of mind are the most intense experiences of my life. They were shocking, at the start, and then they left me giddy with excitement. At the beginning I couldn't control them very well. They'd come and go, wouldn't last long, and I couldn't always enter them when I wanted. Eventually, though, I could drop into a mystical state whenever I liked, for as long as an hour, without ever losing awareness of what was happening around me. In fact, awareness of my surroundings became even more intense and I'd be flooded with compassion for people and things, able to see their experience from what I took to be their points of view. If I went deeper, I'd lose the ability to understand language as the state became more intense, but I could still sense everything in an emotional, visual way. These experiences are spiritually compelling to me. It's like the depth dimension of ordinary reality opens up to me and I fall down into it, flying around in wonder, riding the windhorse."

Maddy smiled at this and Jesse smiled back.

"What do you mean you feel everything you know at the same time?" asked Jenny. "I can't picture that."

"It's a good question, Jenny. I couldn't picture it before it happened, either. It's something like feeling every level of complexity and every perspective at the same time. So what I learned about quantum chemistry and the periodic table and chemical bonding is vividly in my mind at the same time as poetry, everything I learned about general relativity and cosmology and quantum mechanics is right there as well, along with beautiful art and monstrous wars and the rippling transformations of human civilizations and the organs of all bodies and the bacterial underpinnings of life and the vast timescale of cosmic development and the intricacies of biological evolution and the constrained chaos of synaptic signaling—and all of that's co-present with the memory of Matt's first cry and Josh's first home run and Becca's hug and Maddy's courage and Oli's love and your fiery intelligence and Alexandra's beauty, and also with what's happening around me right at that moment. Everything is vivid and I feel it all simultaneously, without any competition among the parts, without any focus on one particular aspect or perspective, without any loss of detail, and with an abundance of meaning."

"It really does sound amazing, and beautiful," offered Oli. "Why didn't you tell us this before?"

"Mmmm..." Jesse said, and glanced at Jerry. "One reason is that it's just my weird thing, a side effect of decades of disciplined brain-training, both through learning and through meditation. It's quirky to be carrying around a vast simulation of this kind and being able to duck in and out of it the way I do. I guess I thought it was a weird private thing and I should keep it to myself." Jesse noticed Chester nod emphatically and had to suppress a laugh before continuing. "A second reason is that there's another whole side to my ability to create and sustain complex simulations. This other side is pretty tender, and I'm quite self-conscious about it. In my mind the two sides have been tied together, so that probably made me hesitate to tell you guys what I've just shared."

Oli looked puzzled, and everyone looked a bit concerned. Jerry looked at Jesse with warm encouragement. Becca was swallowing nervously, but she was also nodding. Jesse pressed on.

"Okay, so the other side of this started almost thirty years ago, a long time before I experienced this mystical state of consciousness. After Becca disappeared, I suffered from serious anxiety and depression, including nightmares so terrifying that I couldn't sleep and couldn't even concentrate during the day. Out of desperation I began meditating to relax. It turned out that I took to meditation like a duck to water. I invested lots of time and energy in meditation training, trying different techniques, and starting to develop my mental simulation skills. Then, five years into my meditation training, I suddenly started to have... hallucinations."

There were gasps and alarmed stares.

"You *what?*" said Josh.

"Hallucinations, Josh," said Jesse. "I was seeing Becca, the way she'd look if she were eleven. Lots of people have visions of loved ones after they die—it's one of the things I studied with Jerry— and because I was hallucinating Becca, I thought it was probably something like that, though we didn't know for sure that she had died. I reached out to Jerry to make sure everything was okay." Jesse looked at Jerry, hoping he'd pick up the story from there.

"I was excited to get your Dad's call, but also a little worried, as you can imagine," Jerry began. "I put him through a full medical workup and a battery of neuropsychological tests. He came out completely healthy, physically, but we still needed to explain the hallucinations. It was, and remains, a diagnostic puzzle. Your Dad didn't experience the disorganized thinking associated with schizophrenia, the mood swings associated with bipolar psychosis, or the paralyzing panic associated with delayed PTSD attacks, though I think it's okay for me to say that he did have experiences like that on a couple of occasions when he was extremely stressed about your missing sister, including right after the first time the hallucination appeared. Other than those terrifying symptoms, which only happened a few times, it looked just like stress-induced psychosis, with symptoms limited to this recurrent hallucination. And the visual hallucination was probably made possible by your Dad's truly bizarre meditation practice. Because he knew with crystal clarity that the hallucinations were simulations, that he was producing them, I concluded that medication wasn't indicated. And that cleared away all of the hurdles for an excellent adventure."

"What adventure?" asked Oli, on the edge of her seat.

"So long as your Dad could manage his psychiatric condition safely, without losing any of his high functioning, in my judgment he was free to cultivate the hallucination, to improve its stability, refine its quality, and explore its behavior. Before long his apparition was talking, had incredibly detailed resolution, interacted with the environment in a physics-appropriate way, and was even being ironic and cracking jokes. Based on the first year of our work together on cultivating the Rebecca hallucination, he and I wrote a paper that describes your Dad's extraordinary case, but I published it without naming him, to protect his privacy. I brought a copy along so you can read it for yourselves if you're interested."

"I can't believe this!" said Matt.

"It is truly incredible," Jerry said, "but I can assure you your Dad is perfectly okay." He pulled two stapled clusters of paper from his briefcase and tossed them on the coffee table.

"During the second year, your Dad somehow used the Rebecca simulation to perform self-therapy of a profound and effective kind. We wrote a second paper about that, and that's on the table, too. As the years went on, your Dad achieved incredible control over the Rebecca hallucination, or simulation—after a while it became impossible to tell the difference. He consistently used the apparition to remind himself that it was an extension of himself, not his actual daughter. Well, almost consistently. There was one experiment that didn't work so well."

Jesse resumed the story at that point, thinking of his exchange with Maddy about panic attacks a few months earlier.

"That experiment was the second time I had, or almost had, a panic attack, the first being right after the first time I saw Becca. On that second occasion, I tried treating the simulation as if it were really Becca and I got extremely scared and anxious. The same thing happened when Josh and Matt and I thought Maddy might have unearthed evidence of Becca's survival and we were wondering if we might actually recover her. That led to two sleepless nights, which can be dangerous for someone like me when combined with extreme emotional stress. Fortunately, Jerry picked up when I called and put me through a meditation routine to get myself back under control. It was a dicey moment."

"What about now?" Josh asked. "Do you still see Becca?"

Jesse paused. It was all or nothing at that point.

"I can see her right now, Josh. But it's not really Becca I'm seeing. It's not a ghost. It's an age-progressed vision of her that I generate and then employ to keep in check what might otherwise be a destabilizing psychiatric condition. It's a useful hallucination that leverages my intensive efforts to cultivate visual simulations."

"Wow. It's still amazing, Dad. I'd give anything to see Becca again, even as a hallucination," Josh said.

"Amen to that," said Matt.

With those reactions from his boys, Jesse suddenly felt free of an enormous burden. He'd told them and they were okay with it. They even saw the beauty in it. And from the faces of the girls, he could see they were in the same place. He didn't have to bear this part of his life alone any longer.

Chester, the one-feathered, otherwise totally plucked, dignity-obsessed chicken, who had never spoken a word the entire time he had been Jesse's power animal, turned and walked out of his consciousness. Becca passed along his parting message: "My work here is done."

As Jesse relaxed, he began talking more about his feelings.

"It is amazing to have Becca with me, even as an extension of my own mind. We've been talking together since she was eleven years old all the way up until today, when she'd be thirty-five. She's grown up in my mind, even if she never grew up in reality. And she's become quite independent of me, with her own feelings and thoughts. I've found it enormously comforting. And we have a profound friendship."

He paused and looked around at his loved ones before taking another step in the series of revelations.

"There's a bit more to this story," Jesse said. "I've been able to see Becca most afternoons and evenings when I'm in a normal state of consciousness, and sometimes she'd appear earlier in the day. For example, she was almost always with me at my daily lunches with your Mom in the long-term-care facility, helping me find ways to be present to her despite her volatile mood and fragmented memory. Lately Becca has been with me for the larger part of each day. Her presence feels totally ordinary to me, and it's been like that for a long time. We're almost all talked out now but I treasure her presence. When I'm in the mystical state I described earlier, Becca is always there, floating with me. But I also see Alexandra, the way she was when we first fell in love. She never talks and she never changes so it's not the same as with Becca. But she does look at me and smile while Becca floats. Sometimes she holds Becca's hand just the way I remember," he said, suddenly tearing up.

"That's so beautiful, Dad," said Jenny, reaching for Matt's hand.

Jerry took over while Jesse composed himself. "The two types of simulation are linked," he said. "My best guess is that your Dad built up his simulation skills first in his meditation practice, and then five years later with the Becca hallucination, and all of that was in parallel with the academic brain training. A lot of work went into both kinds of mental training, that's for sure. When he got to a certain point, the combination of the knowledge and the simulation skills produced the mystical state with its world simulation and the merging of thinking and feeling that happens when he moves around within it. I don't mind telling you that I envied your Dad after I found out about the Becca simulation and confirmed that he was both healthy and managing his psychosis without losing any of his typical high level of daily functioning. But what he's been able to do in the last few years has blown my mind. We have a third paper coming out soon about your Dad's mystical states of consciousness and the way he cultivated them and gained increasingly refined control over them. That paper also covers the way Rebecca has transformed from a simple projection to an independent AI, a living being in your Dad's consciousness, with her own sense of time and novel perspectives on life. I'll send that along when it's published."

"Is that it?" asked Matt, smiling. "Or are there other stunning surprises on this strangest of all afternoons?"

"Well, there is something more," said Jesse. "It has to do with the meaning of all this. You see, riding the windhorse has become my spiritual home. When I'm seeing all of reality as it most truly is..." Jesse paused as tears welled up. "When I'm in the state, with Becca, I'm in solidarity with her, loving her, making sense of her disappearance the best way I can. I can see her whole life, everything I remember and everything that might have happened to her, all together with everything else in the universe. I feel so close to her. And when Alexandra appears, her mind clear and our love strong, I feel... just right. Seeing them holding hands is so comforting. This is my own-most home. No evasive fictions. No supernatural fantasies. Just love threading through the multidimensional possibilities of reality." Jesse started sobbing but caught himself. Jerry put his hand on his friend's shoulder as Jesse stared at both Maddy and Becca, calming himself by breathing deeply in sync with the two of them.

"That's all there is," he said, finally. "I've carried this a long time with nobody except Jerry to support me. I'm so glad to be able to share this with you all now. I'd ask you to keep it confidential because something like this is all too easy to misunderstand. But these experiences are precious to me and it feels wonderfully liberating and special to be able to include you in them."

Becca smiled, and the relief Jesse felt matched the look of relief on her beautiful face.

At dinner that evening, Josh gave a long toast that included teasing his Dad not only for being crazy as a loon but also for not being able to do a serious psychiatric illness correctly. Jesse doubted that any psychiatric patient ever felt so appreciated for what they'd crafted from the bare bones of a potentially dangerous anxiety disorder. He'd never asked anyone in his family, not even Alexandra, to understand his strange form of disciplined brain training, or to read his books; they just let him do his thing. But now Jesse's children had a tangible way to grasp the meaning of what he'd been doing all these years and they were fascinated.

He was more touched by their attention than he'd ever been by academic fame.

THE PRESENT

I've shared this story as though it's about someone else. But it's my story.

Today's the thirty-second anniversary of Becca's disappearance. She'd be thirty-eight-and-a-half years old were she alive to join her family. Matt, Jenny, Josh, and Oli are taking the day off work and coming to Maddy's and my house, as always in this painful moment of the year.

Today is also the summer child's eighteenth birthday, with a family party tonight and a party for Jamie's school friends tomorrow. Jamie graduated from high school last month and is headed to a college in upstate New York in September. Jessie has finished her first year of high school, having survived a couple of stormy years with Jamie before they recovered their earlier closeness, much to Maddy's relief.

Michael has just completed his junior year at music school, delving ever more deeply into the world of professional music. His keyboard skills, especially on jazz piano where he's been concentrating most of his effort, are now out of this world. He's had to tone down his martial arts to protect his fingers but he's still teaching. Willa moved away for college, and she and Michael agreed that they should disentangle for practical reasons. Despite the break, they stayed in touch for the two years they were in different cities, getting together over vacations. A year ago, Willa transferred to a Boston-area university to be near him and they started dating seriously. They recently got engaged and plan to move in together before being married next summer after college graduation. The safe-girl prom date turned out to be the love of Michael's young life.

Walt and Rebecca just finished their sophomore year at different east-coast colleges. Millie, Abby, and John graduated high school a month or so ago, just like Jamie. The twins are headed to the same college; Matt and Jenny wonder whether that's a wise decision. John is taking a year off to detox from high school, exactly as his father, Josh, had done at the same age, and he still has to decide what to do about college. Jake and Kate are done with tenth grade and enjoying a summer free of homework and school activities.

Matt and Jenny are going strong. Matt is fifty and Jenny is turning fifty in a couple of weeks. Married almost twenty-one years, they've gone through their trials but they always seem to choose one another, reinforcing their investment in family and in their shared history. Their careers haven't changed except that Jenny is now leading her creative team of advertising geniuses. Matt found ways to limit his travel, mostly by assigning others to do it, which turned out to be a key move for increasing marital satisfaction. Both still love their jobs.

Matt's autism is harder to see these days, unless you know what to look for. He had to learn the social world manually, as it were, but learn it he did. He's an effective manager of people, kind and supportive despite his lack of instinctive empathy, and always fair. He's respected at work as a result. His intense loyalty to Jenny is a wonderful side effect of his condition and a big strength of their marriage. He can be insensitive at times but unfaithfulness is inconceivable. Jenny knows what she has, and what she doesn't have, and chooses what she has. That's the secret of any long-lasting marriage.

Josh and Oli's careers haven't changed either. They long ago climbed as far up the career ladder as they wanted. To go any higher in social work or in nursing would mean leaving behind people in need and taking on more managerial responsibilities, a prospect that appeals to neither of them. Josh is forty-eight and Oli is a couple of years younger. They have seventeen years of marriage under their belts and are a well-matched and fun-loving couple, having navigated a big wobble early on. Oli is still Maddy's best friend.

Josh is rock-solid in temperament, has excellent judgment, remains superbly empathic, and can be fierce in his defense of the vulnerable people he deals with daily. The only trace remaining of his rocky adolescence is his nicotine addiction. He's never been able to give up the death sticks or the various other nicotine-delivery devices he has tried. He's a bit overweight so the smoking might do him in. I try to accept that as a part of life but it makes me sad. At least he was able to get a handle on his earlier alcohol problem.

Maddy is thirty-six and still living with me. She did take my advice and rented a studio around the corner from our house where she's been aggressively developing her artistic style. Many days I go to the studio with her, sitting in a corner where I read or type or stare through the window at the trees, sometimes riding the windhorse after yielding to the lure of a mystical state of consciousness. Other times Maddy goes alone, building up her ability and willingness to embrace the whole of her life without my immediate presence.

She's been forcing herself to engage the volatile art world. Despite her reluctance, she's seen genuine success, with one gallery exhibition of her sketches and another of her abstract paintings.

Maddy has also dated two people. The first was a woman in her local artist collective, a slightly nutty but intensely loving person. That relationship lasted a couple of months and disintegrated, at least at a superficial level, around Maddy's unwillingness to live permanently anywhere other than in the house in which she was still raising her daughters. At a deeper level, the story was very different, and simpler: Maddy just wasn't fully ready for an intimate relationship of any kind.

The second, a while later, was Bob, a man she met through her exhibition of photo-realistic landscape sketches and pencil portraits. Many years earlier he'd commissioned portraits of his two children from Maddy but they'd never met in person because his former wife had handled the details. He attended the gallery showing and introduced himself to Maddy, showing her photos of the portraits she'd created of his kids. She remembered the sketches immediately, just as she seems to remember everything she's done since escaping her basement captivity. When she asked about Bob's wife, he explained that she'd left him some years earlier for a more exciting man. Before long Bob and Maddy were spending time with one another.

Bob is ten years older than Maddy and both of his kids are in college. He's exceptionally kind and gentle, and was so even before Maddy shared her personal history with him. One woman's boring husband can be another woman's trustworthy rock, I guess. I like Bob and I sense that Maddy can place her infinitely vulnerable trust in him. I think he expands in her wild presence, and they both seem to enjoy that. She's taking things very slowly but I can see her holding back and I don't think it's going to last. In fact, man or woman, I doubt that Maddy will ever choose a lifestyle that involves a permanent intimate partner. She's forcing herself to do it, as a kind of exercise of self-exploration, and I can't picture that changing. But I'd like to be wrong, and she's often surprised me.

One day recently, a couple of months into the relationship with Bob, I was reading poetry in my corner of Maddy's studio, getting slightly high on paint-and-solvent fumes despite the ventilation system she'd installed. Maddy suddenly offered an appraisal of her romantic preferences. As usual, there were no preliminaries; she just jumped right in, while still working blade over canvas.

"Dad, I should tell you that I've finally sorted out my sexual orientation. It's a bit complicated. On the one hand, I like the mind of a good man, but after all these years I still don't trust what he might do if nobody was watching. On the other hand, I love the body of a beautiful woman, but I'm likely to find her emotional life exhausting. I'd settle for the mind of a man in the body of a woman except that it turns out that I like the penis." At this she turned to me and grinned. "I bet you weren't expecting that. I wasn't either! Anyway, what I really need is the mind of a good man, in the body of a beautiful woman that works like a woman's body should, but also with a handsome penis that works like a penis should. So you see, I have it all figured out now."

She looked at me cross-eyed and we both cracked up laughing.

Ten minutes later, she put down her equipment and walked over to the wooden chair near my recliner. She positioned the chair facing away from me and sat down looking at me, her arms leaning on the back of the chair and supporting her head. She stared at me for a few seconds before starting to speak.

"I want to tell you about Bob. He's perfect, really. He doesn't demand much from me. He's not obsessed with sex. He's trustworthy, protective, and kind. He's a good communicator and he's fine with my directness. He can even tolerate my periodic need to get away and be by myself. All that suits me. I like him and I can't think of anything wrong with him. But I'm not excited about a romantic relationship with him. It's like I've rediscovered how to do the intimate-touch thing, at long last, but I still don't really *want* to do it." She paused, pensive. "My therapist says some people just prefer to live without the complications of romance, even if they never had to deal with the kind of problems I've faced. Maybe I'm one of them."

She leaned the side of her head on her folded arms and stared at the woods visible through the window.

"I used to think that if only I met the right person, romantic life would unfold for me, and everything beautiful that Oli says about it would unfold, too. But that hasn't happened. And it doesn't feel like the problem is with my partners. The problem is with me. I just don't care enough about intimacy with a lover." She turned back to Jesse. "What I have with Michael and the girls, what I had with Mom, and what I have with you and my brothers and sisters and their kids—that's enough for me."

Her face scrunched up in frustration.

"But I admit I still feel kind of disappointed and confused. It's like I trained for a marathon, worked incredibly hard for a long time, and actually won the race. But on the other side of the finish line, instead of feeling ecstatic, I couldn't care less. I never expected things to work out this way. Angie can't help and my therapist just says that it is what it is, and maybe it'll change with time. Or maybe not."

I reached for her paint-stained hand and she gently grasped my wrinkled paw in return.

"Here's what I think I know, Maddy. If it's possible and you want it, you'll find a way, because you have that kind of drive. And whether or not you choose the path of a long-term romantic relationship, you'll always find a way to be happy, because you're that kind of person."

"Maybe," she said. "I just thought I'd be feeling more fulfilled at this point, or at least more normal, after everything I've done."

"Kiss the moments as they fly, sweetheart. It's the secret to loving what is, even when it's not what you expect. Kiss the moments as they fly."

She smiled.

"You're a strange old man, with your nuggets of wisdom, you know that?"

"Alexandra would have said so," I replied. Then we squeezed hands and stared out the window together.

"Okay," she said, eventually. "Back to work."

I am now eighty years of age. There isn't a lot to be said for it. Alexandra died more than five years ago, I spend most of my time in my house, and each day involves battling a low level of pain as creaky joints lever me around the ever-shrinking part of my world that I can still navigate alone. What I do have, precious above all else save my family, are memories. Most of my life is behind me, with only a short and tenuous future to anticipate. But my inner world is becoming more richly intense, thanks in part to the way memories accompany me through every moment of my slow days.

On this very early morning, I'm the only person awake in the house. Maddy is asleep with Bob in her room, Jamie and Jessie are sleeping in the room they still share, and Michael is asleep with Willa in his room. I'm standing on the back deck of my house, watching the sky lighten as the part of my planet I know best prepares to turn its face toward the summer sun. I'll see the colors through the trees before everything is ablaze in white light.

I step down from the deck and slowly pace around the house in the pre-dawn glow. I pause under Maddy's bedroom window, thinking about when Becca used to sleep in that room. My mind dances with memories of happy stories and warm hugs and loving goodnights. I see in my mind's eye the indentations in the ground made by a ladder and the deformed window screen lying on the grass. My ears are filled with Alexandra's mournful weeping on the day of the terrible discovery, merged with her demented cries of Becca's name toward the end of her life. My eyes are full of my boys' panic-stricken faces when I woke them that brutal morning. I can feel my pulse racing, my heart pushing blood through my old body, as I relive the acuteness of the grief and the elongated misery and creeping despair that followed. I see the traumatic moment for what it is: the surd of suffering, my family's decisive encounter with evil, the defining incident of our lives, an event without an explanation.

I take a step past the scene of the crime and, for the millionth time, set the trauma aside, knowing that it will never be resolved, never healed, and never, ever forgotten so long as breath remains in any of our bodies.

I complete my circuit of the house, climb back up onto the rear deck, and drag a chair over to my favorite spot. I ease my creaky body down into its cushiony softness and close my eyes in the gloom. I feel the gentle breeze on my face and listen to the birds greet the dawn. I slip into my oh-so-familiar mystical world and ride the windhorse with Becca and Alexandra until I feel the sun on my face. I rein it in, take a deep breath, open my eyes, and emerge into the day. My heart is full of thankfulness for this beautiful world, even for the cruel burden I was once forced to confront and then required to carry my whole life since.

As I sit quietly, I hear a car pull up, and two doors opening and closing. A minute later, my two beautiful boys appear on the deck. They pull up chairs on my left and right, facing the woods, and sit down beside me. My eyes fill with tears of gratitude for my companions in the way of unrelenting sorrow.

"We knew we'd find you back here," Josh says, as he thrusts a hot take-out breakfast sandwich into my cold hands. I smile at them, my happiness plain to see.

"It was right about now that we found out Becca was missing, thirty-two years ago," observes Matt. "We figured you wouldn't be sleeping any more than we were so we thought we'd pop over for Boys' Breakfast before the rest of the day unfolds."

I rest my sandwich in my lap and reach for their hands to give them a squeeze of thanks. Then I lean back in my chair and allow the food to warm my chilled body. Side by side we watch this new summer day blossom into beauty even as it leads us through the stations of agony. We know the rhythm so well but familiarity and repetition never mute the pain. Not even love mutes this pain. But love has surely transformed us, the sorry souls who live in pain.

Love conquers nothing but it changes everything.

Epilogue

The seven years between the time our father completed this true-life novel and his death were relatively free of drama. The world didn't collapse. His children and grandchildren avoided life-changing disasters, despite a few poor decisions. There were several weddings. Both of us boys are still happily married. He became a great-grandfather three times, twice through Michael and Willa, and once right before he died through Kate, who gave birth to her first child right out of college. The rhythm of Boys' Breakfast continued unbroken and we two brothers treasured those weekly times with him. Becca never surfaced but the Becca apparition was with him virtually all the time.

Dad's life became extremely predictable. He no longer traveled. His writing slowed down and shifted to poetry rather than the non-fiction he'd written during his academic career. He spent most of each day with our sister Maddy at their home or in her art studio, a few minutes' walk from the house. His crazy imagination, one of the dominant features of our childhood, yielded to smiling serenity.

His mystical journey continued, though without the aggressive goal-seeking and fierce effort that he brought to the task when he was younger. He'd become comfortable with his bag of meditative tricks and felt no need for novelty or improvement. He'd ride the windhorse whenever he wanted, effortlessly dropping into and out of that unspeakably stunning state of awareness. It's just as Maddy says: he'd become a suburban sannyasi.

What stands out to us about those mystical states, based on what we could induce him to tell us about them, is how ordinary they were in content. They were extraordinary in intensity, yes, but the sum total of the content was nothing other than a couple of dozen smart people could assemble from a variety of university degrees. There were no supernatural secrets, no sacred revelations, no invisible beings, and no intractable mysteries. He fell deeply in love with reality as it actually is and created a characteristically idiosyncratic way to honor what he loved. Of course, a rare mind was necessary to create such a magnificent world simulation, as well as a staggering level of personal discipline and a monumental amount of intellectual work. He probably also needed a certain degree of psychiatric vulnerability, and he may even have required the terrible life trauma that Becca's disappearance was for him.

We once discussed why anyone would go to such lengths to create a mental world simulation when the world is right there to engage for real. But we immediately answered our own question. From Dad's point of view, hardly any of the real world is "right there" for us. The far past, other places, cosmic vastness, the counterintuitive depths of nature, the intricacy of unfamiliar cultures, the existential interiority of every living being, the possible futures of people we love—all of this is hidden from us, almost all the time. We live under a wet blanket of ignorance, our awareness tragically dull. Dad found a way to throw the blanket off and feel the wonder of the world full blast.

He called this his worship. We think that's because he longed to surrender to it, to accept it without imposing demands on it, without inventing fictions to avoid full awareness of what it is. That's what he did with his wife, our mother, Alexandra: he learned to let her be exactly who she was, and he loved that rather than some idealized version of her. To us, Dad's spiritual journey was about learning to love reality as it is, with no illusions and no idealizations—trying your best and then accepting what happens. We think he wrote this book to explain that, and in so doing to make the most sense he possibly could of our sister Becca's disappearance.

They say that grief is sharpest when there's unfinished business or broken routines. We have no unfinished business with Dad, not since we were teenagers. Nothing has been left unsaid. But our routines have been built around his personality, around the house where he and Mom raised us, around special family celebrations on holidays, and around our weekly breakfasts with him. His death has left a chasm in our family. Our feelings are dominated by an overwhelming sense of absence as we wander aimlessly among the shards of shattered life patterns.

It's normal, this dying business, he'd have told us. And we know he'd see beauty in it. The normal is pervasive in our lives and we only glimpse the spectacular in rare moments. But Dad was master of seeing the special in the normal. That was his gift to us as children and throughout our lives: he could *see*! He saw so deeply into the normal that we can barely fathom how spectacular his awareness was. And our incomprehension remained even after he ushered the two of us, with Jenny and Oli and Maddy, into the wonders of his spiritual life. The normal, it turns out, hosts unassimilable depths of wonder, and it was all second nature to him.

Dad would expect this awesome vision of the normal to help us feel better. But knowing this doesn't help us, or beautiful Maddy, or Jenny or Oli, or our children, adapt to the sadness that's flooded us in the long months since Dad died. We all feel flattened by our grief. It just hurts.

A couple of days ago, we were sharing Boys' Breakfast, still trying to deal with the inconceivable contraction in our number from three to two. We were talking about the fact that Dad didn't believe in the continuation of consciousness after death, that he never expected to reunite with his beloved Alexandra, and that he never thought he'd find out what had happened to Becca. We knew what he'd say: evasive fictions, love what is, and all the rest. But the temptation to surrender to hope in some form of personal identity after death was almost overwhelming for the two of us at that moment. And that's from decades-long advocates of the rot-theory of the afterlife.

The temptation felt the same to both of us: there must be some way to register the achieved value of our father's life, of our mother's life, of all our lives. There has to be some balancing of accounts for what happened to Becca, to Maddy and Michael, and to Mom. But Dad never felt that way. We can almost hear him explain why. It is in the nature of things that value is achieved and then dissipates, he'd say. To love reality is to let that fluxing occur with no resistance and no fantasy, and to make the most of the precious moments to create as much beauty, truth, and goodness as we can. Inventing afterlives only seems to bring comfort. Beneath the surface of fictive comfort there lies festering suffering, culminating in the tragic taming of bliss, which should be a wild thing. This self-caused suffering is viparinama dukkha: hanging on when we should let go, fighting the flow when we might be whooping up a joyful hullabaloo under the stars.

ACKNOWLEDGEMENTS

I am grateful to friends who read early drafts of this novel and offered valuable advice as I worked to transition from the non-fiction I've written my entire professional life to the bewitching world of storytelling. I hope that the deep thinking of the non-fiction improves the story-telling, and *vice versa*, but if that's so it's only because of these generous friends. I am especially indebted to my editor Catherine Knepper, who patiently trained me, fed me short stories, passed along countless nuggets of wisdon, and *always* told me the truth.

ABOUT THE AUTHOR

Wesley J. Wildman was born in a quiet corner of Australia, fell in love with universities, and became a professor in the United States. A veteran author of academic and trade non-fiction, *The Winding Way Home* is his first novel. He resides with his wife in Boston, where they raised their two boys. Learn more about Wesley at wesleywildman.com.

www.ingramcontent.com/pod-product-compliance
Lightning Source LLC
Chambersburg PA
CBHW011113100726
47898CB00011B/3062